Coins
2

Easter at the Three Coins Inn

KIMBERLY SULLIVAN

First paperback edition December 2024

Book design by Maxtudio

ISBN 979-8-9868844-6-2 (paperback)
ISBN 979-8-9868844-7-9 Digital Edition (ePub)

www.kimberlysullivanauthor.com

PRAISE FOR EASTER AT
THE THREE COINS INN

"A group of guests staying at a charming Italian inn forges friendships and fresh starts in the second installment of Sullivan's cozy series. ... The novel is well-paced with short, snappy chapters told through multiple points of view. ...This novel evokes a restorative, sun-kissed vacation in the Italian countryside on every page."

-Kirkus Reviews

"A page-turning story of hope and renewal. Sullivan's series-kicker in The Three Coins series is a delightful escape into a world where friendships are forged, hearts mended, and the magic of a beautiful setting can inspire change. ... Whether you're planning a trip to Italy or simply seeking a cozy read, this novel will leave you with a sense of warmth and an irresistible urge to toss your own coin into the Trevi Fountain."

-The Prairies Book Review

"From the start, Kimberly Sullivan excels at crafting a story of transformation steeped in the culture and atmosphere of Europe... Libraries seeking acquisitions which can serve as beach reads, women's group literature, and book club discussion material will find it easy to recommend the ultimately uplifting atmosphere that comprises and permeates *Easter at The Three Coins Inn.*"

-D. Donovan, Sr Reviewer, Midwest Book Review

"A charming array of colorful characters makes *Easter at The Three Coins Inn* a captivating second installment of the richly picturesque Three Coins series. Immersing readers in sun-drenched drama and the relief of an unpredictable and unforgettable holiday, Sullivan›s novel feels like taking a holiday in itself, with the contrasting mixture of fun, anxiety, and relaxation."

-Self-Publishing Review

"A captivating read for fans of women's fiction, romance and drama, *Easter at The Three Coins Inn* is a heartfelt, women-empowering tale of friendship, resilience, and self-discovery."

-Readers' Favorite

"Kimberly Sullivan's captivating story delves deeply into friendship, healing, and transformation. It centers on a group of tourists from different backgrounds who, by traveling to avoid specific individuals and situations, are able to mend their scars and find comfort in the most incredible way."

-Feathered Quill

"Sullivan has deftly illustrated the beguiling setting, making me want to buy a plane ticket immediately. Moreover, the fascinating characters and blossoming friendships will make readers eager to devour the pages. Don't miss out on this one!"

-Reader Views

"Sullivan crafts a beautiful narrative of personal growth, healing, and second chances, all set against the idyllic backdrop of the Italian countryside. The charm of the inn, coupled with the journeys of its diverse characters, makes for a captivating and heartwarming read. ... This is a story that celebrates the power of introspection, connection, and the restorative magic of a peaceful retreat. Readers will be left hopeful and eager for more from Sullivan's world."

-Literary Titan

This one goes out my readers.

Thank you for following me on this writing journey,

and allowing me to create my tales.

Your support means the world to me.

Thank you for reading!

Prologue

THE SAN FORTUNATO CHURCH BELLS CLANGED out the morning hour. The bell tower had been performing that ritual for over six hundred years, but today the melodic notes hung like a promise in the warm air.

The signs had been emerging slowly. The sun set a little later each day. The last snow melted from the surrounding countryside, revealing grass eager to emerge from its hibernation during the harsh winter. The honeysuckle was not yet in bloom, but all the residents knew it was only a matter of time until the sweet fragrance would hang heavily in the air of the ancient town.

The promise of spring transformed the atmosphere. The elderly matrons traversed the ancient, cobblestoned streets with a new spring in their steps, filling their baskets with fresh produce at the market, a whisper of flirtation in their laughs as they chatted with the market sellers.

The old men gathered longer on the *piazza*, allowing the sun to warm their faces. There was a renewed vigor in their voices as they discussed soccer and politics. And, of the two conversational topics, only soccer afforded them pleasure. Todi Calcio may only be *Serie B*, but have you watched that new Brazilian wing run with such speed and shoot with such precision? Have you seen the young, Italian goalie stop every shot? He'd be plucked up by one of the *Serie A* teams soon enough, but only after gaining valuable experience in the heart of Umbria.

It had required patience. But this, finally, would be their year. Maybe the new talent would even catapult the team into *Serie A* to put Rome and Milan in their place, once and for all. Umbrian men, recognized for their skill and strength. All eyes of the nation on their tiny region. After decades of disappointment, this would most certainly be their year. You could feel it in the air.

The greengrocer crossed the square with his crates, pausing before the group to weigh in on the soccer season and the glory that would befall Todi with its new athletic talent. Across the way, the café was doing brisk business as townspeople stopped off for their daily cappuccino and a bit of gossip. The arrival of springtime weather was on everyone's lips.

Easter was approaching. A time of rebirth, of new beginnings. The town was ready to attract the tourists who would once again fill its streets, climb its ubiquitous hills, and enrich its coffers throughout the spring and summer.

Moving beyond the medieval hillside town, with its twisting streets, charming stone homes and towering church spires, one would travel downhill—to the flat expanses below the town. Centuries ago, residents would keep this tract of land under careful watch, attentive to the signs of marauding invaders. Today, the same fields attract a different type of invader—the tourists eager to gaze up, hoping to snap a tasteful Instagram photo of the sunlight setting hilltop Todi aglow.

One impressive stone structure does not date back to medieval times. Nonetheless, it has stood strong and steady for hundreds of years. Five years ago, the main structure and most of its surrounding dépandences were entirely renovated and began welcoming guests as an *agriturismo*. A farm holiday inn. Over the years, it's been building up a steady clientele, both Italians and foreigners.

There are the families who come to escape the cities and to breathe in fresh, country air. Parents who let down their guard as their young children run around the property's large yard, free from the ever-present danger of cars or urban violence in their own cities. There are the arty couples, who love this spot as a base to explore the hilltowns and frescoed churches of Umbria and nearby Tuscany. There are the northern Europeans seeking sun, content to spend hours each day basking in the rays, poolside. The foodies flock here, too. The restaurant and its cooking school have received word-of-mouth promotion around the world, and the sessions are fully booked. Often by repeat visitors.

In the end, these visitors seem to be on to something. From above, the inn spreads out across a sizeable, perfectly landscaped plot of land. The structure, which had been crumbling only a few years earlier, has been restored by loving hands. Odd, admit the locals, that two *americani* could manage it, but credit where credit is due. Even if, truth be told, one would not like to make a habit of crediting foreigners. The inn's stones shimmer in the strong spring light. Freshly painted Provence blue shutters shine pleasantly. Various balconies and small terraces dot the property—boasting a reading nook for visitors, a place to sit and stare at the dramatic hilltown looming up above, or a table to savor the third espresso of the day. And why should they not? They'll never find a perfect *caffè* back home.

A separate structure now houses a spa, where harried mothers escape for pampering, while a kids' center lays claim to the other side of the property, keeping children busy and happy with ceramics projects, farmyard skills and outdoor adventure activities. The local kids who are often called in to support these activities appreciate the extra pocket money.

Paths spread across the property, boasting occasional benches or hammocks that provide the opportunity for guests to extract a book, take a quick catnap, or simply sit in blessed silence. Something far too rare these days for those who choose to live outside of Umbria.

At the center of the property is the fulcrum of activity on a hot summer day. Now drained, the infinity pool helps refresh tourists in the brutal Italian summer heat. Cocktails are served under umbrellas poolside, where visitors can emerge from the pool, stretch out on loungers and, with glass in hand, admire the perfection of the hilltown above them. Soon enough, the temperatures will soar once again, and the pool will enjoy its moment of glory.

Many a tourist have spent a happy week—or two—residing in The Three Coins Inn. Many of them return for repeat visits, hoping to recapture the sense of peace and happiness that envelops them in this little slice of Umbria.

For now, the inn staff are hard at work ensuring that the property shines. Easter kicks off the busy start of the tourist season in Umbria, and, after its winter hibernation, the fully booked Three Coins Inn is ready—and eager—to welcome its guests to this little slice of paradise.

CHAPTER 1

Madison

MADISON HUFFED HER WAY across the bridge. To her left and right, the Scioto River sparkled in a rare display of idyllic, balmy Ohio springtime. Her Manolo Blahnik heels clicked with each step. These shoes had cost her a small fortune, and she'd been expecting to be picked up right outside the Ohio Statehouse building, not schlepping across all of Columbus to get to their van.

There was Max, racing ahead double time, in his sneakers and hauling his equipment over bulky shoulders. How the hell did he expect her to keep up? She needed to get out of this backwater. And fast.

New York was the Holy Grail, but seriously, she needed a major market to get there. Miami, Tampa, Washington, DC. Hell, even Nashville would do. Was it too much to ask to get a bit of damn sun? Yeah, okay. Today was decent. But tomorrow, the snow could start up again. Winter never ended. Ohio was proof you could never have nice things.

Madison had reached the halfway point of the bridge, and the tourist-magnet hairy deer statue that looked out onto the skyline of Ohio's capital city. She stopped at the statue, resting her purse on the deer's metal back and scrounging in her Louis Vuitton bag to locate her cellphone, which was ringing. She glanced at the display screen. About bloody time.

"Hey, Aaron," she responded. "What the hell? I was supposed to be interviewing the Governor about his new economic redevelopment plan, not joining a little coffee klatch with his wife. Exchanging baking tips, for Christ's sake."

"Yeah, about that ..." Aaron's perennially stressed voice reverberated across the line. "Justine was supposed to call you. The Governor's press officer called to cancel as you were taking off. A gas explosion disaster up in Toledo. He left as soon as they got news. They offered his wife as a late substitute." He sighed. "Anyway, that's what the *Get Outta Bed, Columbus!* viewers are going to want anyway. You know they love her."

"I suppose if you're dying for cooking tips, she's great. I'm so bored-to-freaking-hell with housewife tips."

Two women passed by and waved wildly at her.

Madison shot them her megawatt smile, shook her honey blond, artistically and expensively highlighted locks off her shoulder. She knew it must be glowing glamorously in the sun. The women walked on, chatting excitedly. She lowered her voice. "Ah, God. Our viewers are here. You owe me, Aaron. I need juicier stories. It can't always be food, makeup, and fashion tips. Assign those to Allie. She lives for that kind of fluff. I can't take it anymore. I'm ready to stick my head in an oven and have it done with."

She looked out over the city, the sparkling marble of the courthouse, the Nationwide skyscraper. From this angle, with this robin's egg blue sky and bright, optimistic sunshine, the city looked almost appealing. But not quite.

"Did you hear me, Aaron? I want something more challenging than an assignment an intrepid fourth grader could cover adequately for her school newspaper."

"C'mon, Madison. We need to keep up those ratings. Lock in the viewers, then we can speak about more hard-hitting stories. Anyway, get back to the station now and prepare that package for Monday. I'll pick you up at your place at four-thirty sharp."

Madison looked down at her utterly wasted Armani suit. "You didn't even tell me where we're going. What's the glamour scale? Opera in New York? Michelin-starred restaurant in Chicago? A girl's gotta have a clue."

Aaron laughed. "Yeah, well, dial down the glamour meter. Good, old-fashioned, low-key Midwestern charm."

"You're not dragging me out to Amish country, are you?"

He laughed again. "You don't need to dial the glamour down quite that low. Think slow-paced. Rejuvenating ... genuine."

Madison groaned. "Yeah. I was hoping for more than genuine." She slumped against the deer statue, gazing out once again at the cityscape, this time through antlers. The framing didn't make it any less of a backwater. Midwestern charm had long ago lost its charm in her eyes.

When Aaron suggested a whole weekend away, she'd been expecting something ... well ... more. Today, the disappointment of homesteading tips with the Governor's wife instead of a story with teeth that could showcase her interviewing chops. Now "genuine" in lieu of excitement. What a disaster. She gazed across the deer. Max was long gone. Hopefully waiting for her in the van, and not already back in the studio.

She sighed. Another elderly pair of women walked by, waving frantically when they recognized her. With effort, she dusted off that always-at-the-ready, perky smile and made use of it once again. The women tittered and walked on.

"Okay, Aaron. Can't wait to see your idea of genuine. I'll be expecting you at mine at four-thirty. Better get back to the studio now. Bye."

She pushed herself off from her new, best deer friend and tackled the walk in her towering heels. The ones that were supposed to make her look very serious and professional interviewing the Governor. Ensure she was someone he'd remember.

When she'd graduated with her spanking-new degree in broadcast journalism from Syracuse, a TV studio in the middle-of-nowhere Nebraska was an exciting leg up the career ladder. Three years later, the call from Columbus had seemed a tantalizing stepping stone to one of the top east-coast markets. Working her way up to morning host of their highly rated program seemed a natural progression, and she'd welcomed it. But two years in, she was ready to leap into the Scioto, almost on a daily basis.

Something had to give. And soon. But this weekend, she hoped the rejuvenating and genuine location Aaron had arranged could shake her out of this depression.

As she neared the edge of the bridge, feet screaming in anguish, encased in shoes that were made for waiting limos, not urban hiking, she caught sight of the Channel 7 news van. Max was waiting for her in a decidedly no-parking zone. Madison sighed with relief, and, ignoring the screaming pain that accompanied each step, did her best to speed up. The faster she got back to the studio, the faster she could leap out of these high-priced instruments of torture.

"HERE'S TO BOURBON COUNTRY," Aaron held up his drink and clinked glasses with hers.

The restaurant had been a find, she'd give him that. And the old carriage house-converted-to-tasteful hotel was charming. But Lexington, Kentucky? This was their romantic getaway? She really had been expecting something a bit ... more. Even worse, he was combining it with a talk about the contemporary challenges of journalism at the University of Kentucky tomorrow. It was *so* obvious he was getting reimbursed for their little romantic escape-slash-business trip.

She lifted the glass halfheartedly to her lips. She wasn't a straight bourbon drinker, but this bourbon-peach concoction was actually quite enjoyable. As pleasant as her filet mignon and spinach salad dinner. But seriously, Kentucky? This was the romantic getaway Aaron had been promising her? It was their first full weekend together and, frankly, Madison expected something lightyears away from the Bluegrass State.

Outside of the plate-glass window, the two main streets of Lexington maintained steady traffic. Cute, but nothing to write home about. Ever since Aaron had floated this weekend getaway, she'd had something entirely different in mind. New York. Miami. Heck, Nassau had even crossed her mind. Never Lexington. And on a work trip for which the station was reimbursing him ... Was Channel 7 paying for their dinner, too? The very bourbon they were sipping now?

Truth be told, Aaron wasn't even really her type. But the years were ticking by, and if she had to keep hearing news about her former classmates' coups in broadcast journalism, while her own career flatlined, she'd most definitely catapult off that deer statue and into the winding Scioto.

Okay, so maybe it was a cliché that her producer hit on her, but when he started four months ago, he brought with him the whiff of big TV markets. He nurtured her, told her she was going places. Told her he could help her get there. To the center of it all.

And yet, he was mostly getting her to out-of-the-way Columbus motels. And now to their first weekend away together. In Lexington. To make matters worse, each morning, she was still chirping on about makeup and health tips, interviewing the Governor's wife about her favorite recipes while feigning interest.

Madison was always a disaster with men. Always having her heart trampled. At least finding a guy who wasn't a monster, and could also breathe life into her stagnant career seemed a smarter move than her usual cadre of losers. Yeah, he was divorced from a wife who had made him deeply unhappy. Or so he said. Didn't they always? Yeah, she was starting to doubt he was really able to do much to get her into a bigger market. Or maybe he simply didn't want to. Plus, the boss-employee relationship was strictly Verboten, hence, the sneaking around. Her strategic chess move was looking like pretty pathetic Chinese checkers by now.

Aaron leaned over and nuzzled into her neck, whispering, "Can we skip dessert and get back to the hotel?"

She looked at him and tried to recreate the passion she used to feel for him at the beginning. She forced a smile. "You must have read my mind."

MONDAY MORNING, MADISON WAS LAGGING. She hadn't slept well last night after her return from Kentucky, and today's show careened towards disaster more times than she wished to count. One guest bailed. One would not be cut off. Brad, her Ken doll of a co-host, kept jumping in on segments she was supposed to lead and then bumbling his own. It was only seven a.m. and she already had a massive headache exploding behind her eyes. With another two hours of showtime, she could only imagine the state she'd be in by morning's end.

She took another sip of her coffee, trying in vain to channel her dormant perkiness. She needed to get off morning shows at the first available opportunity. Being pigeonholed as a ditz wasn't in her plans for broadcast journalism success, but the longer she languished in the early morning slots, the faster her hopes for recognition as a serious, hard-hitting journalist dissipated.

Aaron was yelling in their earpieces. "Okay, now. Getting your kids enrolled in summer sports programs, call-in with Brad. How to look your sexiest this summer, with Madison. I have to take an urgent call. Jennifer is taking over now."

Brad burst out in laughter, risking a glance at his co-host. "Good thing they prepared you for the sexy segments at Syracuse." The tears were rolling down his cheeks. Makeup raced over to powder his face as the countdown to live began.

Madison did what she did best around Brad. She ignored him. She stared steadily into the camera until they went live, then smiled politely when Brad announced his segment, pretending with every ounce of her being to actually like her egocentric co-host.

Brad was opening the segment and—surprise, surprise— he managed to work in, for the umpteenth time, his college athlete experience playing football for Colgate. She'd had to suppress a laugh last week when the Heisman Trophy-winning Ohio State quarterback looked at Brad quizzically, saying he wasn't familiar with the school, or its football team.

But the elementary-school moms who were the segment guests couldn't knock him down a notch, and so he waxed on about his glorious, halcyon football days while supporting the need to enroll kids in sports over the summer. Two reps of Ohio youth sports programs presented summer offerings, then they opened the line for call-ins. Harried mothers flooded the lines, on the lookout for any temporary reprieve once the school year ended. Had sumo wrestling been the only sports camp on offer, Madison was convinced it would be waiting-list-only by show's end.

The segment wrapped up and they cut to commercial. Brad turned to Madison, eyes shining with mirth. "Now the segment I've been waiting for, when our very own Maddie provides sexy summer tips."

Madison shot him a look, wishing she held the power to turn the pompous blowhard to stone. Sadly, no such luck. She looked down at her notes as the two guests were ushered into the studio. Jennifer was efficiently delivering instructions, and she smiled politely at the two women.

After they went live, Madison tried to inflect the intro with some semblance of interest, but it wasn't easy. She introduced the guests, a perky twenty-year-old influencer and a mom-influencer in her forties. Both gave tips on pool parties, slimming recipes, skincare, and the most flattering—and daring—swimsuits. The ones that would either attract a husband, or ensure the gaze of the husband you already had wouldn't stray.

Madison feigned interest, asking the women questions and trying her best to rein in the girls-breaking-out-the-cocktails-on-spring-break-in-Cancun giggling. But, try as she may, there was no serious angle to this ditzy segment to be had, and, frankly, she lacked the energy to even try. *If you're going through Hell, keep going,* she channeled her inner Churchill. Deep breath, semi-perky smile, shoulders back. "Wow, what a shame we're at the end of the segment. The time flew by. After all those amazing tips, it's time to take audience questions."

Jennifer fed her the details through her earpiece.

"Louise from Dayton wants to know more about diet tips. Baylee, it's all yours."

The young influencer was in rhapsody, sharing with Louise juice fasts, days spent consuming only sunflower seeds, and seemingly every quack diet known to man. Or, more accurately, to women. The positive side of letting her guest drone on was that the segment would mercifully end sooner, with minimal input required from her.

But no, Jennifer was not going to spare her. Madison was instructed to wrap up the diet talk and take another caller.

"Christine from Upper Arlington is on the line. She's not feeling sexy because she fears her husband is having an affair. Christine, I'm sorry to hear that, but I'm not sure if our guests can help you with your concern. We'll have a family therapist joining us later in the week. You may want to tune back in then."

"Oh, I think you and your guests can," said the polished, clipped, very-not-Midwest tones over the line. "I'm afraid I can't wait until later this week."

Madison went into high alert. She touched her earring, a signal to Jennifer. Sometimes they got callers with extreme depression, and they always had a suicide hotline to which they could connect. They were constantly trained about not being too dismissive of the callers, but if the caller became threatening, they could ease into commercial.

"Of course, Christine, why don't you tell us what's on your mind." Madison used her most soothing voice.

Farther down the anchor desk, she watched Brad doing a terrible job of dialing down a smirk. Damnit, she just needed to get through this morning. Get this woman to people who could help her.

"Honestly, I suppose I'd most like to speak with you, Madison. It's not the first time my husband has been unfaithful. Unfortunately, it's always some bimbo at work. But I thought this time would be different. Especially after he nearly got fired last time ..."

"Oh," Madison set down her coffee mug and tried to relax her stunned face. How was she supposed to help this woman? "I ... uh ... I'm sitting here with two talented and knowledgeable social media influencers. I'm sure with their expertise, they can help you far more than I can."

It was clear from their expressions that the women who had been so eager to discuss makeup and diet tips wanted nothing to do with the cuckolded wife.

"But I want *you*."

To Madison's ears, it sounded vaguely threatening. She needed to get out of this hellscape of morning shows, get on to evening shows as soon as possible. Despite wanting to flee offset and away from this dumpster fire, she forced a smile and responded, "I'm here for you, Christine. Tell me what's on your mind."

"You, actually, Madison. Or women like you," came that posh response. "My husband works in television, so he's surrounded by young, pliable women. The ones he promises will achieve all their career dreams ... if only they'll sleep with him, of course. Spoiler alert: He's perfected his technique through years of careful practice."

Madison looked up at Jennifer, in the control room. She could cut this off in an instant. They had already veered way off their segment. Baylee and the mom-influencer whose name she'd already forgotten appeared embarrassed and confused. As was she behind her fake warm and caring smile.

"Christine," said Madison. "I can imagine this betrayal of your trust is heartbreaking for you. But we're heading toward commercial break. I am sure our producer can put you in touch with our couples' therapist. Perhaps she could help you." Madison looked up at Jennifer, signaling her to end this trainwreck of a segment.

"That's the thing, Madison. The therapist doesn't know me from Adam. I need to speak directly to the source of my problems. The young, ambitious morning anchor who'll do anything to climb the broadcast TV mountain, principles be damned. The one who'll screw my husband to push her way to the top."

The venom in the caller's voice was unmistakable.

Madison's usually steady hand shook, and coffee sloshed over her mug onto her St. John's suit. Now she shot deathly stares to the control room. Jennifer had to get this insane woman off the air. Immediately.

"Did you *know* he was married, Madison? When he took you to Lexington to bang you? Did you know he has three kids? Know he couldn't be bothered to go to their little league games while he was ferrying you around Columbus motels with hourly rates?"

The blood froze in Madison's veins. This was Aaron's wife, who was clearly the opposite of the distant ex-wife as he'd claimed. And frickin' hell! He had *kids*?

"How stupid can you be? Didn't you wonder why he went from Miami to Columbus? Not the usual trajectory for a talented producer. Yeah, as you can imagine, he was nailing the talent there, too."

The segment guests stared at Madison, wide-eyed. Brad was no longer glued to his cell-phone screen. His jaw dropped as he gawked at her being humiliated live on local television.

"Yeah, Madison. He doesn't exactly go for the geniuses. But you should know, he never had any intention of helping you. You were a conquest to be bedded. One of many, I should add."

Madison felt every word like a dagger. She was certain she would faint. Once again, she made desperate eye contact with

Jennifer. If there were a time to cut to commercial break, this would be it. But Jennifer stood dumbfounded by these early-morning revelations.

"So, Madison. One final question before I go ..."

Madison realized there would be no reprieve from the control room. She gazed out into space and tried to look encouraging, as she croaked, "Of course, Christine."

Madison stared into the void in terror, anticipating what might come. When it did, Christine's words were loud and clear, so beautifully enunciated to ensure all of metropolitan Columbus heard them.

"Do you ever regret being such a slut, Madison?"

Madison cringed. Across from her, the two women made an effort to look anywhere but at her. At the far end of the anchor desk, Brad fought tears streaming down his face, as he struggled to control his sheer glee at Madison's pain.

Madison fought desperately to ensure her own tears did not spill over. Just when she was convinced she could not hold out anymore, Jennifer cut to commercial break. Madison dissolved into messy sobs.

CHAPTER 2

Heike

APRIL WAS OFTEN GREY in Vienna, but Heike couldn't recall a spring as dreary as this in all her sixty years. She sat at the window as the endless sheets of rain thundered down, cradling her teacup closer to her chest, like a talisman.

She'd canceled the walk she and Ida had planned on taking this afternoon, a New Year's resolution they had both made to lose the extra pounds that were slow to shed after the holiday period. Truth be told, her grumbling about extra pounds were floated more in solidarity with her old school friend. Heike, who used to savor good food, certainly spent much of her life preparing it, mostly forgot to eat it these days. The waistbands of her pants kept getting looser. She simply had the cobbler bore new holes into her belts.

Regular, nourishing meals never used to be a problem. When she worked in the *Beisl*, she ate a hearty, congenial meal with the rest of the staff before opening their doors to customers, but her daughter and son-in-law asked her less frequently to come and pitch in. Her grandchildren were older now, and wanted to help out for extra spending money. And Anneliese and Hans kept telling her it was her time to kick up her feet and relax, that she shouldn't be working so many hours at her age. They always seemed to be hiring young students in their parish to handle extra hours. Heike sighed. She supposed the clients preferred being served by those fresh, young faces, but all the silent nights alone left her feeling strangely adrift.

But wasn't it normal to feel adrift, when your life's work was eased gently from your grasp? Hadn't she and Matthias taken such pride in building the restaurant up from scratch? Hadn't they treated it as a joint project, putting all their heart and soul—and earnings—into it to build something beautiful out of nothing? And yet, since the new year, she'd only been to their labor of love twice. To be honest about it, going there made her feel superfluous.

It was good, of course it was good, that Anneliese and Hans were taking over and molding it into their vision. A more confident vision, focused on the future. She was probably being an old lady, set in her ways. But wasn't a *Beisl* supposed to be about tradition? There wasn't much tradition in the sleek, new chrome furnishings Hans had ordered, nor the mood lighting that made it appear more like a London nightclub than the cheery, family establishment it had been for the neighborhood these past decades. At least Hans had had the decency to deliver some of the chairs and one of the tables to Heike's home, before having them carted away to goodness knows where.

Perhaps it had been foolish to have hoped the cheery, Alpine-inspired furniture would live on. Pass on to her daughter and grandchildren. Stand firmly for tradition in a crazy, fast-paced world. But of course, the younger generations didn't have the same sentimental ties with the past.

After all, Matthias and his brother had built all of the furniture themselves, to save money back when money was tight. Theo was a skilled carpenter. Both he and Matthias had learned their skills from their own carpenter father. She remembered how they'd laughed thirty-five years ago as they placed those polished tables and chairs into the new space. That intoxicating smell of freshly cut wood permeating throughout the room.

Their own father had ventured from their Tirolian village on his first journey ever to the nation's capital. A sturdy mountain man, Heike remembered him filling the door that first night and gazing around him in wonder at the Viennese restaurant his son and daughter-in-law owned. At the Alpine furniture his sons had carved. At the photos framed and displayed proudly on the walls, taken by Heike on hiking trips to Matthias' village. The same peaks in the rosy light of morning, the blinding noon light and the golden warmth of sunset. Shots of cows and lush green grass in summer, the rich oranges, yellows and reds of autumn, and the stark imagery of those peaks after winter's first snowfall. Children donning Dirndls and Lederhosen gathered at local festivals. A hiking trail leading around the bend, into the vast expanse and wide vistas of the rugged Alps.

The familiar sites of the mountain village Matthias had grown up in, where his father and his brother still lived. The homeland of his grandparents and their parents before them— immortalized on the walls of a *Beisl* in Vienna—seemingly a world away from their Alpine hamlet. Photos that would be gazed upon each evening by Viennese patrons, sitting on furniture that would be at home in an Alpine refuge on steep mountain trails.

That face, wrinkled by years of outdoor living, harsh summer sun followed by harsher winter wind, broke out in a heartbreakingly happy smile. Her father-in-law's blue eyes sparkled with a suspicious layer of moistness, a display of emotion rare for this traditional mountain man. "*Ganz toll*," he uttered, an unusual softness to his gruff voice.

Recognizing his vulnerability, Heike quickly turned away, busying herself at the gleaming bar, drawing four beers from the newly delivered taps. When she had drawn four perfect beers, their gleaming, golden color shimmering warmly from those clear, shiny new glass steins, a perfect foam glazing the top, she set them down at one of the tables. She held her stein upwards. "*Prost!*" she declared. "To years of prosperity, and health. And family and tradition."

Matthias, Theo and their father, Stefan, had clinked glasses with her and toasted to the restaurant's success. A man of few words, Stefan expressed his pride in Matthias and Heike embarking on this adventure.

All the work cleaning and setting up the interior meant Heike had not spent as much time in the kitchen, but she did dart in to emerge with a tray containing four steaming bowls of Frittatensuppe and a basket of sliced, freshly baked bread. After all, one needed to christen a restaurant with a meal. They sat in the warm, comforting light of the empty *Beisl*, two-year-old Anneliese sleeping on a miniature camp bed set up in the corner, enjoying the rich broth of the soup and its thinly sliced strips of pancakes. They broke pieces of the bread, soaking it in the hearty broth as they laughed and spoke about their dreams for the future.

Although Heike had been too exhausted to prepare a meat course, it went without saying that her famous Apfelstrudel was ready for them in the kitchen. She left once again, and returned with four slices, each with a dollop of fresh whipped cream.

Stefan pulled a bottle from an interior pocket of his heavy, winter coat and set it before them on the table. The homemade Schnapps he took such pride in. Matthias stood up and rummaged below the bar, returning to the table with four virgin Schnapps glasses. They toasted again to success, the strong Schnapps coating their throats before digging into the buttery pastry and warm apples, the sweet, perfect consistency of the whipped cream.

"*Mein Gott*, it tastes just like Gertrude's," Stefan said softly, sipping again from his glass.

Heike looked down, embarrassed by the flush in her cheeks. She knew comparing her cooking to that of his deceased wife's was the highest compliment Stefan could bestow on her. Her father-in-law had been skeptical of his son's romance with a *Wienerin*. Even worse, a multi-generational Viennese woman, one with an *Amerikaner* as a father. But Matthias marveled at how she had won his father over and how he had accepted that his son would not be returning to Tirol, but forging his life in the big city.

And that night, he accepted their choice to run a restaurant, one that would become an all-consuming labor of love, but would also—after many, many years—earn them a comfortable living and place them at the heart of the neighborhood. Over the years, neighbors came to eat in their restaurant, bringing their infant children, who would grow up under their eyes into young adults who would return with their own young families. Marriages, First Communions, graduations, promotions, retirements, anniversaries. So many of their neighbor's milestones had been celebrated within those four walls. Walls laden with images from the past.

Images that no longer adorned those walls. In their place stood edgy photos of Manhattan, London, and Tokyo. Skyscrapers and chrome to match the chrome of the new, hip furniture. The dim lighting was meant to convey a mood, but Heike had noticed the older clientele struggling to read the menu. As did she.

Then again, Anneliese and Hans appeared determined to steer away from the traditional clientele she and Matthias had built up over decades, in hopes for a younger, trendier public. Apfelstrudel would never grace the new menus, unless it were somehow "deconstructed" and required elaborate explanations from the waiters before allowing the customer to consume it. Beer was, apparently, also out of vogue, replaced by French wines, Japanese gins, and Scottish whiskeys.

Heike took a sip from her tea, long turned cold, watching as the thrashing rain ushered in the lightning flashing across the sky. With the cancelled walk with Ida, Heike realized how few activities tethered her to her days. Her weekly Italian class at the Italian cultural center used to bring her to Vienna's center, and she would sometimes meet up in the cafés with old university friends from a lifetime ago. Back here, Ida was so tied up with her ill mother. If it weren't for their scheduled walks, she would never see her old friend. And the weather certainly didn't help. Worse, so many old friends she and Matthias had spent time with had moved away. How had that happened?

Until recently, she hadn't known what free time was. How she longed for quiet days spent in her rocking chair, with a cup of tea and a book. How Matthias had laughed at her, called her a homebody. Promised they would both be homebodies together one day. But he hadn't kept that promise, had he?

Without the ceaseless pace of activity at the *Beisl*, her days yawned before her. Not those days of the past, always filled with work and a never-ending to-do list. And this dreary weather did nothing to pull her out of her lonely days. Too much time trapped in her own head, closed in this home she once considered her refuge.

She placed down her cup with its frigid dredges of tea, and plucked up a folder. Placing it on her lap, she remembered

Anneliese cutting her short when she'd offered to help out during the busy Easter season. There had been no convincing her daughter. The sparse, modern new restaurant was evidently in no need of relics from the past.

Placing the folder on her lap, she traced her finger over the colorful green, white, and red design. She opened it gently, extracting the glossy brochure. Here was a destination proud to be a relic from the past, with its ancient bell tower and centuries-old stones. The inn looked charming. A restored farmhouse, growing its own vegetables and with some of its own livestock.

She plucked the separate form laying out the cooking course schedule, including preparation of Easter lamb, Italian style. Two years ago, she and Matthias were to have gone here for a holiday, cooking Italian specialties, hiking into the medieval town, drinking Campari on its sun-drenched *piazza*, exploring surrounding towns with their churches and museums laden with priceless art.

But then everything had changed. Plans had been forgotten.

Anneliese and Hans would probably not be happy she was revisiting things. But then again, so little of what she did these days merited their notice. They told her to relax, take it easy.

What screamed out taking it easy more than a two-week holiday in central Italy?

She startled at an exploding thunderbolt. Looking out again at the pounding rain, she pictured herself spending Easter in sunny Todi, the sun warming her skin, the ancient church bells inviting her to make herself at home.

CHAPTER 3

Chris

THE SUN WAS ONLY A FAINT GLIMMER ON the horizon when Chris jolted at the screeching sound of the alarm. He quickly turned it off, trying desperately to cling to the remnant of his dream. White sand beaches, shimmering waves, a delicate Caribbean breeze rustling in the palm trees, and his sun-bronzed and beautiful wife beside him, snuggling into his side. Content in his embrace.

Rubbing his eyes, he turned to see the real-life version now, hunkered up with all the covers at the far edge of their king-size bed. It had been ages since she'd been content in his embrace. And how the hell could a couple conceive a child if they were always on opposite ends of a football field-sized bed? He sighed deeply and sat up, sliding his legs over the side of the bed. Standing, he shuffled his way to the bathroom for a quick shower. Following his time under the hot jets and a quickly guzzled coffee, he'd be right as rain. He closed the door and turned on the taps. All the remaining vestiges of their last romantic, carefree getaway dissipated into the pounding spray.

HE WAS NEARING DULLES AIRPORT. Traffic at this hour was light, and he was alert after two coffees. Good thing he'd packed the night before. Then again, these days, it felt like he was living out of his suitcase more than his actual house. The house attached to an endless vista of mortgage payments. He and Kaitlyn had fundamental differences when it came to money management. He'd been fine with a smaller, more affordable home. What was wrong with a starter home? When had young people decided to skip that stage? It would have taken the pressure off as they fattened their nest egg.

He steered the ridiculous Mercedes she'd also talked him into onto the lane for long-term parking. Another unnecessary expense. Chris had never cared about cars; back when he and Kaitlyn first started dating after college, neither had she. But to his wife, suburban life was one big pressure cooker of keeping up with the Joneses.

Unfortunately, as Kaitlyn's desire for material comfort expanded, her client list dwindled. She used to love designing kitchens for clients in all income brackets, but now she considered a democratic client list a mark of her own insignificance. Only the elite were worthy of her attention. As their expenses mounted, Kaitlyn began turning down work. She claimed it was a sound business decision. Fewer, but more discerning clients. Clients who would pay more. Clients who would pass her name on to other well-heeled couples looking to remodel. Obviously, investing in the future took money, she told him. Did it ever. Country club memberships, charity auctions, volunteer organizations, but only the "right" kind.

He tried to explain to her the women who dedicated their lives to those activities had the means to live like that. And honestly, if her true goal was to work with worthy causes, what was wrong with volunteering with inner-city kids or building homes for impoverished families? It's not as if DC was deficient in either. All the crowd she was running with now wanted to do was nab celebrity chefs for their high-end galas at luxurious venues. The Davos elite of the charity world, feeling superior and lecturing others, without ever actually getting their hands dirty.

So obviously, this had been a sticking point between them. But he hated to see her throw away what had been a good career and serving as a sidekick to the acerbic wives of hedge fund managers and lobbyists. This newfound social climbing also put a huge financial drain on him. He was working nonstop, and something had to give.

Thank goodness for their upcoming Easter getaway in Italy. It had been ages since they'd gotten away, truly had time for one another. No talk of work or bills.

He took his ticket and eased the monstrosity into a parking space in the long-term lot. The sun was streaked with far more rose than inky blue at this hour. Chris took his trolley and computer case out of the car, locked up and glanced at his watch. Time for another coffee. This exhaustion needed more ammo if he was to make it through this week.

AT LEAST THE FIRST DAY'S MEETINGS WENT WELL. Rob had originally told their assistant to book Chris into a high-end hotel, but Chris had put his foot down. No need wasting money on all the trappings, when a more modest hotel would do fine. As long as it had a gym.

Chris had been up early and at the client's office by seven-thirty. He'd spent all day speaking with management and all the unit heads. Tomorrow he'd be back for more, but tonight he would hit his hotel's small but functional gym, followed by an early night.

He did his last set of bench presses and sat up, wiping the sweat off his forehead. It felt like ages since he swam for the University of Virginia, but he liked to stay in shape. Reunions depressed him as he watched old UVA teammates already packing on the pounds, realizing his lifestyle could lead to the same. Hence, his insistence on the hotel gyms. Ideally, at modestly priced hotels.

He spread his towel down on the mat and began his stretching routine on tired muscles. Hard to believe he'd hit thirty earlier this year, and that those college years were truly far behind him. Back then, Rob had been his best friend and fraternity brother, so going into business together had seemed natural, but, truth be told, even if he still loved Rob like a brother, friendship and business didn't always mix. Like spending on high-end hotels. He and Rob never saw eye to eye on that. And Kaitlyn simply went over Chris' head to Rob—asking him to buy expensive company tables at her charity events, to participate in charity auctions to bolster her standing.

It was awkward, Chris having to tell his best friend to stop giving in to his wife. But although their boutique strategy and communication firm was on solid ground, they still had a long way to go for Chris to feel financially secure. The fact that neither Kaitlyn on the home front nor Rob on the business front could understand this was a constant source of stress. Worse, Rob was in charge of the finances, so Chris shouldn't even *have* to be selling austerity to him.

Chris worked through the series of abs exercises, thinking about their new clients, a sports and lifestyle company looking to expand nationally. He wasn't planning to be out here until after his trip to Italy, had been surprised to learn from Rob that it had been pushed up. After speaking to management today, it seemed they'd been equally surprised by the earlier date. But there was clearly a lot to do, so this initial visit would make their May sessions even more productive. Even so, Chris would have appreciated an entire week at home. Since the new year, he'd never been back more than a day or so before hitting the road again. True, he wasn't moving the needle much in convincing Kaitlyn it was time to start a family, but being home a couple of days each month also wasn't helping them to move in the right direction.

Once again, he wiped the sweat from his brow and stood, undertaking his last stretches as he allowed his heartbeat to slow. He gulped from his water. His room, a bath, and a date with his sushi, an ice-cold Asahi, and the Bulls game on TV were on the program before tumbling into his bed.

He threw his dirty towel into the receptacle, snapped up another bottle of water and an apple, and made his way to his room. Letting himself in with his card key, he ran the bathwater extra hot before grabbing his cell to call Kaitlyn. He dialed and waited. Nothing. He WhatsApped, "Maybe you have a committee meeting I forgot about? Up for another 90 minutes or so. If you're back late, let's try tomorrow. Love you."

Next he tried Rob, but without luck. He left a message for his partner and then stripped down and eased into the bath, the warm water enveloping sore muscles. Quickly he soaped up, washed and rinsed his hair and then lay still in the bath, watching the steam rising up. God, he needed a rest. This Italy trip was coming at exactly the right time. And Kaitlyn only knew it was a surprise. If he told her they were going to Italy, she'd probably ask her charity-world friends for their suggestions, and then she wouldn't rest until they had the most exclusive resort in Positano or Cinque Terre, or wherever that uptight pack of lemmings agreed was worthy of their notice.

No way would they select Todi and Umbria. He'd read about it in some airplane magazine, somewhere. It looked perfect. Low key. Relaxing. Beautiful. It would probably be too cool for the pool, but he'd already signed them up for cooking classes and a couple of spa sessions. Otherwise, a week of walks up to explore Todi and their rental car to ferry them around to other Umbrian hill towns, no firm plans. Open to suggestions locals had for them, exactly how he loved traveling. Two solid weeks of alone time, Italian art, great wine and amazing food. Couldn't come fast enough, as far as he was concerned.

And he knew he'd get his own wife back if they could only spend time alone together, away from the life that no longer felt like theirs. Every week, Kaitlyn seemed increasingly seduced by the charity world of her new socialite friends. Italy would coax her away from that superficial world. Remind her of what they had together. What they could have in the future. If he could talk her into conceiving their firstborn in Italy, that would be the icing on the cake. They'd certainly have more time to give it a go than they had in at least the last year. He splashed water onto his face and rubbed his eyes. Were things already supposed to appear so bleak at thirty?

He sat up, opening the drain. As the water began to circle down, he forced himself out of the rapidly disappearing comfort, retrieving his towel from the decadent towel heater. God, he'd love to have one of these at home.

The bathroom steam swirled around him as he combed his sandy blond hair. He examined himself in the mirror. He may not be swimming for hours every day like he did back in college, but the washboard abs and broad, sculpted shoulders weren't resembling those of an old man yet. He still had it.

Chris dried off and wrapped himself in the plush hotel robe. He looked down at his phone. Kaitlyn hadn't even seen his WhatsApp. No blue checks on his message to Rob either, but he doubted Rob was hard at work. Rob may've been his best man and the friend he trusted most, but he just wasn't pulling his weight at their company the same way he did when they began four years ago. That would also need dealing with when he got back.

He looked at the mirror again, at the young, fit man with an exhausted face peering back at him. He shook his head. As knackered as he was, he still had a hot date with dinner and sports on TV. Exiting the bathroom, he retrieved his nigari and sashimi from the mini fridge and flicked on the remote.

ROB MUST HAVE BEEN DISTRACTED SETTING UP THE CHICAGO TRIP. Not only had the company not needed him so soon—although the visit proved to be successful and a good start to the serious work that would soon get underway—but Rob hadn't even realized the company was shut down Friday and Saturday, an annual tradition marking its founding.

Rob had only responded in texted monosyllables to his earlier messages. The man really was distracted, so he didn't even bother involving him with the changes. He arranged hotel checkout earlier, with a credit on his next stay, and he managed a Thursday evening flight that would take him straight to the airport after wrapping up at the company, thereby getting him back at Dulles by ten and forty minutes later to his home.

He hoped Kaitlyn would be home. They hadn't spoken, only exchanged brief messages. He'd surprise her tonight, maybe take tomorrow off and spend the day in bed with her.

As he sat at the airport, laptop propped open, writing up his initial report, he realized just how much he was allowing his work to usurp his life. Yeah, building a business took time, but both partners had to do an equal amount of work, and Rob most definitely wasn't.

They'd just hired a new associate, and Chris had long been suggesting they train her up, that she accompany him on his trips and learn to assess the companies, with him alongside her to help her learn. His hope was that one day she could carry out these assessments on her own. Chris knew Rob was using her to shoulder the burden of much of the financial work. Yeah, they both agreed it would help her understand the business, but Chris got the impression Rob was finding it convenient to palm most of his work off on the eager, young employee.

They called boarding, and Chris packed up his laptop. When he reached his aisle seat, allowing him a bit more comfort for his long legs, and his immediate neighbors had been seated, he opened his laptop to pick off where he'd stopped. Soon the flight attendant passed by and asked that tray tops be closed to prepare for takeoff. He snapped it shut once again and closed his eyes. When he woke, confused, they were already up in the air and the cabin crew was distributing drinks and a sandwich. Realizing he'd skipped lunch, Chris gratefully accepted it.

As he ate, he took a pen from the inside of his coat and began to sketch on his napkin. The church belltower stood at the central point. Soon he began to fill in a town—a jumble of medieval houses clinging to a steep hill. Then he began to draw a wall around the town and olive trees down below. As he sketched away, more ideas came to him and soon his little napkin was brimming with his Italian destination. As it took shape before his eyes, the furrow that seemed to be forming a permanent ridge in his brow smoothed over, his low-grade headache disappeared, and the muscles that seemed to tug his mouth into a frown twitched upward.

The stewardess came to collect empty cups and containers. As she reached over to take his neighbor's empty cup, she looked down. "Oh, wow. That's adorable. Did you just draw that now?"

Chris looked up, startled. "Oh, you mean, this doodle?" He looked down at it, as if with fresh eyes. "Yeah, I do it when I'm distracted."

"It's gorgeous. Are you an artist? A graphic designer?"

Chris laughed. "Much less interesting. Management consultant."

She smiled. "One with an artistic bent, I see. It's Italy, isn't it?"

"Good eye." He looked up again. "It's Todi. I've only seen it in photos, but I'm taking my wife there next month. A surprise."

She smiled again. "You'll both love it. Want a woman's advice? Take that napkin home and use it in the surprise. She'll be thrilled. I know I would if my husband were so romantic with his surprises." She winked. "And I travel for a living."

"Thanks. I think I will." He handed her the items to be thrown away and tucked his napkin into his breast pocket.

CHRIS WAS EXHAUSTED. The day and flight had seemed endless, as did the otherwise short drive home. He stopped off to fill up the tank and pick up a coffee. That would help stave off the exhaustion that threatened to make him drift off to sleep when he should be alert.

He quietly let himself in, relieved to see light from under their bedroom door on the second-floor landing. He glanced at his watch, pleased to see Kaitlyn was still up at eleven. He took off his shoes and padded to the kitchen, where he poured two generous glasses of red wine. Extracting his napkin drawing from his breast pocket, he wrapped it around the stem of the glass he would hand her. Coming home early would be a double surprise—the perfect time to tell her the secret location of their upcoming vacation. Honestly, their departure couldn't come soon enough for him. He was tired of bottling up his excited anticipation. At least they could share their enthusiasm these next two weeks leading up to their flight—conveniently too late for the socialites to weigh in.

With a smile, he walked up the stairs, the thick carpeting muffling his shoeless steps. He hesitated in front of the door. After all, there was no sense in causing his wife to have a heart attack, if the door opened with no warning.

"Kaitlyn," he called out. "I wrapped up earlier—thought I'd surprise you." He pushed the door open with his shoulder.

The first thing he noticed was the bedside lamp casting a glow over his wife's bare limbs. She was dressed in silky, red lingerie he'd never seen. Her auburn hair splayed out on the pillow, on red silk sheets Chris had also never seen before. The second thing he noticed caused him to gasp as if he'd been punched in the gut. "What the f..."

Kaitlyn shot up in bed, shoving the man beside her, clad only in Calvin Klein briefs, away from her bare neck. In her hurry to sit up, her strap slipped, red lace that already left nothing to the imagination falling down to reveal one nipple. Kaitlyn pushed it up hastily, preserving her modesty in front of her husband. Panic shone in her eyes.

Chris felt the same molten rage he'd felt in the pool lanes when an adversary was pulling ahead. Blood pumped through his body as he prayed this was a nightmare he was going to wake from. Hell, he'd even take falling asleep in his car on the road home over this fresh hell.

In that moment, the man turned around and their gazes crossed. "Oh, shit," said the familiar voice.

Without thinking, Chris released his grip on the wine glasses. Ruby red wine absorbed into the expensive white carpet Chris always thought a stupid choice for their bedroom.

"Chris, I can explain," his wife's lover—*his wife's lover?*—said, scrambling for his T-shirt and pulling it over his expanding paunch. "This isn't what it looks like."

His best friend. His fraternity brother. His business partner. His goddamned Best Man. Rob screwing his wife. Behind his back, probably every time he was out of town. This was the same bastard sending him out of town in the first place. How had this never occurred to him?

And Kaitlyn, always pushing him to work more. More money. More trappings of wealth, while she played the society wife.

And screwed his business partner.

The buzzing grew in his ears. He formed his hands into fists. Rob had never been athletic. Was always up for beer pong when Chris headed off to bed in order to wake at five for his morning swim training. And post-college life hadn't been kind to him. Chris would be able to pummel him with no competition, but he purposefully restrained his fists. Better to destroy him with lawyers.

"I don't want to hear it. Both of you, get your clothes on and get the hell out of my house. I've been paying the mortgage singlehandedly the last three years. Start lawyering up, Rob. The business dissolves as of tomorrow."

"Whoa, you're getting way too hasty." Rob held up his hands. "You're angry. I get it. Sleep on it."

"You're right, Rob. I'm tired. Monday morning. Our boardroom. Eight a.m. I'll be there with my lawyer."

"Chris, you're not thinking straight," Kaitlyn pleaded, pouting the way she did when trying to look seductive, unaware of how ridiculous she was. Her big, brown eyes shimmered with unshed tears. "It was one mistake. We drank too much. Nothing happened." Her voice pleaded with him.

Was Rob even the first one? Had he been completely blind?

He turned away from her towards his former best friend. With great restraint, he opened his fists and placed his hands against firm quadriceps, willing them to stay still. "And Rob …"

"Yes?" he asked, eyes hopeful, lips turning slightly upwards.

"Take your tramp with you. I'll arrange for a time for her to come back and get her things through my lawyer."

He looked down at the napkin he'd doodled earlier that night, with its hopeful sketching of Todi, now tinged the blood red of spilled wine. He turned his back on the pair and retraced his steps down the stairs. With long steps, he made his way to his study, switched on the lights, bolted the door, and poured himself a generous glass of whiskey.

CHAPTER 4

Grace

GRACE BLINKED TWICE, CERTAIN HER FIFTY-EIGHT-YEAR-OLD BRAIN was playing tricks on her. But no, the sky was still blue, the sun warm and the flowers blossoming. Durham looked poised for June heat, not gearing up for the first week of April. What was going on?

Market Square was a riot of color, when only last week, it had been blanketed in constant rain. Were the April showers to be replaced by April flowers? What was the world coming to?

Grace glanced at her watch and realized she was running late from her dentist appointment. She didn't want Nicola to have to wait for her. Her old friend was so rarely up in these parts, so this tea and a chat were something she'd looked forward to for some time. She hurried along Silver Street until she reached the familiar staircase on the right-hand side. Quickly, she hustled up, grateful she could still be spry at her age. She burst into the familiar tearoom, relieved that Nicola had not yet arrived.

"Hello, Grace. How are you? We haven't seen you in a while," a familiar voice called from the counter.

Grace smiled. "Hi, Laura, I'm fine. How's that adorable baby of yours?"

The waitress glided over, placing the menu on the table Grace favored, with clear views out to the bustling shopping street. "Still adorable, when he's not being a terror." She cracked a smile. "He's crawling all over the house. Tearing down everything. We know it's a matter of time until he's running around."

Grace chuckled. "That is their talent."

"Speaking of more civilized children. Will your daughter be joining you?"

"Not today, I'm afraid. But an old friend is in town and will be arriving soon. I'll wait to order."

"Take your time. We survived the morning crunch. It's quieter now." Someone called from a nearby table and she took her leave.

Grace gazed out the window at the shoppers and tourists passing by below. She and Ellen often met here, when Kathryn had her piano lessons or was visiting with classmates. But Grace hadn't seen Ellen in a while. Their phone conversations always seemed rushed. She hated to pry, but something Kathryn had mentioned made her wonder if there were problems at home. Grace's son-in-law could be prickly in the best of circumstances, but Grace had hoped this difficult period had brought them together.

The bell rang as someone came up the stairs. Grace turned to see a familiar, well-loved face. Nicola bustled over and wrapped Grace in a big hug. When she pulled back, Grace laughed. "Oh, my. Look at you. Malaga is treating you well. You're so wonderfully tan. Surely it's criminal to be so bronzed in Durham."

She laughed her familiar laugh as she sat across from Grace. "You should come visit. But what's going on here? When is Durham so warm in April?"

"It won't last," said Grace, shaking her head. "Maybe you brought it with you."

Nicola took Grace's hands in hers. "It truly is so good to see you. You know how awful I felt not being able to return for the funeral. But my mother was down for her operation. How are you *really* doing?"

That question everyone asked her. How *was* she doing? The funeral was a blur of shaking so many hands, saying thank you thousands of times, and comforting Ellen as she sobbed beside her.

Grace shook her head. "I really don't know. Things are better than they were, at least ..." She trailed off. Grace was used to the stiff upper lip with most of her friends, certainly with Richard's friends and colleagues, but she and Nicola went way back. Had studied together in this town years earlier. How honest could she be with old friends?

Nicola clutched her friend's hand tighter. She dropped it when Laura came over to take their order and returned quickly with the tea, fresh scones, and elderberry fizz. Nicola spread cream and jam onto her scone. "I know everyone tells you time is the great healer, but it's never easy. Whenever you want, you know José and I would love to have you visit us."

"I know. Thank you." She took deep breaths and kept her eyes down, carefully studying her scone. After a moment, she took a fortifying sip of tea. "To add to everything, Mum's getting worse. She's in the home, with good care, but every time I go there, I'm never even sure if she'll remember me."

Nicola winced. "I'm so sorry to hear that. Your mum used to be so funny."

"She still is. Sometimes." She shook her head. "But those moments are always fewer and far between. Then I don't know what's going on with Ellen. She was devastated, of course. You know how close she and Richard always were. But I get the impression she and Rupert are having problems. They'll be off to Italy for Easter, however, and Kathryn will stay with me. Maybe some time alone together is what they need."

"I hope so," said Nicola, placing a hand over hers. "But after, you need to understand what *you* need, Grace. Malaga has perfect weather in September. Start looking for a ticket. A few weeks away might be what you need. You and Richard never came in the past. I never understood why I could never lure you. But at least it's not a place that holds memories of him for you. José will be away for work most of the month, so it will be a real girls' holiday. What do you say?"

Grace smiled and took another sip of tea. "Maybe. It might be time ..."

"It definitely is. Now let me show you a photo of Clara; she's *such* a teenager now. And believe me, she's *all* Spanish in temperament."

Grace studied the phone and then looked up. "She's always been so pretty, but now she's drop-dead gorgeous. How's José handling the boys buzzing around?"

Nicola chuckled. "About as well as you can imagine a Spanish father would handle it." She finished her tea. "Now, while we have this Spanish-like sunshine, I want to take a walk with you to the castle to see our old dorms."

Grace knew she'd feel better with her old friend back. A walk down memory lane—even if those memories were decades ago—was exactly what she needed right now.

"WHAT DO YOU MEAN, YOU NEED TIME ALONE? I thought Italy was time for you to be alone?" Grace sat in her kitchen with Ellen, pouring tea. The sunny, balmy weather from a few days ago was already a distant memory. Rain now thrashed at the windows. Grace had baked her daughter's favorite biscuits that morning, knowing she would stop by, but Ellen hadn't even registered them.

"Things ... uh ... were kind of rough even before Dad ... before Dad ..." Ellen stifled a sob.

Grace patted her hand, her heart aching for her daughter.

"I guess the shock put things on hold for a while, but now we're back where we were before. This is the worst time to take a trip."

"But you can cancel, surely? Postpone? I can still take Kathryn."

"No." Ellen shook her head. "Rupert doesn't want her to see. Not that you could miss the tension in the house. Kathryn's a smart girl, but we need time alone. We have a couples' therapist lined up. Rupert has time from the university during Easter break, and Kathryn's on term break. It's the best possible time."

Grace bit her tongue and stayed silent, waiting for Ellen to reveal the plan. Rupert always devised the plan, generally without Ellen's input, and even more stridently on issues where Ellen had the most experience.

"So Rupert thinks ... I mean, Rupert and I think, it would be best if you and Kathryn go to Italy and take our place. Then we can fully concentrate on ... on trying to work things out."

"Italy? Kathryn and I?"

Ellen rubbed one hand over her face. "It's not like we'd be sending you to Rome, or Naples. It's a little village in Umbria. The place looks fabulous. You can walk into town. There's plenty of space, a game room for the kids. Ping pong, billiards, that kind of thing. There are cooking classes, too. I think that would be brilliant for Kathryn."

Grace chewed her lip. She'd been counting on Kathryn also being able to visit friends, keep up her sports activities. She was such an athletic girl. Grace wasn't sure if so much time in proximity with her grandmother was really what a twelve-year-old girl wanted. What if there were no other kids there? Would she be homesick?

Ellen looked at Grace, a layer of tears causing her bright blue eyes to glisten. Pain was etched on her pretty face. "Please, Mum. We need to make this work. It'll be too hard with Kathryn around. Just two weeks."

Grace sighed. She reached across and touched her daughter's cheek. "Of course, darling. Don't you worry about us. Kathryn and I will have a wonderful time, won't we? Two girls off to enjoy ourselves in Italy."

CHAPTER 5

Emma

EMMA SIPPED HER CAPPUCCINO. She swore the smartest investment the hotel ever made was their high-end coffee maker. At least, *she* got tremendous enjoyment out of it each morning.

She looked out the window at the early-morning spectacle playing out. It was still early April, but they were firmly in spring. It had been a rough winter, with lots of snow, but the days were growing longer, and that springtime scent was in the air when she walked out into the vegetable garden each morning. Emma loved to listen to the birds, who were making their way back to the Italian peninsula after their winter journeys to Africa. By next month, the swallows would be swooping through the sky. At this rate, they may even be able to open the pool for the May First weekend. Touch iron, as the Italians said, for luck.

She savored this time of silence, before the household began to stir. Chiara, of course, had been back in Rome the past two years, studying economics at the university, dancing in her free time, and staying at Emma's apartment, the one she'd purchased after putting the Aventino home on the market. In exchange for free rent, Chiara had to welcome her mother whenever she wanted to stay a few days in Rome.

Being back in Rome had also been good for Chiara, allowing her to get closer with her father once again. Yes, Dario was still running around after women half his age, but he also made time for his children once again, and for this, Emma was grateful. Marco and Valerio had spent time in Rome over several vacations, and their father had taken them to soccer games and spent quality time with them. A welcome change from the past.

Today, Marco and Valerio could slumber later than usual. This afternoon, they would have soccer, but a sleep-in was more than deserved by her twelve-year-olds. The twins had adjusted wonderfully to village life, quickly making new friends and enjoying their reduced traffic existence. Everywhere they needed to go could be reached by foot or by bike, a big change from their native Rome.

And she? Well, to be honest, sometimes Umbrian life seemed a bit provincial. But on those occasions, she'd hop down for a few days to Rome, see friends, try out new restaurants, get to the theatre, see a couple of exhibitions and—yes, why not?— throw a few coins in the Trevi Fountain. After the brush with familiar city life, she was always content to return to her new life. Her Umbrian life.

She examined the Easter week calendar, checking and cross-checking the reservations, and inputting into the system the airport pickups, the cooking class schedules, the dinner reservations.

A kiss on her cheek roused her from her concentration. She soaked in the familiar scent of aftershave.

"*Buongiorno* to my lovely wife. Tell me, do we really have to get back to work next week?"

"'Fraid so," she laughed. "But haven't these past three months been blissful?" She turned and gave Mark a kiss. "Nothing like running a hotel with no guests."

"Yeah, I know. A stress-free existence. If only we could afford to do this all the time. Keeping the restaurant open last month for dinner reservations kept some cash infusions running into the place. But it also gave some time to Annarita and Giuseppe with the new baby." He stroked her cheek. "But it's time. The Three Coins Inn needs to open again to paying guests. Tell me the lineup next week." He rubbed his hands together, like he did when he helped coach the local kids' soccer team.

Emma smiled up at him. Even after four years together, and three of those married, she couldn't believe how lucky she'd gotten on her second chance at love. After Dario trampled on her heart, she'd been so convinced she was done with men, but rekindling her relationship with Mark had done wonders for them both. And, despite all their fears, their kids—after a few hiccups—had adjusted relatively well to their new, blended family.

Emma turned back to the guest reservations. "Yeah, so we're completely full Easter week. The Japanese tour that comes through every spring will be back. Easiest clients ever. You remember Mr. Tanaka. He'll have them going early each morning, off exploring Umbria and Tuscany. They only have one cooking class with us, and Easter dinner here. Breakfast has to be arranged early for them, in time to hop on their coaches, but, otherwise, a piece of cake. They only sleep here.

"We have a couple from Ohio. A TV news producer and his wife. She's fully booked in the spa, and he has organized them both for cooking classes.

"We have an Austrian woman here for two weeks. She speaks perfect Italian, but says she's half American. Would prefer Italian, but will go into the English cooking classes, if that's all we have. A few spa sessions, too.

"Another American couple, from Virginia. Signed up for cooking classes and spa sessions.

"And the last was supposed to be a British couple—some town up north. The name escapes me." She looked down at her notes. "Oh, yeah. Here it is, Durham. They just called. Something came up for his work. They can't come, but the wife's mother will come with their twelve-year-old daughter. A grandmother-granddaughter spa session, and cooking classes together. Isn't that nice?" She looked up. "Maybe Marco and Valerio will be excited to have someone their age here."

"Maybe." Mark smiled. "If she likes playing sports." He tapped a finger under one entry. "Is that Tiffany and Simone, I see?"

Emma smiled. "Yes, Easter weekend only. They'll visit Simone's parents in Perugia Easter Monday, but they wanted to come for the weekend here. Tiffany was away last time I was in Rome. So, I'll be so happy to see her. It's been too long." She turned around and slipped her arms around Mark's neck. "Are you sorry the girls won't be down?"

"Yes, but they have their cousin's wedding. And they've promised they can make it a week for May First holidays. I'm holding them to that."

"It'll be great to have them here again. I'll try to see if Chiara can manage to come up to see them, too." She smiled. "You know she considers them bonus sisters."

He stroked her hair off her forehead. "Everything has been a bonus since finding you again, Emma," he whispered. "Hey, you know we're still technically on holiday. Why don't you come back to bed for a bit before we get to work? Starting in a week, we won't have that luxury ..."

She laughed and whispered in his ear, "I thought you'd never ask."

CHAPTER 6

Madison

MADISON LOUNGED BACK IN THE CUSHIONS of the new place on North Front Street that had been getting rave reviews. Her friend, Amanda, was joining her in a boozy brunch. Perhaps not a wise idea, but she'd locked herself in her apartment all week after the Show From Hell.

From her plate glass windows, she gazed down enviously at the Scioto Riverwalk, at the myriad of families, lovers, schoolkids, and joggers passing by all day. Paralysis had set in. Madison was too scared to go out for groceries. Too scared to get to the gym. She cancelled all her plans.

The shame she felt as she slinked out of the studio Monday morning was crippling. Brad had been more than happy to take over the rest of her segments, and, of course, Janice, the new newsreader, could hardly hide her excitement at jumping in to substitute for her. Then again, who could blame her? She would have been the same at her first job. Hell, she'd be the same today if she could sub for a shamed anchor in a top-ten market.

Madison still hoped all the excitement would wear down by this week. They had already asked her to take a few days last week and this Monday. Her agent, Rita, had been caught by surprise, out of town, but she returned late last night and had already arranged to come to Madison's apartment later that day.

Rita knew nothing about Madison's brunch outing with Amanda, had been adamant she needed to stay put in her apartment. But really, not everyone watched the morning shows. It would probably all blow over soon. She'd go insane if she had to stay cooped up in her place another day.

Amanda was an old college friend, now working for the local paper. She wouldn't betray Madison. And Madison desperately needed a sympathetic ear right now. Her email was filled with vitriol. Say what you want about Midwestern politeness—it seemed all bets were off the table where infidelity was concerned. She had stopped logging the insults. *Whore. Jezebel. Prostitute. Hussie. Conniving bitch. Satanic slut.* She'd heard it all. This brunch was a way to escape the hate. At least for a few precious hours.

Madison sipped her Bellini. Brunch cocktails were the best part of Sundays. Maybe starting her day with alcohol would have deadened her emotions and helped her through the early morning assault last Monday.

"Enough about me. You saw the on-air meltdown. I need good news." She paused when the waitress brought over the eggs Benedict, studying her a little too closely for Madison's liking. This was such a stupid idea. They were probably gossiping about her, too. "Tell me what's new with you and help get my mind off my own problems."

Amanda laughed and took a deep sip of her Bloody Mary. "What do you want me to say, Madison? A girl's gotta work hard to top you."

Madison groaned. "I deserve that. But seriously. What's new in the world of print? Any job openings?"

"You wish," said Amanda, tucking into her waffles. "Print's been dying for a while. As you know. But there's been a big trade-union scandal I've been assigned to. Mum's the word, but I'll let you in on it when we've done more digging."

"God, I wish I were doing hard-hitting pieces. Not just hair and makeup tips. And now I'll be suspended from hair and makeup tips for a few more days."

Amanda had already worked her way steadily through much of her Bloody Mary. Their bar bill was always substantial when Madison joined her for brunch.

"I dunno. Are you sure it's just a few more days' suspension? Only a week? It seems a bit lenient for that kind of transgression."

Madison leaned in closer, flicking her perfectly coiffed locks over one shoulder. "Are you saying everyone's decided I'm in the wrong?" She glanced around quickly to ensure no waitresses were in the vicinity. "Yeah, okay, I made a mistake with the producer. But he just arrived. How was I to know he was married? Married with kids?"

Amanda shook her head, her eyes glazing over. "Yeah, not sure many people are gonna buy that. He left Florida for problems with womanizing. I mean, why would someone go from a bigger market to a smaller one? You didn't check that out?" She giggled. "Not much of a reporter, are you, Maddie? Plus, your whole audience is made up of housewives. How do you think they like the idea of their beloved morning host breaking up happy families? To them, all families are happy until the evil temptress hones in on her prey. Gotta admit, it's not a good look." She leaned back against the cushions, peering at Madison through drooping eyes.

Okay, so Amanda was a bit of a lush at their brunch get-togethers, but could she be right?

Jennifer had been cagey about asking her to go home and rest a few days while it blew over. No one had ever actually said she could return on the following Tuesday. She'd just assumed that to be the case since they said they'd be in touch Monday. But what if Amanda, tipsy as she was, had accurately assessed the situation? What if viewers weren't ready to forgive her?

She met her friend's gaze. "So, you think the audience will punish me, but allow him back?"

Amanda nodded. "Sorry, not what you want to hear, but I think that's exactly how it'll play out. He's not in front of the camera. And you'll be seen as the Jezebel breaking up a family."

Madison peered down into her half-finished Bellini and the eggs Benedict growing cold on her plate. Suddenly, the thought of eating or drinking made her stomach roil. She needed to get back home and prepare herself for Rita stopping by.

Taking out her credit card, she signaled the waitress. She looked at Amanda, forcing a smile. "Hate to cut things short, but time flew. My agent will be coming over soon. Can I help you find a cab on my way back?"

THE PACING WAS BECOMING A HABIT. Back and forth before the plate glass window. Observing the world from above, while separate from it.

She hated to admit it, but Amanda was probably right. Aaron would be forgiven. Of course he would. She'd have the big, red scarlet "A" emblazoned across her chest forever. And her audience would not be swayed. In New York or Miami, maybe it would blow over. But not here. She felt the panic well within for the umpteenth time that day. The mantelpiece clock kept ticking away loudly. Still no sign of Rita.

The buzzer rang and Madison clutched her heart. God, she had to hold it together. An attack of nerves in front of her agent certainly wasn't going to improve anything. Rita was hardly the supportive, mothering type. She approached the door and answered the intercom. "Sure Mike, send her up." She closed her eyes and took deep, restorative breaths. Channel that inner confidence.

At the open doorway, she struggled to morph her rictus grin into something that looked warm, natural. The elevator dinged and Rita floated out. Her Saint Bart's tan looked incongruous in central Ohio's April. Madison held her arms out in welcome, and Rita bestowed her habitual air-kisses. Madison ushered her in, seating her on the leather couch overlooking the views Madison had been obsessively tracking these past days.

Rita settled into the couch, tossing her Hermès bag beside her and leaning forward, pinning Madison with that sharp-eyed gaze that could stop the young woman's heart mid-beat. "So, nothing better to do than hook up with the industry's most famous womanizer? What was going through that head of yours? Clearly, not much."

Sitting in the armchair opposite, Madison became endlessly fascinated by her hands, clutching them together, observing as they trembled of their own accord. Head bent down, she whispered. "No, I obviously wasn't thinking."

Rita breathed in through her nose. "Madison, I know you're frustrated you're not moving up as quickly as other reporters. But did you honestly think sleeping with *Aaron* was going to get you ahead?"

Madison looked up and met that intimidating gaze.

Rita held up one bony, bejeweled finger. "And before you think of lying to me, do *not* even attempt to tell me you were in love with him. How his own wife can even stand that blithering idiot is beyond my comprehension. I certainly hope she was smart enough to find a higher-IQ individual to father her children." She sighed. "What do I always tell you?"

"Hard work, up the ratings." Madison focused on a point beyond Rita's head. "Become the trusted morning host. Build up a following to catapult me to the evening anchor chair."

"Yes, and yet you blew it all on a roll in the hay." She stood and paced to the window. "Worse, one who we know was substandard and was using you for easy sex."

Madison looked up and breathed in, fending off the tears she knew were building up within. She would not break down in front of Rita. She would not. "But … but," she stuttered a few times before finding her voice. "Do you think I can go back on Tuesday? Or, if they need a bit more time … Thursday or Friday? Surely it's better to get back there sooner. Smooth things over."

Rita shook her head slowly, shoulder-length hair swishing luxuriously over Pilates-toned shoulders. "You will go nowhere near that studio for quite some time."

"Won't that make it all worse?"

"Poor, little, clueless Madison. Did I teach you nothing?" She extracted her phone and clicked it, handing it to Madison.

Madison looked. There she was at brunch this morning, apparently splattered all over Twitter. "Maneater on the prowl in Short North, scouting out her next prey." "Wives of Columbus, lock up your husbands. She's baaack!" Madison looked in disbelief at the photos. Retouched, obviously. Her blouse wasn't that low. Her lips not that red. They really had it in for her. Or they were desperate for clicks.

Rita was observing her coolly. "That will only grow worse. We can't control the narrative if you go back. You need to take some leave. A long leave. Far away from here."

Madison slapped her hands on distressed-jeaned legs. "What do you mean far away? Foreign reporting?" she asked hopefully.

"No." Rita shook her head. "No reporting. A break. Time for reflection. Time to let this work its way out of the collective psyche. Pray some bigger, better scandal emerges in the meantime. No, my dear." Rita returned to the couch and sank into the plush leather. "You are bound for Italy."

Madison felt her entire forehead furrowing in confusion. "Italy. Why Italy? For how long?"

Rita placed a long arm over the edge of the couch, her jewels and golden bangles catching the light of the chandelier. "Why not Italy? Poetic justice, really. Aaron and the Missus were to travel there for a two-week cooking class in the hills of Umbria. Too late for them to cancel. It was Christine to suggest you take the tickets."

"Christine? The wife? Why?"

"I imagine to get you far away. Management have already agreed. I suspect the wife knows a thing or two about trying to keep her husband in a job. Cooperating with the network to smooth things out. Regardless, the end result is the same. You're on a plane next Friday. You will land in Rome and be driven up to Todi, where you will spend two full weeks in a little Umbrian hill town, learning to cook pasta. When you come back, you will be modest and contrite. You'll say you fled because of the embarrassment. The shame. Italy gave you time to reflect. You're Catholic, right?"

Madison nodded.

"Even better. Seeking redemption. You go up to the local church, light some candles, kneel in prayer. We'll manage to get some photographer to snap a few photos we can use later. Viewers can handle redemption stories. Particularly when the cheating husband was hardly a paragon of virtue."

Madison sank her head into her hands, willing the tears to wait until her agent's departure.

Rita slid over and placed a hand on one shoulder. "You messed up, Madison. Messed up big time. This is your only chance to claw your way back. And hey, it's not like we're sending you to Pyongyang. Two weeks in Italy is a pretty easy penance. Behave yourself." She reached into her purse and extracted tickets and some type of hotel brochure. "Study these. Pack up. For God's sake, no more brunches. Stay inside. Order your food in. Your next outing is the cab taking you to the airport. We'll speak on Wednesday, okay?"

Madison nodded mechanically as Rita air-kissed her again and sauntered to the door with a jaunty, "*Arrivederci.*"

Madison slumped into the couch and allowed all the pent-up tears to roll down her face, unchecked.

CHAPTER 7

Heike

HEIKE WOKE WITH A START, momentarily confused about her whereabouts, until she caught sight of the countryside speeding by. Decidedly Italian countryside. Her heart beat a little faster as a hilltown came into view, its hulking castle ruin dominating the town clinging around it. Austria also boasted ruined castles, but they were not interchangeable with those of their southern neighbor. Even after a lifetime of traveling around Europe, she delighted in the changes in landscapes, architecture, and styles when one crossed borders. The new languages caressing your ears. The new flavors stimulating your tastebuds.

Despite her pleasure in being back in Italy after such a long absence, these night trains were so discombobulating. Last night she'd boarded her train at Südbanhof, and chugged out of Vienna. Heike never lasted long in the couchettes, with the comforting rocking making her eyelids heavy and hastening her voyage into the world of sleep. When the conductor announced the breakfast trays would be making their rounds, her cabin-mates opened the window screen, and Heike had been amazed at the change in vegetation, the decidedly Italian-and-no-longer-Austrian towns whizzing by on the changed landscape.

Heike and Matthias were supposed to come here together. But now, she was here alone.

Heike sighed and smiled politely to her cabin-mates. She attempted to tame her hair, but there was no point in trying to make a real difference before she had her needed jolt of coffee.

The conductor came back with his trolley, handing out trays with a cappuccino and an Italian cornetto, along with a small glass of orange juice. Heike tried not to make a face. After all, she'd be eating too much in these days—a spare first breakfast in Italy would do her good.

The caffeine was greatly appreciated. She sipped from the paper cup and looked again out the window. The other cabin passengers were chattering away in Japanese and, she thought, Polish, so she allowed it to become white noise as she watched the landscape speed by.

Her daughter and son-in-law had not been pleased with her news that she would be spending the holidays in Italy, in the same region she and Matthias had long planned on visiting. But she was tired of feeling like an extra wheel in her own family. Made to feel useless in the restaurant she and Matthias had built up over the years. Yes, perhaps it was right that the new generation wanted to take it in a new direction. But it hurt. It hurt to feel excluded from the only life she'd ever known. It hurt to feel somehow shunned from the local community they'd built around the restaurant, a community that crumbled rapidly when her restaurant changed from being a popular local magnet to a trendy spot that actively worked to attract clients from other parts of Vienna.

This break would be good for her. Time to put things in perspective. Time to brush up on her rusty Italian and to enjoy cooking classes. Time to return to a country where she and Matthias had often vacationed together. For a long time following his death, Heike hadn't felt ready to return. It would still be hard, but she felt stronger now. She would still miss him—she always missed him—but now she didn't have to fear dissolving into tears every day.

It was time.

The hotel was small enough that the faces of other hotel guests would become familiar, at least to exchange some words each day. And she could walk into Todi and take buses to nearby towns. On holidays, she and Matthias had always enjoyed basing themselves in Italian regions and exploring the surroundings. Sadly, they'd never squeezed in enough vacation time—always assuming they'd have time when they started retreating slowly from full-time work at the restaurant. How foolish to pin all that future happiness on something that would never come to be. Why hadn't they taken a month off each year—closing down for July or August? Other restaurants did so.

Heike sighed. It didn't do to dwell on bad choices. Wasn't she taking more initiative now? Making up for lost time? And she loved Italian cooking—those cooking classes would help when she was back home. No longer cooking for her work, but inviting friends and neighbors to dine. She needed to get herself out more, rebuild friendship groups. The *Beisl* had been her whole existence. Now she would have to learn to take charge of her second act. New hobbies, new friends, new adventures.

This trip was her first, modest step.

She examined the timetable. She would get off in Florence and switch to the regional train that would carry her to

Perugia. There, the hotel had arranged for a car to take her the last forty minutes to Todi.

She'd arrive in time to freshen up before dinner and an early bedtime. Her daughter and son-in-law hadn't thought she was capable, and yet, here she was. Taking on Italy alone. She turned back to the window, watching another picturesque, medieval hilltown speed by.

CHAPTER 8

Chris

WHAT THE HELL? The more he chewed it over in his brain, the less sense it made. His wife and his closest college friend. His best man, for Christ's sake. How could they have done this to him? Was laughing at him when they were in bed together part of the fun?

Chris shifted in his cramped economy-class seating, trying in vain to stretch his long legs as much as he could under the tiny seat space. He swore they kept moving the seats closer together with each passing year. As each generation grew taller, airlines pretended they were transporting hobbits.

He looked at his watch. Still hours to go until he reached Rome, where a shuttle would be waiting to take him to the Umbria property. The hotel had been understanding when he'd canceled his wife's reservation. For a while, he'd considered canceling his own, too, but it was too late to get the deposit back. And hell if he didn't need a radical escape from the dumpster fire his life had become. He didn't think he'd be very good company, doubted he'd be Miss Congeniality in his cooking classes, but he needed to shake things up.

The last two weeks had been miserable. Yes, he'd kicked Kaitlyn out. The house was in both of their names, but he was the one footing the monstrous mortgage payments the past years. She'd be back in his absence to gather most of her things, but his lawyer had already delivered news that Chris' intention was to sell the property as soon as possible and to split the proceeds, with an eye to the disproportionate mortgage payments from Chris' side. Let Kaitlyn hire her own lawyer. The two professionals could hash it out while he was a continent away.

Since Kaitlyn had left, Chris had been shell-shocked. He never would have accepted it well. But honestly, an affair with some random guy she'd met would have been easier than his best friend. How could the two people he loved most have betrayed him so cruelly?

Here Chris was, trying to convince Kaitlyn it was time to take the next step, have a family. And all along, she'd been screwing Rob. Under his nose. In his own damn bed. What kind of a person did that?

And Rob. He couldn't even think about the guy without wanting to split his skull. They'd gone through everything together. Rob knew how much Kaitlyn meant to Chris. He was constantly telling Rob how much he wanted to be a dad, for Kaitlyn and Chris to embark on this new adventure. Chris remembered Rob slapping him on the back over beers, telling Chris he was a better man than he was. That he was sure Chris and Kaitlyn would make amazing parents. And then, on the side, he was banging Chris' wife?

Chris knew it started about a year ago—about the same time Rob was apparently inventing nonstop travel for Chris. Even this latest—the Chicago trip. A face-to-face wasn't necessary so early on with the clients. But looking back, it all made much more sense. The back-to-back trips. "Checking in on" clients, who didn't understand the necessity any more than Chris. All of it to get Kaitlyn's bed empty—all the better for Rob to maneuver into during the cuckolded husband's absence.

God, no wonder he wasn't sleeping well anymore. Wasn't doing anything well anymore. He'd kept up the pretense for two weeks. Going into the office, wrapping up loose ends with clients, prepping the new hire on work to be done in his absence. He'd even put together an initial strategy exercise for the Chicago firm. Through his lawyer, he had conveyed to Rob he wouldn't be returning after his holiday. Rob could buy out his half of the business, or they could dissolve it. Rob had tried to waylay him one evening. Said something about "clearing the air."

Chris was still taller, stronger, and in better shape than his former friend. He clenched his fists before taking a deep breath and informing Rob to contact him exclusively via his lawyer.

The whole situation scared the hell out of him. No wife. No job. No house. But if he walked away from this steaming pile of horseshit, he'd exit with his sanity intact. At least, he hoped he would.

Chris shook his head. And now two weeks in Italy. Hoping running away from his problems would make them go away. The cabin was quiet, almost all the passengers asleep or quietly watching films. When the flight attendant walked by with a tray and asked if he'd like water or wine, he gratefully accepted the wine. Sipping it quickly, he hoped it would help slow his thoughts and allow him to slip into much-needed sleep. Chris prayed every mile he traveled away from his own life would result in more inner peace and clarity. God knows, he was in desperate need of it.

CHRIS DID MANAGE TO SQUEEZE IN a few hours' sleep before landing. But even that couldn't make up for all the sleepless nights these past weeks. The first thing he needed to do during this holiday was to get into a normal sleep rhythm.

He shifted from one foot to the other to jolt himself awake in the long passport line. The airplane coffee hadn't done much to wake him up. Judging from the line, all the non-EU world was passing through Rome as this line progressed at a snails' pace, while the Italian and EU citizens' line sped along at a steady clip.

Announcements were coming over the intercom system in singsong Italian. Kaitlyn would have loved ... Oh, shit. There he went again. How did one erase eight years of history in one fell swoop? Chris had to get his head around it this week. Start pushing memories out of his mind. That level of betrayal didn't allow for nostalgic memories. He'd invested way too much time in his wife, his best friend, and the business he and Rob had built from the ground up. He had no idea what he was going to do when he got back to the US, but this time away would give him the needed headspace to start figuring it out.

"*Buongiorno*," said the uniformed officer from behind the plexiglass. "Passport please."

Chris hesitated. He'd been so absorbed in his own head, the same problems he'd been hashing out these past days, that he hadn't even realized he'd been inching towards the passport control until he was directly before the border guard. He recovered slowly, reached inside his coat, extracting his passport. He placed it on the countertop.

The officer placed the passport through the scanner and stamped it. He looked up "*Benvenuto*—Welcome to Italy. I hope you'll enjoy it."

Chris smiled and tucked his passport away once again before following the signs to the baggage carousel. He'd rethought this trip a thousand times, but more than ever, he was convinced he needed this break. Needed to regroup before he returned and completely cut ties with his old life. Italy would be a good place to allow for introspection.

He looked up at the baggage claim video display board, saw his flight was at belt seven—just across the room. As Lady Luck would have it, situated right next to a coffee bar. With a spring in his step, he walked over. Life would look much better after a genuine Italian cappuccino.

AN HOUR LATER, A FRAZZLED CHRIS emerged, luggageless, into the arrivals hall. Thank God for the cappuccino, because everything had gone downhill from there. After waiting for the very last bag to be plucked off the baggage carousel, Chris accepted the fact that his own luggage was, quite decidedly, not there. A worker with rudimentary English signaled him towards an office with another horrendous line.

There he waited, ever less certain about his decision to come to Italy, to finally have his moment in the cramped office. A woman with rudimentary English and a bored voice, pointed to various illustrations of suitcases and he pointed to the model closest to his, provided her with the baggage check claim and the address of where he would be staying in Umbria. She handed him a form, a number to call to follow up on his bag's journey and their—hopeful—speedy reunion in the same country. He tried to mentally recall what he'd packed in his overnight back. A clean shirt, two pairs of boxers, and an extra pair of socks. That wouldn't last him long.

He sighed as he exited the office, spotting the coffee bar where he'd experienced such a sense of optimism earlier this morning. Now his feet dragged as he strode away from the baggage claim area in search of his long-suffering driver.

He examined the placards all announcing visitors. English names, French names, German, Japanese. Studying them all, he grew exhausted. Was all of humanity passing through Rome today?

Finally, he spotted a sign indicating Chris Larson, way in the back. He released a sigh of relief he hadn't realized he'd been holding in. One goddamned thing had gone right today. He walked decisively towards the man, a spring in his long strides. He needed to believe things would get better.

THE DRIVER'S ENGLISH WAS ATROCIOUS, but his lack of ability didn't curb his enthusiasm and loquaciousness. He'd sympathized with Chris' situation, but said it happened all the time, adding he was certain the suitcase would be delivered in the next days.

He promised the hotel owner was a similar height and build, though certainly not so *muscoloso*, and that he could probably lend *Cristoforo* some clothing. The chatter continued at breakneck speed, half in English, half in Italian, and a sizeable portion appearing to be in a made-up language combined from both.

Chris' exhaustion made it far more difficult to follow this odd conversation, and to attempt to make sense of it. He looked out the window as they drove ever further from the airport, modern housing structures speeding by. "How far is the airport from Rome?" he asked slowly.

"Not so far. *Quaranta* ... uh ... forty minutes. Depend on how many cars. Rome is always full of cars. Many, many cars. Better in Umbria." He thumped his chest. "I am from Umbria. My father from Umbria. His father. My *bis bis nonni*. You will like it Umbria. Much, much more beautiful than big city of Rome."

Chris was finding it exhausting. Ugo, this man in his early sixties, seemed a nice guy, but the jetlag and wrangles with baggage claim were taking their toll, and Chris was finding it hard to concentrate.

"I'm sure I will love it. Umbria." He rubbed his eyes. "I just thought it might be nice to see some of the Roman monuments before the long drive."

Ugo shook his head. "You want to see the many, many cars that fill Roman streets? Make the city crazy crazy? You come from crazy crazy American city?"

Chris felt the lurking pangs of a headache. "I do not live in crazy crazy city, but outside of one. Maybe a bit like Umbria. Without all the history."

Ugo smiled. "Okay, Sunday traffic no so bad. We cut through center, then you can to see some of Rome before I take you to better place."

Chris smiled. "Okay. That sounds good. *Grazie.*"

"*Prego.*" Ugo pointed to the odd structures in the distance. "That is Square *Colosseo.* Mussolini built it and whole *quartiere,* EUR. To be new Fascist ideal city. All Fascist architecture. Now offices, museums."

They continued their drive and Chris looked out from the window, trying to follow Ugo's explanations. The road became bigger, with more traffic.

"This street is for you. *Cristoforo Colombo.* Busy, busy all day."

"Ah, Christopher Columbus, I assume." He sat up straighter. "What's that wall?"

"*Mure aureliane.* Walls go all Rome. 18 kilometers. Aureliano. He is Emperor, Ancient Rome time."

Chris looked up as they drove through them. The walls formed part of this major traffic artery now, modern and ancient converging. He looked up at the towering pine trees with their fluffy umbrella tops. They lined the roads. Ugo was maneuvering into the left lane, and Chris made a point of ignoring the cars and scooters vying for the same space, angrily honking on their horns. Thank God Chris hadn't rented a car himself. He was still undecided if he'd do so in Umbria, but no way would he be ready to do battle with Roman motorists right after a long flight. They turned off the Christopher Columbus road and began a descent. Chris sat up straighter as he saw hulking ruins emerge on the roadside. "Oh, wow! What's that?"

"*Terme di Caracalla*. Most famous baths of Ancient Rome. You want to see? I park?"

"Oh, yes. Please."

Ugo pulled into a spot. The views were spectacular from here, along the fence. Chris got out of the car and looked down. How big it was!

Ugo materialized beside him. "All Roman cities has *terme*, but Caracalla most big and best in whole empire. Now ruin. But imagine all marble. All mosaic and fresco. People ... they to come here for baths and sport." He nudged Chris on one bicep. "You *atleta*, no?"

"*Atleta* is athlete? Yeah, well ..." Chris sighed. "I used to be. Swimming."

"Ahhh... *nuoto. Sì.* Here more for *atletica leggera.* Running, discus, wrestling. All the best athletes. They come here to train. Olympic athletes, too. Baths. Sports. Place to speak and see friends. Center of life."

"Oh, wow. And today, can you visit?"

"*Sì.* Tourists they come see ruins. In summer play opera."

Chris took a deep breath. "*Grazie, Ugo.* This is so beautiful."

Ugo smiled and his eyes sparkled. "You happy? Good. No worry for suitcase. You come. We see more. Then we go better Umbria."

Chris chuckled. "Okay, if this is the consolation prize, I can't wait to see Umbria."

They got back in the car and continued their descent from Caracalla. Ugo pointed out the Coliseum in the distance and the Circus Maximus, where the chariots raced. They drove alongside it with the Palatine, the ruins of the palaces of ancient emperors looming up above them. Chris felt his despair dissipating with each scenic view.

They continued on, and Ugo pointed out the Ancient Roman temples, before they turned right onto a road flanking the river.

"This road it is called *Lungotevere*—along the Tiber. See there. The island. The broken Roman bridge. On island. That is hospital. On right that is Jewish temple. And neighborhood called the Ghetto. On other side of river Trastevere. Lots and lots of tourists. I no go there. All Americans now."

Chris laughed. "I guess that's made for me."

"And over there. Other side Tevere, that is ancient bury place Emperor Hadrian. Now part of Vatican. Behind it you see Vatican. Where Pope Francis lives. You go there. It is new country. Vatican City. But you no need passport."

Chris straightened in his seat, face pressed to the window. This was his first time to Rome, and he hadn't even planned a stop off here. What was he thinking? He continued following Ugo's explanations as they drove along the Tiber, Chris' excitement rising with each tantalizing view. Eventually, they veered away from the Lungotevere, and Ugo explained they would be driving out to the Via Salaria to reach the highway.

"You enjoy Rome visit?" Ugo smiled.

"I did. Thank you. How far is it from Todi to Rome?"

"Oh. Not bad. About two hours. You can come back in day. Mark and Emma organize trips to Rome if people want. My daughter. She speak good English. She make trip for hotel guests. But you will too much like Umbria. Not want to leave."

Chris looked around him, at the constant motion and spectacular buildings. "Maybe you're right, but in hindsight, I probably should have booked more than two weeks in Italy. Maybe I was in too much of a hurry to get back."

"Maybe you decide to stay? Become Italian. Real Umbria man."

Ugo laughed and Chris joined him.

Chris leaned back in his seat, drinking in the view. He forgot, even if momentarily, his broken heart. He banished from his mind his cheating wife and the former best friend who had betrayed him. He was in Italy. Two weeks to enjoy himself and his surroundings, to forget about the shitshow playing out across the ocean.

Free of baggage in more ways than one, Chris felt anticipation with each kilometer bringing him closer to his holiday.

CHAPTER 9

Grace

KATHRYN HAD HELD UP HEROICALLY ALL DAY. They'd left Durham early. Ellen had driven them to the Newcastle airport, where she bid a tearful farewell to her daughter. Luckily, the tears had been few and far between on Kathryn's side. Clutching passport in hand, she was excitedly speaking to Grace about what she had been reading about the area and the things she'd want to see, how this was so much better than staying with her grandmum in Durham, how all her friends took exotic trips for their holidays.

Grace had heard about all of those friends and all of those trips in detail as they waited for the flight from Newcastle, after they boarded, and as they were going through passport control in Amsterdam. There was a bit of time before their Rome flight, and Kathryn asked for a hot chocolate and a brownie at Starbucks. Grace and Kathryn sat together, and the words continued to flow from Kathryn's mouth, non-stop.

Grace smiled. Her granddaughter really was a force of nature. She knew Ellen and Rupert were constantly obsessing over perceived problems with Kathryn. And Grace knew, intuitively, that the role of grandmother was far less stressful than the role of parents. But really, could Ellen and Rupert not embrace their daughter more, and worry less about making her into someone she was not?

To Grace, Kathryn was perfect. If, perhaps, a bit overwhelmingly vivacious. Still, she enjoyed listening to Kathryn prattle on. Silence had reigned far too long in her own home and her own life since Richard's death. Honestly, she'd long ago relinquished being vocal. Or being an active participant in life rather than a quiet bystander.

Her role with Kathryn was mostly picking her up, ferrying her around occasionally. But now that they were here together, Grace fully realized what a lovely opportunity this would be. Two whole weeks with her beautiful granddaughter. She was sorry Ellen and her husband were having problems. Of course she was. True, she had never warmed to Rupert, but she did want them to work things out. For Ellen's sake. And for Kathryn's sake, of course. But for now, she was pleased to have this two-week time with Kathryn.

She laughed when her granddaughter told a funny story about a recent football match, when the girls turned up at the wrong pitch. Tears streamed down her cheeks at the clever impersonations her granddaughter was making, and she realized it had been some time since she had laughed so hard. It was about time she started living once again.

Looking up, she saw their gate was now showing on the screen. "Hurry up, Kathryn. Drink the last of your hot chocolate. We should get to our gate."

Kathryn looked at Grace's almost full cup of coffee. "But you've hardly touched your coffee. Will you take it with you?"

Grace wrinkled her nose. "My dear. We are going to Italy. I'll hold out for much better." She stood. "Now, let's get up or we'll miss our flight. *Andiamo*."

THE TWO FLIGHTS AND THE LONG DRIVE from Rome meant they only arrived in Todi at the end of a long day. The exhaustion hit the young and old travelers alike, and both Grace and Kathryn were stifling yawns as their chatty driver, Ugo, said they were nearing the hotel. It took concentration to listen to him, with his "original" English. But ever since he'd hit the borderline with Umbria, he'd been singing the praises of their new home for the next two weeks. Not only was he an Umbrian man, but his father, and grandfather, and all his ancestors before him.

Grace checked herself before asking if he could trace his roots all the way back to the Etruscans. With her luck, he probably could, and she and Kathryn would hear a lengthy diatribe. Well, perhaps she alone. Kathryn had fallen asleep in her lap long ago. Truth be told, Grace would have been happy to join her, but it seemed rude. She suspected Ugo might spend as much time alone as she did to be so animated to speak to other human beings. Or was that simply a part of his job? Regardless, Ugo was right on one count. Umbria did look pretty spectacular.

She admired the cypresses and all the medieval hilltowns they passed. When Hugo pointed ahead, indicating Todi, Grace caught her breath. So stunningly beautiful, arched against the late afternoon sky, already turning a dusty pink. She tried to rouse Kathryn, who rubbed her sleepy eyes and woke only slowly. But when she did wake up, Kathryn's expression was as enthralled as Grace imagined her own was.

"That's Todi?" whispered Kathryn. "That's where we'll be staying these next two weeks?"

Grace squeezed her hands. "Not too bad, is it?"

"It's beautiful!" exclaimed Kathryn. "Wait 'til I message my friends."

Grace's brief brushes with preteens in 2019 had taught her that social media postings were the most important aspect of their existence. While she actually applauded Kathryn's artistry in taking photos, she did wonder at the sagacity of her daughter and son-in-law in allowing her social media access. But she was only the grandmother, after all. Regardless, a little less technology during this vacation would be a blessing.

The medieval town grew ever closer. Ugo turned off onto a small dirt road, driving slowly. "We're almost here. You'll see the *agriturismo* hotel just between those trees. And you, Signorina Kathryn, should know it is an *agriturismo* because they do grow food and have some livestock. They'll let you help, too, if you'd like."

Kathryn clapped her hands together and smiled up at Grace.

Yes, it was a treat to have her this holiday. Grace kept her eyes fixed on the point Ugo indicated, and soon the hotel materialized. Oh, it was beautiful! Grey stones. Red tile roof. A picturesque, little fountain gurgling at the entrance. Todi floating above it. The views must be fabulous in the mornings and bright afternoon light.

"There is a path going up, up to town," said Ugo. "To go up is much difficulter than down."

"I would imagine so," said Grace, craning her neck up to the church bell tower high above them. As if on cue, it began to toll the hour, the clanging reverberating across the peaceful countryside. Oh yes, this was perfect. What her soul needed.

Ugo had reached a little parking area, and he was bringing the car to a halt. He turned back. "Now you go ahead and check in. The owners, Mark and Emma, will be waiting you. I can to carry the suitcases."

"That's awfully kind, Ugo." Grace unlocked the back seat to step out. "Are you sure?"

"*Sì, sì.* Go off."

Grace smiled and breathed in deeply. Fresh, country air, yet different from back home. Beside her, Kathryn slipped her hand in Grace's and sighed.

"It's so pretty. I'm so happy we came." Her face glowed in the dusky light.

Grace smiled. "So am I, my dear. Shall we go in?"

Kathryn nodded, her chestnut ponytail bouncing with the effort.

They walked together up to the big oak entrance door, slightly open. Grace pushed it open. "Hello?" she called out tentatively. She stepped inside and looked around her, at the terracotta tiles, the dark, wooden ceiling beams. A couch and comfortable armchairs were gathered in a circle around an enormous fireplace. Inviting bookshelves groaned under the weight of numerous novels Grace assumed were for borrowing during one's stay. A chessboard was set up on a table. Another table, in an opposite corner, had a shelf filled with board games beside it. The whole atmosphere looked so cozy and welcoming, a place where guests were probably encouraged to interact and meet one another. At least, she hoped they were.

On one edge of the room, a large glass wall looked out at the town above. The sun was hanging low now, and sunset was not far off. But this view must be spectacular throughout the day. What a perfectly positioned hotel.

She located the desk, with its computer and cubbyholes for keys. Behind the desk was a huge, framed photo of Rome's

Trevi Fountain. It was, after all, The Three Coins Inn. An odd name for an Umbrian hotel, but charming nonetheless.

Grace approached the desk and called out once more, "Hello!" A woman came into the room from a doorway to the right of the desk. She was tall and slim, with blond hair twisted carefully into a French twist. She wore a cashmere cardigan that looked a bit warm for the weather, but then again, not everyone judged temperatures by northern English norms. Perhaps this was unseasonably cool weather by Italian standards, for all Grace knew. The woman smiled, and her whole face lit up. She was remarkably beautiful.

"You must be Grace Bradford," she said, extending a hand to Grace and shaking it. "I'm Emma. How lovely to meet you." She turned to Kathryn. "And you are most certainly Kathryn. I saw you're twelve—like my own twins. They're on a school trip, but back in a few days. I'm sure they'll be thrilled to meet you."

Kathryn smiled, and Grace felt relief. She'd hoped there might be other children around for when things became too dull with one's grandmother. This was certainly welcome news.

Emma slid behind the desk and asked for their passports. "Italian rules," she explained. "We have to register all guests with the police." She clicked away at the computer then excused herself to make a copy. "There." She handed back the documents. "I left the door open for Ugo, so I know he's already left your bags in your room. Shall I give you a quick tour around, and then bring you up?"

"Yes, thank you," said Grace.

Emma walked beside them. "Did you have a good trip? You must be tired."

"A bit long, but all worked out well. Wonderful to have had Ugo waiting for us. That made everything so simple."

"I'm so pleased," said Emma. "Well, you've seen our living room. It's still chilly in the evenings, so we'll set a fire tonight." She opened a door. "Here is our dining room. You have breakfast and dinner in here."

Kathryn was looking up at the huge chandelier. "That looks very old."

Emma chuckled. "It is. The chandelier and the central table and chairs both came from local castles. We knew we had to have them. So when you're sitting here tonight, you can wonder how many knights and ladies sat there before you."

Kathryn smiled. "Cool."

"I agree. It is kind of cool. Please, follow me." She walked to a doorway and opened it. "This is quiet now, but will soon be a hive of activity. This is our kitchen." She looked at them both. "I know you will both be in our cooking classes, so you will do those here, with our chefs Giuseppe and Annarita. Actually, Annarita just had a baby boy—he is adorable—so we are all telling her to take a bit more time. But she lives just on the other side of the wall around our property." She waved vaguely out the window. "So you might see her coming with an absolutely adorable baby, if you're lucky. They also have an older girl, who is often our little mascot in the family." She smiled. "A real family affair."

Grace looked around the large kitchen, filled with the dwindling afternoon light.

"If you'll follow me." Emma was holding open a door to the outside. "This is our kitchen garden. We are just starting to get things prepared for spring planting. But in the summer, we have our own tomatoes, eggplants, zucchini, and spinach. Sadly, it's too early for you to enjoy them, but those are all cherry trees. And figs over there." She indicated them with one hand. "My sons would have loved picking those with you. They certainly eat their fair share, but again, too early."

"How lucky to pick your own cherries," said Kathryn, examining the trees.

"You may not want to say that to Marco and Valerio, my sons. Do you see all those trees over there?" She pointed to the distance. "Those are olive trees, and in the fall they have to help us harvesting all the olives. Days and days of work." She shook her head. "They certainly don't think they are very lucky then. But you all get to enjoy our olive oil at dinner. I assure you, it's delicious. Now, let's see some things that might interest you, Kathryn."

Grace looked around her. It truly was picturesque out here. She hoped the weather would cooperate, because she'd love to spend some time out in this nature. Emma was up ahead, with Kathryn. Grace had to scurry to catch up to where they were standing beside a large infinity pool, covered for the season.

"Will you be opening the pool?" Kathryn was asking.

Emma laughed. "It's a bit early, but I'll speak to Mark, my husband, about plans. He takes charge of the pool. We usually open in May."

"Kathryn, don't be rude, darling. It's probably so cold in the evenings that you wouldn't even want to dip your toes in."

Kathryn turned to her grandmother. "It's probably warmer today than it is in Durham in June. And we always swim there all summer."

Emma shook her head. "I get it. My sons are equally impatient to start the swimming season." She indicated two separate buildings. "Here, on the left are spa treatments that can be booked with me. The full list is in your rooms. To your right might be something you'll enjoy, Kathryn."

They walked together to the door, and Emma opened it. The interior walls were stone and there were tall wooden ceiling beams. The room was filled with bean bags, Nerf guns, a ping pong table, a foozball table and a big train set.

Kathryn looked around, her eyes aglow. "This is great."

"Marco and Valerio spend a lot of time out here. I'm sure they'd be happy to play with you, if you'd like." She walked back out, closing the door behind her and indicating a field. "And when you get sick of foozball, we also have the real thing."

"Oh, wow!" Kathryn's eyes shone with joy. "You have a real football pitch? Full-sized goals?"

"The boys love it, of course. But I must admit that many of the adult guests spend a lot of time out here, too. If you prefer tennis, there are also courts nearby. I can help you rent court time."

"Oh, no," said Kathryn. "I love football. I play in my city. My mum didn't tell me you had a pitch here."

"You've made my granddaughter very happy," said Grace.

"My sons, too. They'll be thrilled. Now, back there we have chicken coops and a sheep pen. We have neighbors helping with that, but guests are welcome to stop by, or to help out. That path you see over there takes you up to Todi. It's all uphill, about twenty minutes or so. There's also a public bus, if you prefer not to walk."

"Oh, no. We'll walk," declared Kathryn.

Emma met Grace's glance and the two women exchanged a knowing smile. "Well, let's go see your room, shall we? I'll leave you to rest and unpack. Dinner is served at eight thirty. You only have one other guest this evening, a nice American man who came in yesterday. We have other guests arriving tomorrow, but I hope you'll enjoy the relative quiet this evening."

They walked back to the building and climbed up the stairs to their room.

"SURE, MUM. IT'S FABULOUS HERE. Grandmum and I love our room. I have my own little bedroom nook. And the window looks out at the town. We haven't been yet, but we'll walk in tomorrow. Right, Grandmum?" Kathryn looked up from her cellphone. "Oh, and there's a football pitch, too! You didn't tell me that! I can't wait to play."

Grace smiled at Kathryn's enthusiasm. They had unpacked and Grace had taken a bath and felt revived, while Kathryn watched some sports match on Italian television. They had been about to head down to dinner when Ellen called, not taking into consideration the later Italian dinner hour. But still, it was wonderful to see Kathryn so excited, and Ellen would naturally want to know her daughter was settling in. Settling into the holiday she was supposed to have enjoyed with her husband. The nice surroundings made Grace forget the turmoil dominating her daughter's life. She hoped, for Ellen's sake, they could use this time to work things out.

"Okay, Mum. We need to get down to dinner. We can talk tomorrow. Grandmum sends love, too. Goodnight!"

Kathryn closed the call, then looked up at Grace. "Are you in the mood for pasta like I'm in the mood for pasta?"

"I am indeed." Grace plucked her sweater from the bed and they walked down to the dining room. In the big space, there was one lone man sitting at the large table under the grand, medieval chandelier. His sandy blond hair glowed in the lights of the chandelier's illumination. "Oh, good evening," said Grace as they approached. "Are you the fellow guest tonight—the one Emma told us about?" The man stood. He was handsome and extremely tall, with broad shoulders. He was wearing jeans and a Georgetown sweatshirt.

"I am. A pleasure to meet you. I'm Chris Larson. Please, call me Chris." He shook Grace's hand.

"How nice to meet you. I am Grace Bradford, and this is my granddaughter, Kathryn. We're here from northern England—

Durham." She looked at his sweatshirt. "Are you a student at Georgetown?"

The man looked momentarily confused, before looking down at his chest. He laughed. "Oh, no. I'm afraid the airline lost my luggage. Mark, the hotel owner, has been kind enough to lend me some of his clothes until I have my own."

"How dreadful," said Grace. "I hope they'll deliver them soon." The table was so large that they would have to yell at one another from opposite sides, so Grace and Kathryn positioned themselves next to him.

"May I pour you some wine?" He held up the carafe. Grace nodded and he poured into her wineglass. He held up his own. "*Salute*," he said. Holding his glass aloft.

Grace held hers up, too. "*Salute*. So Chris, do you speak Italian?"

"Sadly, not at all. You just saw it all on display there. How about you?"

"I'm afraid not."

"And you, Kathryn? How do you like Italy?"

"It's my first time here. Mum and dad were supposed to come, by they couldn't, so they sent Grandmum and me."

Chris smiled and his face transformed. He was a strikingly good-looking young man, but Grace appreciated the warmth he conveyed when he smiled. She may have been wrong, but earlier she had detected a profound sadness in his gaze. Then again, maybe they were all simply tired from the travel.

"You're lucky to have time with your grandma." He winked at Kathryn. "I remember mine spoiled me an awful lot more than my parents did."

Kathryn squeezed into Grace's side, something she had been doing a lot less in the past two years as she entered those preteen years.

"Mine, too. Anyway, Mum and Dad are fighting so much recently that it's good to be away." She took a big gulp of her water.

Grace squeezed her granddaughter into her quickly. Her gaze crossed that of Chris' and they exchanged a knowing look. The moment was interrupted by a young woman coming in with a big platter of bread. More than bread, Grace noticed with enthusiasm, with bruschetta. Bread piled with bright red tomatoes and deep green basil, shining with golden olive oil, and other slices of oven-warmed bread drizzled only in golden olive oil.

The waitress smiled. "I hope you're hungry. I have your bruschetta, all with our own olive oil, while we prepare your first dishes. Tonight we have a choice of *fettuccine al ragù di cinghiale*—that is wild boar sauce—or *zuppa di faro*. That's a typical Tuscan barley soup."

"Oh, my," said Grace, her stomach grumbling in anticipation. "I have no idea. They both sound so good."

"I've only beaten you by a day," said Chris, "but I had the pasta in wild boar sauce last night and made them promise to offer it again today. I can highly recommend it."

"I've never eaten wild boar," said Kathryn, no traces of her earlier melancholy on her glowing face.

Grace smiled. "Alright then. It sounds like we'll all have to give it a go. Pasta with wild boar sauce it is."

They passed around the bruschetta and Chris filled Grace's wine glass once again. The food was delicious, and the wine a welcome addition to the long day. The conversation flowed all throughout dinner, sounding much more like three longtime friends rather than two parties that had only met that evening. Although only having preceded them by a day, Chris had walked up into town and understood the lay of the land. He promised to walk up with them tomorrow after breakfast.

Grace was also pleased to see that Chris, a former college swimmer, and Kathryn, a football-mad athlete, quickly slipped into sports banter. Kathryn's love of sports so annoyed her parents, but her granddaughter's enthusiasm and energy had always filled Grace's heart with pride. Her own father had been mad about rowing, up early every morning to take the River Wear by storm. She always appreciated that same competitive gleam in Kathryn's eye. Certainly, the trait would serve her well in a life that threw everything at you.

Grace sat back happily in her seat. Her face glowing, her stomach full, her body toasty from the crackling fire and the sense of happiness and goodwill emanating from around the table. She examined the striking, medieval chandelier. Who knew how many medieval banquets it had witnessed? Grace, who had been somewhat cautious about this solo Italian holiday with her granddaughter, felt only a deep satisfaction that these two weeks would be a very special time together for them both.

CHAPTER 10

Annarita

GIUSEPPE MADE AS MUCH NOISE AS HUMANLY POSSIBLE in their kitchen, clanging the dried pans as he put them in their proper places in the cabinets, clicking windows to see if they were locked, bolting the doors. Annarita shook her head; her husband was so predictable.

Looking down, she observed Sebastiano's downy head as he nursed, and her heart filled with an overwhelming sense of love. Three months old. How had it flown by so quickly? She'd felt the same with Giulia, but somehow, with the second, a mother better understood the need to slow down time, to not always be wishing along the next milestone, but to implore time to stay still in order to fully enjoy those precious first months of a new baby's existence.

Annarita heard her husband's heavy footfalls on the wooden staircase and she smiled. It was odd, when they usually ascended together, to have him returning from work alone. A moment later, Giuseppe opened the door cautiously, catching sight of the nursing baby before his gaze crossed with Annarita's and a smile lit up his face.

"*Tale padre, tale figlio.*"

She laughed quietly. "You're telling me? The acorn most certainly doesn't fall far from the tree with this one. Sebastiano has been nursing nonstop tonight. I don't remember Giulia being this insatiable at this age."

"True," Giuseppe said as he came to the bed and changed into his pyjamas. "But, aside from these late-night feedings, it seems he's been sleeping through the night these past two weeks. I'm afraid to curse things by saying it out loud, but let's hope it keeps up."

"You and me both ..." She pushed her wild curls behind her ear with a practiced swoop. "I had gotten used to sleeping in one whole stretch throughout the night. I guess I am too old to start doing the sleepless-nights thing again."

"You're too old, *mia cara*? What does that make me?" Giuseppe folded his clothes and placed them down on his bedside chair, changing into his pyjamas and slipping under the covers beside her. He gave her a gentle kiss on her temple, and propped himself up on his elbow, looking at his nursing son. "I thought we were so lucky to have Giulia. I know it was asking a lot to have another, so close together, but can you believe how fortunate we've been? He's so perfect." He stroked Annarita's face. "And so are you."

"I feel there's a whole other scale of romanticism to say words like that to a wife still recovering from a bruising labor, sleepless nights, and around-the-clock feedings. All of it so, so worth it. *Grazie, amore mio.*" Trying not to disturb Sebastiano, she snuggled beside her husband's solid form.

"Did Giulia get to sleep without problems?"

"Like a light. I read her two stories, but she was already drifting off before we were halfway into *Goodnight, Moon.*

Thanks for leaving the wild boar sauce. Fettuccine with wild boar sauce is rapidly becoming Giulia's favorite. But I'm not sure her pediatrician has okayed introducing wild boar in her diet yet."

He grunted. "*Ridicolo*. She's an Umbrian girl. It's part of the essential food groups."

Annarita shook her head. Five years ago, when she had been certain her family back in Yonkers was right and she was destined to become an old maid, she'd met Giuseppe. Met him here in Todi, when Emma suggested she leave Rome and come to the new hotel to be Giuseppe's sous-chef. Poor Emma hadn't anticipated how Giuseppe would react to having an *americana* in his kitchen. Thank goodness he'd overcome his initial stubbornness, because their work together in the kitchen quickly transitioned into love.

They'd been married in Todi, with a wedding reception at The Three Coins Inn that the town still talked about. They'd moved into Giuseppe's cozy stone home neighboring the inn. Deciding that age was not in their favor, they'd quickly had two children—a joy Annarita had feared might be beyond her ability to attain. And their work at Emma and Mark's inn continued to be rewarding and challenging. Annarita, especially, loved teaching cooking lessons, and delighted at the Christmas cards and postcards she received from former guests, recounting how the recipes they learned were served to their families and neighbors in far-flung locations. This was exactly the life she'd dreamt of when she'd been struggling to make ends meet as an English teacher in Rome, being deserted by one disastrous boyfriend after another.

Even today, Annarita still awoke occasionally with uncertainty, before feeling Giuseppe's solid presence beside her in bed and then turning to see first Giulia, and now Sebastiano, slumbering peacefully in the cradle beside her.

Only then could she relax. It wasn't just a dream. It was her life. Busy, full, exhausting, messy. But happy. Always happy.

Annarita looked down, realizing Sebastiano had drifted off into his milk coma, a contented look on his slumbering face. Gently, she shifted out of bed and gingerly lifted him up, placing him softly on his back in his cradle. She pulled his blanket up.

She slid back into bed and her husband slipped one arm under her neck as she snuggled in close. "So, the first week back after the winter closing," she whispered. "I know you had two new guests today, how did it go?"

Giuseppe chuckled quietly. "You know a lot for a woman who is supposed to be on maternity leave through June."

"You and I both know I'm gonna stop in a bit before that. Not full time, but I need something outside the house, too. And this is—as you know—quite literally outside the house."

"True." He smiled. "So we still have Chris, the American. Like Giulia, his favorite is the boar sauce fettuccine. He was supposed to come with the wife, but cancelled her trip. From what I've seen, however, he seems to be pretty happy to be on vacation without the wife. Poor guy, I understand him."

Annarita leaned back and gave Giuseppe a gentle punch in the arm. He chuckled quietly and pulled her tighter.

"We had another switch in guests. A couple from northern England ... can't remember where ... sent the grandmother and granddaughter in their place. They're going to do cooking classes and I've already forgotten their names. Caterina is the girl—or whatever the English is for that. She looks smart. Hope she actually wants to do the lessons. The *nonna* looks nice, too, but I need to see the name to remember ..."

Annarita shook her head. "Giuseppe, you're a genius in the kitchen, but a PR disaster. You need to learn the names, where they're from, what their goals are. Some personal details to discuss with them. Do they want to entertain friends? Do they need a bit of change in their lives? Did they love to cook as children and lost that habit over the years?"

He kissed her on the top of her head. "That's why I need you, *amore*. But right now, we'll make do. Sebastiano needs you even more than I do. And you'll be back in time for the busier summer season."

Annarita had her arguments to make, her worries that Giuseppe needed to step up on the customer care, but honestly, her fuzzy mommy brain couldn't capture all those thoughts in a coherent way. Right now, she needed sleep far more than struggling to form logical arguments. As her eyes drifted downwards, she promised she'd continue the discussion with her husband the following day.

CHAPTER 11

Madison

MADISON SAT, JETLAGGED AND BORED, in the backseat of the crappy car. Ugo droned on and on in that thoroughly annoying English. Up and down, up and down, the cadence lulling her to sleep. Really, why should she be bothered to hear Ugo's father was an Umbrian, and his father, and his father before that going back probably to the start of the Roman Empire? Was the fact that your ancestors were hicks something to crow about? Not even one of them had the gumption to pick up and make it somewhere more exciting!

She knew something about hick ancestors stretching back generations—and how important it was to break the cycle of geographical lethargy. Her own family came from backwoods Indiana and had no intention of ever leaving. When she announced she would be going to school at Syracuse, she might as well have announced she was colonizing Mars. The Eurorailing summer raised more eyebrows. She'd worked her ass off to earn enough money for that trip, still regretted not having added a semester abroad, too, but her stints at the radio station and local TV studio were more important.

As Ugo drove her past Rome, she instantly regretted spending the time out in Umbria rather than a city she never managed to reach during her Eurorailing summer. But, in the end, she hadn't done the choosing. Aaron and Christine had done that. In more ways than one.

That slimeball Aaron hadn't even had the decency to apologize to her. He handled everything through Madison's agent. Rita received the details, the changed reservations. A double room for use by a single. Transport to and from the Rome airport. Christine's spa treatments bought and paid for. Even sessions in some ridiculous cooking class. As if. No way were carbs passing her lips this vacation. She worked hard to be a size four and she damn well was going to stay that way, no matter how much pasta those crazy cooks tried to ram down her throat.

She patted her carry-all bag filled with keto bars. She had Rita email over a list of Madison's dietary requirements, so the pasta pushers at this boondocks hotel would have to make do. In two weeks' time, she would be back on her show and fitting into her old wardrobe. Being lighter by a few pounds would be a plus. Seriously, why did everyone say you put on weight in Italy? Discipline. Discipline and the spa. And no pasta. She had this.

"*Signorina* Madison?"

Oh, no. Here was Ugo rattling on again. Did that man never take a break? What if a girl wanted to admire the view in silence? True, she wasn't doing much view-admiring on this trip. She may be in beautiful Italy, but her mind was firmly in Columbus—clawing back what was hers. What would still be hers if that pathetic worm Aaron hadn't ruined it all for her.

There was no hope of peace and quiet. Ugo kept droning on. She'd managed to mostly ignore him up to now, feigning sleep.

"You see we approach Todi now. We say Hercules build Todi. Only strong, strong man can build such most beautiful city."

Madison rolled her eyes. Okay, at least it wasn't Kentucky. It was pretty picturesque. But she wasn't here to *ooh* and *ahh* over Italy. She was being banished here against her own will. Out in the sticks, she'd hide away from the public and strategize to get her svelte self back in her morning anchor chair.

Rita said she'd have to return repentant. She could do repentant. She could channel the whole spiritual retreat schtick if that would get her back in her audience's good graces.

Maybe the hotel could find her a local priest. One who spoke English better than Ugo. Or maybe Ugo-level English could work to her advantage. A story of retreating to this backass place in Umbria, confiding in a smalltown priest. Repenting for her sins. Damn, that was broadcast gold. They'd be eating out of her hands in central Ohio.

Madison shook her head and allowed her diamond drop earrings to swing from her lobes—probably catching that golden, late afternoon light. She glimpsed a guarded look at herself in the rearview mirror, accidentally catching Ugo's gaze.

"You hear me founding my town?"

Madison looked momentarily confused. Then she smiled her television smile, wide, dazzling, and entirely devoid of emotion. Ugo would be simple enough to mistake it for interest. "That story is *fascinating*, Ugo. Wow, you must be so proud of being able to trace your family back so far. I know I would if I came from a place this beautiful."

Ugo beamed from cheek to cheek. Men always wanted the same thing. Affirmation. Affirmation of their prowess, their talent, their intelligence. Didn't matter if it was some TV exec back home or a peasant farmer-airport taxi driver here in Umbria. They were always the same.

She turned back to the window. Even if she had zero desire to be here, the town was remarkably pretty. The steep church tower thrust into the blue sky, the defensive walls encircled the picturesque town. Okay, maybe she could stray from her spa and strategy sessions tomorrow. Do a little exploring. They probably did a decent aperitivo in town. Why not? After all, Aaron was footing the bill.

She smiled at the irony. Here she had complained about Kentucky, but in the end, she was getting Italy out of him. Minus the annoying guy. If it weren't also minus the job, it would be perfect. Two weeks of penance, and she'd have her job back. She was certain of it.

The car slowed and Ugo eased into a parking area. "Here we are. Welcome to The Three Coins Inn."

Madison shook herself out of her thoughts. The Three Coins Inn. What a tacky name. But the place itself looked inviting. Old stone walls, striking views of the town high above. A large property with lots of trees and flowers. A small fountain gurgling pleasantly before the entrance. Yes, she supposed this would do. It's not like she was here to hang out and make friends, but this would serve as a comfortable Operation Restore Madison's Career base.

God knows she needed a place to lick her wounds and rebound. Far from prying eyes. And out here in the middle of nowhere was about as far away as anyone who counted, anyway. Yes, she looked up at the spacious inn again, this would do nicely for her purposes.

She thanked Ugo, mentally counting down the minutes until she could be rid of him, once and for all. She graced him with a tight smile as he said he would drop her bags in her room as she checked in, and pointed her in the right direction. She muttered a gentle thank-you and practically sprang from her seat. Free from the endless commentaries. Right now, she only wanted to check in, get the keys to her room, and draw a long, hot bath. This had been an endless day, and she needed her wits about her if she were to strategize her next moves. Tomorrow, she'd be rested and more prepared.

She sauntered into the hotel entrance. A huge lobby area. Comfortable couches, a blazing fire, exposed wooden ceiling beams the length of the room. Tasteful, welcoming, but not the modern, minimalist lines she favored. But had cool arrived in Umbria? She doubted it. Anyway, not her choice—she was simply interloping on the save-our-marriage romantic trip philandering Aaron and pain-in-the-ass Christine had arranged.

She rang the bell at reception. A blond woman in expensive clothes materialized. Definitely fifties, but pretty, polished. Madison liked her look—seemingly ready to step into the chair, the well-loved and experienced evening anchor. At least, until her younger, sexier clone could shove her out, slipping her own trimmer, more youthful derrière into that warmed-up seat. A week earlier, she'd been that ambitious, young would-be anchor, waiting anxiously in the wings. And now, here she was in Umbrian Hicksville.

The blonde smiled, and Madison did her best to meet her halfway.

"You must be Madison Moore. American from Columbus. Am I right?"

Madison smiled her false megawatt smile. "Got me there. And you are ...?"

"Oh. Where are my manners?" She wiped one hand across her forehead. "Emma Patterson. Hotel owner. I am afraid we haven't actually met. I was in touch with the previous occupants and ... I believe .... with your agent, to change everything to your name. Regardless, we're thrilled to have you with us these next two weeks."

Madison gave the woman a tight smile. Why was she gushing on? Where was the room key already?

"Now, to check in, I will need to photocopy your passport, then I can get you set up in your room. If you'd like to freshen up, dinner is beginning in the dining room." She smiled. "I can assure you, your fellow guests are charming. Everyone speaks English, too. Well, except for the Japanese tour group we have eating with us tonight. I will be happy to introduce you to the other guests."

No way would she be stuffing her mouth with carbs tonight, forced to make conversation with strangers.

She took a deep breath. "Thank you. It was Emma, right? Yeah, tonight I'm tired. It's been a long day. A warm bath and early bedtime sounds perfect. Tomorrow I'm booked for a massage and facial at the spa, right? My agent said she'd spoken to you."

Emma opened a second book on the counter, placing her finger under a note. "Yes, it says here, eleven-thirty. Facial and massage." She looked up and met Madison's gaze. "But if we keep those times, you'll miss your cooking session."

Yeah, like she'd be spending any time slaving away in a kitchen. Good luck with that.

Aaron and Christine paid for it, but it didn't mean she had to attend. Well, okay. Maybe the last day for some plausible Instagram photos to supplement her cover story of time away for reflection. Yeah, the audience would eat that crap up when she got back on her show.

She tilted her head and handed her passport over. "Maybe later in the week. I need tonight and tomorrow to get acclimated." *And it may possibly take the full two weeks before I join the Love Boat fun group activities on the Lido deck ...*

"Oh," said Emma, quickly masking her surprise. "Well yes, of course." She tapped the passport on the countertop. "As I said, I'll need to get a copy of this. Only a moment, I'll be right back."

Madison stood at the counter, feeling bored and sorry she had to be here. Yes, she knew Italy was more exciting than Columbus. But she wanted to be working. Didn't want Brad usurping her role. He'd be all smarmy with the temporary co-host, hinting that the show worked better without Madison. Doing all he could to ensure her ouster became permanent. And here she was, in the countryside of Umbria, helpless to do a damned thing about it. She rubbed her temples.

She really, really did not want to be here. But Rita was so insistent, Madison hadn't had much choice. Things might seem better, or, at the very least, less like a flaming disaster, after a good night's sleep and a spa appointment tomorrow.

Laughter and chatter drifted out from a back room. The dining room, Madison assumed. Ugh, she really would have preferred a hotel with more privacy. This wasn't going to be all forced togetherness, was it? She didn't have the energy to have to chat up fellow guests. All she cared about was getting her job back. As soon as humanly possible. If they called her this second to relieve her of her misery, she'd endure two hours of Ugo droning on and on about the utopia that was Umbria to get to an immediate flight back, jetlag be damned. She wasn't about to set that goal back by refusing to keep her eyes on the prize. Italy, its food, and its charm could wait.

She checked her watch. How long could it possibly take to make a photocopy of a document? A warm bath was screaming out to her. Desperately. Shrilly. She more than deserved it after her long day. She flicked her bright blond hair over her shoulder. Luckily, she'd seen her colorist before the proverbial *merda* hit the fan. Her life was a shambles, but her hair looked great. Figured.

She turned at the sound of footsteps behind her. Instinctively, she clutched her purse closer. But it was ridiculous. She was in the peaceful Italian countryside, not walking alone in the city at midnight. Entering the inn was a decidedly unthreatening middle-aged woman, wearing an optimistic floral dress.

"*Buona sera.* Good evening."

Both greetings seemed conveyed in the perfect accent. But what did Madison know? She didn't speak Italian, aside from a few choice words.

"Hi," Madison responded, with a decided lack of enthusiasm. Even to her own ears, she sounded rude. But it didn't stop the forward momentum of the woman, a wide smile forming across her nondescript face.

"I'm so excited to be here," the woman sang, standing before Madison and thrusting out an expectant hand.

Madison fought an inward sigh, instead offering her own in exchange. She shook this strange woman's hand. "Nice to meet you. I'm Madison."

"*Gerne!* What an absolute pleasure," gushed the woman. "I'm Heike. From Vienna. Have you been? Lovely city, but such a distance. Took me two trains and a long drive to get here. *So* relieved to be here." She giggled. "But what am I saying? You sound as if you're American. I'm half American, too, by the way. My dad. Stationed in Vienna after the war. Fell in love with my mom. But you must be so exhausted after your long trip."

I am after listening to you. Madison stared in confusion at this woman, who had met her two minutes earlier and uncomprehendingly had felt the need to share her entire life story. How would she survive two whole weeks with these people? "Hi, Hike. Yeah, sorry. A bit tired now. Waiting on my key to get up to my room to catch some shut-eye."

Heike giggled. "Oh, of course! I understand, Madison. But my name is Heike. Hike—eh. I know, German names are tough. Even my own dad didn't pronounce it perfectly. Oh! Is your spine simply tingling to be in Italy? Mine is! It always had that effect on me. I'm sure we'll become the best of friends."

Yeah, I wouldn't count on that, Frau Uber-friendly Hike-eh. Miraculously, Emma returned with Madison's passport and key. Madison smiled at her gratefully—as a desert-island dweller would observe an approaching lifeboat.

"Why, hello!" Emma exclaimed to the new guest. "You must be our guest from Vienna. Welcome to The Three Coins Inn. We're so happy to have you."

"Not as thrilled as I am to be here!" exclaimed Heike.

Madison thought she had stifled her groan, but realized she hadn't when two pairs of eyes stared at her. *Oh, hell.* "Please don't think me rude." *As if I would give a damn if you did.* "But I am falling asleep on my feet. Could I get that key from you, please, Emma?"

"Oh, of course. You're in Room ten. Directly upstairs from where we are now. Shall I accompany you?"

"No!" Madison yelled, far too stridently. "No, I'm sorry." She purposely softened her voice. "I'm just exhausted. Ready to tumble into bed. I can find my way. I see the stairs right there."

Emma smiled. "Yes, of course. I will have time to show you around tomorrow. Breakfast is served until ten. We hope to see you well rested." She smiled.

"Of course." Madison tried to match her smile, but knew hers was hollow. "Good night, Emma, Hike."

"Good night, Madison. *A domani.* See you tomorrow," said the new arrival.

Madison gave a curt nod to both women and trudged up the staircase, grateful Ugo had carried her bags to her room. She already anticipated the softness of her bed, following her bath, and doubted the boisterous chatter from the dining room would keep her awake for long.

As Madison reached the staircase, she heard the Austrian woman whisper, "Poor dear. She looks absolutely knackered."

CHAPTER 12

Heike

THE WHOLE TRIP HAD BEEN EXHAUSTING, and Heike was beginning to feel her age. Running the *Beisl* had kept her young. Organizing the orders, the cooking, the daily contact with their customers—those who came from all over the neighborhood, those who no longer felt comfortable in the chic, new restaurant with low lighting, expensive, edgy furniture and unfamiliar foods—had kept her focused and filled with energy. All that energy seemed to have been sapped from her these past months.

This vacation would be a first step in busting out of this rut she'd been stuck in for too long. Of course, she would have preferred being here with Matthias, but at least she was here. That should be enough.

The driver placed her suitcase inside the door, then turned to take his leave. In the silence of the countryside, she heard the car crunch over the gravel. The lobby was entirely empty except for a tall, glamorous blond woman dressed in stylish clothing in the lobby when she entered. Heike greeted her.

"*Buona sera*. Good evening."

The woman turned, a wary look on her pretty face. "Hi," she responded, with a decided lack of enthusiasm.

Heike chose to ignore the bored tone of the woman's voice, and to meet it with forced jollity. "I'm so excited to be here," she said, thrusting out an expectant hand.

After a moment's hesitation, the blond woman shook Heike's hand. "Nice to meet you. I'm Madison."

"*Gerne*! What an absolute pleasure. I'm Heike. From Vienna." She prattled along nervously. She knew she was gushing, but she couldn't help it. She so wanted this holiday to unfold pleasantly. Was tired of all the silence in her home and desperately eager for company. But she realized trying too hard might be off-putting to the young woman.

Their hostess, Emma, joined them and Madison was clearly eager for her key. Despite her beauty, the young woman appeared dead on her feet. She waved off the innkeeper's attempt to accompany her to her room and headed up the stairs after a hasty goodnight.

Heike waited until Madison had reached the staircase, and then whispered, "Poor dear. She looks absolutely knackered."

The innkeeper smiled at her. "You know how it is with those transatlantic flights. They always knock me out, too." She smiled. "It truly is a pleasure to welcome you. I'm Emma. My husband Mark and I run the inn." She held out her hand.

"I'm Heike Schneider. Absolute pleasure to meet you. We spoke on the phone, I believe. In Italian, before I realized you were American, too."

"Yes, of course. Your Italian was so good. And you're American, too? American and Austrian?"

"American GI dad. Austrian mom. Classic postwar story. But I didn't spend much time in the US. Occasional trips to visit extended family, but I really consider Vienna home."

"How interesting. Good news for your English: many of our guests this week are English speakers. But I can guarantee our chef, Giuseppe, will be thrilled you speak Italian so well. His American wife usually joins him for those classes, but she just had their second child." She winked. "We are all trying to push her into taking a longer maternity leave."

"Oh, how lovely. Those days seem so long ago, but they fly by."

Emma nodded. "They certainly do. You'll meet my youngest from my first marriage, twin boys, when they return from a school trip. They're twelve and live here with us."

"Oh, that's delightful," Heike exclaimed.

"Now, you must be exhausted by your trip, but will you be up to joining us for dinner? We'll start service in thirty minutes, but the guests are enjoying an *aperitivo* and talking about their days. Such a fun group this week. I'll be delighted to introduce you, should you wish."

Heike felt her heart thrumming with excitement. "Oh, absolutely! Though I would love to get up to my room first." She extracted her identity card and handed it to Emma.

"Thank you. Let me make a copy of this and return to you at once to show you to your room."

Emma took her leave and Heike was free to observe her surroundings. She wandered around the large living space. She noted the fireplace not in use tonight, the overflowing bookshelves. She carefully surveyed their collection, already eager to pluck one of the Italian titles to keep her language skills current.

For years, she'd attended classes at Vienna's Italian cultural institute—she and Ida both. It had been their escape when the kids were little. Something to keep her mind engaged.

They'd delighted in the films and cultural events. Matthias had indulged her—as he had with their annual trips to Italy, where she could practice her skills while he would beam with pride at her talent. Following his death, she hadn't had the drive to attend the weekly conversation classes. Then Ida's mother fell ill, and she no longer had the time, either. But those classes had been a needed escape. She'd grown close to their teacher and the other women in the class. She sighed. Maybe it was time to return. After all, she certainly had the time now.

She turned to survey the rest of the room. Cozy, welcoming. Exactly the type of place she'd wanted to stay. She heard a sound behind her and saw Emma returning with her document and a key.

"Come, let me show you to your room. Then you'll have time to freshen up and rest before you join us back down here again for dinner." Emma walked to the door and picked up Heike's suitcase, then the two women walked together up the steps.

ALL VIENNESE THINK OF ITALY BATHED IN WARM SUNLIGHT, but the April evenings in Umbria were still cool. After unpacking her items and resting a few moments in the comfy window-side armchair, Heike had changed from her light floral dress into more sensible slacks and a light sweater that better fit the cooler evening temperatures.

Feeling more prepared for what might be a drafty dining hall, Heike brushed her short, sandy blond hair and swept a light lip gloss over her lips. She surveyed her handiwork in the mirror. Not as rumpled as when she'd arrived, but definite room for improvement after a good night's sleep. For now, the thought of a delicious Italian meal, and being served by others, rather than battling it out in the kitchen, sounded absolutely perfect. She smiled at her reflection, plucked up her room key and let herself out.

Voices rose up from below, flitting through the stairway as she walked down. She heard laughter, the clink of glasses. Emma had mentioned the dinner service was yet to begin, and the guests were enjoying *aperitivi*. She thought she had hurried, but had she been wrong? She looked down at her clothes again. Nothing special, but not embarrassing either. She hoped she hadn't misread the atmosphere, and that this was a casual environment. She hadn't packed elegant clothes.

She entered the dining room, struck by the cozy fire blazing in the enormous fireplace at the opposite end of the room and the heavy, medieval chandelier above that cast light throughout the room. Below the chandelier was a large, medieval table and heavy benches. They looked to have come from a castle. Smaller tables and chairs were scattered throughout the room. Those seemed to be populated by a large Japanese group. Listening, she could hear them chattering away in Japanese. Certainly, they would not want to be joined by someone with whom they'd have to make an effort to converse. Hadn't Emma said there were many English-speaking guests this week, too?

Perhaps she would have done better to have waited for Emma to accompany her to the dining hall, to introduce her to the others. She hadn't wanted to be a bother, and yet, here she was, clinging to the doorway. Afraid to step over the threshold and introduce herself to the fellow guests.

Had Matthias been with her, he would have plunged right in. Even with his appalling English and nonexistent Italian, he was the life of the party wherever he went. The wide-eyed, good-natured mountain boy, genuinely enthralled by any new surroundings. Jolly, boisterous, with an addictive laugh and a smile at the ready. Her rudder. And here she was, rudderless and adrift. And alone.

Just as she was wondering if she could retreat from this boisterous dining hall without anyone noticing, an older woman speaking and laughing at the big table looked up and met Heike's gaze. The woman smiled, and her face lit up. She motioned Heike over. Heike sucked in a breath, trying to display more courage than she felt.

She walked over to the table and forced a smile.

"Why, hello!" said the older woman, looking up at her. "You must be our new Austrian guest. Emma mentioned we must look out for you if she was busy with other guests or running in and out of the kitchen. So nice to meet you. I'm Grace. Sorry for appearing rude, but my knees aren't what they used to be, and getting out of this bench is a bit of a chore."

Heike chuckled. "No need to explain to me the loss of teenage flexibility. I'm Heike. So nice to meet you." She held out her hand, and Grace shook it.

"I hope you will join us for dinner, Heike. Wonderful to welcome someone new. I arrived yesterday, with my lovely granddaughter, Kathryn."

A pretty young girl looked up. Dazzling blue eyes observed her, a long ponytail swayed side to side.

"Wonderful to meet you, Kathryn. I have a granddaughter, too, and a grandson, back in Vienna."

Grace clasped her hands together. "This is our first solo trip, but we're having a brilliant time, aren't we dear?" She looked back up at Heike. "We come from Durham, in northern England. And I would like to introduce you to Chris. Chris joins us from Virginia, and he has been here the longest. This is your third day, isn't it?"

The man across the table laughed. Younger and fitter, he managed to hop out of the bench and reached across to shake Grace's hand, wrapping her hands in a firm, and, truthfully, somewhat crushing handshake.

"Welcome, Heike. Glad to have you here with us in paradise."

She giggled. He was extremely young and incredibly handsome. When he smiled with those dimples, her heart melted in a way it hadn't in what seemed like decades.

"Will you come sit here next to me?"

Heike fought a schoolgirl blush and walked around the table, slipping into her space on the bench. "This is quite the grand table and chandelier, isn't it? It seems like something out of King Arthur."

"Emma says she purchased it when they were fixing up this property—and that it did, indeed, used to be in a castle," said Grace. "I love it."

"Me, too," said Kathryn. "Heike, wait until you see dinner. I've been eating so much since we arrived. And Grandmum will be taking me to the cooking classes. So I can show my mum and dad back home what I learn."

"What wonderful news. I'll be in those classes with you. I cook a lot back home. My husband and I started a restaurant, and I'm the cook. But it's all Austrian food, so Italian will be a nice change."

"Oh, no. This was supposed to be for fun." Chris chuckled. "But now we have a professional in our midst. Kind of ups the ante."

"Not unless we're doing Schnitzl and apple streudel ... in which case you'll be absolutely crushed." She winked. "But for our purposes, I think you're safe. Anyway, I'm retired now. My daughter and son-in-law run the restaurant now, so who knows how rusty I'll be."

"I doubt that," said Grace. "But we're so happy to have you with us."

The waitress came out with dishes of creamy risotto with radicchio and carafes of red wine and water, still and sparkling. She distributed them on the wide table, then returned with the parmiggiano. She came back and forth, distributing serving dishes until all the tables were served.

Heike was eyeing the course, a curl of steam rising from its depths. It looked spectacular. Chris began pouring wine into all of their glasses. Even Kathryn got a tiny bit, and she looked positively ecstatic at her elevation to grown-up status. At one of the Japanese tables, and older man stood up, wine glass in hand. He clinked his wine glass with his spoon, and the dining room went silent, faces swiveled in his direction.

"I do not wish to disturb your meal," he said in accented, but precise English. "I come here every year to The Three Coins Inn, and they always make us feel so at home. We Japanese—like the Italians—love our food." He translated, and the tourists he was accompanying laughed at this. "We are happy to enjoy this beautiful place and wonderful food with you. A toast to us all. In Japanese, we say *kampai*." He raised his glass again and everyone followed suit.

Calls of "*Kampai! Salute! Cheers!*" echoed throughout the space. Heike saw the smiles around the room, felt the goodwill of all the guests. The fire crackled in the dining room fireplace as she and those around her enjoyed the creamy risotto. Heike felt tears prickling at her eyes. Matthias could not be here with her, but in some sense he was. And she was so grateful to have come to Todi, even if alone.

CHAPTER 13

Chris

CHRIS AWOKE WITH THE LIGHT STREAMING IN. He turned to observe his bedside clock, gazing groggily at the clock's hands. 8:30. The last two mornings, he'd still been jetlagged, waking at four or five a.m., then trying hopelessly to coax his body back to sleep. Finally, he'd admit defeat and rise, changing into his sweatpants and sneakers—dutifully delivered by the airline. He'd wait for the pink fingers to mark the morning sky, a promise of imminent sunrise. He'd set out on his morning jog to Todi's center—still quiet at that early hour, the cafés still setting up, the school children still enjoying their last moments of shut-eye.

Chris loved seeing the town on these early-morning jogs. From its center, he could look down at The Three Coins Inn and wonder at the twist of fate that had brought him here. Brought him here alone.

Since that awful night, he had stood firm in his resolve to refrain from contact with the two people who had brutally betrayed him. Truth be told, that early-morning wakefulness wasn't due solely to jetlag. Chris kept replaying that awful night in his mind. Feeling the pain carving into his heart.

How could they have done that to him? The woman he was building a life with. The best friend he trusted with his life. Both of them laughing at him. Sending him off on useless travels, freeing themselves up to carry on their affair. If he hadn't returned early, without informing Rob or Kaitlyn, he never even would have known. He'd still be the cuckolded husband, working his ass off to keep Kaitlyn presiding over her ridiculous throne as wannabe society queen. Damn, his stupidity never failed to floor him.

He swung his legs over the side of the bed and walked over to the window. No jogging this morning. The sun was already long up, and it looked like a beautiful day.

Last night had been fun. It was an eclectic mix of guests at The Three Coins Inn. Different ages, different circumstances in life, but they all hit it off well and quickly came together as if they had been old friends. Chris had been a little cautious about coming here on his own, but right now, he was happy he'd overcome the lingering sense of discomfort. A group of strangers who knew nothing about him, his recent humiliation, the crumbling of his marriage and—let's face it—his career, that's what he needed right now.

The physical distance from Virginia helped, too. Yes, he'd need to start thinking strategically about his next steps. But for now, this was enough. Enough that he didn't feel panic about his life imploding. Enough that he didn't suspect everyone was looking at him and laughing at him. Or worse, pitying him. Enough that he didn't have to worry about bumping into Rob and Kaitlyn as he was running errands.

The sun shone down on the medieval town of Todi, the town looking exactly the same, strong and steady for centuries.

Who knows what horrors it had witnessed over the course of history, and yet it still survived. He was starting to believe he would, too.

Chris' stomach began to growl and he turned from the window. A quick shower before he went down to get breakfast. Another carefree day in Umbria awaited him.

THE DETRITUS OF A DELICIOUS BREAKFAST was scattered round them. If he kept eating at this rate, he might return with an expanding waistline. Then he'd start to resemble Rob.

Kathryn interrupted his thoughts. "Do you remember you promised to play football with me today?"

Grace clucked her tongue. "Kathryn, that's very rude. Chris is here on holiday. He doesn't have to go out to the football pitch with you."

Chris smiled. "Oh no. It would be a pleasure. I didn't go for a jog this morning and I was just thinking about, with the rate I'm eating all this great food, how my jeans will be getting tight on me if I don't up the sports. Anyway, I know from Emma that her sons are coming back—so my soccer skills," he chuckled, "that'll be football skills to you—won't be desired for much longer."

"No!" exclaimed Kathryn. "Two-on-two will be even better. But Emma said a friend of the twins is coming today to practice on the pitch. A girl." She looked at the clock. "She should be here soon. But she doesn't speak English. So there'll be three of us."

"Only if you're sure," said Grace. "Chris, my granddaughter can be quite persuasive, but feel free to say no if she tries to strong-arm you. She can play alone with the local girl and you can enjoy your free time."

Chris chuckled. "Oh, don't worry about me. No one has to really twist my arm to play sports. I was a lot like you as a kid."

He looked at Kathryn, and watched as the girl's entire face was transformed by a glowing smile. For a moment, he sensed something amiss. Were girls today teased if they like sports? But it was probably nothing. "Hey, if you want, I can go change into my sweatpants now and we can head out to the pitch as soon as the twins' friend arrives. Your grandma and Heike can come along. You ladies are welcome to join in, if you'd like." He winked. "But otherwise, I noticed there are some comfy looking hammocks out there."

"That does sound nice, but Chris ..." Grace trailed off. "I promised to walk up to town with Heike. Show her around. Would it be alright if we brought you and this girl over, and left for town while you play?"

Chris smiled. "For me, it's fine. I promised Emma's husband I'd join him later at a sports bar around here. A match we both wanted to see, but that wouldn't be until after lunch."

"Oh, we won't be gone long," said Heike. "And Kathryn and her young friend can return back here whenever they finish. Play in the game room until we're back. Grace was so nice to agree to show me around. But we would be back well in time for lunch. Are you sure that's alright for you, Chris?"

"No problem." He gave Kathryn a little punch in the arm. "Look forward to seeing what the female Ronaldo has in store for me."

Kathryn grinned, and they all decided to go up to their rooms and then meet in the lobby twenty minutes later.

KATHRYN REALLY WAS A FEMALE RONALDO. While Chris had spent hours—and hours on top of that, and more hours piled on top for good measure—in pools and weight rooms throughout his childhood, youth and college years, he wasn't a natural soccer athlete. Yeah, he played sometimes with friends. But Kathryn was quite exceptional. She told him she mostly played with the boys in her town, but that co-ed teams would be ending soon.

It didn't take much to see Kathryn was a gifted athlete. She possessed impressive footwork, was strong and swift, she had a clear vision of the whole field that Chris could only imagine was laser-honed with a whole opposing team, and she was competitive as hell. Even when there were only two of them.

Chris, who prided himself on his athleticism, at a certain point raised his hand in surrender, threw his sweatshirt on the ground and placed his hands into the T of timeout. "Have mercy on an old man," he laughed.

He lay down and closed his eyes, feeling the warmth of the April sun against his face. When he opened his eyes, he admired the bright turquoise skies, punctuated by the bright green cypress trees.

"Okay, lazybones," said Kathryn, standing above him and bouncing the soccer ball from her knees with impressive dexterity. Her new friend, Luisa, was answering a call from her mother.

Chris sat up. "You know, you really are very talented. I hope you have good coaches who are encouraging you. That's one of the things that made a huge difference to me in swimming."

Kathryn slumped to the ground. "Up until now, I have. But now I have to change age categories, and I'll be with the girls' team. I'm hoping it'll be as challenging. Playing with the boys made me a lot better. And I ..." She looked off in the distance. "Well, I don't think my parents are that supportive about me continuing with the sport."

He shook his head. "Really? You're really gifted. That's the kind of athleticism you can't teach. Seems a shame not to cultivate it."

Kathryn lay down on the grass now, too, looking up and avoiding his gaze. "That's kinda the problem. Mum and Dad haven't told me to stop. Not point-blank." She sighed. "But they make it clear what they think. Constantly. Especially Dad. He's … uh … kind of into fighting all kinds of social justice battles. Wants me to join him on all these marches." She rolled her eyes. "Climate justice. Marriage equality. Universal basic income. Honestly, I don't even know what that is. He thinks sports are a waste of time."

"Oh," said Chris, staying silent. Better to let her express the thoughts that were bothering her, without interference from an adult she hardly knew. And who'd blurt out what he really thought about selfish parents who politicized young kids' lives.

"It's … Well, it's hard if your parents don't support you in what you love. I'm a good student, but I don't love school like I love being out on the pitch. Training with my mates, scoring goals, running until my lungs burn and I'm certain I can't run another step … but then doing it." She was clutching the soccer ball tightly into her chest. "There's no feeling like it in the world." She looked at him from the corner of her eye. "Is that how you felt with swimming?"

He chuckled. "It's *exactly* how I felt about swimming. Life sucks, objectively, when you decide to be competitive in sports. I was up every morning way before the sun came up. First workout at five a.m. Then practice after school. Weight training. Meets away almost every weekend. I logged every workout. Everything I ate. I wasn't around for most of the parties. Missed my high school prom for an important swim meet." He tilted towards her, propping himself up on his arm. "But I seriously loved every single minute of it. Nothing beats pushing yourself to the max. Winning your race. And you're never able to stop. Your latest victory doesn't mean anything the following week. It's all up for grabs, and you need to prove yourself again. There's always someone hungrier and ready to take your place."

He sat up and placed his arms around his knees, looking up at the medieval town, looming above. Tried to pinpoint where Heike and Grace were. Hoped Grace appreciated what talent her granddaughter had. A child could still achieve greatness if someone believed in her. If her mother and father wouldn't, Chris hoped Kathryn could rely on her grandmother's support. She deserved one family member who believed in her and supported her dream.

"The thing is, when you spend so much time training, you learn to pinpoint those with talent." He looked directly at Kathryn. "I'm not a soccer player, but you clearly have it. I'm sorry your parents aren't behind you one hundred percent, but please don't let that stop you." He stood up and took up a second soccer ball, bouncing it far less expertly over his knees. "You're so young now that you won't fully understand. But you're only young once. You only have one chance. I didn't make the cut for the 2012 Olympics in London. Didn't miss by much, but my coach was on board for making sure I got to Rio in '16."

Kathryn sat up. "What happened? Did you make it?"

Chris bounced the ball down on the ground. "Didn't even try. I gave up. All those years of sacrifice … for nothing. I realize now I should have gone all in. Prepared for my next shot. But I'd met a girl and swimming felt less important." He shook his head. "Now I realize it was all a mistake, but I didn't listen to my coach back then." He reached for her shoulder. "Kathryn, if this is your dream, go for it. The world needs a female Ronaldo." He smiled. "Now—are you ready to start again?" He looked over at Luisa and waved. "*Calcio*, Luisa?" The young girl ran over to join them.

Three players, one American, one English, and one Italian, ran around the pitch full speed, in the shadow of medieval Todi.

CHAPTER 14

Grace

GRACE FELT HER BREATHS COMING HARD AND FAST. The walk up felt like a mini Mount Everest. She wondered if it would get any easier during her stay here. She peeked at Heike, climbing up beside her, somewhat heartened that the Austrian was struggling as much as she was. Yesterday, she had hiked up with Kathryn and Chris and, frankly, next to those two athletes, it had been downright embarrassing.

They reached the top, to both women's visible relief.

"Oh, my," said Heike. "And to think my husband comes from an Alpine village, and long ago we used to spend holidays hiking up challenging peaks. And now, I'm winded on the walk up to Todi."

"To be fair, it's a pretty steep hike. I was up here yesterday with Chris and Kathryn. We discovered a cute café out on the main *piazza*. What about catching our breath with a cappuccino and some cold water?"

"Not sure if so many coffees are a great idea, but how can I say no to a cappuccino under this sun? Lead the way."

"I have to warn you. The hills don't stop because we're in town. This whole town is up and down tiny alleys and steps."

Heike laughed. "Okay, well a good thing I have my walking shoes on."

"Let's see if I remember. Luckily, the town's not too big." Grace retraced the path she'd taken yesterday, following Chris. After many twists and turns, and what seemed like endless stairs to her groaning calf muscles, she emerged with relief onto the monumental Piazza del Popolo. "Whew. This is where I wanted to get us. And see there." She indicated tables set out under the warm sun. "That's the perfect place for a short break. To rest our legs before we explore town."

Heike's face broke out in a smile. "Oh! It's absolutely perfect. I know a cappuccino here will taste even better."

"Isn't that always true?" Grace smiled. It felt wonderful to be here, and she strode with confidence to the tables bathed in golden sunlight. Especially after a lifetime of never taking the lead. She sank into one of the seats. "The only danger is my muscles may revolt and refuse to get up from this perfect spot."

"Mine, too, I'm afraid." Heike smiled at the waitress, who walked over. "*Buongiorno, abbiamo trovato questo posto idillico. Per piacere, volevamo due cappuccini e una bottiglia di acqua leggermente frizzante.*" The waitress smiled and took her leave.

Grace whistled. "My, my. You're a dark horse. I didn't know you spoke Italian. I've been torturing everyone with my English. Where did you learn?"

Heike smiled. "Don't be fooled. It's not that advanced. But I love Italian and started studying it in Vienna when my daughter was small. Rather strategic on my part. My new hobby was a convenient way to get me out of the house for a few hours, one day a week. I kept it up over the years, and my husband and I came down to visit on holidays. But it's so rusty now. Hopefully this holiday can help revive it."

The waitress returned, placing their coffees, bottle of water, and glasses down on the tabletop and taking her leave after chatting a moment with Heike.

"She said it has been a quiet winter, but the tourists are starting to make their way back for the Easter holidays."

"Yes," said Grace. "I imagine they are. It must stay busy all through the summer. I feel so fortunate to be here. My daughter and son-in-law arranged this holiday, and then couldn't come at the last minute. Such a treat for Kathryn and me to take their place."

"How fortunate to spend time with your granddaughter. It's a good age. My husband and I used to take our grandchildren—a boy and a girl—out to his mountain hometown for a week each summer when they were little. But that died off when they approached the teen years and being out in the mountains with Oma and Opa was no longer fun."

"Oh, my. The teenage years. I recall them with my daughter. I must admit I'm not fully prepared for that with Kathryn." Grace stirred a packet of sugar into her cappuccino and took a sip. "Oh, this is wonderful." She tilted her face up to the sun. "I shall recall this moment when I am back in rainy, springtime Durham." She smiled at Heike. "Could your husband not join you on this holiday?"

Heike placed her cup down firmly in its saucer. The smile vanished from her face and she gazed at the Duomo, directly across from them. "I certainly wish he could have. We were to come together. But he ... he died. Six months ago. I was not sure I had the strength to come here on my own." She shifted her gaze down, looking at Grace. "But I'm glad I did."

Grace placed her hand over Heike's. "I am glad you did, too. You're very brave to have come. I'm a widow, too. A year and a half ago. I should have started traveling solo earlier, but ... well..." She trailed off. "I was a bit paralyzed."

"I'm so sorry for your loss." Heike took another sip of her cappuccino. "It's hard, isn't it? Everyone treats you like you're breakable. Everyone avoids the topic. Some days I wonder if my husband of thirty-seven years ever existed at all. My closest friend is now caring for her bedridden mother. And my work used to provide an outlet, but everyone felt it would be better for me to retire. I didn't have the strength to argue." She swiftly rubbed the corner of her eye. "But somehow, it's made my world seem so much smaller."

Grace nodded. "I think that describes it perfectly. Your world can become smaller. My husband was a university professor." She chewed her lip. "And so much of my life was caught up with his. My best friend lives far away, in southern Spain, although she's always inviting me to visit." She poured more water into each of their glasses and took a sip. "I know I need to do something to shake things up." She smiled. "I'm becoming a bit of a recluse. If it weren't for weekly church services, grocery runs, and accompanying Kathryn to sports events, I'm not sure I would venture far from home." She held her cappuccino cup up. "Maybe we should toast to new beginnings."

"Oh, I like the sound of that." She clinked her ceramic cup gently against Grace's.

"Now," said Grace. "We were here too late for the San Fortunato church yesterday. I think it was closed for the lunch hour." She glanced at her watch. "Should we finish up here and go over to see it?"

"*Assolutamente*," said Heike, draining her cappuccino and smiling up at the sun.

CHAPTER 15

Mark

MARK SNUCK UP BEHIND EMMA and kissed her on the cheek. "Sorry those fence repairs took longer than expected, but it's all completed now. Fixed the chicken coop, too. Now I can help you and Giuseppe with anything you need."

Emma turned and placed a hand on his shoulder. "Everything's under control. It's still a quiet week—what with the Japanese tour group mostly returning only to sleep and to eat breakfast the next morning before they head off on their tour bus. Anyway, we have a soft week. Although certainly not the Japanese themselves. Gosh, seeing their schedule on paper exhausts me." She started taking out plates. "And the core group is off to a good start. They're all tight and spending a lot of time together. All except Madison. She seems to mostly be in her room. Keeps asking for salads and gluten-free, ideally calorie-free, foods to be sent up to her room." She smirked. "Not sure she's even met the other guests. Between us, she seems to be a bit of a spa junkie."

"Well, by now, we know the type. If that's what they want ..."

"Yeah, I know. Up to her. I just have an idea she'd like the other visitors this week. I really like them. Anyway, cooking lessons start tomorrow. She's signed up. If she wants to, maybe she can break out of her bubble."

Mark tapped her nose. "Her business, Emma."

"Yes, I know I'm a hopeless meddler ... especially after such a long hiatus. But the season's kicking off well. I'm hoping Giuseppe and I can convince Annarita to take a little more time off—come back in July when Sebastiano is older, and she'll feel more rested." She smiled. "Not sure we're winning that battle, however."

"You know Annarita. Once she's made up her mind ..."

"Uh-huh," she chuckled. "I know. So—you going to see the game this afternoon?"

"Yeah. Even talked Chris into joining me."

"Oh, good. He's been fabulous with the guests, but I bet he won't mind a little male company."

Mark smiled. "Nor will I. As I wait for Marco and Valerio to come back."

Emma wiped her hands on the towel. "They're going to be so sorry to miss the Derby. I'm happy they'll be back tomorrow. From the little I've seen, I think they'll have an able soccer mate in Kathryn."

MARK AND CHRIS entered the sports bar a short distance from town. The place was packed. Mark weaved in quickly through the crowds and nabbed what appeared to be the last table. Chris smiled before crossing the room to join him.

"You can tell you're a local."

"No kidding. For the big matches, this place is always packed. You should come back for the European Cup or the

World Cup. Then they move the screens outside, set up picnic tables and everyone hangs out there."

A waiter came over and took their beer order. Mark spoke to him for a couple of minutes before switching over to English and introducing Chris.

"Welcome. Hope you'll enjoy it here in Umbria. Who're you cheering for tonight?"

Chris smiled. "Don't know the teams that well. But if you tell me sports are on TV, I'll come."

"Good man," the waiter slapped him on the shoulder, before returning to the bar.

"So who *is* playing?" asked Chris, once the barkeep was safely out of earshot.

"Rome and Lazio. The two rival teams from the same city. It's called the Derby when two city teams play one another." He raised his eyebrows. "There'll be some high spirits tonight."

"No danger of me starting a fistfight for two teams I didn't even know existed five minutes ago. But thanks for bringing me."

Their beers arrived, and Mark held his up, clanging glasses with Chris in a toast. "*Salute.*"

"*Salute.* I think that might just be my first Italian word. *Calcio* being my second, which is helpful today."

"Cheers and soccer. Both good ones," said Mark. The two teams took their place on the field, escorted by young children in oversized jerseys. The match began and the entire pub started cheering on their preferred side.

By half-time it was still 0-0, but it had been an energetic game. Mark ordered two more beers, and they arrived quickly.

"I admit, I never watch professional soccer at home, but this is pretty exciting. You've found yourself a great sports bar," said Chris.

"I agree."

Chris sipped his beer. "I'm so glad I came. You and Emma have an amazing place. I was … uh … thinking of cancelling my reservations after—well—a disaster at home. But I'm so glad I didn't bail in the end."

"I'm sorry to hear it. Anything you want to talk about?"

Chris looked across the room, at the boisterous crowd, almost all men. He took a deep breath. "Have to be honest. It's been two weeks and I've been avoiding talking about it at all costs. But why the hell not?" he took another big swig. "My wife and I are splitting up." He avoided Mark's gaze. "This was a surprise. For me. We were supposed to come to Italy together. I'd been after her to start a family. Thought this would be a romantic setting. Time together. Something we haven't had in ages." He rubbed a hand over his eyes. "Yeah, finding *my wife* in bed with *my best friend* somewhat put a monkey wrench into those plans …"

"Ouch." Mark felt horrible for their guest. He hadn't guessed Chris had been running from such turmoil back home. But with this knowledge, he was even more impressed by how Chris had thrown himself headlong into life at the inn.

"Yeah, tell me about it." Chris took another sip. "As the cuckolded husband, you can probably imagine exactly why I've been playing my cards close since the … big reveal, shall we say? What the hell am I saying? How could you imagine? Emma seems amazing." He slumped deeper down in his chair.

Mark nodded. "Emma is amazing. But a few years ago, I was exactly in your shoes."

"*You?*" Chris was observing him with a confused stare.

"It's what brought Emma and me together. We were both the spouse with cheating partners. And not only with the best friend. Emma's first husband and my first wife … shall we say … were using Hugh Hefner as their role model." He smiled. "I can laugh about it now, but I assure you, back then, I was gutted and humiliated. But desperately trying to keep my family together. My girls were young. And Emma. Poor Emma. She was raising three kids on her own, with her husband never keeping his promises to his kids while he pursued young women."

"Oh, man. Sorry. I obviously had no idea."

Mark clutched Chris' shoulder. "I get the stage where you are now. But believe me, as much as this hurts your ego, it's better you found out now than after starting a family with a woman like that." He shook his head. "She wasn't going to change. Take it from me."

Chris sighed. "You're right. I know it sounds awful, but you've made me feel a lot better. Ever since I arrived, I've felt so much better."

"You're coming someplace new. Meeting new people—people who don't know you from home. A break is sometimes the best thing to get you back on track. Ironically, Umbria did that for me, too."

Chris shook his head. "What do you mean?"

Mark sipped his beer, thinking back to that time not so long ago. "I'd given up on thinking my wife would ever change, but I worked for her father's consulting company in Amsterdam. I inherited a property in Umbria—the property that's now our hotel. I'd been in love with Emma back in grad school ... at Georgetown, your neck of the woods. But I never got anywhere because she came to Italy and fell in love with an Italian. Her first husband. I got my second chance when we were both licking our wounds. That was almost five years ago—and, believe it or not, I'm now thankful my wife cheated on me. We were miserable together, or, at least, I was. My ex wound up giving me my chance at happiness with Emma." He smiled. "We got it right the second time around. Something tells me you will, too."

Chris sighed. "Thanks, Mark. You've made me feel a hell of a lot better."

The pub grew quiet and the bartender turned up the volume with his remote. The second half was beginning, and in the first five minutes, Rome scored. Half the bar went wild, the other half grumbled.

Mark leaned in. "Don't tell anyone, but I've actually become a huge Rome fan. But not so much that I want to start getting into soccer arguments with everyone, so I pretend I'm neutral."

Chris chuckled.

"Hey, that's pretty good." He looked down at the drawing Chris had done with a ballpoint pen on a bar napkin. He'd drawn two of the soccer players going after a ball. One a Rome player, and the other with Lazio's distinctive stripes. "I didn't know you were an artist."

Chris shook his head. "I'm not. I just like to doodle. I used to love art, but it didn't seem practical when I was at college. I did business. But sometimes I wonder if I made a mistake."

"I don't know, if I could draw like that, I'd be doing it all the time. I'm a stick-figures-only kind of guy."

"*Gol!*" screamed the entire bar.

Mark and Chris looked up as the Rome team was going wild, embracing the young striker who scored his second goal of the afternoon.

CHAPTER 16

Madison

MADISON FINISHED THE CAPPUCCINO that had been brought to her room, alongside a fruit cup. It really was better than anything she could get back home. Her days were falling into an easy, predictable rhythm. Every morning she requested room delivery, then went to the spa. Somehow, in this way, she'd avoided all the hotel guests since her arrival.

Oh, she heard their conversation and laughter wafting up from the dining room while she picked away at her salad. Italy was a foodie's paradise, but she was counting calories as rigidly as she did in Ohio. This afternoon she was supposed to go to a cooking class. Breathe in the calories from all those carbs. As if.

But keeping herself apart from the other guests, ignoring the beauties of Italy surrounding her, it wasn't getting her one step closer to her goal: a return to her old life. While it's true the difference in time zones did not work to her advantage, it was clear to Madison that Rita was assiduously avoiding her calls. She sat around for entire days waiting for Rita to return Madison's increasingly desperate messages.

Once in a while, she did wonder if it wouldn't do to take her mind off it—joining the guests, walking up to Todi, exploring some of the surrounding towns. It was, after all, her first visit to Italy, and all she knew was the inside of her comfortable room and every inch of the spa space.

But, thanks to her chats with Angela, her masseuse, she learned about Viterbo and its hot springs, only about an hour from here. The former spa of the popes, apparently. Ugo's daughter, Patrizia, would drive her there and walk around Viterbo with her. So she would actually see some of the country today as she waited for news. And Patrizia spoke English well, Angela had promised.

She would tell Emma to cancel her presence at the cooking lesson. It should be no skin off Emma's nose—Aaron already paid for it. But every time she spoke to Emma, she got the odd sense the older woman was disappointed in her. As if she had to partake in the orchestrated fun the inn offered. What was it, summer camp? Surely they had guests who longed for privacy and solitude.

Yes, a day away would be good for Madison. It would also stop her from obsessively texting Rita and sending emails. She would bring her cell along with her, of course she would. She'd be ready to speak as soon as the call came that the station was ready to take her back. But maybe a whole day away would clear her head better than she'd been doing these past two days. Her blood pressure still soared every time she thought of that young seat-warmer filling her anchor chair. She checked social media obsessively, praying the studio was falling apart without her. It only made her more depressed.

And for what, really? How the hell was she supposed to know that Aaron was married?

Legally, she was sure she could fight her station. But she'd have no career to return to after a decision like that. Rita had already made that abundantly clear. Madison had no choice but to slink away and lay low for a while, hoping things would smooth out and she could return. Slice it any way you wanted, it was a crappy position to be in. Cappuccino cup in hand, she stood and looked out the window. It was shaping up to be a beautiful day. Bright blue skies, birds chirping from the trees dotting the property, the medieval towers and turrets beckoning high above. Tomorrow she would get up to see Todi. She sighed and turned away from the window.

For now she needed to pack a swimsuit, toiletries, and she'd better charge her cellphone battery to maximum. She wouldn't want to miss Rita's call.

THE WARM WATER IN THE POOL was glorious with the sun shining down. The Thermal Baths of the Popes had been a real find. Patrizia had more than just driven her here. She brought her, chatting along the way, and had even accompanied her on the spa packet. She said she'd just be bored waiting around and claiming she loved this spa.

It turned out Patrizia had studied in Viterbo at the university and sometimes came back to visit friends. This pool had been where they'd unwound as students. She promised Madison it was spectacular with the frigid January and February temperatures, when you wanted to loll here all day until your fingers were pruned up.

Madison thought it was pretty fabulous in April, too. She enjoyed her time with Patrizia, who worked as a translator of English and French into Italian. Mostly legal and business documents, but she also worked with a wide range of clients. And she took on group or individual tours from the hotel when

Emma and Mark needed a helping hand. Her father, Ugo, was the regular driver picking up clients from the Rome airport.

Patrizia laughed. "Papà's English is atrocious. But he so loves chatting with visitors that they rarely mind."

Madison squirmed uneasily in the pool, realizing she'd been among that minority. She hoped Ugo hadn't expanded on the disdain Madison had shown to him when speaking to his daughter.

Apparently not, because Patrizia seemed quite friendly. Truth be told, Madison hadn't realized she'd been lonely until that day as she chatted with Patrizia on the drive to Viterbo. Maybe it was a mistake waiting around for Rita to call. After all, Rita had said to keep a low profile for a while. Hell, she was in Italy. Why not enjoy it as she waited for her heralded return?

"So," said Patrizia, beside her in the thermal pool. "What's it like to be a glamorous television journalist?"

Madison laughed. "Well, most of my life is decidedly *not* glamorous. I'm up by four every morning. Does that sound like a lifestyle to envy?"

Patrizia splashed her face and shook her head. "Not for me, definitely. I'm so not a morning person. But the fame must be nice."

Madison leaned her head back against the pool's edge. "Yeah, I guess it is. But the thrill is wearing off." She leaned back further, letting her legs float up, looking up at the sky. "You know, when you're in college, you have your whole life planned out. Honestly? I wanted to be famous. I come from such a little, boring town."

Now it was Patrizia's turn to laugh. "Yeah, I may get you there."

"Well, that's what I've been fighting for. My agent ... she's in new salary negotiations right now. So it's a good time for me to lie low, let things move forward during my absence." A white lie, surely. But wasn't that better for all? "But for the first time, I am wondering. Is this even what I really want?"

"Well, makes sense you want to reflect. Have some time to relax. See Umbria—and beyond, if you want. Want to head down to the rest of the circuit? We can come back here to the pool again."

"Lead the way. I surrender to the local expert."

Madison and Patrizia went to the leg circulation treatment favored by the Ancient Romans, walking in circles in a cold pool followed immediately by a hot one. They walked through both for about fifteen minutes, before moving onto the Turkish bath tucked into a picturesque grotto. Madison felt the humid air working miracles on her lungs.

"Oh, my," exclaimed Madison.

"This is fabulous. I know," agreed Patrizia. "Can't you feel how amazing this is? I don't even favor the Turkish bath. I generally prefer the dry heat of the sauna. But this is really special. No wonder the medieval popes spent so much time here."

"Men of taste," agreed Madison, breathing in deeply.

"What do you say if we wrap up here in a few minutes then head back to the pool? When we decide to call it quits, I'll give you a guided tour of Viterbo. I'm biased, but I really love it. The medieval popes did, too. You'll see a lot of the buildings they built."

"That sounds perfect, Patrizia. I'm in your hands."

LATER THAT EVENING, Madison collapsed onto her bed. It was only nine thirty, but she was wiped out. She and Patrizia had returned to the warm, thermal pool following the amazing Turkish bath. They floated in that toasty, volcanic water and Madison felt all her worries floating away.

She really liked speaking to Patrizia. She was funny, irreverent, and far more well-read than Madison. Madison had once enjoyed literature but hadn't read much since she had begun in the early morning news grind. She vowed to check out the Three Coins Inn lending library when she returned. New leaf, and all.

Following the thermal pool and showers, Patrizia drove the short distance to town. And what a fantastic town Viterbo was. Grand squares, ornate palaces, spectacular views. Patrizia ferried Madison around, throwing out dates and historic events that made Madison's head spin. But she loved every minute of it.

Patrizia almost had a conniption when she discovered Madison had been in Todi three days and hadn't even bothered to venture up to town. "What the hell are you waiting for, girl?"

And she'd been right. Madison had been moping around long enough. Here she was, for the first time in her life in Italy, on an all-expenses-paid trip. About time she turned herself over to the local rhythms and enjoyed herself.

She pushed herself up from bed and changed into her nightgown, padded to the bathroom to brush her teeth. Returning to her room, she slipped under the covers and plucked her new novel from her bedside stand. Patrizia had suggested it when they returned. A modern Italian novel, translated into English, called *I'm Not Scared*. Patrizia had promised her she'd love it. Why not? When in Rome ... or Umbria.

Madison cracked open the spine to start reading, immediately engrossed in the tale set somewhere in southern Italy. She raised her gaze only once to observe her cellphone. She placed the novel momentarily on her chest as she switched it off.

Before returning to her reading, she realized with a sense of wonder that she hadn't checked for a call from Rita even once today. Smiling with the knowledge that her phone was down for the count, Madison turned her attention back to Michele and his harrowing coming-of-age story.

CHAPTER 17

Heike

HEIKE OPENED HER ROOM, deposited her bags on the bed, and collapsed into the armchair. She'd positioned it precisely before the large window. From here, she could see the expanse of the property and a sliver of Todi up above.

She had a perfect view over the soccer pitch in the distance. Kathryn was running around at full speed, dodging two boys who appeared to be of a similar age. Could these be the twins Emma said were returning from a school trip? It certainly looked as if the three children were well matched, all soccer mad and having the time of their lives out in the fresh country air.

Heike grinned. Grace would be so pleased for her granddaughter. Although Kathryn was having a good time, Grace was worried she didn't have any children around her own age. And now to have found companions who loved sports like she did, Grace must be feeling some relief.

It was always like that, wasn't it? When your grandchildren outgrow that moment when spending time with you is enough for them. She sighed, recalling how she and her own grandchildren spent hours in the kitchen, baking cookies and Apfelstrudel, telling stories. How she would take them to the marionette shows in Vienna or out for cake in one of the city's grand cafés—and how those outings would result in faces filled with joy and wonder. Those days were long, long gone.

Heike turned back to the three children running around, watching as one of the boys scored a goal, then threw his arms in the air in joy. And now Chris was walking by, probably from a trip to town. Kathryn seemed to be introducing him to the two boys. Soon enough, Chris was part of their group, and they were playing a two-on-two match. Kathryn and Chris against the twins. Heike chuckled. He really was a good sport, always ready for fun. He would make a great dad one day. She hated to be one of those old ladies who pried, but at one point, when she asked if he had children of his own, he responded that he didn't. But his gaze was filled with such naked longing that she could feel a sudden ache in her heart.

She didn't ask any more personal questions of that nature. He wore no wedding band, but she could see the slightly paler strip of skin where one might once have rested. He stroked that point sometimes, when he didn't think others were observing him. She wondered if he even knew it himself. Heike feared there might be a tale of heartbreak there, and did not wish to meddle unless he wished to share. She certainly knew what that was like.

She took a deep breath. Watching the four of them running around made her legs tired. Yesterday, she and Grace had climbed up and down those treacherous hills of Todi. She had taken an evening bath to soothe her sore muscles. Today, they had done the same on a trip to Deruta—famous for its ceramics.

The bags scattered all over her bed were filled with colorful pottery. Heike was still not certain how she would get it all back on the train. She may have to make a trip into the town post office to have some of it shipped, but she had time to decide before her departure. All the colorful designs had been too lovely to resist. Grace, who was flying back, would have a much harder time of it.

They really had had a lovely time walking around the town, admiring the ceramic staircase, stopping for a cappuccino— or two. And always talking and laughing. Heike had forgotten how much fun she used to have, before Matthias' death, before management of the restaurant had been taken from her, before she lost contact with so many friends, before she spent so many hours alone in her home. Once, quiet time alone had been a luxury. Now it was a constant.

Maybe she'd be sick of the guests after another week and a half together, but for now, it was magical. She especially enjoyed spending time with Grace. She had the impression that, as a widow, too, she understood the struggle, how hard it was to wake up without your beloved husband. She slapped her thighs and pushed herself up from the comfortable chair. And now, it was time to reclaim some of that dormant energy. This afternoon was their first cooking class.

THE KITCHEN WAS FULL. Madison had bowed out—not that Heike had exchanged two words with her after their brief meeting at check-in, but Grace and Kathryn were there, as was Chris. All donned green aprons. There were ten from the Japanese tour group. Apparently, they were splitting shifts—another ten would attend tomorrow's session. While the kitchen was spacious, it certainly wasn't made for such numbers of students. But everyone was good-natured, and that made the atmosphere more pleasant.

Emma started off on translation duty, but soon enough the phone was ringing and she had to take off. Giuseppe was warm and funny, but his English was not up to the task. And, of course, the situation was more complex because few of the Japanese group spoke English, and the guide was valiantly attempting to handle simultaneous interpretation of Giuseppe's pidgin English into Japanese.

At this rate, they'd be here until midnight.

The third time Emma exited to answer the phone, Heike piped up in Italian, asking Giuseppe if she could assist.

"*Parli l'italiano?*" he asked, a look of relief spreading across his face. "It is usually my wife to do this, but we have a new baby. My English is a disaster."

"*Non ti preoccupare.* I'm happy to do it. I speak so little Italian in Vienna. But please," Heike implored, "speak slowly. I'll tell you if there is vocabulary I don't understand."

And so, order began to reign amongst the chaos, as Giuseppe demonstrated and Heike explained his instructions in English. It soon became apparent to Giuseppe that he also had a skilled chef in the kitchen with him. Heike told him she and her husband owned their own Viennese restaurant. The furrows eased in his forehead and she helped him to make the rounds of the students as they spread out the flour on the countertop and added eggs, trying to make it into a dough before taking a rolling pin to it. She stood behind Kathryn and taught her how to get the right consistency, how to ensure it would roll out correctly under the rolling pin, if one applied correct pressure. The girl had a knack for it and grinned up at Heike gratefully.

The Japanese tourists were having fun, laughing and chatting away in Japanese, snapping photos. The guide was working from her English, interpreting into rapid-fire Japanese.

Giuseppe taught the group how to cut the pasta into long ribbons. The guests laughed when theirs looked far less professional than those Giuseppe created with ease. Chris was finding it particularly challenging. Heike showed him the trick to rolling the dough out correctly. "Your first time making pasta?"

"My first time making more than a hard-boiled egg. I've never been much of a cook."

"It's not rocket science. I mean, at the highest levels, it's an art. But anyone can learn to cook. You'll get the hang of it. After all, Giuseppe has a week and a half to whip you into shape."

He chuckled. "You're not doing such a bad job, either. I knew about your chef background, but not your Italian. Both are impressive."

Heike shook her head, self-deprecating to a T, and moved on to help the Japanese who seemed to like the sound of her name, calling out Hai-kei, with natural ease. But Chris' comments made her feel better. She'd been feeling so useless in recent months, wondering what the purpose of widowed life was. Once again today, Heike was glad that she'd garnered the courage to come alone. She needed this.

The Japanese tour guide called out to her, again, and Heike hurried over.

Chris

THERE WERE NO TWO WAYS AROUND IT. Chris was a disaster in the kitchen. And yet, despite his atrocious skills, he'd had so much fun. Heike had to help him substantially to complete his part of the pasta. Heck, even Kathryn had chipped in to make him appear less pathetic. Together, they'd created the *ragù* to accompany their misshapen pasta. Regardless, Chris hadn't laughed harder in weeks.

Heike had encouraged him, telling him it was to be expected at the beginning. At the same time, she held out promise that he could improve with a little practice. Maybe it was ridiculous, but he clung to that hope. The communal dinners in these days had done much to squelch his inner despair.

After so much unhappiness these past weeks, sitting around the table with this group of strangers—people whose paths he would never have crossed had he not come here to Umbria—had somehow managed to revive his positive outlook once more. Cooking, something he'd never cared much about, now seemed like a challenge he wanted to conquer. It was good to feel a sense of pride and confidence again. Even if it was exclusively in the kitchen.

Alone in his room, it was harder to escape from all the decisions he faced. Chris had been forced to hire two lawyers before his departure. One who was in contact with Kaitlyn about the divorce, the other to extricate Chris from his business. Since that horrible night, Kaitlyn had been sending him texts and email messages that he hadn't even bothered to read. He simply forwarded them to his attorney. Cheating on him was bad enough. With his former best friend was unforgiveable.

Chris tried—generally without success—not to think about what his life would have been like had he not met Kaitlyn and fallen head in heels in love with her. If he hadn't married her so quickly and upended his life.

For so much of his existence, swimming had been at the core. He'd had a late growth spurt and really reached his full height and the capacity to fill out in strength training during his freshman year at college. He'd always been good, but the college years were when he started to become great. Around him, friends flirted and parties raged every night. His friends were used to him bowing out early, drinking only rarely, never giving in to the late-night pizza or junk food. Hell, he was in bed old-man-early each night during the season, and not much later in the off-season.

He was the first at practice, the first into the weight room and the last out. Conference championships, NCAA championships. He became obsessive about each new challenge. The World Championships and Olympics had always been his goal, and his coach believed in him. He knew it took an obsessive mindset to reach those levels. He knew girls and parties would always have to take a backseat to those objectives.

When his freshman roommate, a fellow swimmer, got homesick and moved back to Australia only a month into the school year, Rob had taken his place. Decidedly not an athlete, unless you counted beer pong as a competitive sport—and Rob most certainly did—Chris admitted that Rob helped him break out of his competitive shell. At least, occasionally.

Later on in the year, when Chris had the chance to room with a fellow teammate, he'd chosen instead to stay with Rob, and had done so the next three years, both in the dorms and their fraternity. If only he'd chosen differently all those years ago.

If only he'd refused to meet Kaitlyn's ultimatum, shockingly early in their relationship, and continued swimming competitively. After all, in sports you only got one shot at youth. Once it was gone, it was well and truly gone. A new generation poised to scoop up the accolades and medals. No second chances.

Foolishly, he thought he'd been sacrificing his dream for love. More fool he.

No wonder this trip to Umbria and its ability to shove his messy life into the recesses of his confused mind was a Godsend.

The consequences of real life awaited him at the conclusion of this holiday. But that did not mean Chris was any closer to confronting the two hulking elephants in the room. Learning to perfect the quintessential Italian fettuccine was, by any means of the imagination, far more preferable.

"WATCH OUT FOR THE MISSHAPEN FETTUCINE. They're bound to be made by Chris." Kathryn dissolved into giggles.

The others seated around the table laughed at the joke, and even Chris broke out in a smile. What else could he do? He really did spot his misshapen creations among the big, family-style bowl being passed around the table.

"That may be," he agreed. "But mine are by far the most tasty. And I have it on good authority tomorrow is gnocchi, where lumpiness is an art." He looked around the table. "All of you will be *begging* me for help, but I'm gonna ignore you."

"Getting off the topic of talented chefs," said Grace. "Heike and I had spoken to Ugo, after he took us to Deruta today. We decided to go see Orvieto, and he said he could drive us there tomorrow and get us back in time for cooking class. Would you like to join us?"

Kathryn tugged his arm. "Please come! Emma showed me photos of the old Etruscan well we'll go down. And there's supposed to be some scary Last Judgment scene in the cathedral."

"Signorelli," said Heike. "It'll have you on your best behavior for a long time after seeing that."

"Will you come?" asked Kathryn.

"Will there be space for all of us in Ugo's car?" Chris asked.

"It'll be a bit crowded," said Grace. "But you need more legroom, Chris. You can take the front. We can all fit in the back. It's not such a long drive, anyway. Ugo says it's less than forty-five minutes. And, if we have time, we'll stop at a lake on the way back. It's on the road."

"I've been there before," said Heike. "Lago di Corbara. It would be nice for a short walk— the weather's supposed to be perfect tomorrow. We're hoping to leave at nine-thirty. Will you join us, Chris?"

Chris looked around at the two women and one girl all gazing expectantly at him. He smiled. "Why not? This is my first time in Italy. May as well see as much as I can." *After all, that was my plan for my wife and me. To explore all around us in our rental car.*

"It'll be so much fun to have you with us," said Kathryn, twirling the pasta on her fork. She grinned. "And if you still have energy when we return, Grandmum told me I can duck out early from cooking 'cause Marco and Valerio will have their football friends here and we'll play a match."

Chris' melancholic thoughts dissipated before Kathryn's enthusiasm. "I'll probably have to bow out of that one, but I'm looking forward to the trip with you tomorrow."

And he truly was. If you'd told him even a week ago that he'd be having fun hanging out with two new friends about his mother's age, and one of their granddaughters, a twelve-year-old girl, he would have declared you certifiably insane. And yet, these women, and Emma and Mark, and—why not?—even Giuseppe, who tried unsuccessfully to hide his wincing every time Chris was let loose in the kitchen, they'd all helped him emerge from the darkness these past two weeks.

Speaking to Mark the other night had had a tremendous effect on him. Here he'd been feeling like a fool these past weeks, ashamed to tell anyone about the disaster that had befallen him. But just look at Emma and Mark. From what Mark told him, both of them had suffered betrayal far worse than what Chris was experiencing. But to see them now, one would think they'd always been together. Mark had said it himself—that their cheating spouses had done them a favor. And that their second chance was so much more fulfilling than their disastrous first attempt.

Life had a way of pulling a fast one on you, as Chris was learning. But this time away was also providing him with needed perspective. And things weren't looking half as desperate as they had only two weeks ago.

All these thoughts flowed through his mind as he finished up the second course, the roasted vegetables drizzled in olive oil, followed by fruit, dessert, and after-dinner *digestivo* that Emma promised to serve in the living room-lobby. A blazing fire awaited them. Although the days were warm, the country evenings were still cool, and the guests welcomed the cracking flames. Not necessary, but comforting.

Kathryn pulled Chris into a game of checkers in the comfy leather armchairs strategically placed before the fireplace. Emma appeared with a glass of Chris' favorite *amaro* (a recent discovery) and he sipped it thoughtfully, pleased once again he hadn't pulled out of Italian plans in the end.

Head over the board, studying his next move, at first Chris didn't see Mark towering above them.

"So sorry to interrupt your game. Chris, would you mind if I speak to you a moment in my office?" He patted his son on the shoulder. "Marco wouldn't mind taking over the game, if that's okay with you."

Chris shook his head, slight confusion furrowing his brow. "No, of course not." He placed down his *amaro*.

"Bring it with you." Mark gestured him to follow.

Together, the two men walked to a door beside the lobby desk. Mark ushered him in and gestured for Chris to take a seat on a large couch.

Mark took a seat beside him, brandishing a large folder. "So sorry to interrupt, but I was thinking of our conversation the other night."

Chris sipped his *amaro* and gestured to the folder. "Are you feeling sorry for me and ready to present me with a stack of hot women in Todi, just dying to meet me?"

Mark chuckled. "Don't get your hopes up. Far from it. It was actually your artistic talent that piqued my interest." He opened the folder. "When we started this hotel four years ago, we had a local man design a logo for us." He shuffled through papers. "We had so much on our plates. Renovations, Permits. New website. Booking guests. Moving here. We didn't really like his work, and we left it to languish." He plucked out a packet with a logo concept and handed it to Chris.

Chris studied it carefully, trying to make sense of it. It's true he had abandoned art long ago, but the design was truly terrible. He looked carefully at the fonts fighting one another for attention, at the busy design, at the utter lack of any empty space to relax the gaze. Even on closer inspection, it was pretty dismal.

Mark rubbed his hands together. "Look, you're not going to insult us with your brutal honesty. We know it's awful. We never used it. But at the same time, we never did anything about it." He took the paper and turned it face down. "The Three Coins Inn was my wife's idea. She met her closest friends at a movie screening of the 1950s film *Three Coins in the Fountain*. It led, in some ways, to us being together. Same for Giuseppe and his wife, Annarita, who met Emma at that movie. You haven't met her yet. And then there's Tiffany, the third friend, who lives in Rome with her boyfriend. They joke the film kickstarted their new lives. Just like the women in the film. So when Emma insisted, I couldn't say no. She liked the idea of a name that might bring luck to our guests." He smiled. "New friendships. New love. New insight. New directions in life. That sort of thing." He shook his head. "Maybe there is something to a name, because we've had plenty of people form tight friendships here. And even the blossoming of some new relationships, or patching up those that had derailed." He smiled. "But we need a logo that's not an embarrassment. We send out flyers and emails and Christmas cards. We present at local fairs, and it would be great to have an attractive design with The Three Coins Inn that we would be proud to put on display."

"Well, yeah. What you have is major cringe. I entirely agree you should invest in something you're proud to display. I'm not sure how you think I can help out, however. It's not like I know graphic artists here."

"Actually," Mark sat back in his chair, stretching his legs out on the Turkish carpet. "I think you do. I saw what you drew at the sports bar."

"What I drew at the sports bar?" Chris shook his head, confused. "When we were watching the soccer match?"

"Yes," said Mark, leaning forward, his arms on his knees. "The little sketch you drew. You said you always loved drawing but had given it up."

Chris sat in stunned silence for a moment. "I mean, yeah. I did. But I haven't drawn in years. That was just a silly doodle. I haven't done any graphic work in ages. You want to hire a professional."

"Look, I know you're on holiday. I know you've had a rough time and want a bit of a break. But I saw what you threw together quickly. You have a real sense of style. I like the idea of a concept through a tourist's eye. We would pay you, obviously, even if we don't use the logo in the end. But I thought it might be fun to see what you could come up with." He chuckled and placed a hand over the turned-over paper. "It certainly can't be worse than what we've got."

Chris laughed, too. "That's true. But you're setting the bar awfully low there." He leaned back and looked through the window at the inky sky. "I mean, I haven't drawn in years. I may be rusty. Can I think about it and get back to you tomorrow?"

"Absolutely. We're glad you're considering it." He held up his glass of grappa and waited for Chris to do the same. Clinking glasses, Mark said, "*Salute!*"

"*Salute!*" returned Chris, his mind swimming with ideas for a logo he could design, utilizing a talent he'd allowed to atrophy for years.

CHAPTER 19

Grace

GRACE, KATHRYN, HEIKE, AND CHRIS ALL STOOD in front of Orvieto's Duomo, admiring its beauty. The golden mosaics of its façade sparkled in the morning sun. The white and blue stripes ran down its length on either side of the cathedral. The tiny group admired the masterpiece, silenced by its beauty.

Grace was the first to break the spell. "Ugo told us how beautiful it was, but it really is different standing here before it."

"I can't believe I've never bothered to come to Italy before," said Chris, his eyes never straying from the façade. "I'm not sure exactly why that is."

Heike laughed. "You're so young. You have your entire life ahead of you. Consider this your introductory visit. The first of many to come. I predict Italy will become a central part of your life."

Chris grinned. "I like the sound of that."

"It's still early, so we can see those Signorelli frescoes without the crowds," said Grace, "but I'm drawn to that empty outdoor table at the café, with perfect cathedral views. Should we nab it before anyone else does?"

"A woman after my own heart," said Heike. "Cappuccino time. Again."

Chris was distracted by something across the *piazza*. "Can I join you in a minute?" When they nodded, he headed off at a brisk pace, calling over his shoulder. "Would you order me a cappuccino?"

They settled in at the table, the warming sun so pleasant on this clear April day. The views across the *piazza* to the Duomo were perfect. And Grace knew she wouldn't be enjoying this same sun back in Durham for some months still. If at all. She smiled over at Kathryn when the waitress arrived and her granddaughter asked for a *cioccolato caldo*, in what sounded, to her ears, like perfect Italian. Since Marco and Valerio's arrival, she'd been out playing football with them and their friends, and she already noticed Italian words slipping into Kathryn's vocabulary.

Ellen and Rupert would be proud of their daughter when she returned home. At least, Grace hoped they would be. It seemed they so rarely were. She shook her head and tried to dispel negative thoughts, instead focusing on the here and now. Kathryn was buried in a guidebook, and Grace squeezed her granddaughter's hand. "Tell us what we should know about the Duomo."

"It says it's perched up at three hundred meters, and you can see it clearly from the surrounding countryside." She looked up. "You remember how easily we saw it when we were driving here? Ugo pointed it out."

Grace smiled and nodded, recognizing the mature young woman her granddaughter would one day become, and wishing she could preserve the traces of the little girl still trapped within.

"The guide says it's among Italy's greatest Romanesque-Gothic cathedrals." Kathryn looked up as Chris slipped into the empty chair, placing a plastic bag on the table.

The waitress arrived with their order of cappuccini and a hot chocolate.

"Oh, good," said Chris, "I didn't miss much. Keep going, Kathryn."

"Work began on the cathedral in 1290, under Pope Nicholas. It says it's the main cathedral of the diocese of both Orvieto and Todi. Oh, wow. It took three hundred years to build. It says here work was completed in 1591. The golden mosaics on the façade were started in 1321 and added to over the years. Most of what we see now were done in the fifteenth and sixteenth centuries."

Everyone gazed up at the façade as they sipped their drinks. Chris pulled a sketchpad from his bag and opened it to the first page. He then extracted new art pencils and began to sketch. Kathryn stopped reading from the guidebook and they all watched Chris' progress in silence.

Grace was seated next to him and observed how absorbed he was, capturing the stripes running down the length of the Duomo. He seemed to have forgotten he was seated beside them, lost in a trance.

It was Kathryn who broke the silence. "Wow, Chris. I didn't know you could draw."

He looked up, seemingly surprised to be surrounded by other people. He placed down his pencils and took a sip of his coffee. "It's been such a long time since I've done it. I only started again a few days ago. I guess with swimming, and work, and ... and... well, life ... I gave up on it a while ago." He grinned. "Being in Italy inspires me to pick it up again, or try to, anyway."

Kathryn peered across the table. "If I drew even half as well as you do, I wouldn't constantly be struggling for a decent grade in art class."

Grace shook her head. It was true. Poor Kathryn hated art. She'd come to Grace's house numerous time with her sketchbook for projects, almost in tears. For the granddaughter and daughter of university professors, Kathryn was somewhat indifferent to her schoolwork. She only lit up with sports, but her grades were pretty good in most classes, art being the glaring exception. Sadly, Grace was unable to support her in that area.

"I'm no expert, Kathryn, but I can teach you some tricks that may appease your teacher. I always loved art, but I gave it up a bit too soon. I liked graphic arts and design in college and should have taken more classes, but swimming and my business classes didn't leave much free time." He took another sip of his coffee. "Maybe it's not too late to get back to it."

"Of course it's not too late," said Grace. "I think it's fantastic Italy inspires your creative vein. Isn't that what travel is all about?" She looked at her watch. "I hate to be the drill sergeant here. But if we want to see the cathedral and see its Signorelli frescoes, and still get to the San Patrizio well Kathryn learned about in class—and do all this before the lunch Ugo booked for us, maybe we should get a move on." Grace signaled the waitress, then looked at the others. "I hope there will be plenty of other opportunities for outings and coffee together in the sun, but this one's on me." She smiled at her group of new friends as the waitress approached and she plucked euro bills from her wallet. Across the *piazza*, the golden glow from the Duomo's mosaics intensified with the angle of the later morning sun.

Grace felt a deep sense of peace as she admired the perfection of this cathedral, watched the furrow in her granddaughter's brow as she studied the historical details of the cathedral from the guidebook, and saw Heike observing the frantic drawing Chris was undertaking on the page.

Only two weeks ago, Grace had felt lonely and useless in the town she'd lived in for decades. And now, here she was, abroad in a country where she didn't speak the language, with new friends she had met only a few days ago, yet feeling fulfilled and content in their presence. Almost as if she'd found her home.

GRACE'S FEET ACHED as she stretched her legs out beneath the table. What a blessing to be seated in this restaurant. She'd been certain she couldn't manage another step. They'd had a delightful morning. After the cappuccino, they'd gone to see the cathedral and its impressive Signorelli frescoes. They'd all stood before it, transfixed, observing the demons as they dragged the damned into a hell of writhing terror. Kathryn's eyes had grown big as saucers. Chris had immediately found a spot to sit and began sketching. Grace had, surprisingly, felt a profound sense of peace before the images of sinners forcefully dragged down into their brutal, fiery fate.

"Didn't you love the well?" Kathryn was asking the group.

Grace stifled a groan. The architecture and harmony of the curving stairs had been spectacular—especially such a level of detail carried out in a sixteenth-century well. But her legs were already feeling the pain. She feared what shape she would be in tomorrow. Perhaps she could pop into the chemist's for some arnica. Better yet, perhaps she could speak with Emma about booking a massage for tomorrow. She had not yet explored the onsite spa, but it was feeling urgent.

Her gaze crossed with Heike's, and a look of understanding passed between the two women.

"Kathryn dear, the well was absolutely lovely, but you know we are not all as sprite and athletic as you." Heike winked at Grace. "You and Chris were bounding up and down those steps and, generally, putting your elders to shame. Umbria is stunning, but these hills are placing a heavy toll on my old legs."

"I love it here," said Kathryn. "There's so much to see. The food is incredible. And at home, my dad tells me I only play sports so much because I was born in the wrong body, and I maybe I identify as a boy." She lowered her eyes. "Here, no one tells me that. I can just play and have fun."

Grace sucked in her breath and slid her shaking hand under the table.

The *tagliere* arrived at the table, laden with local salame, prosciutto, and cheeses. The waitress set it down on the table.

After an embarrassed silence, chatter resumed around the table. Grace suspected the others wished to avoid the topic as eagerly as she did. Grace felt deep shame, and intense pain for her granddaughter. She loved her own daughter, but knew she was weak and followed Rupert's lead, even when Rupert did not need affirmation, but rather someone to stand up to him.

Grace's husband, for all his faults, always considered his son-in-law a pompous ass, with limited intelligence. In this, they were in perfect agreement. But Ellen was so head-over-heels in love, so convinced she'd found the perfect ideal of her beloved intellectual father, mistakenly put her trust in Rupert. And now, poor Kathryn was suffering the consequences of that misguided trust.

She'd done her best, but a grandmother never had the same influence as the parents. But how dare they make her beautiful granddaughter doubt herself, only because she was a talented athlete?

"I'm sure you've misunderstood, Kathryn," said Chris, returning to the earlier remark. "How would being good in sports make you less of a girl? I was on a team alongside some of the most talented female swimmers. They were like you. Strong, athletically prepared. Competitive as hell." Chris placed the meat and cheese on his plate and took a piece of bread from the basket before passing it on to Heike. "You should be proud of your talents. Your parents should be, too." He looked over at Grace. "I know your Grandma is."

Grace smiled at him. But Kathryn's dilemma was real. Grace needed to speak to her daughter when she returned to Durham. Why weren't girls simply allowed to be tomboys today? She'd certainly been one at Kathryn's age. Yet one who was nowhere near as athletically talented as her granddaughter.

The food made its way around the table, and Grace found herself suppressing her inner rage.

"Thanks, Chris," said Kathryn. She squeezed Grace's hand beneath the table, and Grace's heart soared.

Her granddaughter was sure to be a stunning young woman one day, one who turned all the young men's heads. Even better, one who could go head-to-head with them on the pitch. Her granddaughter could play college soccer, maybe even play on the professional women's team. Should that not be something to celebrate? Grace certainly thought so.

Thank goodness Chris and Heike seemed to think so, too. Especially Chris, who understood about nurturing athletic talent. What a relief Kathryn was having such a wonderful time with Marco and Valerio this week. The poor girl. While her whole home life was potentially imploding, Grace was relieved to know she was enjoying this holiday.

But the problem with Rupert remained. With his progressive views and his desire to impress the more extreme professors and crusading students, would her son-in-law convince his daughter she was confused about her gender primarily for social justice bona fides? She hoped not. Kathryn deserved so much more. She was his daughter—not a showpiece for his cause *du jour*.

Yes, it was clear that Grace would have to protect her grandchild, but she felt tremendous relief that an athlete like Chris could help convey what a rare talent Kathryn possessed. She looked at her lovely granddaughter as her plate of pasta arrived. She saw Kathryn's blue eyes sparkle. Saw her wide grin and glowing skin. Her beautiful, talented, athletic granddaughter. Grace knew she would do anything to protect her.

CHAPTER 20

Emma

EMMA SWITCHED OFF THE BATHROOM LIGHT, beelined to bed, and slipped under the goose-down cover. Soon enough it would need to be packed away. They had been up late tonight, playing cards and laughing over glasses of grappa.

Some of the Japanese tourists had stayed later, joining the group, even with the language barrier. The tour guide spoke English well and answered questions about the favorite places they had seen.

It had been a jovial evening. Marco and Valerio had joined the group. They rarely did so, mostly preferring to retreat from the guests, keeping to themselves in the family apartment.

Mark was reading a novel, one of those spy thrillers he loved so much, and which were certain to send Emma off to sleep if she read more than two pages. She placed a gentle hand on Mark's arm.

He looked up from his book and planted a soft kiss on her cheek. "I have to admit, I thought they'd be chatting all night, and I've been dying to stretch out here before drifting off. It's been a long day."

"It has," Emma agreed. "The phone is ringing off the hook for the next set of guests. Dietary restrictions. Changes to pickup times."

Mark chuckled. "I knew what I was doing when I tracked you down and forced you into marrying me." He placed his book down on the night table and turned to Emma, wrapping his arms around her. "How would I have managed this hotel without your incredible organizational skills?"

She tapped his nose. "Your handyman's skills ain't so bad, either. And I see how a lot of the male guests like to chat with you. I think it's been nice for Chris, especially. He's pretty surrounded by women this week."

"True, but he seems to be enjoying the company. And I told you how he confided to me that he's headed towards divorce. I don't think he's shared that with the guests, so don't say anything."

"Of course not. Why would I? That's for Chris to share. Or not. So, tell me, did he agree to trying his hand at a logo?"

"I hope so. He seemed interested. Anyway, can't be worse than what we already have."

"You've got that right." Emma shook her head and snuggled into Mark's embrace. "Anyway, I like Chris. He's great at playing soccer with Marco and Valerio, too. They adore him. And the twins seem to have a sweet spot for Kathryn, too."

Mark smiled. "Smart boys. She's pretty, and she's a terror on the soccer pitch. What more could twelve-year-olds ask for?"

"You're right on that. They're taking her to the Todi youth league tournament tomorrow. I had to have Grace sign the release forms. Kathryn's so excited about it. It seems her parents aren't very supportive about her sports skills."

Mark shook his head. "How could they not be? She's a natural. If my daughters had been that athletically gifted, I would have been cheering them on all the way."

"Well, Marco has already asked her if she'd stay in Todi. He says the girls' team really needs her."

Mark cocked one eyebrow. "Sure he doesn't have ulterior motives?"

Emma chuckled. "It would be the first girl he's shown interest in that way, but it's about the right age. Why not?"

"Almost teenagers. And now girls." He shook his head. "I'm too old for this."

"Aren't we all?" Emma sighed.

"And what about that Madison? I'm not sure I've even seen her."

Emma clucked her tongue. "She's keeping herself to herself. A shame, but her choice, as you reminded me. I love that so many of our guests become close-knit, but we have to offer privacy to our guests who want it. And Madison most certainly seems to want it. I've given up on wanting to draw her in. I'll help her have that peaceful vacation she desires."

Mark reached for her hand and laced his fingers in hers. "You're right, Emma. You always are." He rolled on top of her and kissed her. "I know you're probably as exhausted as I am right now, but what about a little nocturnal exercise?"

"Your mind is always in the same place." She returned his kiss. "And I love you for it." Emma switched off the bedside light and wrapped her arms around her husband's broad shoulders, all daily concerns forgotten.

CHAPTER 21

Madison

THE SUNLIGHT TUMBLED THROUGH THE WINDOW as Madison cracked one eye open. She stretched out, hands grazing the high-thread-count sheets. This bed was much more comfortable than hers at home. Maybe it was time to invest in another mattress.

But would she be able to afford a new mattress? Fears of poverty quickly snapped her out of her dreamy state.

She turned over to examine the bedside travel alarm before startling and shooting straight up.

Ten o'clock? She swiped one hand over her face. How was that even possible?

Her head swiveled to the window seat positioned with its views up to Todi. She glanced at the half-finished bottle of red she'd indulged in last night. Throwing her arms over her head, she fought off the tears threatening to break free.

The late-night call with Rita. After days of stalking her agent, messaging and emailing, Rita had finally called Madison.

Around one in the morning Madison's time. Madison had been tossing and turning, her mind whirling too fast to allow sleep to claim it. She welcomed Rita's ring tone, fantasizing she may be asked to cut her vacation short, called back to the morning show right after the Easter holiday weekend.

Her enthusiastic voice rang out, despite the late hour. But her wide smile quickly faded. Rita laughed when Madison asked if she were needed back in the studio. "Actually, I was going to ask if you wanted to extend your stay in Italy. We're not getting anywhere in negotiations. I thought a little more time away might help talks move forward."

Madison sat in stunned silence as Rita explained the studio was none too enthusiastic about having her back. Rita was putting out feelers with other stations, albeit smaller markets, to see about openings.

"Only a Plan B, mind you," she assured Madison, in a voice that held little genuine assurance.

Madison had begged. Damn it, thinking back, she'd even blubbered. But Rita hadn't budged at all. She suggested they check in Monday to see where things were. Madison had choked back tears and said goodbye.

As soon as she'd clicked off the phone, she tore into the bottle of red that had been a welcome gift, unopened on her dresser until that moment.

She poured it into one of the two glasses and sat before the window, peering out into the blackness, guzzling down glass after glass of a wine meant to be savored, as the tears streamed down her cheeks. Her mind dwelt on the failure of moving backwards, to markets even smaller than Columbus. The tears flowed faster.

Now, the morning after, her head was pounding. She pushed herself up from the bed and padded to the bathroom, digging aspirin out of her cosmetics case.

EVEN IF SHE'D SLEPT THROUGH BREAKFAST delivery, Emma had arranged for Madison to have a cappuccino and her customary bowl of fruit in the dining room before her spa appointment. No way would she get through even a stress-free massage on a stomach still roiling from last night's overindulgence without a jolt of caffeine.

New day. New start. Full body massage and facial. Jacuzzi. Sauna.

The spa was a real find, but as Madison sipped her cappuccino, guilt nibbled its way into her conscience. No, she hadn't planned on being here, but, for good or ill, it was an all-expenses paid vacation. To a country where she'd never been before. Shouldn't she make *some* effort to see something of Italy? In four full days on her first visit to the Italian peninsula, she'd only ventured outside the hotel once. To another spa. Although, to be fair, she had enjoyed that day and the walk around Viterbo. She'd relished Patrizia's enthusiastic explanations of the city once favored by the popes. They'd laughed and talked. Patrizia had even asked her to contact her if she wanted to see more towns in Umbria or Lazio. Should she take her up on the offer?

The other guests appeared to have formed a tight bond. She often heard them laughing at their cooking classes, the ones Madison always avoided as she rushed back to her room after spa treatments—certain Rita would be calling and demanding she book the next flight back. She noticed their chatter floating up into her open window as they ate dinner together, while Madison consumed her grilled vegetables alone in her room.

Why? Why was she always alone? Why did she choose to be hiding out, cloistered in her hotel room, when around her everyone appeared to be having fun? Perhaps a watched phone never rang. And even when it did ring, it bore only bad news.

She gazed out the window, at the sparkling blue sky and the medieval town, stalwart on its perch. She glanced at her watch. Time to get back to her room and then to the spa. But with weather this perfect, maybe she should venture up to see Todi this afternoon. It was too ridiculous to cast her gaze on it every day, while never having even taken the time to visit it. She breathed in deeply and pushed herself up from the medieval table, ignoring the dull pounding in her head that the coffee had managed to diminish, but not fully banish, from her skull. Yes, today she'd explore the town.

New day. New start. Full body massage and facial. Jacuzzi. Sauna. And Todi.

MADISON GROANED WITH PLEASURE as she emerged from the sauna. Angela had been a miracle worker. All the tension knots—and there had been many—had been smoothed, her shoulders felt amazing, relaxed and fully kneaded. She'd been skeptical when she'd first seen the tiny slip of a girl, wondering how she would have the strength to deliver a vigorous massage. Angela was living proof that you could not judge a book by its cover. When Angela ran her magical hands over Madison's tense shoulders and back, Madison purred with pleasure as the accumulated stress melted away. Today had been no exception.

Now, post-massage, she felt the bubbly water caress her skin. She rested her head back on the jacuzzi's edge, closed her eyes, and stretched out her long legs, feeling the jets work their magic. Of course, her legs hadn't experienced much of a workout in these days, with her walks consisting of sojourns from her room to the spa only a short distance away in the garden. After all, Christine had booked daily treatments. It was probably only to escape that preening ass of a husband, but far be it from Madison to look a spa gift horse in the mouth. Regardless, today she'd take her massaged and pampered legs up to the top of the hilltown, finally visit the twisty streets of the medieval town, enjoy views down below, and find time to enjoy an aperitivo on some perfect Italian *piazza*. Hopefully with some handsome, unmarried Italian guy at the table next to hers ...

Rita had told her to post photos on social media, but she hadn't had the heart until now. She was terrified of the harsh responses that could accompany her attempts. Maybe it was the relaxation talking, but it seemed time to emerge from her forced hibernation. At least somewhat. Baby steps.

MADISON STRETCHED OUT on the smooth wooden bench, her neck firm against the hard headrest. The dry heat shrouded her and she closed her eyes. God, she loved saunas. Right after this, she'd go up to her room, shower, and head up to Todi. Yes, this would be better than hunkering down in her room all day, especially after yesterday's disastrous call.

She paid attention to her breaths—in, out, in, out—in the welcoming silence of the sauna. She flinched when she heard the creak of the door and a blast of cold air. Instinctively, she sat up and turned to the arrivals. Two older women stood in their robes, apologetic looks marking their faces.

The familiar one spoke. "So sorry. We must have startled you. May we join you here?" She held a hand to her chest. "I remember you're Madison. We met briefly at check-in. I'm Heike. And this is my new friend, Grace."

Madison fought the groan welling within. Only a few more minutes of solitude. Was that too much to ask? The women stood expectantly. The silence had stretched out too long to be considered comfortable. She nodded and pointed to the door. "Sure, please close that and come in."

The two women looked relieved, claiming their places on two wooden benches.

Madison leaned back down onto the sweltering wood. Ten minutes more and she could escape up to her room, shower, and go see Todi.

"So, Madison," said the Austrian woman, indifferent to the unwritten spa rules that one should not disturb strangers in saunas. "Where have you been hiding these days?"

Madison counted to ten, closed her eyes, and spoke in a measured voice. "I haven't been hiding. I came here to rest, and I've been doing that."

"Fair enough. Grace, maybe Madison is on to something. I'm not sure I've ever had such an amazing neck and shoulder massage. Should we splurge for the full-body massage? Is it worth it, Madison?"

Madison gave up the fight and opened her eyes. "Angela's a real pro. I've been getting her massages every day. *So* worth it."

The other woman smiled. "I could use that. What do you think, Heike? Shall we book?"

British accent, thought Madison. *Okay, Grace is the Brit. Heike the Austrian. I suppose I should make some effort. It's only ten minutes.*

"Sounds great. But not today," said Heike. "We have Kathryn's soccer match, of course. And tomorrow the trip to Spoleto. And the Good Friday menu for our cooking. Saturday, maybe?"

"Saturday's perfect," said Grace.

How the hell were these old ladies leading such an active social schedule out here in the boondocks? Zheesh, this place really was like a cruise ship, chock-full of fun activities people felt forced to take part in. Hearing her name, she was pulled from her thoughts.

"Madison, we should have mentioned there's a group of us going to Spoleto tomorrow. Ugo will be driving us. You may have met him. Charming fellow. I'm sure one more wouldn't be a problem, if you'd like to come along."

Ugo, charming? "Oh," Madison sat up, looked carefully at the women for the first time. Grace was older, but very attractive. She was the one Madison had seen with the young girl, Madison imagined her granddaughter. "I ... uh ... I haven't been on any trips. Except one day in Viterbo, with Ugo's daughter, Patrizia."

"Oh! She'll be our guide in Spoleto," said Grace, nodding. "We haven't met her yet. She couldn't join us in Orvieto, but we got around quite well on our own, didn't we, Heike?"

Heike smiled. "That we did. What a lovely day. And so much fun with Kathryn and Chris." She turned to Madison. "Kathryn is Grace's granddaughter. Beautiful girl, and such a promising young athlete. You may have seen her out playing soccer each day with Emma's twins. And Chris, of course, is a fellow guest. American, too. You might have seen him. Tall, handsome. Kinda hard to miss. And such a nice young man."

Madison fought a groan. Maybe these people were all genuinely nice, but it felt overwhelming. She hadn't signed up for sleepover camp. What was wrong with a polite smile in the breakfast room each day, and then giving everyone their space? No forced togetherness. She unclenched the tight fists she'd been forming and uncurled her fingers at her side, feeling the solidity of the warm wood. She sat up straight, looking pointedly at the clock over the door. "Oh, my. Where does the time go? Ladies, it has been so lovely chatting with you, but I'm afraid I need to make a work call."

"Oh, yes," said Heike. "Emma told us. A television journalist. How glamorous!"

Yet another reason not to mix with the guests. She had enough pressure without having to handle grilling from strangers. She offered a tight smile, the same one she flashed at overly forward fans, as she stood and gathered her towel.

"Don't feel under pressure about the Spoleto trip. You can let us know later tonight," said Heike with that hopeful look. "The others are going, but there'll certainly be room for one more. We were going to ask you, so it's really good luck bumping into you here."

Madison felt pressure building behind her eyes. "Yes, what excellent luck. I'll certainly let you know by this evening. Enjoy the rest of your spa time." With relief, she reached for the door, stepping out of the sauna and relishing the chance to once again be alone.

MADISON was huffing by the time she reached the top of the staircase, thrilled to discover that her fears the steps would never end were unfounded. How on earth did people climb up and down so many steps each day? She'd seen the fellow guests—even not-exactly-spring-chickens Grace and Heike—making their way here. Thank goodness she'd had the presence of mind to exchange the high heels she'd first put on with lower heels. But even those had been a challenge. Something told her fashionable shoes would never see the light of day in this cobblestoned hilltown.

She began to wander the narrow, twisting streets. Though small, the town was filled with people: young children carrying school backpacks, mothers with baby strollers, young couples and elderly matrons. All seemed to be busy popping into shops, chatting, and winding their way through the narrow streets. Madison allowed herself to be nudged along with the flow. She admired the colorful shop windows, boasting wines, cheeses, and cakes.

She looked at the stone buildings that had been built in medieval times and housed centuries' worth of residents and shopkeepers. She listened to the chatter in singsong Italian, taking comfort in the knowledge that she didn't have to understand or even make an effort. Her only purpose in this centuries' old town was simply as an observant spectator, watching life play out around her. Utterly devoid of responsibility. It felt freeing.

She emerged into a sun-drenched square. In one corner, two little boys were kicking a soccer ball back and forth. The largest building was unmistakably a church. She gazed at its façade. Its open doors beckoned and Madison groaned her way up a few more steps to enter. This was her first medieval church, and yet the familiar scent of candle wax and incense surrounded her like a comforting, familiar blanket. She was rarely at church today, but she'd spent every Sunday at mass growing up. Her mother insisted.

When she was young, she'd loved it. As she grew, mass felt longer, what she had to give up—sleepovers, outings with friends—so much more appealing. But every Sunday, her mother insisted they leave early to get seats in the front of the church. One's Sunday best was always worn. Hymns were to be belted out, as if God judged you by the strength of your vocal cords. Adequate time at the end to chat with Father Robert and other churchgoers. Teenage Madison was always embarrassed, knowing she would be forced to make conversation with the families whose homes her mother cleaned. It was always the worst when they had children who went to school with Madison, and she saw those privileged classmates observe her with pity as they gently urged their parents to hurry before they would be late for brunch reservations at the country club.

Madison and her mother never dined at the country club.

They stuck to the tradition Madison had loved as a child, and which now filled her with shame. Her mother would park their battered Ford Pinto in the parking lot of the local Dunkin' Donuts, where her mother would insist on a prominent window seat before ordering one chocolate donut and black coffee for herself and one Boston Kreme and chocolate milk for Madison.

Madison had long outgrown chocolate milk and the caloric Boston Kreme. But her mother seemed to relish this time spent together, when she'd ask Madison all about her week, recount her GPA, and what her guidance counselor had said to her. Her mother's eyes sparkled as they never did throughout the rest of the week, her pride in her daughter's accomplishments so raw and naked, that Madison vowed she would never disappoint her. The donut felt like sawdust in her mouth, sawdust washed down by sickly sweet chocolate milk that had seemed the height of sophistication at age five. But it meant so much to her mother that she was willing to pretend it meant the same to her.

The scent of incense mingling with the stuffy air of the cathedral broke the floodwall on those distant memories. She proceeded through the church, her heels clicking in the silence. She paused to admire the copy of Michelangelo's *Last Judgment*. When she reached a bank of candles, she dug a euro from her purse, dropping it into the offering box. Lighting a candle, she recited a Hail Mary, the irony not lost on her that she should be accompanied by a professional photographer capturing a private moment to make her more likeable to her irate morning audience. She preferred the privacy as she uttered her final "Amen," and watched the flicker of the candle. "You would have loved it here, Mom," she whispered, turning quickly from the candles and making her way down the silent aisle.

Madison emerged into the bright sunlight, blinking like a mole ascending from his crepuscular den. Her hands trembled, her breathing skipped a beat, but she walked slowly down the steps, taking comfort in the chattering crowds, the bright blue sky. Her gaze swept across the sundrenched *piazza* and paused on café tables set out where they could observe and be observed. One table was free and Madison weaved her way to it, sinking down into the chair. She extracted sunglasses from her purse. The shades allowed her to better observe the activity on the pretty square as she enjoyed the warming rays.

It really had been a good idea to venture out of the hotel spa. The young waitress served the neighboring table and then turned to her. "*Che desidera?*"

"I don't speak Italian," Madison said, eyeing the colorful orange drinks drowning in luscious ice the other table had just been served. "I'll have that," she said, pointing to the glasses.

"*Sì, certo,*" said the waitress, nodding.

Madison tilted her head to the sun, closing her eyes behind the sunglass lenses. A feeling of wellbeing surged through her. Aaron may have been a lying, cheating bastard who ruined her career, but at least he had the foresight to book this holiday she could now enjoy. Otherwise, she'd hide away by crashing with friends in Syracuse or heading back to visit distant family in Indiana. This was decidedly better.

There was a gentle cough and Madison lowered her head and opened her eyes. The waitress stood before her, the drink balanced on her tray, She placed the drink on the table, and Madison eyed the ice cubes greedily. The waitress placed down a small bowl of olives on the table.

"Thank you," said Madison, and the woman smiled and departed. Madison held the glass up to the light, watching the rays refract through the orange-red liquid, setting it aglow like a happy, optimistic jewel.

"*Salute*," said a man's voice behind her, close to her ear. "I love admiring the color of an aperol spritz, too. Never fails to put me in a good mood."

Madison shifted in her chair, looking back at the man. He was similarly contorted to face her. Sunlight shone in his blond hair. His broad shoulders bulged against a short-sleeve polo shirt in forest green. Judging by his accent, American. A soft southern drawl.

"Sorry to disturb you, but I heard you speak English and I recognized you from the hotel. The Three Coins Inn. You're staying there this week, aren't you?"

Madison observed him closely. "Oh, yeah. I think I've seen you playing soccer with the kids. I met the grandmother of the young girl today. Grace, I believe."

He chuckled. "Grace's granddaughter is Kathryn. And she's a formidable soccer opponent." He reached a hand across. "I'm Chris, by the way. Chris Larson. Wannabe Italian by way of Virginia."

Madison smiled, the first in a while. "Madison Moore. Working in Ohio, but happy to be on holiday here." She shook his hand.

"Do you mind if I join you? Not sure my back can handle twisting this long."

She hesitated for a moment—today seemed to be filled with uninvited guests encroaching on her bubble of isolation—but then indicated the chair across from her. "Please."

He stood and gathered his glass and backpack, striding the short distance to her table. Madison couldn't help but notice how tall and well-built he was. Easy on the eyes, too. Exactly what she did *not* need right now. He sat down, stretching his long legs out before him.

"So, Madison. What brings you from Ohio to Todi?"

This was exactly why she'd been hiding out. Avoiding people in the first place. At least at the spa they were well-trained to never discuss work, potentially torching their poor clients' blood pressure, tensing up their muscles, and doubling their work on the massage table. These were the risks of unwisely breaking away from self-imposed hermit status.

She stared out over the *piazza*, at the cathedral she'd visited earlier, now glowing in the afternoon light. She kept her eyes fixed in that single spot, assiduously ignoring his eager gaze. "Contract negotiations that haven't gone as well as I'd hoped. It was a good time to put a little distance between me and work, and take all that holiday time I've accumulated while I let it sort itself out." From the corner of her eye, she saw him squirm in his seat.

"Yeah, I hear you. I'm co-owner of a boutique consulting firm, and trying to sell my half. Hiding out here suits me, too."

She noticed his jaw tense. He was looking in the distance, too. Her journalist interest was piqued. Probably something he didn't want to discuss any more than she wanted to discuss her own disaster playing out in faraway Ohio. Better that way.

"And is Todi helping?" She turned and pinned him in place with her winningest smile. The one that used to drive audience views. Until it didn't. "Keeping your mind off business concerns?"

Relief washed over his face. "Yeah. Yeah, it is. Nothing like being in a town with centuries of history to realize your little problems aren't all that important in the grand scheme of things."

Madison tilted her head. "Music to my ears. Shall we toast to that?" She held her glass aloft, the golden afternoon sunshine illuminating the orange cocktail. "Here's to enjoying Italy, and not talking shop."

His lips tilted upwards, displaying attractive dimples when his face broke out into a full smile. He lifted his glass up and clinked gently against hers. "Couldn't agree more. *Salute*, Madison. To Todi. And Italy. And escaping daily life."

"*Salute*, Chris. To Italy and escape, it is." She sipped her refreshing drink and observed all the other people at nearby tables doing the same. The square was filling up with all the locals and tourists out on the later afternoon *passeggiata*. A sense of wellbeing filled her from within. Not the temporary boost she got emerging from hours in the spa, but something deeper. Something fueled by intense gratitude, something she hadn't felt in a long time.

Yes, her personal life was a nightmare right now. Her reputation shot. Her career in the toilet. And yet, as she sat on this luscious *piazza*, drinking this simple drink, listening to Chris enthuse about all he'd seen and loved in Italy (and how had he managed to see so much in such a short time?), she felt fortunate to be part of the pulsing life and activity all around them.

She smiled at this handsome man as he recounted some humorous detail about a trip he'd taken with the other hotel guests, and she soaked in the details and the atmosphere. Surreptitiously, she switched off her cellphone. If Rita called, she would not be available.

She angled her face up to the warm sun, took a deep sip of her gently bitter drink, and allowed her handsome companion and Todi's charm to set her long-battered heart aglow.

CHAPTER 22

Heike

HEIKE SAT IN THE ARMCHAIR by the window. The sun
streamed in, warming her as she gazed out at Todi high above.
Her skin tingled after a morning at the spa. She usually prided
herself on not caving in to trendy fripperies, but it had been
pleasurable to be pampered, for once. And Angela knew what
she was doing, as she managed to knead those knots out of
Heike's shoulders. Sitting here, so relaxed, Heike felt like a
young girl again. A young girl meeting fellow student Matthias,
back in those heady days of the University of Vienna, when
everything had seemed possible.

How quickly it could all slip through your fingers. And, years
later, you would find yourself all alone. Unwanted. Unneeded.

Talking to Grace had helped. Maybe it did make a difference
to speak with people who hadn't known you your whole life, to
give you the needed perspective.

Grace was dealing with the death of her own beloved
husband, too, and a daughter whose life seemed to be

imploding. Listening to Grace, it sounded so similar to what she observed with Anneliese. When she was allowed to observe at all. With what speed she'd gone from owner of their local *Beisl* to unemployed, widowed *Hausfrau.* How had it happened, exactly? Why had she allowed it? It would have never happened if Matthias were still alive. Yet, she alone was to blame, allowing herself to be bullied into irrelevance.

This holiday provided her with the distance to see it more clearly, to speak with Grace, who had so many similar concerns. Meeting Grace had been such a miraculous stroke of luck. Only a week ago, Heike had been sitting in her home, feeling lonely. Now she was out and about, speaking with a new friend more than she ever managed to do with old friends and neighbors back home.

And yes, the cooking classes, walks to Todi, and conversations with the other guests had been exactly what she'd needed to rouse herself from the loneliness that had settled into her bones in these past months. She gazed up at the warming sun. An escape from still chilly and wet Vienna hadn't hurt either. She sighed deeply. And that spa! Not to be overlooked. Perhaps she'd been too dismissive of pampering. Surely, once in a while wouldn't hurt.

Heike glanced at her watch. Another half hour before she would meet Grace in the lobby and they would walk together to see the town soccer match. Kathryn had been invited by the twins, and she was over the moon. Grace confided in Heike that Kathryn was blossoming on this holiday. She'd been hesitant to take her on holiday, but it had been the best thing for the young girl. Unpleasantness might await her on their return, and so, she was especially appreciative of these carefree days.

Heike kicked off her shoes and lay back on the firm bed. Not much of a napper, she was not concerned about drifting off to sleep. But resting during the day, something she rarely did as a busy mother, wife, and business owner, was becoming a cherished part of her day in recent months. She felt her breath becoming more shallow and her mind clearing itself. She took deliberate breaths. In, out. In, out.

The shrill buzz of the phone broke her relaxed concentration, She sat up, confused. Slow to react, she reached for the phone beside her bed.

"*Pronto?*"

"*Mutti,*" Anneliese's voice rang out across the line.

Heike hadn't spoken to her daughter since her departure. She'd sent a few WhatsApp messages and photos, but heard almost nothing in response, and planned to call on Easter.

"Anneliese," Heike recovered quickly, now fully concentrated on the call. "What's wrong? Are the children okay? Hans?"

Heike's daughter sobbed. "Yes, everyone is fine. Physically. It's …" she paused. "It's the restaurant."

Heike closed her eyes and breathed in deeply, attempting to stave off the anger and frustration she felt coursing through her body, that same body that was so harmoniously relaxed mere moments earlier.

"*Mutti*? Are you there?" Anneliese's pleading voice urged over the line.

Heike sighed. "Yes, I'm here."

"I … I need to ask you for another loan. The restaurant. It's in trouble. Hans is afraid we may go under if we can't obtain the needed liquidity."

Heike squeezed her thumb and forefinger at the bridge of her nose, willing away the tension. "Anneliese, I bailed you out four months ago. With a so-called loan you never made any attempt to pay back. In fact, since then, I've seen very little of you. And you're telling me you want a second loan now?"

The young woman sniffled. "*Mutti.* How can you be so cruel? Running a restaurant is hard work. It takes capital. Surely, you can spare some money. Hans and I will pay you back."

Heike looked out at ancient Todi, gleaming in the afternoon sun. "I know how hard running a restaurant is. Your father and I did it successfully for years. We never asked for loans from anyone. We worked *hard*. We understood what the neighborhood wanted. What you are offering is not what anyone in Hirschstetten wants."

There was a sharp intake of air on the other end of the line.

"I could give you a second loan. And a third. And a fourth. You would never pay me back. And you would also not turn things around to make your restaurant a success."

"How *could* you, *Mutti*?"

"I speak the truth. Your father and I slaved for years. Built a good life for ourselves, through hard work and determination. I could give you all the fruits of our prodigious labor, but you and Hans would squander it." She clenched her fists in anger as she gazed out the window at the medieval town on a hill.

She'd only been gentle with her daughter, even after she and her husband had greedily tugged away everything Heike and Matthias had built stone by painful stone. Mourning had taken a toll on her, weakened her resolve to fight back. She'd even forked over hard-earned retirement investments, hoping against hope her daughter and son-in-law wouldn't lose that, too. And now, it was clear they had.

On the other end of the line, a sharp intake of breath. "That is so unfair. If Father were still alive, he would have wanted to help us."

"If Father were still alive, you and Hans would have never wrested a successful business away from us only to turn it into a failure." Her own words shocked her. How long had they been nestled in the deepest recesses of her brain? Ignoring what was before her very eyes. What she wanted to believe. But grieving could no longer be an excuse for being taken advantage of by her own daughter.

Heike took two long steps to the bed and sank down to the mattress. "Anneliese, *Schatzi*, I know this criticism will sound harsh, coming from me. I've always been gentle with you. Perhaps too gentle. But distance has allowed me to see things more clearly."

"No," Anneliese interjected, her voice breaking as the sobs washed over her. "You are being petty and spiteful. Hans is trying. He is trying so hard. But it takes seed money, at least until things get off the ground."

Heike shook her head. "Oh, my darling girl. Things will never get off the ground. We *were* successful, offering our neighbors what they wanted. A welcoming environment. Familiar foods. A place for family occasions, a well-earned dinner out, a chance to see friends. Genuine, warm, traditional." She closed her eyes. "Hans came in and ignored the market. He created a fusion restaurant no one wanted. You chased away all our clientele, when it took us years and years for us to build that up. Half of them won't even speak to me anymore."

"That's not fair …" her daughter sobbed.

"It pains me to say it, but it is fair. You chased them away without having new clientele to replace them. Your restaurant might work in central Vienna, but clients aren't going to come all the way to our neighborhood for a pretentious restaurant. The prices are too high. The decor and atmosphere so cold. You tried. But it hasn't worked. I can't loan you more money I will never see again."

The sobs grew louder, but while Heike's heart broke for her daughter and her disappointment, an enormous weight lifted from her own chest. She had been living with it so long. It had mingled with the grief of the loss of her husband and best friend, the loneliness, the regret in watching a lifetime of work dismantled piece by piece for a project destined to end in failure.

Heike breathed in, feeling the air seep deep into her lungs. Squaring freshly massaged shoulders, she felt an odd sense of pride. She'd told her daughter what she'd long needed to hear. It didn't make it any easier, but at least it was a first step to finding a path forward.

"*Schatzi.* I know you're upset. But you grew up in our restaurant, too. You know I'm right. This was Hans' dream, but I suspect you knew it was not the correct strategy for the neighborhood. Please, just think about it. We can speak when you are less emotional."

"But please ..." she sobbed. "Please won't you consider it? Just a small loan?"

"No, *meine Leibling.* Do not ask that of me. Please reflect on what I have said. If you are honest, you will realize I am right. And we can look for a way to come back from this failure. Let's talk again at Easter. See if you've had time to think about it." She concentrated on speaking in gentle tones. She knew Anneliese shied away from any criticism, not unlike herself. But her daughter needed to trust her own instincts, not always bend to her husband's blustery will. "And darling, please give all my love to the children."

"I will," said her daughter, her voice breaking once again. "We'll speak soon, *Mutti.*"

"Goodbye, my love."

Heike placed the phone down. She looked down at her feet and sighed. The relief was real, but her heart was still breaking for the pain she had inflicted on her daughter. But what were her choices? She and Matthias had consistently set aside money for eventual retirement—a retirement they would never be able to enjoy together. Despite her misgivings, she'd dug into those savings to fund her daughter and son-in-law in their dreams. And they'd subsequently repaid her by pushing her out of her restaurant and their lives, and losing the entire customer base Heike and Matthias had built up after decades of careful cultivation.

This even caused a rift with many of the neighbors, who had come to depend on a local restaurant to gather and to see neighbors. In her time of grieving, Heike tired of being criticized by these neighbors, of hearing her daughter criticized. This is when she started spending more and more time home alone, wallowing in her grief, when she needed to get out more to reinsert herself into life. She'd stopped participating in church activities, no longer ventured to the center for her Italian classes, found excuses to not meet old college friends for coffee at their favorite cafés. Slowly, calls and visits stopped coming. And poor Ida was wrapped up in her own concerns, with her mother's health taking a turn for the worse, and even their morning walks fell by the wayside. It was enforced solitude entirely of her own making.

But this time away—even if only for a few days—made her see things with a new perspective. Made her braver. Her daughter and son-in-law could no longer rely on her to finance a restaurant destined to lose money. Her money.

Painful as it was, she would need to speak with Anneliese when she returned. Speak to her without Hans hovering nearby, always eager to jump in and take control, even when he had no idea what he was doing. It drove Matthias mad, how his son-in-law, with no restaurant experience, was always lecturing his father-in-law on how his business strategies were so old-fashioned. She and her husband had both ignored it, for the sake of marital harmony for their daughter. And, at the time, Hans had some well-paying sales job and was frequently traveling. The grandchildren were small back then and such a pleasure to have around. And it was easy to ignore the unwanted, yet infrequent, lectures. Hans lost his job around the time of Matthias' death. Heike was at her lowest point, practically unable to make it through the day, let alone to make rational decisions about her future.

But now she was clear-eyed. And not one euro cent would be invested into a business venture she should have stood up against at the outset. This holiday was giving her the distance and perspective she'd lacked for too long.

She sunk her head into her hands. Despite the newly developed backbone, it didn't ease her conscience knowing her daughter and grandchildren might somehow suffer. How had things spun so quickly out of control after losing Matthias? None of this would have happened if he hadn't died. She felt the familiar flood gathering behind her eyes and did her best to stave off the tears. Not now.

A knock at the door distracted her.

"Heike, dear ... are you there?"

Grace's voice, Heike noted with relief. She forced her back straighter. Willed her voice to sound firm as she called, "Oh, Grace. Took a bit of a catnap there. I haven't forgotten our outing. Will you wait for me in the lobby? I'll be down in two minutes."

"Of course. Take your time." Footsteps receded in the hallway.

Heike stood and strode to the bathroom, examining herself in the mirror with a critical eye. She splashed cold water on her face and wiped it off gently with the thick towel. She reapplied her face cream and swept a nude gloss across her lips. Not ideal, but a brisk walk would get some color back in her cheeks.

Slipping on her shoes, she scooped up her keys and pocketed them, before closing the door firmly behind her. She descended the stairs at a rapid clip, willing her mind back to Todi.

WORRIES ABOUT GETTING SOME COLOR back in her cheeks were unfounded. The strong sun glared down on the edge of the pitch and Heike cursed herself for forgetting sunscreen. Or a hat. April in Vienna was never this hot.

She stood beside Grace, both women wearing red and white scarves that Marco and Valerio had given them. Apparently the under-thirteen league boasted the same color scheme as the professional league in town. She and Grace were among the sizeable crowd of parents, grandparents, siblings, friends, and townspeople cheering the Todi youth league on.

The enthusiasm seemed to be working. The Todi team was crushing neighboring Pantalla, five to one. And The Three Coins Inn was the epicenter of goal scoring. Valerio scored two, Marco one, and the huddle was still formed around the latest Todi scorer—a lovely English girl from Durham.

Grace's eyes glistened with tears as Heike placed an arm around her new friend's shoulders and laughed. "Look at her go! Even scoring against Italian lads."

Grace smiled broadly, checking her phone to ensure she'd captured the impressive goal and the congratulatory huddle Kathryn elicited from her new teammates. Grace tapped the screen to rewind the rapid kiss teammate Marco placed on her cheek in the excitement.

"Well, I'll be ..." laughed Heike. "I bet he's not doing that often in the matches."

Grace chuckled and then flashed a thumbs-up when Kathryn looked their way, elation glowing on her pretty face. "It's a real treat she was able to play. This is a benefit—collecting money to support the girls' team in the towns, too." She pointed. "See ... each team has two girls playing. Todi's second girl player has the flu, so Marco offered up their guest, arguing she was a temporary Todi resident."

"That she is," agreed Heike. "You must be so proud. Look at her on the pitch. She's fearless. And fast. Amazing footwork, too."

Grace sighed, her eyes never straying from her granddaughter. "She works so hard, but I sometimes feel her parents don't appreciate it." She pulled her team scarf tighter. "Or, more precisely, my son-in-law doesn't appreciate it."

Heike stayed silent as she observed the hard set to Grace's jaw, the twitching at her temple. Frustrations with sons-in-law were nothing new to her. Grace would share, if she wanted to, in her own time.

A familiar voice called their names, and Heike turned to see Emma, a matching scarf around her long neck, arms extended. "That was amazing!" she reached in for a hug with Grace, and then another with Heike. "What a goal! I don't think the team will want to allow Kathryn to return to Durham when her holiday is up." She winked. "And judging from that celebratory kiss, I'm guessing Marco will be leading the charge."

Grace chuckled. "I caught it all here on film," she said, pointing to her phone.

"Oh, good. I missed it. Signora Ranucci filled me in. Will you send it to me?"

Heike felt a sense of warmth and belonging welling within as the sun warmed her face and they cheered on Todi to victory. Just as Emma was explaining something about the history of the team, another red-clad player charged to the goal and made a corner shot. The goalie flew through the air, but it soared just beyond his fingers.

The team and crowd erupted in a wave of red, as the final horn sounded and Todi claimed victory, six to one.

THE PIAZZA DEL POLOLO WAS CROWDED, every table filled. Kids in uniforms were eating ice cream. Parents were chatting and clinking glasses of *aperitivi*. Those who didn't fit at tables spilled over to the edge of the *piazza*, laughing and talking.

Grace had one eye on Kathryn, surrounded by Marco, Valerio, Luisa, and teammates as they licked their ice-cream cones and laughed in the golden, late afternoon sun.

Heike felt the warm sun on her face. "If you didn't know it, you'd think Kathryn was a local. What language do you think they're speaking?"

Grace chuckled. "Good question. She woke me up in the middle of the night, yelling out Italian terms in her sleep. I have to assume they're football terms. I only understood *Gol!*"

"Good for her. It shows something about a personality to blend in so well to a new culture so rapidly, to immediately find friends and be welcomed into the group. Even in another language."

A smile played on Grace's lips. "It does, doesn't it? Kathryn could use that. Her parents ... well, they haven't been wholly supportive of her goals." She held up her aperol spritz and toasted with Heike. "To victory."

"*Alla vittoria*," said Heike, sipping her drink, grateful for all the cool ice. "I remember Kathryn mentioning it the other day. Why don't her parents support her? Do they worry sports takes away from her study time?"

"Perhaps somewhat," said Grace, sliding one long finger along the rim of her glass. "But I'm afraid it's more complicated than that. Rupert, my son-in-law, is so desperate to be seen as a progressive professor. I have to admit, I don't even understand exactly what he teaches. It's all 'decolonize this,' 'gender is a social construct' that. Hoping to get more standing at the university."

"Oh," said Heike. "It all makes me feel so old. University seemed much more straightforward in my day."

"You're telling me," said Grace, with a tight smile. "Richard couldn't stand him. My husband was an economist, numerous prizes, book awards, and accolades. A bit of a snob, if I'm being honest. He always called Rupert a pompous ass behind his back. Made fun of his victim studies."

"Oh, I see." Heike took another sip of her drink.

"The good news is, my son-in-law never realized when he was being made fun of. And, believe me, my husband took full advantage of that. He said he would never suffer fools. And he felt his son-in-law was an extraordinary fool. Ellen, our daughter, was so close to her father, but she pretended not to understand. She did everything to support her husband's career. Dropped out of her own doctoral program in art history to make Rupert's life easier. Richard was furious, of course. To be honest, so was I. But then she fell pregnant with Kathryn, and it made more sense to have the time to dedicate to her little girl."

Grace reached for the potato chips at the center of the table, looking beyond Heike's shoulder. She sighed. "It felt they had reached a compromise, but then my son-in-law kept getting involved with progressive causes. Durham was a hotbed of student movements. Still is. Rupert often seemed more strident than the students he taught. Everyone oppressed. The evil, capitalist, colonial power of Great Britain was apparently thwarting opportunities for everyone. You can imagine the fun dinner conversations that sparked. Richard would always retreat to his study the second the pudding was cleared away."

Heike nodded. "My son-in-law isn't that bad, but I know the type."

"It was fine when he was running on about the cause *du jour*. Attending marches for every perceived injustice. But things started to get uncomfortable as Kathryn grew older."

Heike looked into the distance, at the group of tourists filing into the *piazza*.

"Ellen spoke with me, of course. I knew their marriage was strained, even before Richard's death. I would often collect Kathryn from school, or accompany her to football, to allow my daughter time to work things out." She shook her head. "She was always the one trying to work things out. Then the sports became another source of tension. Kathryn started getting better, dedicating more time to training. That was about the time there were a lot of lectures on campus about being nonbinary. How courageous it was for parents to support those children." She took a deep sigh. "Around that time, Rupert started suggesting that's why Kathryn was so into sports. Always hanging around with the boys. Because she wasn't comfortable being a girl."

Heike's sharp intake of air startled her.

"At first, my daughter refused to listen to his ideas, but the more he pressed, the more she gave in. It felt like Rupert wanted to have a gender-confused daughter for prestige among his students, his fellow faculty members. But I kept telling Ellen, Kathryn is just a tomboy. To not start confusing her with these ideas. To give her time to grow up."

She sipped her drink, and Heike noticed the slight tremor in her hand.

"Things were coming to a head around the time Richard died. His death was so sudden. So unexpected. And Ellen was such a daddy's girl." Grace looked up at an airplane flying high above. "She was suffering. She withdrew even more. And my son-in-law increased his influence with Kathryn." She rubbed her eyes, stayed still for some minutes with her hands obscuring her face.

Heike knew about leaving someone time for their grief, staying close, but not pushing them to "Cheer up" or "Move beyond it." After all, she'd been in this strange limbo for the past six months. She looked up at the town hall, where a small wedding party was gathered for photos. The bride and groom looked older. Perhaps second marriages. Or maybe even love the first time around. Who knew? Even if she'd found true love once in her life, the language of the heart was still a mystery to her. The bride looked radiant on the stairs of this perfect square, her new husband, family, and friends gathered all around. The elegance of the wedding party clashed with the dirty soccer gear of the players scattered across the picturesque *piazza*. But surely embracing the complexities of life—young, old, celebration, grief—was what this public space was all about.

Grace dropped her hands, placing them flat on the table. "I'm sorry for that."

Heike dropped her own hand over one of Grace's. "Please don't apologize. Not to me. I lived in a fog for so long after Matthias' death. No need to explain."

Grace wiped away a tear. "Thank you." She reached for her drink and took a decisive sip before placing it down and breathing in deeply. "It's nice with you, Heike. Not to have to explain myself. You understand." She smiled slightly and turned back to the town hall. "Look at them. They have no idea what they're getting themselves into, do they?"

Heike tilted her head and observed her new friend, her brow furrowed with a darkness that flashed in her eyes, before shaking her head and chasing it away.

"Still," Grace continued. "I feel some responsibility in allowing it to happen. I did intervene, but belatedly." She sighed. "I picked up Kathryn more frequently after football, had her for dinner, under the pretense that it was too lonely dining alone." She shook her head. "That's when I learned Rupert had started taking her to a child psychologist, who was also filling her head with ideas about her so-called confusion." She tilted her head towards the place on the *piazza* where Kathryn and Marco were seated.

In their identical uniforms side by side, Kathryn and Marco were staring into one another's eyes. Kathryn laughed at something he said. Marco brushed something off her shoulders. Grace could see how his fingers lingered there. Years later, she still recognized that spark of first love.

Heike smiled. "It does seem a bit of an Italo-Anglo crush has developed at The Three Coins Inn."

Grace turned back and nodded. "As often happens around this age. The worst of it is, Rupert will probably be devastated his daughter is merely conventional."

"Oh," interjected Heike. "I wouldn't be so sure. I think everyone lives in fear of not being open enough to new ideas. But it's such a trying age, isn't it? I look back at myself at Kathryn's age. I was so shy and confused. So afraid of becoming a woman. I didn't have half her confidence. She's going to be fine. You'll see. Your son-in-law will come around."

Grace sighed and took another sip of her drink. "I hope you're right. But I'll also be more vigilant." She nodded. "And ensure my son-in-law's views are not the only ones Kathryn hears. This trip has been good for her." She turned back to the animated tween couple again. "New friends, a new language, seeing that her sports skills are appreciated, exploring a new place. No matter what awaits her at home, this trip has made her stronger." She turned back to Heike. "And it's been good for me, too. It's been good to make a new friend. I'm so glad our vacations at The Three Coins coincided, Heike." She held up her glass. "Shall we toast once more? This time to friendship."

Heike felt a warm glow burning in her heart, a sensation that had been absent for too long. This trip had been good for her, too. She'd needed a change of scenery, a kickstart to live life again. She smiled at her new friend, hoping this friendship would last beyond their Todi stay. She held up her glass, clinking it gently against Grace's. "I'll never say no to friendship."

The wedding party applauded the bride and groom before setting off for the wedding dinner. Kathryn, Marco, and the rest of the team were up on legs that should have been more exhausted, and were gently kicking the soccer ball back and forth while laughing and chatting. Across the *piazza*, young and old traversed as part of the afternoon *passeggiata*. Canes and baby strollers promenaded in equal measure. The crowds increased, the conversations and excited cries of children rose through the air, the warm sun shone down on them and Heike felt that inner glow expand as she embraced it all. The energy of the *piazza*. New love blooming. Friendships being created. Life being lived.

And she, once again and after what seemed so long, finally a part of it.

CHAPTER 23

Chris

THE SUN WAS ONLY A BRIGHT GLIMMER on the horizon as Chris sat at his window-facing desk, his laptop open. Since he'd arrived and overcome his jetlag, he'd miraculously been sleeping well, but this morning had been an exception. He'd woken at four a.m., and no amount of tossing and turning, not even the chamomile tea he'd brewed this morning in the electric kettle had managed to return him to his slumber.

There was still time before breakfast and loading their van for today's trip to Spoleto, and he'd been avoiding it long enough. His lawyers were in the trenches, handling the divorce and the sale of the company. It didn't look as if Rob had the funds to buy him out, and the slacker didn't like the alternatives: either bringing in a new partner, taking out a large loan, or dissolving the company altogether. Chris' only concern was for their ten employees, but they were young and talented and Chris had already promised them great references and a few phone calls to potential firms if a buyout or a new partner could not be arranged.

Now his hand hovered over an email he longed to delete. Damn, he really needed a coffee before dealing with this. He looked out the window again, the orange glow on the horizon intensifying, as dawn prepared to break in Umbria. Umbria. Being half a world away definitely helped put things in perspective. Entire days passed where he almost forgot his deep humiliation, the pain only creeping back late at night, alone in his room.

Being in Italy helped to distract, but Chris couldn't push the reality of the shambles of his marriage and his career out of his mind forever. He looked down from the brightening sky and turned his attention back to his computer screen, his finger hovering over the laptop's touchpad as his heart, despite his best attempts, thrummed wildly in his chest.

He breathed in, out, in again. Channeled the intense focus he used to have on the diving blocks before his competition. Without allowing any more self-doubt to creep in, he clicked into the message with a split-second reaction that used to accompany the starting gun.

Words. Words from her.

He breathed in deeply once more and plunged in.

Dearest Chris,

I'm sitting here thinking of you. I wish you'd take my calls. You keep letting them go to voicemail. Please. You'll have to talk to me eventually.

I know you're furious with me right now. You should be. I'm furious with myself.

I don't know why I did it. Fighting boredom? Routine? I never should have started anything with Rob. It was meaningless. I don't love him. I love you. I've always loved you.

Maybe it was the pressure of you wanting us to start a family.

I didn't think I was ready.

I sit here and think about the surprise you had planned for us in Italy. The incredible time we could have had together, if things had gone differently. Maybe we could have talked it over then, away from all the daily stress. We've been apart so much this year. That's not an excuse. I know what I did was wrong, but so much time away from one another hasn't helped.

Chris, we've been good together. If you can find it in your heart to forgive me, I know we can be good again.

Please, Chris. Answer my calls. Don't be driven by anger. We can work this out. Keep the house. Keep the business you worked so hard to build. Keep our marriage intact. Don't we deserve another shot?

I love you. I always have, and I always will,

Kaitlyn

Chris sat motionless, staring out the window. The sky was filled with ever bolder fingers of light. Oranges, pinks, and light blues painted the morning canvas. Another day. Another adventure.

And yet, his old life was trying to tug him back.

He dropped his head into his hands. Yes, eight years was a long time. He'd given up everything for Kaitlyn. His dreams of swimming professionally to build a future with her. A family. And at first, they'd seemed to want the same life. But even before she betrayed him, things were shifting in the wrong direction.

Yes, he'd been obsessed with getting the business off the ground, but he was doing it for them, for their future together. And at the same time, his wife fell in with the socialites and no longer appreciated what they had. She always needed more. And he was expected to deliver.

Even a year ago, he would have done anything to save his marriage. He'd willingly sacrificed for Kaitlyn because he truly loved her. Believed in her. And now?

With a sigh, he clicked out of his email and firmly shut the laptop. Standing slowly, he gathered his clothes and made his way to the bathroom for his shower. Breakfast would be served soon, and he had a busy day before him.

CHRIS KNEW HE WAS BEING antisocial at breakfast. Everyone was in a good mood following yesterday's victory against their hometown rivals. Kathryn's eyes were absolutely glowing and, despite his distractedness, he noticed that Marco had joined breakfast and didn't appear ready to allow Kathryn out of his sight. Chris smothered a smile. A first crush may have been long ago in his case, but memories of those feelings of elation and confusion still made him smile. Marco was clearly a young boy of good taste.

But Marco had some complicated, prearranged school project with a classmate that was due after the Easter holidays. Kathryn would be joining the adults in Spoleto without her new, lovestruck shadow.

He'd gotten away with his moodier demeanor claiming, in truth, a night of poor sleep and the need for a few coffees to get the engine roaring. In truth, his participation wasn't strictly required. Grace and Heike were thick as thieves, chatting away like old friends who'd known one another their whole lives. And Marco and Kathryn seemed to be storing up for the long hours of separation, laughing and chatting a mile a minute. It was easy for Chris to remain silent.

The only one not at breakfast was Madison. She'd been aloof since they all arrived. She was keeping to herself, never eager to join the group. In fact, yesterday out on the Piazza del popolo, he'd had to look twice to ensure it was her. But their talk over an aperitivo yesterday had been pleasant. Afterwards, they'd meandered over to panoramic Oberdan Gardens and caught views over Todi, bathed in that otherworldly, golden afternoon light. They'd talked about everything and nothing. Their impressions of Italy, how far away it all seemed from their lives back home, long-ago college days. His senior year at Virginia had been her freshman year at Syracuse and they'd laughed, recalling a meet he'd attended on the upstate New York campus, where the real sport seemed to be trudging through the snow to reach the pool. Not an easy task for a southern-born and bred guy like him. She'd felt he'd captured Syracuse winter accurately.

He was going to invite her to climb the San Fortunato belltower, but glancing down at her impractical shoes, he thought better of it. How the hell had she made her way up to town in the first place? Those shoes made their joint descent necessary, with Madison leaning heavily on his still well-muscled arm. Hell, he hadn't minded at all. But what possessed a woman to climb up to a medieval hilltop town with heels like that? Women still mystified him sometimes.

But all in all, it had been fun. He'd had a great time with Heike and Grace. And Kathryn, of course. And after the visit to the pub and the sketches he was working on for a new visual for the inn, he and Mark had been getting closer. But still, he had to admit that being with an attractive woman, even if there was no other intention from his side, somehow boosted his bruised ego. He couldn't help but notice the local guys casting envious glances his way as he passed them down those monstrously steep streets, a beautiful woman quite literally clinging to his arm.

After the humiliation his own wife subjected him to—his wife and former best friend subjected him to—it felt like the universe was finally taking a bit of pity on him. But then, Madison hadn't appeared for dinner, like she said she would, and he felt a vague sense of disappointment.

He glanced down at his watch and realized Ugo would be picking them up soon. If he still wanted to brush his teeth and pack a few items in his backpack, he'd need to hurry. He gulped down his second cappuccino and ran up the stairs, two at a time.

WHEN HE RETURNED TO THE LOBBY and stepped outside, Chris was surprised to see everyone was waiting for him in the van. "Oh, wow. Sorry to have held everyone up."

"No problem. No problem," said Ugo. "Emma was preparing me second espresso of morning. Good again to see you, Chris." Ugo's smile was wide. "I introduce you to my daughter, Patrizia. She speak English better her *papà*."

A slim woman, her long hair gathered in a ponytail, stepped around the van to shake his hand. "So nice to meet you, Chris. I'm so pleased to join all of you in Spoleto today. *Papà* has an errand to run, so I'll be showing you around today."

"Lucky for us," said Chris. "Shall I get inside?"

"Please," said Patrizia. "We're all ready to go."

Chris slid into the first row, next to Kathryn, who smiled at him and then looked back at her phone, swiping through photos of yesterday's game. Grace and Heike were spread out in the back seat, chatting away, oblivious to the others.

"Road trip!" shouted Heike, with youthful enthusiasm.

Chris smiled. This outing was what he needed to put Kaitlyn and her strategic regrets, most likely following concerns about a sudden socioeconomic slide downwards, out of his mind.

Ugo, freshly caffeinated, slid into the driver's seat, turned on the engine, and pulled out of the driveway. Through their open windows, they heard a commotion behind them.

Chris turned to see Madison at the inn entrance, shouting and waving her arms. Ugo stopped and Patrizia stepped out of the car as Madison approached.

"I thought you said you wouldn't be joining," Chris heard Patrizia say through his open window.

"I know. I changed my mind."

"Madison, Spoleto's not as steep as Todi, but there's no way you'll get around with those shoes. Let's go see what Emma has." Patrizia turned to the car. "*Papà, un attimo soltanto.*"

Ugo shook his head.

"Well, this is a nice surprise," said Grace. "We've only met Madison in the spa. I'm glad she can join us today. Chris, she's American. Like you. You may not have met her yet."

"I have actually," Chris said, turning back. "I recognized her up in Todi yesterday afternoon. Introduced myself. I mentioned our trip today, but she didn't seem interested."

"Hmm," said Grace.

Chris caught the hint of a smile on the two women's faces and he turned to ignore it, peppering Kathryn with new questions about the match and the players.

His door opened, and Madison stood before him, looking chic in a taupe fitted shirt and slim pants, a loose scarf knotted elegantly around her neck.

"Hi, Chris. Would you mind scooting in one?"

He moved over to the empty space beside Kathryn, ignoring his cramped legs, and Madison took possession of his window seat.

"Emma kitted me out with these Italian designer sneakers." She rotated one slim ankle for him to see. "Not bad. The good news for you is at least today you don't have to do all the heavy lifting to ensure I make it down the hills in one piece." She smiled and her whole face glowed.

Chris met her comment with a smile. Ugo started the motor and they took off. Deep inside, Chris felt an inexplicable sense of disappointment.

"EACH SUMMER, SPOLETO HOSTS an international music festival," said Patrizia. "It grows in popularity each year. You need to book hotels way in advance. There are always quite a few of those concertgoers at The Three Coins Inn. Maybe you can come back one day." She turned and led the way to the Duomo.

Chris recalled long-ago college days, where the tour guides were so adept at walking backwards while speaking to their charges. Patrizia possessed this same random skill. She could even finesse it walking up and down Spoleto's steep, cobblestoned streets. A whole new level.

"Was she this turbocharged when she accompanied you to Viterbo?" Chris asked Madison, who was lagging behind.

"Oh, God, no." Madison shook her head, still walking decisively, as if she were still wearing heels. "But then again, we spent the whole day at the spa, only a quick jaunt into town. So no chance to run around like the Tasmanian devil."

Chris chuckled. "Speaking of Tasmanian devils. Look at you in your sporty new shoes."

"Watch it, jock boy. Some of us aren't used to running marathons in our free time. And we don't all have three-meter strides like you. I'm getting the hang of it." She looked down. "But they're not bad. Maybe I'll have to pick up a pair before I head home."

"Already thinking of home? Do you leave after Easter, or do you stay on another week?"

"Here for the long haul. Another week. How 'bout you?"

"Same," said Chris. "But Italy's kind of growing on me. Can't believe the first week is almost over." He gazed over the picture-perfect town bathed in golden sunlight, and took a deep breath. "I'm not really in any rush to leave."

Madison winked at him. "Let's see if you still feel that way after a full day of Spoleto's Marathon Tour. She really is making sure we earn our lunch."

He laughed out loud, relieved to see the Duomo before him. "Yeah, she really is. Look, we made it." He looked back, trying not to get distracted by how Madison's hair caught the sun's rays and formed a golden halo. He tried to ignore her slim figure, with its perfect curves, and the sparkle of mirth in her clear blue eyes. *Female distraction is the absolute last thing I need now,* thought Chris, as he turned back to the church and attempted to ignore Madison's musky perfume so close behind him.

CHAPTER 24

Grace

GRACE WAS LAUGHING SO HARD she feared her sides would burst—a real possibility after all they'd eaten. The remains of their meal was scattered around the table. The waitress had come to clear the dishes, but she was meting out jokes instead. After discovering their various nationalities, every joke initiated with an Austrian, a Brit, an American, and an Italian walking into a room, with the Italian always outsmarting them all.

They were silly and childish, but told in the waitresses' singsong English and exaggerated facial expressions, they were all cracking up like schoolchildren. Kathryn, the only actual schoolchild present, had tears of joy running down her face. Grace suspected Kathryn would be reversing nationalities and telling the same jokes at school. It warmed Grace's heart to see her so entertained. Kathryn deserved this. Joy in her life. An absence of bickering at home. Freedom of criticism about all the unique qualities that made her the extraordinary young woman she was. Grace smiled inwardly. How special to be on this holiday with her.

She looked around the table. How wonderful to be on this holiday, with all these people who were strangers to her a week earlier, and whom she now considered friends.

Patrizia had pushed them hard—perhaps a bit too hard this morning. But she had done an impressive job of presenting beautiful Spoleto to them. Once they had caught their collective breath after trooping behind her, and honestly, only Kathryn had been up to the task, they'd had a fantastic time. The monumental fourteenth-century bridge, the first-century Ancient Roman arch, the spectacular Duomo and its Baroque interior, the art gallery and its collection by Perugino, and his local apprentice—entirely new to Grace—Lo Spagna. She sighed happily and stretched her legs under the table, surreptitiously kneading a sore muscle. She may need to book a massage to recuperate tomorrow, but it had most definitely been worth it.

To her side, Heike and the waitress had slipped into Italian, with Patrizia joining in. Her friend spoke fluently in Italian, laughing and joking with the locals. What a talented woman. And yet, she'd confided in Grace that she'd been living like a hermit since her husband's death. How wonderful for Heike if this trip could spark that joy for life Grace was certain had been buried deep down unnecessarily. She hoped she and Heike could maintain this friendship they'd been forming over this week. Grace needed a fresh start, too. She should finally visit her friend Nicola in Spain. And, perhaps, even her new friend in Vienna.

After all, she'd let a small piece of herself die after burying Richard. Heike wasn't the only one living like a hermit. Grace had confided to Heike she felt positively envious of her new friend's Italian, contemplated taking an Italian class in Durham. New classmates. New challenges. Perhaps, like Heike, a little shake-up was all she needed.

"Grandmum," said the voice beside her. Grace looked over to see the rosy cheeks and sparkling eyes of her beautiful granddaughter.

"Sorry, Kathryn. I was daydreaming." She grinned. "And kneading my poor, aching muscles. I no longer have your levels of energy." She chuckled. "Probably never did, if I'm honest."

"That's okay," said Kathryn. "There are so many hills and cobblestone streets in these towns. Guess it keeps all the older people in Umbria fit."

Grace nodded. "That, it does. Maybe we should come back sometime to explore more and keep me in shape."

"Oh, yes!" gasped Kathryn. "Could we?"

Grace smiled at the naked longing in her granddaughter's eyes. Someone was feeling the first bloom of almost-teenage love. "Well, we're still on our holiday, so let's save that discussion for another day, shall we?"

"Did you notice," Kathryn said, lowering her voice, "how slow Chris was today?" She nodded her head to the other end of the table, where Chris and Madison were deep in conversation, their blond heads close together as they spoke, seemingly unaware of the rest of the table.

Grace recalled that long-ago ability to form a cocoon around oneself, even in the most chaotic surroundings, when you were with someone who made your pulse beat faster. Those days seemed like ancient history.

"Maybe he's found a new girlfriend," whispered Kathryn.

Grace drew closer. "It's not nice to whisper about people when you're sitting with them. You wouldn't like it if someone said it seems you've found a new boyfriend, would you?" She registered the flush wash over Kathryn's cheeks, and she caressed her granddaughter's arm gently. "When possible, it's best not to jump to conclusions. Our friends will tell us their news when and if they're ready. For now, it's nice that Madison is joining us, rather than spending all her time alone." She cast one more glance their way, appreciating her granddaughter's perceptiveness. Why not? Two attractive, single young people. She didn't know Madison well enough yet, but Chris was so kind and interesting. Amazing that he was still single. He deserved to find someone.

"Do you think they have dessert here?"

"You may be the only one with space, Kathryn, but I'm certain they do. Let's ask, shall we?" She clasped the girl's warm hand in her own, too aware that very soon, Kathryn would no longer allow her to do so. Taking advantage of every opportunity afforded her before that moment arrived would be her main priority now.

CHAPTER 25

Annarita

ANNARITA ROCKED IN FRONT OF THE crackling fire. The days were warm and, technically, it was no longer fire-setting weather. But there was still a nip to early evening air and she was too aware that the hot weather would soon arrive, and fires would be a thing of the past until next October.

There was so much she, a reformed city girl, enjoyed about rural life. And this was one of them. She looked down at Sebastiano, who suckled greedily at her breast. Motherhood was inextricably tied with her new life in the country. Annarita, who had despaired at ever becoming a wife and mother, woke each morning, grateful to know she was the mother of two. And yes, that gratitude even extended to predawn waking to soothe her daughter, sobbing from a scary dream.

Giulia had had such a night yesterday, and she'd fallen into her bed after an early dinner. That's how Annarita found herself alone before a roaring fire, nursing her baby in blissful silence. Silence was a rarity nowadays.

The ring of her cellphone broke that blissful lull. She extended her arm to the sidetable, enduring her son's disgruntled protestations. *Tale padre, tale figlio.* Like father, like son. He would not be discouraged from his meal despite a brief interruption. Clasping the edge of the phone, she retrieved it and noted the caller before answering and putting it on speaker.

"*Ciao bella.* You have an uncanny knack for calling me when the *ometto* decides it's time to eat."

"Oh, am I disturbing you?" said the voice over the line. "I can call back."

"No, Tiffany. It's perfect. Giulia's asleep. Giuseppe's at the hotel. And Sebastiano will drift off into his milk coma the second he's full. It's the perfect time to call. I'm a woman of leisure in my rocking chair before the fire."

"Fire? Is it still fire weather? Maybe I didn't pack correctly for Perugia."

Annarita cracked a smile. She remembered when packing for Tiffany would have taken about four or five of the old-time Saratoga trunks. Today, her friend was far more practical. But still, no reason to scare her. "No. You're fine. It's quite warm here. That's just me, trying to drag out fireplace season to the bitter end. Which'll probably be next week. How're things in Rome?"

"Got warm all at once. At this rate, we'll be at the beach soon. We're both excited to get up to see Simone's family for Easter. His mom has a slew of friends, family, and charity committees I have to meet while there." She chuckled. "She still thinks I'm the one she has to win over to get us back to live in Perugia."

Annarita laughed. "And yet it's her own Romanized son. Every time I see him, his Roman accent is stronger. Giuseppe says he'd never pass for an Umbria boy anymore. I'll tell him no poking fun at him while he's here. I can't wait to see you on Monday. I just wish it weren't for only two days."

There was an intake of air on the other end. "Yeah, that's why I'm calling. Simone's mom is taking it hard we're staying such a short time. The idea was Saturday and Easter Sunday with them, Easter Monday and Tuesday with you, and we'd get back here Tuesday evening. I already called Emma to let her know. May First falls on Wednesday this year, so I asked her if there was anything free, and we'd make it for a luxurious, long weekend. Wednesday to Sunday. Talk about a super-*ponte*."

"Oh, no. So we have to wait 'til May to see you? What did she say?"

"That there was a cancellation, and she'll keep it free."

"Well, that's good news, at least."

"So Simone and I will have more time with you, Giuseppe, Emma, and Mark. Chiara even told me she'll be going. We'll drive her up."

"Oh, Emma will be thrilled. Marco and Valerio, too. It's been a while since she's been back."

"So, do you forgive me?"

"What's to forgive? The important thing is you're coming here. We miss you. That's all." Sebastiano stopped nursing and she extracted him gently from her breast, laying him on her lap, his angelic face perfect in repose. She slipped her nursing pad back in, snapped her bra, and pulled up her nightgown.

"I miss you, too. I know we'll have a great time seeing you. And seeing the kids." There was a pause. "That's Simone calling. We're meeting friends for drinks. Give a kiss to Giulia and Sebastiano from Auntie Tiffany."

"I will, Tiff. Talk soon."

"*Ciao*."

Annarita soaked in the pleasant silence, the fire crackling in the ancient stone fireplace. Her gaze slid upwards to the mantel. The wedding photo of Giuseppe and his first wife still held pride of place in the center. Giuseppe had offered to take it down when Annarita moved in, but she had refused, saying Luisa had been an important part of his life, and deserved to be remembered and grieved properly. Giulia was old enough to notice now. When she'd asked, Annarita had explained to her that the nice lady was her *papà*'s first wife, and that she was in Heaven now, looking over all of them. She'd been too young to truly understand, but she referred to the smiling woman on her father's arm as *zia* Luisa.

Around that photo had sprouted a haphazard collection of frames paying tribute to Annarita and Giuseppe's life together. A wedding photo from right here at The Three Coins Inn. A culinary prize they had earned together, awarded at Todi town hall and presented by the mayor. Photos of their growing family. Visits back to New York. Annarita sighed happily. All those years she'd suffered her mother's constant haranguing that she wasn't yet married, and that time was running out. Annarita shook her head at the strange twists of fate.

A deep tenor sounded from outside the house. Turandot. *Nessun dorma.* She'd become knowledgeable of many arias during her marriage to an enthusiastic tenor. The door opened and Giuseppe greeted her. She placed her right index finger over her lips, and then pointed down to the slumbering bundle in her lap. Giuseppe smiled and reached down, scooping up his son and whispering that he'd tuck him into his crib.

He returned down the stairs and slid onto the couch beside her, clasping her hand in his. "How are you doing?"

"All's fine. Giulia and I had an early dinner. She was so tired after waking up last night. I didn't even make it through a page of her bedtime story. How's everything at the hotel? Did you eat?"

"I did. And it was an easy night. No cooking classes. They were all exhausted after Patrizia conducted a combined ultra-marathon-death-march through Spoleto."

Annarita shook her head. "Remind me to convince Patrizia to take up babysitting trips with the kids when they're older. Can you imagine how they'd return home, exhausted?"

Giuseppe chuckled. "She's great. Knows her art and architecture. Is an encyclopedia about all things Umbria. But that girl has to slow down. She's exhausting our guests."

Annarita stood up from her rocking chair and slid in beside her husband on the couch. He placed his arm around her and she rested her head on his shoulder. "On the topic of exhaustion. Let's enjoy this a bit while the fire burns down, and then head up to bed. I didn't follow Patrizia around Spoleto today, but I feel like I have."

Giuseppe pulled her in tighter and planted a kiss on her temple. Annarita felt awash in happiness, concentrating on the glowing flames of the family hearth.

CHAPTER 26

Madison

MADISON WOKE TO THE CHIRPING of birds flowing into the window she'd left open last night. She checked the bedside clock. Eight o'clock. Wow, she must have fallen into bed, exhausted after Patrizia's Ironman tour of Spoleto, before nine last night. Almost twelve hours of sleep. When had she last done that?

She stretched her arms luxuriously over her head. Her gaze fell on her cellphone and she placed one hand over it and allowed it to hover there, mid-air. In the last twenty-four hours, she hadn't checked obsessively for calls or texts from Rita. What was getting into her?

Decisively, she retracted her hand and sat up in bed, head against the headboard, soft sheets and the comforter caressing her legs.

Life. Life had gotten in the way of her near-constant worries.

Life outside the television studio. Away from the superficiality of her profession and the people who engaged in it. Most of her first week here, she'd obsessed about what was happening back in Columbus, desperate to get back. Well, truth be told, she was still desperate to get back. But she was here, wasn't she? Her first visit to Italy. Things *would* smooth over, she was certain of that. But while waiting, why not enjoy where she was?

Yes, the spa was helping her to relax, that was true, but going up to Todi and visiting Spoleto with her fellow guests yesterday had felt invigorating. Sitting by the phone wasn't going to make Rita call any faster.

Flicking her hand quickly, she clutched the phone and tapped in. No. Nothing. She sighed, then pushed herself higher against the headboard.

Flipping through her photos, she found a shot of the steep road up to Todi, the San Fortunato belltower, shot from below, the elegant Piazza del popolo. The aperol spritz set aglow by the golden afternoon sun. Clicking into Instagram, she set up a gallery, flicking through the perfect shots once more. Rita had said to lie low, but then again, Rita wasn't even taking her calls. No work. Tourism only. Proving to her followers she wasn't hiding under a rock, but having the time of her life.

Maybe she could put out feelers. If things didn't work out at her station, she'd start looking at other markets. The longer she stayed silent, the more she looked like the guilty party.

She started typing:

> Can't believe I've never been to Italy. Perfection.
> So much to see and explore.
> What if I'm tempted to stay forever?
> #Italy #Umbria #HidingAwayinBeauty

Before she could reconsider, she sent it off, switched off her phone and picked up the room phone.

"Oh, hi Emma. Madison here. Wanted to let you know, no need to send up the cappuccino and fruit this morning. I'll be coming down for breakfast."

"Wonderful. We'll be happy to have you. Everyone's a bit late after your busy day, but they'll make their way down. See you soon."

Madison hung up the phone and pushed herself out of bed. She turned on the television, raising the volume on a television news program. She didn't understand a word of it, but the melodious strains of Italian accompanied her as she entered the bathroom and ran the water for her shower.

BREAKFAST HAD BEEN FUN. After their adventures of yesterday, Madison had been accepted into the tight fold, and they laughed and joked much as they had at yesterday's lunch. The twins, Marco and Valerio raced in, wearing their soccer uniforms and tossing a shirt to Kathryn.

"Are you done with breakfast?" asked one of the twins.

Madison was hopeless at keeping them straight.

"We've got a scrimmage to prepare for Monday's match. We're gonna be late." He turned to his brother and rattled something off in rapid-fire Italian, with wild gesticulations to match the speed of speech.

Madison smiled inwardly. She hadn't heard them speaking Italian, but, of course, they were half Italian, half American. Living here, it made sense their common language was Italian. She'd been impressed to listen to Heike chattering away yesterday in Italian. She spoke so well. She was bilingual, too. German and English. Madison thought back to useless Spanish classes in high school. The one semester she'd taken in college because she was forced to. Would she even be able to compose a couple of sentences to hold up a conversation today? Some of her college friends had spent a semester abroad, but she didn't want to lose time when she was interning at local stations, building up her resumé. Semesters abroad were merely a distraction.

A lotta good that did her in the end. Nose to the grindstone, building up her resumé, gathering contacts and recommendations. And for what?

Anyway, there'd be time for all this later. Now, Italy, it was. Maybe she could consider it making up for lost time.

Now the twins were yanking on Chris' arm. "But you promised," one whined, sounding much younger than he was.

"Honestly, Valerio," said a weary Chris.

How could he tell them apart? Especially when they were wearing the same exact uniform.

"I completely forgot. I'm a bit worn out from yesterday."

"We need a ref," said the one who must be Valerio. "It's not all day, just a couple of hours."

Just then, Emma stepped in from the office, arms folded across her chest. "Valerio, you can't annoy our guests like this. If Chris wants to rest, he can rest. You'll have to find someone else."

Now both boys were looking at him with puppy-dog eyes, and Kathryn moved closer, too. You had to hand it to them. Those kids were insistent. And manipulative. Even without knowing him well, she could see Chris break down to their demands.

"Nah, it's okay. I did promise them, Emma," he turned to their host. "And I remember the days when we needed refs who didn't show. It's okay. Give me five minutes to finish my cappuccino and grab my backpack, and I'll meet you out front."

The twins and Kathryn broke out in loud cheers and sprinted from the room.

Emma shook her head. "You're too good to them, Chris. They take advantage. This is your holiday, too. I'm sorry Mark is out getting the car serviced, otherwise I would have subbed you out."

Chris chuckled. "No problem. They're great kids." He clapped his hands together. "And we have to ensure Todi dominates the competition on Monday. I'm sorry, ladies, not to join you today. Any chance in meeting on the *piazza* later for an afternoon *aperitivo*?"

"That sounds lovely, Chris. How is five?" asked Heike. "Ugo is taking us shopping. Madison, would you like to come?"

"Oh, yes," said Emma. "He's bringing you to the outlets. Madison, they have the brand of shoes I lent you. You told me you'd like to buy some. You're welcome to keep mine until you have your own." She looked down at Madison's heels. "Those aren't going to work on these hills." She smiled. "Trust me on this one."

"Oh, do come," said Heike. "It'll be fun to have a girls' shopping trip."

Shopping with two women her mother's age hadn't really been at the top of her list, but why the hell not? What else did she have to do? And she did want a pair—or two—of those shoes. "Sure," she smiled. "Why not? Just us girls."

THE OUTLET WAS HUGE. Although Madison was supposed to be saving money, she'd found two outfits she simply had to own, and the smart dress sneakers Emma had lent her in two different colors. If she was meant to feel guilty, however, she was far outdone by Grace and Heike, who carried far more shopping bags than she.

Much to her surprise, the day had been a lot of fun. Instead of splitting up, Grace and Heike had insisted on waiting as she tried on clothes, and commenting as she modeled them. Their comments were insightful. She paid back the favor when they tried on their own clothes, and helped to find the most flattering styles for them.

And all three women purchased the same shoes.

"I know it's ridiculous we all have matching blue shoes," said Grace, as she tilted her walking shoe-clad right foot left and then right. "But I love this color, and I also love the idea we'll each be wearing these on the streets of Vienna, Durham, and Columbus when we return home." She laughed. "And we'll think about our Umbrian shopping outing!"

"When you say it like that," said Madison. "Maybe it's worth being triplets for the next week. But they are fabulously comfortable. And so stylish. I can't even believe I was climbing up the hills of Todi in my heels."

Heike arched one eyebrow. "Neither can we."

"If it weren't for Chris, literally lending me his arm, it would have taken ages to get back down," said Madison, slipping the shoes off and placing them into the box.

Heike and Grace exchanged a knowing look and smiled. "That must have been real torture, having a man like that come to your rescue," deadpanned Grace. "He's so weak and unattractive." Heike and Grace giggled like a pair of schoolgirls.

Madison looked at them both, guessing her stare was not amused.

"Okay, perhaps that was unfair," said Heike. "But we're probably your mother's age. When we see two handsome young people, who are also nice, our instinct is to push them together. Of course, it's none of our business. You could have a boyfriend. Chris could be secretly married, for all we know. It's just healthy meddling, don't take us too seriously."

Madison placed her shoes back into their box, her hair falling over cheeks she feared may have grown rosy. "No boyfriend. I'm single." She looked straight at the two women.

"But I'm also not looking. Now, should we go pay for these?"

They walked together to the counter to ring up their purchases, Heike chatting and laughing with the salesgirl.

THEY HADN'T PLANNED ON lunching. After all, they were eating so much at The Three Coins Inn that missing one meal wouldn't hurt anyone. But when they passed a small restaurant, a waitress was ferrying two plates of *caprese* salad, and all three decided they absolutely had to have one.

Their bags spilled around them at the table. Madison stretched out her long legs. Honestly, and despite her new, comfortable shoes, she was exhausted. This brief respite was exactly what she needed, especially if, as they'd planned, they'd be hiking up to Todi later for *aperitivi*. With all the drinking she was doing on this holiday, she was starting to morph into her friend, Amanda.

"Are you two as exhausted as I am?" asked Madison, pouring more water into her glass and gulping it down. "Who knew shopping was so wearying."

Grace shook her head. "I think it's everything combined. New place, new people, new language. Our senses are always working overtime, and it hits you, all of a sudden."

Their glasses of wine arrived at the table, and the women clinked them together. "*Salute.*"

Madison laughed. "I hope that *salute* and *vino* won't be the only Italian I learn on this holiday."

"What's the problem?" Grace shook her head. "They're useful words."

"How did your Italian get so good, Heike?" asked Madison.

"You forget, Austria and Italy are neighbors. My husband and I used to come down a lot for holidays. We both loved it here. And I've long taken classes at the Italian Institute in Vienna … although I stopped recently. I need to get back."

"I'm impressed," said Madison. "I love the idea of studying a language. The time commitment scares me."

The waitress arrived, the color of the Italian flag displayed on the plates she placed before them. The white of the mozzarella, the bright red of the tomatoes, and the vibrant green of the basil, with the added touch of glimmering yellow olive oil.

"Oh, this looks fabulous," said Grace. "I'm glad we stopped for lunch." She cut a piece of the tomato and mozzarella and took a bite, chewing, her eyes widening. "Heaven."

"Funny, but since we're speaking about language. Our Viennese dialect uses the word for Heaven–Paradise for tomatoes. So you're not far off," said Heike. She turned back to Madison. "If you want to get a leg up on your Italian, come to our cooking class. Giuseppe can't make it past five words in English before slipping into Italian. You'll get a crash course."

"It's true," laughed Grace. "Not sure I'll make any progress in Italian, but between my kitchen-related vocabulary and Kathryn's soccer terms, we've gotten a real head start." She sipped her wine. "But if you only stick to recipes and soccer terms, we're fluent."

"That's already way beyond me."

The buzz of the restaurant surrounded them as they talked and laughed and ate. Coffees followed their meal, and Madison was shocked when she looked at her watch. They signaled the waitress to pay, scooped up their purchases, and sprinted to meet Ugo at their designated meeting place.

Madison had never been happier to own a new pair of practical designer sneakers.

CHAPTER 27

Heike

THEY NABBED THE LAST FREE TABLE outdoors on the busy Piazza del popolo. Getting back had taken longer than they had planned. Then they had to stop off at the inn to deposit their purchases. By the time their weary legs carried them up the seemingly endless hills to Todi's central square, the afternoon *passeggiata* was well underway, all tables but one taken.

Thank goodness Madison was fast in her new, sensible shoes. The heels she favored would have set them back even longer, and hopes for an outdoor table would have been nonexistent.

All three women sank gratefully into their chairs, relieved a fourth was already in place and that they wouldn't have to go table to table to beg. Heike, Grace, and Madison all tilted their faces towards the late afternoon sun, delighting in its warming rays.

"This is great, isn't it?" asked Heike. "A day of shopping, and now lounging out on a picturesque square on a sunny afternoon to drink cocktails. And then returning back for yet another scrumptious dinner."

"Life is tough," agreed Grace. "I looked at the forecast in Durham this morning." She shook her head. "You don't want to know."

"Ha. I can guarantee Vienna's not any better."

Madison sighed. "Don't even try to compete with Columbus for worst weather ever. We win hands down. All year long."

The waitress approached their table.

"Oh, dear," said Heike. "Should we order now, without Chris? Let me WhatsApp him."

The waitress reached them and Heike responded to her greetings, letting the other women know he would reach them soon and asked them to order. Aperol spritzes were ordered all around.

"We're a dull bunch with our drinks selection," said Grace.

"That might be true, but they're so *pretty*," Madison said with a smile. "I know when I go back home, I'll have images of me sitting on this square, bathed in sunlight, with a bright orange drink in my hand."

"Who can argue with that?" said Grace.

A tall figure approached the table, and all three women looked up. "That was fast," said Heike. "Did you sprint up to town?"

Chris shook his head. "Pretty much. Those kids wouldn't let me go. After reffing the scrimmage, they wanted to stay doing drills. They wore me out after a bit. Would have kept me there all night. Running up the hill to you lovely ladies seemed the far more pleasant option." He slumped into his chair. "Grace, your granddaughter has energy to burn. When she's older, if she wants to play soccer in college, I hope you'll also consider American schools. I could see her on the team at my alma mater."

"Oh," Grace looked genuinely surprised. "It seems so far off, but I hadn't even considered American schools. But I know you have the athletics programs within the school. We had a neighbor recruited for cross-country." She tilted her head. "That could be an option."

"As you said, you have plenty of time. But we can speak when you're starting to think about it."

The waitress returned with their drinks and placed them on the table, alongside savory snacks.

"Well deserved after a long day on the pitch," said Chris, holding his glass aloft. "Ladies, *salute*."

They all clinked glasses and sipped their drinks, soaking in the mood on the bustling *piazza*.

"Do you do this as much at home?" asked Chris. "Take time out of your busy day to just sit out with friends and observe life taking place around you?" He leant back in his chair, stretching his legs out under the table.

"Admittedly, no. But, to be fair, Viennese weather works against me on that one."

"Ha. Try Durham."

"Ohio puts you all to shame. I win again."

Chris smiled. "Okay, I had that one coming. I guess it's that these few days have me feeling less stressed. Reevaluating everything." He took another sip of his drink. "You know, I'm currently selling the company I poured so much sweat and tears into these past years. I guess I was thinking about splitting up with my business partner and starting a new firm on my own." He looked around the large square. "Being here makes me wonder if that's even what I want."

There was silence at the table, and Heike noticed his pained look. Matthias had always looked the same when he felt he had overshared with others. As she had with her husband, Heike felt the need to jump in. "Madison, I don't know if you've all seen, but Chris has a real talent for drawing. Mark asked him to design a new logo for the hotel. I can't wait to see it." She smiled at him. "And he was sketching away while we were in Orvieto. I still have that drawing of the Duomo on my dresser. I'll frame it when I'm back in Vienna."

"No, I didn't know about your drawing," said Madison. "But Chris, I think you're right. I don't take much time away from work. In my business, you have to worry others will elbow in and take your seat at the table, before it's even cold." She laughed, but it sounded bitter. "There's something to be said for distance. And rest … And getting a new perspective."

"I think," said Heike, placing her drink down. "It's harder for young people like you. You're so caught up in building your careers. We were there once, but I do think it's important to take time out for yourselves. I'm grateful my husband and I did travel and take vacation together." She sniffed. "But I wish we hadn't saved so many plans, thinking we'd have all that time to do things in retirement." She looked off at the staircase leading up to the Santa Annunziata, at the sun shining off the rose window, probably creating a spill of colorful light filtering in. "Do as much as you can when you're young. You'll have fewer regrets when you're my age." She blinked quickly, staving off tears.

Warm fingers clutched her shoulder. Strong, comforting. She looked up to see Chris looking at her with kindness in his bright blue eyes. It hurt so much not to be here with Matthias. But how lucky was she to meet this interesting group of guests who could shake her out of her lethargy?

She took a deep breath. "Here I go, getting all maudlin. I propose another toast." She raised her glass, and the others followed suit. "To new and beautiful places. To *piazze* drenched in sunshine and the sounds of life ringing all around." She smiled. "And to the great luck of meeting new friends. At any age."

They clinked their glasses together and talk shifted to the Easter dinner they would be cooking and to trips they wished to take before their halcyon days of vacation in Italy came to a sudden end.

CHAPTER 28

Chris

CHRIS OBSERVED WITH DISGUST his flurry of WhatsApp messages. At least half a dozen from Kaitlyn, asking if they could try again, each subsequent message sounding more desperate than the last. Two messages from that weasel, Rob, asking if he wasn't being hasty selling the firm. Rob couldn't afford to buy him out and didn't want to work with a new partner.

"Yeah, no wonder there," Chris muttered after throwing his phone down in fury. "You haven't done an honest day's work in the past two years. A new partner means you'd have to get your butt in gear without me bankrolling you and working my ass off so you can do jackshit except for screwing my wife."

He dropped his head into his hands and took slow breaths. How had his life become such a mess? He and Kaitlyn were supposed to have been here together, exploring Italy, taking cooking classes together, hopefully on their way to starting their family.

This wasn't at all how he had imagined this vacation back when he'd booked it.

But even if this wasn't what he'd planned, he'd made the right choice to come alone. Away from everyone who knew him and his old life. Who would judge him and pity him. Here, Heike and Grace knew nothing about his failed marriage. He didn't know Madison well yet, but neither did she. Mark knew, of course, but he'd been through it himself and didn't judge. He watched Mark and Emma interacting together, all the small signs of affection and complicity between them. They'd had spouses and children before, but when things fell apart, they were able to rebuild their lives and love again. From what he observed, neither appeared to maintain any rancor for their exes. He observed Emma the other day as she spoke with Valerio about an upcoming visit with his dad. It seemed natural. Unemotional. Mark had mentioned it hadn't always been that way, that Emma's husband had left her devastated, but that together they had left all that pain and anger behind. Maybe there was hope for him, too. But right now, he harbored only hate for his former wife and his former best friend.

He would call his lawyers on Monday, a holiday here, but not back home, and ensure all was on track with both the divorce and extracting himself from his business.

Chris turned his attention back to the sketchings he'd been working on these past days – ideas for the logo and visual design for The Three Coins Inn. He'd been surprised to discover Todi had no fountains, so he'd had to use the inn itself. He picked it up and held it under the desktop light. It had been ages since he'd drawn, really drawn. But at the risk of sounding arrogant, he was quite pleased with his efforts. He tucked his work into a rigid folder and slid it under his arm before picking up his room key.

He could only hope Mark would be pleased, too.

CHRIS SAT BEFORE THE FIRE, a whiskey in his hands. Strictly speaking, the fire wasn't necessary. It had been a warm day, but as evening descended, the mercury dropped. Mark said he enjoyed a warming fire as he was going over accounts for the hotel, and this would likely be one of the last occasions to enjoy one, with the warmer weather setting in soon.

Chris tried—and failed—to not feel like a nervous schoolboy. For crying out loud, he wasn't even a graphic designer, he'd only agreed because Mark had asked him. What did it matter if Mark liked his work or not? And anyway, it's not like it could be worse than that garbage an actual designer had put together for their grand opening.

Mark took a sip of his whiskey and tilted his head left and right, examining Chris' work.

Was that good? Bad? Chris looked miserably into the amber liquid in his cut crystal glass, his knee jumping up and down and causing ripples on the whiskey's surface. *Oh, what the hell.* A little liquid courage. Chris took a sizeable sip. It burned as it went down his throat, but he noted its smoothness, its peaty scent. This was definitely the good stuff. Chris placed the glass back down on his stilled knee. Definitely calmer.

Mark looked up and Chris almost let his glass slip to the floor. He was used to closing deals with important businesspeople, managing large accounts. Why did the opinion of one innkeeper have his stomach tied in knots like some college kid on his first job interview?

But he knew why. It wasn't a simple business deal. It wasn't an impersonal business pitch, where a firm would select either him or a competitor. He'd either work with them or move on. This was about him. *His* design. *His* artistic ability. Something he'd let go long ago, even though he loved it, because it cut too close to the bone.

Just like swimming. It was all or nothing. Putting yourself on the line. Your whole body attuned to the starting pistol. One day at the top of the podium, soaking in the applause and the admiration, certain you belonged there. No one ever saw the hours and hours of practice, of sweat, tears, and pain that allowed you to ascend to that lofty step. But there were days you didn't get there and your rival did. Seconds faster, mostly split seconds faster. Him instead of you soaking in the applause as the medal was placed over his neck, and you were seething with anger and kicking yourself within. How had you let it slip through your fingers? All those ringing alarms at 4:00 a.m. All those killer workouts in the weight room. The massages and the ice baths, waking up in the dark for yet another day of more brutal training.

The artwork you slaved over, were certain would be a bullseye, but the client hated it. Hated you.

The consultancy never felt as personal. Business was business. It wasn't putting yourself out there in the same way. Putting *you* out there, one-on-one. The doubts had set in once Kaitlyn maneuvered into his life, and his bed. She wanted a stable relationship. A stable income stream. House, cars, the American dream. Some part-time work as he pursued his dream as a professional athlete wasn't what she had in mind. Nor was his side interest in graphic design. The business degree, consulting. Those were what she convinced him counted most. The swimming championships simply provided him with that veneer of athleticism that melded well with the business world, with the rapidly expanding bellies of the business owners who relived their high school glory days every chance they could.

Kaitlyn was less than impressed when he didn't return victorious, was always sabotaging his efforts to train harder for the next meet. Looking back, he'd lost that hunger then. Began withdrawing from that hyper-vigilant state of competitiveness he'd dwelled in since junior high. It only took a slight distraction, but once you lost that all-encompassing drive to win, others surpassed you. His college coach had continued coaching him postcollege, as he was aiming at nationals. When his coach noticed the hunger fading, he sat him down, but Chris was too lovestruck to really consider what he'd be giving up. Competitive sports were a cruel master. The years ticked by, and it wasn't like piano lessons you put on hold or improving German with lessons you could always take later. Either you gave it your all in your younger years, or you buried those childhood dreams and pretended they'd never meant all that much to you. That you'd gladly traded them for love. For love with a woman who cheated on you with your best friend. He took another sip of his whiskey as he stared into the flames.

"Chris? Chris, did you hear what I said?"

Chris snapped his neck up. Mark was staring at him, his designs spread across Mark's desk.

Mark chuckled. "You were a million miles away. Penny for your thoughts."

Chris covered his face with one large hand, then let his arm drop on the leather armrest and shook his head. "Not a good place. Divorce garbage awaiting me back home."

Mark nodded knowingly. "I hear you. I had longer than you to deal with it. Betrayal after betrayal, promise after promise. I felt pretty stupid hanging in there so long that it was a relief at the end." He looked into the fire. "And then there was Emma. It seemed I was being given a second chance I couldn't afford to screw up." He looked up. "But for you, it's still raw. It's like ripping off that Band-Aid. You need to do it, but it still hurts. Don't worry if it hits you when you least expect it."

Chris nodded, not quite trusting his voice.

"But," said Mark, observing him closely, "onto better news. These drawings." He swept a hand over the scattered designs. "These are amazing."

Chris felt his heart jump up to his throat. *Amazing*? Had he heard correctly?

"You've captured the atmosphere we want to convey so well. Elegant. Relaxed. A place to forget your troubles and to meet new people. I love these."

No, Chris hadn't misunderstood. Mark really liked the designs. *His designs.*

Mark smiled. "Emma'll be tickled that you were able to work in the fountain and coins."

Chris slid to the edge of his chair. "Gotta be honest with you, never even heard of *Three Coins in The Fountain* before. Emma talked my ear off one morning, how the film changed her life, introduced her to new friends, even led her to you. She was so passionate about it I had to work it in, but I couldn't help noticing that Todi has no fountains."

"True. But this is even better, you included our little fountain. Hands around a table enjoying drinks, the view up to Todi on high. I love it. I'll show it to Emma tonight, but I'm sure she'll love it, too. And if she agrees, we'd love to buy this from you and have it as our own visual design, include it on our website, on new printing of brochures, Christmas cards. We'll be involved with some tourism trade fairs, so we'll need designs for signage, that kind of thing. But I'm getting ahead of myself. Let me speak to Emma, and we can talk tomorrow."

Chris' head was spinning. How would he even charge for his work? He couldn't invoice this through a business he was trying to sell. What were even going rates for design today? And, more importantly, might other people want to buy his designs? Could this become his new project when the sale of the business went through? It had been years since his design classes. He'd certainly need to learn a lot of new software, get caught up on trends and changes to the industry. But he wasn't over the hill just yet ...

There was a knock on the door. Mark yelled out, "Come in."

A man with short dark hair and a light, navy blue sweater and jeans walked in. Chris pegged him for American right away, even before he opened his mouth and Chris heard the gentle drawl.

"Am I disturbing you?" the man asked. "Emma was running out when I came in, and she said to knock." He held out his hands. "But it's not urgent. I can come back another time."

"No, Scott, great to see you." Mark got up and strode across the room, reaching out and shaking his hand. "Chris is a guest here. We were just talking." He clasped the man's elbow and nudged him into the room. "Scott, I'd like to introduce you to Chris. Chris Larson."

Chris extended his arm to shake the man's hand. This man—Scott, wasn't it?—was staring at him oddly.

"Scott, we're having whiskey. Can I get some from you?"

"Sure. A little. I have to drive up to Perugia, but a finger'll do fine."

Mark poured another glass. "Chris, you might detect the accent of a neighbor. Scott's from North Carolina. Been here with us in Todi for what, about nine—ten months?"

"About right. Project started back in July. No idea where the time goes anymore ..." He accepted his glass, and held it up. "*Salute*. And here's to a small world."

Chris held his glass aloft before joining in a sip. "How so? You mean because a guy from North Carolina and another from Virginia find themselves here in Todi?"

"Nah. I mean because old rivals meet up years later ... in little Umbria."

Chris observed him closely. Scott's hazel gaze pinned him in place.

"You don't remember me, do you, Chris?" He looked over at Mark. "We swam in the same conference back in college—the Atlantic Coast Conference. Chris here swam for UVA, I was at Wake Forest."

"No way," Chris observed him closer. "Scott Henderson. The Fly."

"Ah, so you do remember." He laughed. "I was afraid these greys sneaking through," he ran a hand through his hair, "were making me look like an old man."

"You were a couple years ahead, right?"

"I was a senior when you were a freshman. Scared the crap out of me, if I'm honest. Killer Butterfly, this guy." Scott looked at Mark, indicating Chris with one thumb. "He was a beast in the pool. Good thing I was on my way out." He chuckled. "But I did keep track of your progress, through teammates and following meets. NCAAs, All American. I was convinced you'd go pro, but you didn't seem to stick with it long after school."

Chris felt the blow to his stomach. Even if a punch had never been thrown, it may as well have been. His reaction was physical when he realized the chances he'd thrown away. Without asking, he stood up, crossed the room, and poured another finger into his whiskey glass. "Yeah," he said, back still turned to them men. "Bit of a cliché, but a woman got in the way of my plans."

"Haha. They always do."

Chris swiveled and returned to his chair.

Scott held up his glass and smiled. "I hope she was worth it."

Chris grimaced. "We're getting divorced, so I can say with some certainty that she most definitely wasn't." He sipped his drink, hoping his voice didn't sound as bitter out loud as it did in his own head.

"Sucks, man. Sorry to hear it."

"Hey, Scott," said Mark, standing up from his desk. "You're breaking the cardinal rule of our inn. No dwelling on problems from home." He smiled. "We created this environment to help people escape from daily life. Enjoy a deserved break. And Chris here, he's been allowing his artistic talent to percolate in Umbria. Take a look." He plucked up two of Chris' designs and handed them to Scott, stepping back and leaning on the edge of his desk.

Scott placed his whiskey down on a side table and examined the drawings. Chris fought the urge to squirm like an embarrassed seven-year-old when a teacher was reviewing his writing.

"This looks amazing," said Scott, looking up from his examination. "I've been teasing Mark forever about those God-awful graphics he had. When we set up our university program, we'll have a design department. I told him we could do something a million times better. But you've nailed it, Chris." He smiled. "Not only a gifted athlete, but a gifted artist as well."

"Thanks," said Chris, stunned by the compliments. Two people praising his work. Were they merely being polite? Or did he have what it took to become a graphic artist? With his life in such limbo, he'd cling on to any hope.

"I'm not just saying that to be nice. You're talented." Scott placed the designs on the couch beside him. "I don't know anything about your circumstances now, but since you're going through a divorce, you may be eager for a change. We're looking to hire graphic artists to teach our students here in Todi."

Chris felt confused, and feared it showed on his face.

"I should have mentioned," said Mark, moving over to the couch and sitting beside Scott, careful to not disturb the designs occupying the space between them. "I met Scott when he first came to Todi. His situation was a bit like mine. He came to work on an old property that needed to be renovated. It had to be converted to a study-abroad complex for an American university." Mark smiled. "But unlike me, he had an obscene budget willed to him from a generous donor."

Scott shook his head and smirked. "What can I say? Generous, it certainly was." He looked at Chris. "After graduating, I got into college administration. Started working for Lakeview University. About a year ago, a wealthy alumnus died and left us his luxury holiday home in Umbria. He'd worked with the university to provide them with this gift in his will. They knew they would receive it, but he died much younger than they expected. They sent me over to handle the development, and I'll be rewarded with a promotion—Director of our Italy program." He laughed. "If you told me that back in our college days, I would have laughed in your face."

"Scott's being modest," said Mark. "He came over here with vague instructions, but the property looks fabulous. Emma and I met him early on because, well ..." he turned to Scott. "Fair to say you were a little lost?"

"More than fair," agreed Scott. "But, as Mark mentioned, I had a sizeable budget, so with Emma and Mark's help, I got some great workmen on the job and the place is looking pretty impressive. At the end of August, we'll have our first students coming over to do a semester or year abroad. Not bad for a college student, living and studying in a luxurious villa, complete with a gym, vineyards, and swimming pool with views over the valley." He looked up at Chris. "We'll have a graphic design program, so if you had any interest in teaching, maybe we could talk."

"Oh, wow," said Chris. "I don't know what to say. I'm not a real graphic artist. Not really. I've been working in business consulting ever since college. My own firm. Art was only something I did on the side."

"If these designs are anything to go by," said Scott. "I'd say you have an impressive talent. It might be hard going from business consulting to academia, but our start-up status allows for more flexibility." He laughed. "And I already know you're competitive as hell in the pool and driven, so I can imagine you would see this as a challenge. And deliver."

Chris sat in stunned silence. Being offered a job in Italy by an old swimming competitor was not on his holiday bingo card.

Scott looked at his watch. "Anyway, hate to love you and leave you, but I need to get up to Perugia for work. I'll be back after the holidays." He looked up. "Mark, would it be okay if I give you a call Wednesday night?"

Mark nodded. "Of course. You know you're always welcome."

With a quick goodbye to both men, Scott strode out of the room.

Chris sat in silence, feeling surreal. His designs, the new visual look of The Three Coins Inn, were still laid out across the desk and on the sofa, where Scott had left them. He'd met someone who knew him from his competition days. And Scott had suggested he might be able to apply for an academic job. A job in Italy.

Could things get any weirder than this?

Sensing Chris' confusion, Mark smiled and offered up his glass, with the dregs of the spirits that had filled it earlier. "A toast to that small world?"

Chris laughed and leaned over to clink glasses. He sat back and welcomed the warmth of the fire. This was shaping up to be a very strange night.

CHAPTER 29

Grace

GRACE WOKE EARLY on Easter Sunday and tiptoed around quietly, making herself a tea to drink in bed. Kathryn was fast asleep in the single bed. Grace had placed the huge Easter egg Emma had bought for Kathryn on her bedside table. When Grace protested, Emma told her it was a tradition whenever there were children staying during Easter—and that she'd been shopping for the twins anyway. It looked so pretty in its shiny, colorful wrapping. Kaitlyn would be thrilled.

Today, they would all be hard at work in the kitchen, cooking the traditional Easter lamb. Grace tiptoed back to her bed with her mug and crawled under the covers, wrapping her fingers around the warm ceramic. Kathryn looked so peaceful in repose, her chest rising and falling. She would be going with Marco and Valerio to meet with her new friends on the Piazza del popolo later this morning after the kids went to Easter mass at the Duomo, but she promised to come back to join the cooking. Emma had arched one eyebrow when she commented that, for the first time, Marco had asked to join the cooking course, too. "I'm guessing," she said with a grin, "there's some other interest sparking his burning desire to prepare *abbacchio*."

All the adults were studying Kathryn and Marco with interest, while attempting not to be observed doing so. Preteen love was the sweetest. And Kathryn was already wondering aloud when they could get back to Umbria, or whether Marco would like to see Durham and its soccer clubs.

Grace took a sip of her tea. It seemed luxurious to lie in bed with her tea, but breakfast wouldn't start for another hour, so she was pleased to laze a bit longer while her athletic granddaughter enjoyed her well-deserved sleep.

She cracked open her novel and placed her mug on the bedside table, stretching out her legs and luxuriating in the idleness.

As she turned the page on the chapter she'd just finished, her phone began to vibrate. Ellen's name appeared on the screen. She looked over to Kathryn to ensure she hadn't been disturbed, but the girl slumbered on.

Grace plucked her phone from the bedside table and hurried to the bathroom, closed the door and sat on the edge of the tub, before responding.

"Happy Easter, Ellen. It's awfully early for you."

"Happy Easter, Mum. I couldn't sleep. How are you? How's Kathryn?"

"Oh, she's doing marvelously. I know she's WhatsApped you photos. She's joined the local football team, although the hotel owners' sons are American ... so, *soccer*, and she's made so many friends that way. They hang out together on the main town square, laughing and chatting ... goodness knows in what language. But she's really integrated well in such a short time ... and, I don't know if she's told you, but there's a boy she likes. And he seems pretty crazy about her. He's the son of the inn owner. A very sweet Italian-American boy."

Grace heard a sharp intake of air on the other end.

"No, she didn't say anything ... but maybe you misunderstood. Kathryn shouldn't feel trapped in her gender. She may be fluid, and we want you to be open to that. We told you we didn't want gender stereotyping ... being forced into thinking she needs to have a boyfriend because society expects it of her."

Grace sighed. "Ellen, I'm fifty-eight years old. I'm not going to be buying this nonsense. You're simply parroting whatever fad Rupert has picked up in the faculty lounge this week. Kathryn is a lovely young lady, very content to be a girl. Beautiful, intelligent, and an extremely skilled athlete. And now she has her first serious crush. I am not confusing her. You and Rupert have been confusing her. And it needs to stop now." Grace took a deep breath. "She does not need this artificial stress in her life."

Loud sobs emitted from the other end of the line. "Oh, Mum, you're always criticizing Rupert, even if he has my—and Kathryn's—best interests at heart. But the couples' counseling ..." she sobbed again, "It's not working. I think ..." she sniffled and blew her nose, "I'm afraid when Kathryn returns, her father will have moved out. We'll be doing a trial separation while we work things out."

Now the sharp intake of air came from Grace's side. She caught sight of herself in the bathroom mirror. She closed her eyes and breathed in deeply. Her daughter needed her support now, not the honest-to-God truth. There was a time for everything. "I am sorry to hear that. I know how much you wanted the counseling to work, but maybe the time apart will be best for having space to think things through."

The sobs on the other end of the line grew louder. "Oh, Mum. This wasn't what I wanted."

Grace heard her daughter blow her nose, followed by more sobs.

"I wanted ... well, I wanted what you and Dad had ..." A choking sound came over the line. "You set the bar so high. Dad was such a great father to me. And your marriage was so strong. All my friends envied me. I thought I'd have the same." She dissolved into more sobs.

Grace looked up and, once more, caught her gaze in the mirror. The gaze of a liar.

Taking another deep breath, she gathered her strength to whisper comforting words to her daughter. Words her daughter wanted to hear.

THE FRUIT TREES WERE BEGINNING to bloom. Grace walked through the rows of fig and persimmon trees and the dew-splattered grape vines. The grass was dripping in dew. Emma had been awake and had leant Grace her wellies. How odd for an Englishwoman to be so unprepared. But, until now, Grace hadn't been out on dawn walks in the still-wet fields.

She walked over to the chicken coop, listening to the gentle clucks emanating from the hen house. They had been consuming many of the eggs produced here. Nearby was the sheep pen. Grace had also enjoyed all the wonderful cheeses she knew were created on the farm. Emma said they had a local man who took the sheep out to graze each day, who was also their shearing expert and made a delectable cheese that people travelled far and wide to purchase. Sometimes, the twins accompanied him. She'd laughed when she explained to Grace how her city boys had fully adjusted to their country reality when they'd moved to Todi four years ago. The vegetable garden, the fruit trees, the farm animals—she and her Roman boys knew nothing about it, but they'd learned. Chiara, her oldest, had been closer to university age and had been there only a short time before returning to Rome to study. Grace paused at the pen, watching the sheep beginning their day, the tiny lambs testing out their spindly legs in comic jumps.

The twins had taken Kathryn out here to help with their chores. She'd proudly told Grace how she'd helped to gather the eggs prepared for their breakfast, that she had helped to prepare the vegetable garden.

Country life wasn't only a balm for the twins. Kathryn was taking to it, too. Leaving in a week would be hard on her. Doubly hard returning to a fractured family. Grace sighed as she watched the lambs frolicking around. Fears about what a broken family would mean for her own young daughter had often dominated her thoughts years ago. She sighed and glanced up at hilltop Todi. The sun was creeping higher in the sky, shining down on those ancient stones, setting them aglow.

Years later, in the heart of Italy, she understood it wasn't the end of the world. Ellen would survive this, too. So would Kathryn. And she'd be there to support both of her beautiful girls. It would be a type of penance for the courage she once lacked.

She turned back to the inn, her boots pounding through the slick grass, the early sun caressing her face. As she neared the hulking stone structure, the soothing sound of water gurgling in the fountain pacified her troubled thoughts. Just then, Emma emerged from the front door, the early morning light setting her golden hair aglow. In her hands, she clasped two ceramic mugs. She placed them down at the table beside the fountain, and indicated the chairs that had been wiped down in Grace's absence, now sporting fresh cushions.

Emma winked at Grace. "I saw you returning. It's still quiet, no one will miss us if we enjoy a cappuccino together before all hell breaks loose with breakfast and our Easter preparation." She slid across from the chair she'd indicated.

Both women sipped their coffees and looked at the fountain's play of water. Grace smiled at Emma, and gazed once more at the town rearing dramatically above them. The companionable silence was lovely and her heart, so heavy with preoccupations following her call with Ellen, felt lighter and carefree in the fresh Umbrian air. The gurgling water calmed her, the coffee warmed her, and she felt a sense of peace radiating within.

THE DAY HAD FLOWN BY in a flurry of activity. Grace's apron had come untied and she adjusted the belt, knotting it tighter. After the difficult morning phone call, the day had progressed quickly. She'd allowed Kathryn to sleep later, Ellen felt it would make more sense to speak on Easter Monday, when she'd be more pulled together, although she insisted she did not want to say anything about the separation until Kathryn returned, knowing it would only upset her and wanting her daughter to enjoy her holiday.

Kathryn had gone with Marco and Valerio to meet her new teammates and friends up in town before they returned to their family dinners, and now Kathryn took her place in the kitchen, with a suddenly interested sous chef, Marco, diligently peeling carrots alongside her. Emma kept peeking in, shaking her head in amusement and winking at Grace. According to Emma, today was Marco's first cooking class attendance. His presence also meant Heike could spend more time cooking and less time translating for Giuseppe. Grace was alongside Heike, and she really was a wonder in the kitchen.

Of course, all those years running her own restaurant gave her a decided edge over the rest of them, but it was the joy she emanated as she was mixing ingredients, testing flavors.

Grace had always been a reliable cook, but never a skilled one. But watching Giuseppe and Heike, and Annarita when she came over to help, provided her with a new outlook on cooking.

Kathryn had been enjoying testing out new recipes, and she was already suggesting dishes she and Grace would have to cook for her family when they returned. Grace smiled inwardly, hoping Kathryn could develop that nonchalance in the kitchen that seemed to produce such superior dishes with an elegant ease. It seemed a worthy skill to accompany one through life, and she was proud to see her granddaughter developing skills superior to her own.

Heike had promised to teach Grace and Kathryn the secrets to a perfect Apfelstruedl, and that would also be a new addition to their repertoire when they returned to Durham. Grace looked over at Kathryn, giggling with Marco as they sliced mountains of garlic, feeling guilty the girl knew nothing about what awaited her back home. But her granddaughter was bright. Could she sense it? She hoped Ellen and Rupert could break it gently to their daughter. It would certainly be throwing a funeral shroud over the glow of happiness and the excitement of blossoming first love Kathryn would be celebrating on her return.

"Why the long face?" Heike slid up beside her and Grace startled.

"Oh, my. Off in my own world."

"I think I know what's bothering you," said Heike. "It's the same for me." Heike took a deep breath. "The holidays are always the worst. I so wish Matthias were beside me helping prepare this dinner. He so loved Italy and Italian cooking. These were the types of holidays we were supposed to be enjoying together in these years."

Grace grimaced. "Richard certainly wouldn't have donned an apron to prepare Italian specialties. He'd have been holed up in our room, typing away his latest journal article. Regaling us all on his new economic theories over dinner."

Heike chuckled. Luckily, she hadn't seemed to pick up on the bitterness in Grace's tone.

Heike wiped away a tear with her wrist and placed a warm hand over Grace's. "Still, chef or not, you know I'm here to listen if you ever want to talk. I went this morning to Easter mass and lit a candle for Matthias. It helps me to feel closer to him." She shook her head. "Silly, I know. But we do what we can ..." She slapped her hands on her legs. "Anyway, feel free to join me to light a candle if you think it can help."

"Thanks, Heike. I'll keep that in mind. But it's not Richard on my mind." She lowered her voice. "It's my daughter and son-in-law. I got a call this morning and it seems things have gotten worse, but my daughter doesn't want to worry Kathryn during her holidays." She sighed. "I guess I'm worried about the homecoming."

Heike grimaced and looked up at Kathryn and Marco. "Oh, I see. That does have to be weighing on you. But try not to let it eat away at you. We always spend our time worrying about the next hurdle. Believe me, I'm as bad as the next one." She grabbed a bowl full of potatoes and wielded the peeler as a samurai handles his swords, with quick, precise strokes, stripping ribbons of potato peels from the tuber with remarkable speed and grace. "Believe me, if things are rocky when you return home, you'll need to draw upon the relaxation and tranquility you felt here more than ever."

Grace looked up and smiled. "You're right there. I think this holiday will be a fount of strength when I return home." She picked up another peeler. "I must be a glutton for punishment, trying to peel potatoes next to you."

Heike laughed. "Yeah, years of drudgery in the kitchen will do that to one. Some talents, it's better to never develop."

The pile of potatoes grew higher as activity swirled around the kitchen and laughter and conversation filled the space.

THE DINING ROOM WAS BEAUTIFUL. Candles dotted each tabletop and the large fireplace mantelpiece. There were large, colorful, wrapped chocolate eggs for Kathryn and the twins. Another was for little Giulia, who was joining the dinner with her parents. Infant Sebastiano slept in a bassinet at the edge of the room, oblivious to the commotion around him. Sleeping skills like that would serve him well in life, thought Grace. The chocolate egg was Kathryn's second, so she'd be on a sugar high today. But if someone deserved some joy on this holiday, it was Kathryn.

The pappardelle with wild boar they had all cooked together was the first course. Annarita carried out the steaming bowls and rested them on the table, to be passed around and served family style. Annarita, Giuseppe and the waitress would not be serving dinner tonight. They joined Mark and Emma and the guests for an Easter dinner together. Soft jazz played on the sound system, mingling with laughter and the clinking of glasses.

Grace looked around her at all the familiar faces: Emma, Mark, and Annarita, chatting animatedly with guests. Giuseppe beside Heike, so he could speak Italian. Kathryn flanked by wide-eyed Giulia on one side, clinging to her every "big girl" word, and attentive Marco on the other, equally enamored. She noted Chris and Madison, beside one another in earnest conversation. Thinking back, she realized they'd spent most of the afternoon cooking together, deep in conversation. And why not? Maybe Cupid's arrow would strike more than just her granddaughter on this holiday.

Emma and Mark helped clear the dishes as Giuseppe came in with the huge platter of traditional Easter *abbacchio* they had all learned to cook that afternoon. Annarita followed him with a bowl filled with potatoes with the rosemary they'd picked in the garden, rich red tomatoes with basil they'd also picked in the garden—the basil, not the tomatoes—roasted zucchini and eggplant, drizzled in their golden olive oil produced here on their land, and fresh ricotta cheese they produced from their sheep.

Mark indicated to Marco and Valerio which bottles to select from the sideboard and, to Grace's surprise, the boys each expertly opened a bottle, sliding the corkscrew out like trained sommeliers. They went around the table, pouring for their guests with a practiced air. Grace stifled a smile when Marco materialized by her side to pour into her glass with an expert wrist twist.

The candlelight flickered over the bounty on the table and she observed all of the happy faces. Giuseppe clapped his hands together. "We all work hard to create this. *Mangiate!*"

They did not need to be told twice.

LATER THEY SAT, STOMACHS FULL, before a blazing fire in the living room. The traditional Easter Colomba cake they had made from scratch had long since disappeared. The guests were happily lazing on couches and comfortable leather chairs, nursing their grappa and amaro.

After far too much wine, Grace should have refused, but held in her hands a frosted glass of limoncello. Annarita said it was made in a seaside town with an exotic name, south of Rome. Sperlonga, that was it. Apparently, Emma and Annarita had met there, alongside another friend who lived in Rome. And that random meeting had changed their lives.

Grace looked around at all these now familiar faces and felt recognition. All these strangers who were touching her life as well. Kathryn, Marco, and Valerio were sitting apart from the group, laughing, chatting, and drinking cocoa piled high with marshmallows as they played Monopoly. Kathryn probably did not imagine that her grandmother noticed her hand brushing against Marco's every time they exchanged money or property cards, or that he was always finding excuses to whisper into her ear.

On the couch closest to the flames, Madison and Chris were deep in conversation, almost oblivious to the rest of the room. Grace had the impression that, not unlike Marco, Chris was finding excuses to lean in closer as he spoke to Madison. Madison may have seemed a bit prickly at first. A bit of attitude. Keeping herself to herself and prancing around, divalike, in designer heels not fit for Umbrian hilltop towns. But she had softened, grown friendlier with her fellow guests. And, thankfully, converted to more practical walking shoes during her stay.

Annarita and Giuseppe had long returned home to put little Giulia to bed, even if she would have rather stayed up late to sit on Kathryn's lap and soak in the attention from an exotic, grown-up girl. But her eyes had been drooping and Sebastiano was due for a feeding, so they said their good nights. Emma and Mark sat side by side, chatting softly.

And she and Heike had just been speaking about a visit to Vienna. Grace had traveled only where Richard had arranged for them to go, places generally connected to economics conferences. And Vienna had never merited a visit, at least with her in tow. Heike was enthusiastic in promoting her city and all the things they could do together there. And why shouldn't she go? At her age, it seemed odd to finally set off on adventure, but going to Vienna to visit Heike and Malaga to finally spend time with Nicola seemed important first steps in breaking with the past. This vacation was uncovering the courage she'd forgotten she'd possessed as a young girl. She glanced up at Kathryn, pleased her granddaughter would never fall prey to the same destructive patterns.

A spoon hitting against a glass broke the chatter in the room and all attention focused on Mark, now standing in front of the hearth. "Three Coins guests … I have an announcement to make." Mark smiled and placed down his glass, plucking a binder up from the table. "When I was clever enough to convince Emma to leave Rome to come here with me to Umbria and become my better half in managing this inn, we were completely overwhelmed." He swept one arm around the room. "At the beginning, it did not look *anything* like it does now. That is all thanks to Emma's masterful work overseeing the workmen in renovations. Between that work, permits, setting up bookings, and making a name for our new business, we may have let other things slide." He made a grimace as he held up a flyer. "And that includes this embarrassment of a logo."

Grace squinted at the ugly design, with its clashing colors and unimpressive graphic work and fonts. It was hard to imagine such an unattractive visual in use for such an elegant inn. And Emma, who had such impeccable taste, surely never okayed such a design.

Mark smiled ruefully. "As you can imagine, we never used this, simply set it aside and moved on. And there was so much to compete for our attention." Mark placed the design face down on the table. "But it was always on the back burner, so when it came to my attention that we had a guest with hidden artistic talents …" He stared pointedly at Chris. "… the idea to revive the logo returned."

Chris shifted in his seat. Grace imagined he hadn't realized his work would be showcased before all this evening. The children edged closer, Kathryn sat beside Grace on the couch and slipped one hand into hers. Marco and Valerio took places on the floor. Everyone was concentrated on Mark and the designs he held in his right hand.

Mark flipped one of the pages over and everyone stared.

"That's our front yard!" yelled Valerio.

And it was. The table where she and Emma had sat together just this morning, sipping cappuccino before the fountain and looking up to the light setting the hilltop town aglow. Chris had placed glasses of wine on the table, with coins falling from the air into the fountain. Hilltop Todi reared against the vast sky.

Grace sighed. "Chris, it's beautiful. " She broke the silence of the room. "You've captured the atmosphere perfectly."

Chris looked at Grace, his eyes glowing. He was such a tall, fit man, bursting with confidence and good humor, but Grace had the impression he was ashamed to have his work on display for the room. He'd been the same when they had been admiring his sketchings in Orvieto. Quick to brush off any compliments, saying he was rusty and would have to ease his way back into art.

Mark smiled. "We couldn't agree with you more, Grace. Emma and I love it. We're going to have it incorporated into our website and brochures. Our business cards. Even a banner we use when we set up at local fairs to advertise the business." He nodded over to Marco and Valerio. "In a few short years, you two will be representing us at those events."

Grace didn't think she imagined the active twins squirming. Unless there was a football pitch nearby, she doubted standing still at a table in a market square all day would appeal much to the twins. Then again, people changed. After all, long ago she'd been a young woman filled with energy, independence, and ambition. And look how that ended up.

"Chris, Mark and Grace are right," said Heike. "It's beautiful. You've captured the atmosphere perfectly. That will look wonderful as a visual for the inn."

"Wow, you really can draw," said Madison, sitting by Chris' side.

Madison placed a hand on Chris' forearm. Grace didn't think she imagined Chris' glow of happiness at this recognition.

"Even better that we're all in agreement," said Mark. "Let's raise a glass." He placed the design down and picked up his grappa. "To the artistic talents of Chris. And to The Three Coins Inn's beautiful new design." He held his glass aloft. "And a Happy Easter to our guests and new friends."

Everyone held their glasses to strains of "Happy Easter!" and "*Buona Pasqua.*" Grace sipped from her limoncello, observing the big grin on Kathryn's face, the warmth that permeated the room, the crackling of the warming fire, and her new friend, Heike, beside her.

She was very pleased fate had led her to this destination. She leaned back on the comfortable, well-worn leather couch and allowed the homey atmosphere to wash over her as the yellow liquid trickled down her throat and warmed her from within.

CHAPTER 30

Emma

"I'M BEAT. BUT THE DINNER was lovely," said Emma, delicately smoothing night cream over her cheekbones. "Our guests will all return home making a mean *abbacchio* for their families and friends."

Mark chuckled. "That, they will. I'm exhausted, too. If only we could sleep in a little later tomorrow."

"No hope of that." Emma met his eye in the vanity table mirror. "Such is the thankless lot of an innkeeping family. Now I'm understanding how spoiled we were while the hotel was closed. That recuperation time is key." She placed the cap back on the face cream and turned around to face him. "Hope that bed is a lot warmer than out here. It's still nippy in the evenings."

Mark folded back the sheets on her side of the bed, and she raced over and slipped in, resting her bare feet against his.

"Ooooh! Your feet are freezing."

Emma laughed. "And yours are warm. Don't be selfish—share with your wife."

He kissed the top of her head and wrapped her in a warm embrace. "Always."

"It really is a nice group, isn't it? I have the feeling a lot of friendships are being formed that will stretch well beyond this two-week holiday."

"And by that, you mean more than just Marco and Kathryn?"

"That's another whole layer of complexity. He's going to be devastated when Kathryn leaves for Durham. He's already asking when she can come back again to visit. Or if we can go up to explore northern England." She lowered her voice to a whisper, even if the boys couldn't hear them from their room on the other side of the owner's suite. "It might not be an easy return for Kathryn in any case. Grace confided in me this morning that Kathryn's parents are separating." She sighed. "That poor girl will get the news on her return. Obviously, we're not to say anything. And especially not to Marco."

Mark winced. "That's horrible. Kathryn doesn't deserve that. But I suppose it is better to let her have her holiday. It's not like she could change anything."

"I agree. But it's not easy on Grace. Keeping it secret from her granddaughter, even if she agrees it's for the best." Emma shifted over on her back, looking up at the ceiling. "We both have firsthand experience of what a split-up does to the kids."

Mark took her hand. "It's true. But ours bounced back. Marco and Valerio have a much better relationship with Dario now. Chiara, too. And I never badmouthed Lieke to the girls. I know it took some time to accept us, but they do now. They're excited to get down here for a longer holiday in July. And you know how close they are with Chiara. How they see the twins as bonus little brothers."

Emma shifted to her side, brushing a lock of Mark's hair from his forehead. "I know. But it never makes that initial shock easier, does it? I always hate to see someone else go through it. Especially a girl as sweet as Kathryn." She took a deep breath. "But from what Grace confided, it hasn't been easy on her. It seems her father is quite pushing the idea that Kathryn's confused about her gender. According to him, that explains why she's so obsessed with sports. Why most of her friends are boys. He's been taking her to a psychoanalyst who has been suggesting the same."

"That poor girl."

"I agree, but between Kathryn's crush and the separation, it seems Grace finally has her daughter on board to stop seeing this therapist and to end this discussion."

"Well, it's not our place to interfere. But make sure Grace knows Kathryn will be welcome to return anytime she wants, Grace and Kathryn both."

Emma nodded. "I'll make sure she knows. On to better news. Tiffany called today, and she and Simone will definitely be up for a few days around May First. Simone will have to return for classes, but she says she can extend her stay for a week. And she'll drive Chiara up, so we're all set. Chiara will stay all week, too. Then she needs to get back to classes."

"But do you think we can get her to come back in July when the girls are here?"

"I know she wants to. It all depends on where she gets her internship, and how much time she could have." She kissed him. "We'll work it out. Now, I've got to get to sleep if there's any hope of me waking up tomorrow to prepare breakfast. *Buona notte, amore.*"

Emma switched off the light, and her eyes had closed before her head even hit the pillow.

CHAPTER 31

Madison

THE SUN WAS ONLY A SLIVER on the horizon when Madison rose. She'd been on a strict diet since her college days, when even the Syracuse University television studios proved that, yes, the camera truly did add ten pounds.

Last night's feast had been delicious. And decadent.

Not used to eating so much, or honestly, not used to eating enough for basic survival on a daily basis, she hadn't slept well. She was still feeling full, but she was returning for a spa appointment this morning. A facial, a massage, the sauna, and the Turkish bath would probably set her right as rain.

A quick shower and an early coffee would get her off to a good start. After all, there was no hope of falling back to sleep. Then again, she'd been sleeping far more than usual. Cutting back on social media had helped. No more late-night scrolling. Not following the latest news had added more time to her schedule. And all the walking and climbing ensured that she tumbled into a deep sleep the second her head hit the pillow—no need for the chemical assistance that had become far too prevalent in her life in recent years. She hadn't even packed sleeping pills and would dispose of those in her medicine cabinet when she returned home.

This whole week had been far more stabilizing than she had imagined. Once she'd joined the fellow guests, she'd started eating well, working exercise into her daily routine, and, to her great surprise, she was enjoying conversations and spending time with her fellow guests. Heike was interesting. An Austrian-American who spoke fluent Italian, she had a knack for cooking and was Giuseppe's helper in the kitchen— patiently explaining recipes and tips in the kitchen, and translating Giuseppe's rapid-fire Italian. Madison had always been a disaster in the kitchen. Then again, she grew up with a mother who didn't realize that alternatives existed to Lean Cuisine ready-made meals. Now, while she still needed work, she could—if pressed—make a decent fettuccine from scratch and a fresh tomato sauce. After endless practice, because it had become the guests' favorite meal, she could even manage a passable wild boar sauce. That would bowl over most of her friends in Ohio. Heike had patiently walked her through the steps numerous times. She had a knack for explaining things in a simple way for kitchen-challenged students like Madison.

And Grace, who seemed like a boring, older British lady, turned out to be interesting, too. She was well-read and enjoyed recommending books she thought Madison might enjoy. She mentioned she hadn't really travelled much on her own and was enjoying the freedom. And she was a loving grandmother. It was heartwarming to see how close she was with Kathryn, and how she encouraged the girl and gave her confidence. Madison could have benefitted from a loving family like that when she was growing up. Her mother had tried, but so much energy went into making ends meet. Raising Madison alone after Madison's dad bailed on them both couldn't have been easy.

And then there was Chris. Handsome, athletic, funny. She didn't need any romantic entanglements. Certainly not now. But something about him intrigued her. He seemed so different from most men she'd met. Not superficial at all, but genuinely confident and down to earth. A gentleman. The kids adored him, and he seemed to truly enjoy playing sports with them, even helping with the coaching of the local soccer team. How many men of his age—those without kids of their own—would do that? But why was he thirty and still unattached? He'd made no mention of a serious girlfriend, past or present. That, in itself, seemed odd. But then again, Madison really didn't need romantic complications. Time spent with someone as sweet and easy on the eyes as Chris should be enough. Simple and uncomplicated should be her guiding words now.

Reluctant to climb out from under her warm covers, she turned to her phone on her bedside table. She'd become far less obsessive checking for word from Rita over the past couple of days, and it was doubtful she received Easter tidings. She flipped on her phone, noted the lack of correspondence. Last week, she would have been devastated, but now, although still feeling a pang of disappointment, she placed the phone face down and stood up from her bed. She stretched and watched as the sky grew brighter, the hilltop town beginning to glow.

A shower and coffee would do the trick. Sliding into bedside slippers, she shuffled to the bathroom.

MADISON AND EMMA SAT IN THE LIVING ROOM, nursing their second cappuccino of the morning. At first, they ventured out to the table beside the fountain, but the early morning air was still nippy and they raced back in to the warmth of the inn.

Emma even set a fire, and both women sat on the soft leather couch, cradling their coffee cups and gazing into the orange-blue flames.

"This won't last. The heat'll hit all at once, usually in May, and then there'll be no need for this fireplace 'til October." Emma sipped from her cup. "I remember before the heating was in place here, and we were doing work in this inn, we only had the warmth of the fireplaces. That was one frigid winter."

She smiled as she gazed into the flames. A type of smile Madison knew all too well. One that made her suspect Emma was reliving memories that had nothing to do with the intricacies of construction work and more to do with how she and Mark staved off the cold in those days.

"How long have you and Mark been together?"

"What?" Emma's concentration was broken. "Oh, goodness. We went out on a few dates many years ago, back when we were grad students together. But then I met my Italian husband. Mark and I met up again almost five years ago, after my divorce. He had inherited this place from his aunt, and he and I worked on it together. Kind of rekindled an old romance. We married almost three years ago."

"Oh, wow. You seem to have been together so much longer. Then again, I really have never had a relationship that's lasted that long."

"It's probably hard with your work, being so recognizable. And I imagine you work long hours," said Emma. "Do you enjoy being a news reporter?"

Madison looked into the dancing flames, pondering Emma's question. "I always did. It's all I ever wanted." She traced one finger around the rim of her ceramic mug. "But for the first time, I'm not feeling the same passion." She sighed. "Half the time, I'm not even sure I *like* television news. And then ..." Madison looked around. The others were still asleep.

She was tired of keeping everything inside. "It's just ... there's a lot of pressure. To get ahead. I've watched so many former classmates rise quickly to big markets, and I felt stuck in a midlevel city. Wanted something bigger. I uh ..." Her heart began racing. Why was she telling an almost complete stranger about her shame? "I'm not really here hiding out because of contract negotiations. I met this guy at work. The new producer. We started dating. Well, maybe dating's an optimistic word." She kicked off her shoes and tucked her legs under her, placing her mug down on the side table. "I wasn't in love with him, but he was nice, had worked in a big market. I thought ... well, I thought he could help launch me in a market like that, too. Maybe I'm not as much of a star reporter as I thought I was. Turns out I had no idea he was married. With kids. His wife found out about us." Madison swept one hand over her face. It was embarrassing, but also freeing to say this to someone. "Let's just say, you may have noticed mine wasn't the name on the reservation."

Emma placed down her cup. "No, it was a husband and wife from Columbus, but she called saying they wouldn't be able to come. That they would transfer the reservation to someone else, and someone would be following up with your details."

"Yes, my agent. Rita. I know she made the arrangements. I wasn't looking forward to being banished, to be honest. But maybe this has been good for me." The fire was warm on her skin, and probably masked the heat she could feel pricking her cheeks. "I've never been to Italy before. At first, I was just planning on hiding away at the spa." She chuckled. "And I do love your spa—I'm headed there in a bit—but then I started meeting the other guests, going on some of the trips. And I'm feeling less like the exile I was sent here to be."

"Oh, that's a terrible way to look at it." Emma clasped Madison's hand in her own. "We're so pleased you're here.

Anyway, why should you be exiled? You're single. He's the married one sleeping around. Is he still there?"

Unbidden, a tear escaped and Madison wiped it away. "Yeah, that's a bit of a double standard. He's on leave, too. But it seems he's going to be back at work next month. June at the latest. And my future at the station is still unclear."

"Why am I not surprised?" Emma was shaking her head. "Some things never change."

"My first days here, I was obsessively waiting for news from my agent. Now a whole week has gone by. I should know what's in store for me at my return."

"If your channel is making it so difficult on you, can't you go to the competition? Or another city?"

"Running away?" She shook her head. "Yeah, it does look like that might be the only option. I was hoping time would help, but they say my poll numbers have plummeted. I have some decisions to make this week …" She trailed off and watched the flames, concentrated on the crackling of the wood. Did she even care anymore? For the past years, she'd been laser focused on working her way to a top market, but now that she'd stepped away from it all, it all seemed less important. Madison sighed and turned back to Emma. "I just don't know what I want."

Emma smiled. "It seems you have a lot to think about. Listening to you, I'm sorry my friend Tiffany couldn't make it this weekend as she'd planned. She, Annarita, and I met at a hotel on the Italian seaside and became close friends. She was trying to be a dancer on Italian television programs. And … well … she had a lot of producers and television execs who took advantage of her, or let her know the casting couch was the only way to get where she wanted to go. She took a step back and started to realize she wasn't even convinced she wanted TV success that much." Emma got up and stretched. She walked to the fireplace and removed the andiron from its place, stoking the fire. "Today, she's concentrated on teaching dance classes in Rome. One day, she'd like to open her own studio. She's incredibly talented—dances in performances, too. The school has a reputation for putting on great performances in some of Rome's historic theatres. My own daughter trained there. And Tiffany is in a great relationship with a wonderful man."

"Yeah," said Madison. "She does sound like someone who would understand where I am now."

"I know it's not the same, but Angela will be reporting to work in about a half hour. Want me to push your spa appointment up? Sounds like you could use the relaxation and reflection time."

"Do you know what?" Madison stretched out her legs and twisted her ankles right to left. "Thanks to you I have far more practical shoes. The stylish, sporty sneakers. I'm gonna do something I never do. Take a nice walk to clear my head. I'm going to tackle those stairs and hills up to town and enjoy the early-morning views. I might even get my third cappuccino of the day out on the *piazza* before returning to my spa appointment."

Emma smiled and strode over to the couch to pluck the cups and plates from the side tables. "Thatta girl. Go conquer Todi, while I conquer the breakfast crowd. Thanks for the fireside chat."

"Thanks to you, Emma." She watched the older woman leave the room, then stood and stretched before the fire. She had some hills to climb.

ANGELA WAS A MASTER AT HER CRAFT. Madison's calf muscles had been aching after her morning excursion, but Angela's massage had worked wonders. Now the masseuse was easing the tension from her shoulders and back. Aaron may have been a jerk, but he and his wife leaving her these prepaid spa appointments *almost* made up for having exploded her comfortable life. Almost.

The talk with Emma this morning had been therapeutic. Holding everything in wasn't doing her any favors. The charming setting and fellow guests were certainly distracting her, but the stress was building within. As was all too evident to Angela and her magic fingers. She knew Emma wouldn't say anything, so it had helped to get it all out to someone who wouldn't judge her.

And despite her sore muscles, the early morning hike up to town had been a good idea. There was something about seeing the town in the early morning light, before the crowds and the hustle of daily life set in. She stood at the ramparts at the Oberdan Garden and watched the sun glittering against the town as it gained strength. The green expanse in the distance glowed. The church bells of San Fortunato broke the silence of Easter Monday, not a holiday back home but one here that delayed the activity on town squares.

Despite the holiday, her preferred café on Piazza del Popolo was open, even if she was the only client at this early hour. She sat at a table outside. The chilly morning air was less evident after the brisk walk up. When the young waitress approached her, she ordered a cappuccino. She leaned back in her seat and observed the empty square. A delivery man crossed one side, wheeling crates of food, probably for a restaurant preparing an Easter Monday feast for its customers. Emma had told her the holiday was *Pasquetta*, "little Easter," and that it was a typical day for taking trips to see nearby towns. Tourists would probably emerge in Todi come late morning, but for now, she had it almost to herself.

Her cappuccino arrived. Madison thanked the waitress and sipped it, watching more locals filling up the *piazza*. A priest walking up the steps to a cathedral, an old woman dressed in black and sensible shoes slowly making her way up the same stairway, albeit more slowly. A harried mother crossed the *piazza*, a baby screaming in the carriage she pushed. She stopped for a moment, manically pushing it back and forth, a look of desperation on her face. It seemed to do the trick, because the wailing tapered and then ended. A look of relief washed over her young, but tired, face before she continued her journey across the square.

Madison smiled as she observed all this life around her, feeling a part of it. She sipped the last of her cappuccino and felt the rising sun warming her face before the easy trip downhill to her spa appointment.

"Ma-dee-sone ..." a voice sang out, lengthening the vowels.

Madison startled. She was face down and jerked up, looking around the room.

"Shh ..." the woman's voice continued. "You fell asleep during our massage. You must have needed the rest."

"Oh, my. I guess I was exhausted. I was up in town this morning. I was thinking about that while you were getting the knots out of my shoulders. I can't believe I drifted off."

"It means you were relaxed. It also means I'm doing my job well. I have another client now, but you're scheduled in the Turkish bath. Mariella will accompany you there."

"*Grazie*, Angela." Madison followed Mariella into the shower room and rinsed the massage oils from her body under the tropical rain shower she'd grown to love so much. She truly must be exhausted to have fallen asleep on the massage table. Mariella was waiting for her with a thick robe as soon as she exited the shower and then accompanied her to the Turkish bath, prattling on all along the way. Madison smiled at the young woman's enthusiasm, but was too tired to join in.

She thanked her, disrobed to her bikini, and slipped into the Turkish bath.

Her muscles were so relaxed, even if she had apparently been asleep for half of the massage. Maybe her chat with Emma that morning had been even more mentally exhausting than she'd imagined. After all, she'd been holding it in for so long. She sat against the colorful tiles of the bench. Mariella mentioned that all the tiles in this room had been created in nearby Deruta, apparently a town known for its ceramic work. Hadn't Grace mentioned traveling there and not knowing how to transport all her new purchases? Madison's skin was beading with the humidity, her bikini already damp from the steam. She breathed in deeply again.

Next Saturday, she'd be headed back home. She would have to have a call with Rita to find out what was in store—one way or another. The Scioto luxury apartment's lease was up soon. She had planned on renewing it, but certainly now would be a good time to get out if her local job prospects were destroyed. Rita couldn't keep her hanging for long. Maybe she would have to try a new market, even if she were damaged goods. And she'd have to build up once again. Start from scratch. The very idea exhausted her.

Madison pushed herself up and stepped out of the steam bath and into the shower, before descending into the Jacuzzi. True, all these things would have to be arranged. She would call Rita in the next days and tell her she needed certainty as she returned home. But she was tired of ruining her days stressing about her fate in Ohio. She was in Italy now. In a spa. Following this, she would dress in her room and decide what to do for the rest of the day. Tomorrow she knew a daytrip was planned for Gubbio, and she had already expressed her interest to Emma, so she knew she was on the list. Emma had told her she'd love it, that it was a picturesque, medieval town.

That they'd book lunch in a popular trattoria. Madison placed her head back and felt the bubbles along the length of her sore legs. The problems all remained in place, but Columbus seemed very far away right now.

She hadn't factored the sauna into her spa time today, but it had beckoned as she dried off and was headed into the locker room. And, why the hell not? Into her second week of her holidays, her days of pampering were clearly numbered. Unless she got a handsome settlement and until she could get a new job, who knew how much scrimping she'd have to endure?

She closed her eyes and stretched her legs out along the warm wood, breathing deeply in and out. She felt her heartbeat slow as her body relaxed in the dry heat.

The door opened and a gust of cool air entered. "Oh, I'm sorry. I didn't realize anyone was here."

She cracked one eye open. Chris stood in the doorway, taking up the whole doorway, to be precise.

"No problem. Come on in. There's room enough for two." She pulled herself up and leaned against the wooden wall, swinging her legs in front of her.

Chris sat on the bench adjacent to hers. He leaned his head against the wall and sighed.

Even at rest, Madison couldn't help but notice his broad shoulders, bulging biceps and washboard abs. Definitely a former swimmer. But one who still kept himself in shape. She forced herself to look away, closed her eyes and rested her head against the wooden wall. The last thing she needed now were complications. Nice guy. Nice to look at. That was enough.

"Wow," said Chris, issuing a low moan of pleasure. "This is fantastic. I just had a neck and shoulder massage by Angela. That woman works miracles. Better than the ones we had back in college on the swim team."

He opened his eyes and smiled, forming dimples that made him even more appealing. Why did he have to break into her solo time? Up until now, she'd had the place all to herself today.

"Is it your first appointment with Angela? I haven't seen you here before."

"I know. My mistake. I'd actually booked spa visits when I made the reservation, but never bothered confirming times. Emma told me I needed to slot them in." He rubbed his shoulder. "But now that I see how well she does, I'll definitely get back. I think she took a good ten years off me."

Madison laughed. "Yeah, I know what you mean. Same here, every time I go." She shifted, leaning against the far wall and stretching her legs across the bench. At least she knew she looked good in this bikini. She may not be interested, but it wouldn't do to not be looking her best in the sauna with such a handsome man. Even if she was definitely *not* interested. "Anyway, didn't Emma say you've been roped into coaching duties today with your youth soccer team?"

"Ha. *My* youth soccer team. It's starting to feel that way. I already have a million messages from the actual coach. Going over strategy in broken English. Why do you think I'm here? Relaxing before all the stress begins. We're playing Orvieto today. This is a huge game for the kids. The twins and Kathryn are convinced we can crush the 'big city' kids."

"How big is the 'big city'?"

"According to Emma, about twenty thousand, so we're talking megacity levels compared to Todi. Let's hope our competition is soft and lazy as a result of those big city ways."

Madison smiled. "You're a good sport to get so involved. Especially on your vacation."

Chris shook his head. "Nah, I get it. I was sports obsessed at that age." He grinned. "Probably still am, if I'm honest. It means a lot to them, and it's not that much time. Hey, you should come to the game today. We're playing at the local soccer field. Since it's Easter Monday, the whole town will come out. I'm told the village women will come bearing local specialties and everyone will celebrate together. You'll enjoy it."

She looked over at him, at a trickle of sweat dripping down his forehead. At those washboard abs that glistened in the heat. The blue eyes that sparkled. "I ... uh ... I hadn't planned on it."

"Oh. Well, no pressure. I know Grace is coming. Heike said she'd be there, too. And Mark and Emma, of course. Giuseppe said he'd take Giulia along, because she always wants to tag along whenever Kathryn is doing something. And Annarita said she's been going on about Kathryn as Todi's first girl soccer star and insisting she has to go cheer for her. Annarita will try to come with the baby, if she can manage it. So, you see, you'd be all alone here at The Three Coins Inn."

"Means I'd have the spa all to myself. No need to share the sauna space with intruders."

"*Touché.*" He closed his eyes and leaned against the wall. "But I hope you'll at least consider it."

"I'll see what I can do."

"Are you going with us tomorrow to Gubbio?" asked Chris.

"Definitely. Emma's been telling me all about it. Another medieval hilltown. I can't wait to see it."

"But don't you think they're all fantastic? All these perfect hilltowns? It's my first time here, but a part of me wishes I could stay."

Madison observed him again. She wondered what his story was. Impossible someone like him didn't have a girl— or more—fawning over him at home. He'd said he was a management consultant. Maybe one sick of the daily grind? Or maybe, much like Madison herself, he was running from something.

"Judging from your design unveiling last night, your artwork is pretty good. Maybe Todi needs more graphic designers."

Chris chuckled. "That was fun, but I can hardly create a job out of it. I haven't drawn for years. Only a bit of fun—since Mark told me they needed a new logo. I was happy to take on the challenge. And believe me, I'm thrilled they'll use it as the visual for the inn. But I'm a decade behind when it comes to changes in the industry, software, all the rest. I wouldn't even know where to begin. Guess it's just a dream." He grimaced. "More management consulting for me."

"I can't tell if you're serious or not. Anyway, seems you'd always have a job as youth team coach, if you want it."

He wiped the sweat beading on his chest with his towel, and Madison tried not to stare too obviously.

"True. You take the wins where you get them. And speaking of wins, hope to see you there this afternoon, Madison." He stood. "If I'm going to be in time for our pregame session and warm-ups, I'd better get going. See you at four at the pitch!" With a dimpled smile, he was off.

She watched his broad shoulders and toned glutes as he walked away. Madison was grateful the hot sauna masked the flush spreading across her cheeks.

CHAPTER 32

Heike

HEIKE LIT THE CANDLE, shaking out the long match she had used. She watched its glow in the cathedral, flickering alongside other votive candles offered on this Easter Monday. The mass, while not full, had been well attended. Heike had left the inn early to walk up to town, politely telling Emma she didn't need any breakfast, that she wanted to make it up to Easter Monday mass at the cathedral.

The mass had eased her pain, somewhat. All night she'd tossed and turned, not journeying any closer to sleep. When a faint light began to glimmer on the horizon, Heike gave up all together and rose from her bed. She waited for some time in her room, reading and gazing out the window until the bedside clock hit a more reasonable time.

Now she watched that candle flicker and sank down to her knees on the wooden kneeler, crossing herself and mumbling familiar prayers. A tear trickled down her cheek, followed by another. Why did it have to be so hard, when she was finally getting better? But each date hit her like a Mack truck, and forced her to begin the process anew.

She felt the familiar tightness in her chest. The ache in her heart. Maybe one day these pains would fade, but she feared it would take a long time.

She looked up to the familiar fresco. The souls in anguish, confronting their fate. She observed the pain and horror she felt within, reflected on their countenances as they were dragged into the pits of Hell.

The saints, all depicted with the instruments of their torture. Her eyes never failed to seek out the image of Saint Bartholomew, holding his flayed skin in one hand. That slack, flayed face, forming the countenance of its painter, Michelangelo. No matter how many times she prayed in silent contemplation, her gaze stopped at that image. But today, she shouldn't be thinking about the fate of Bartholomew.

"Heike," she heard a whisper behind her. She turned to see Grace standing hesitantly at her back. She reached up to swipe away a tear, hoping Grace wouldn't notice, but the pain glowing in her friend's eyes made it clear she already had.

Heike stood and Grace placed a gentle hand on her shoulder. "I shouldn't have disturbed you while you were praying. It just surprised me, seeing you here. I hadn't yet seen the fresco." She looked up. "So when I saw the mass was ending, I waited for the parishioners to clear out and then came in. But please," she waved her hand. "Don't worry about me. I didn't wish to disturb you."

Heike shook her head. "You didn't. You aren't." She looked up. "Pretty amazing, isn't it? A partial copy of Michelangelo's *Last Judgement*, right here in Todi."

"I know. I didn't know it was here. Emma mentioned it, and I came up to see it. I'll need to take Kathryn this week. But today she's all tied up with football. Was off with the team before the match this afternoon." Grace craned her neck to see better. "But she'll love this. I need to return with her. At least until I can take her to see the real one in Rome."

Heike chuckled. "You'll never have the real one almost to yourself like you do this one. I've been here almost every day, and I'm often alone."

"Oh," Grace sounded surprised. "You mentioned lighting candles, but I didn't realize you were here daily."

"Not always for mass. I came this morning for the holiday service. But I light a candle and say a prayer. Today is April twenty-second, and I couldn't miss that." She looked at Christ in the center. Not the sinewy, loving Christ of most depictions, but the musclebound version created by Michelangelo, his right arm raised to the eternal fate of the damned.

"I'm sorry. I'm not Catholic, so I may be missing something. What is the significance of April twenty-second?"

Heike looked up again, at the swirl of colors and figures, Heaven and Hell mingling on one wall. "It's Matthias' birthday," she whispered. "He would have been sixty-two. It's the first birthday I celebrate alone, after his death." She forced a smile, happy she could not see the strained attempt. "We were supposed to be here, celebrating it together."

"Oh, Heike. I am so sorry. I didn't realize ..." Grace put an arm around her shoulders. "I feel terrible barging in to your moment of silence. Shall I go and leave you alone? I'll see you back at the inn. Whenever you're ready."

For the first time since she'd woken that morning, Heike felt a glow of happiness within. "If you wouldn't mind, I'd love if you could get us a table at the café. I'll only be another couple of minutes. And a cappuccino with you out on the Piazza del popolo would cheer me up."

Grace smiled. "Of course." She squeeze Heike's hand, and whispered. "I'll go right now to get us a table, but please take your time. I'm happy to wait."

HEIKE AND GRACE SAT OUT ON THE SQUARE. The waitress recognized them now and asked them if they'd like their usual cappuccino.

Grace had smiled. "I don't even speak Italian, but when I'm being asked if I want *il solito*, it makes me feel like a local."

"That it does," said Heike, leaning back in her chair and looking at the cathedral on the edge of the square.

"I really am so sorry for having disturbed your silence. I should have left when I saw you in prayer."

Heike shook her head. "No, I had come to do what I meant to do. I wanted to attend mass and light a candle. You are helping me to take my mind off of it." She fidgeted with the sugar packets in their container. "That's important, too. I didn't think I could handle this trip. Handle it all alone." She sighed. "You see, we had selected the hotel together. Matthias and I loved Italy. We'd been to so many regions, but never Umbria. He wanted to see Todi and Spoleto ... and Gubbio, where we'll go tomorrow. I feel guilty doing this on my own."

Grace nodded, and Heike imagined she understood.

"It's just ... we put it off two years ago." She dabbed at her eyes. "You're so busy ... with life. Raising kids, working. In our case, we poured so much into the business. We always thought we'd have more time later. The two weeks in Umbria for his birthday was part of our plan to factor in more time away. We wanted to start scheduling in more time for us."

The waitress returned with their drinks, and Heike thanked her.

"You never really plan for when you won't be able to be together. He was only two years older, and he kept in such good shape. We were so convinced we'd have ages." She sipped her cappuccino. "I wouldn't normally go on like this. But you know better than anyone else what I mean."

Grace was silent on the other side of the table, staring into the froth of her cappuccino. Heike had done it again. Poor Grace was already dealing with the probable breakup of her daughter's marriage, handling the fallout with Kathryn. And here was Heike, piling yet more on to her plate-load of woes. What a friend she was. She sipped her cappuccino. Placing the cup down on the table, she gathered her strength.

"I'm so sorry, Grace. I'm feeling sorry for myself because it's my first birthday without Matthias. Since you're a widow, too, I knew you'd understand. But I know it's not right dragging you into my melancholy." She sighed. "I know you have a lot worrying you back home. It wasn't fair of me to add to your burdens by reminding you of how much you miss your husband."

Grace picked up her cappuccino and took a slow sip. She was slow to place it back in the saucer and her knuckles were white from gripping the ceramic so hard. "But that's just it." She looked out across the *piazza*. "I don't."

"You don't mind I dragged you into my grief? I'm so relieved, Grace. Thank you."

Grace sighed. Took time to scan the entire square, before meeting Heike's gaze. "No. You misunderstood me. I'm not upset because I don't miss my husband. I'm tired of pretending I do."

Heike heard her own intake of breath. "Uh ... you mean, because you've managed to overcome your grief faster than you imagined?"

Grace took a deep breath and lifted her cappuccino, taking a slow sip, then swirling the cup before taking another. She studied the sugar packets with great attention. Heike wanted to break the silence, but forced herself to wait for Grace to feel ready to explain.

Grace placed her coffee cup down on its saucer, leaned back and placed her hands neatly folded on her lap. There was a sheen to her eyes as she looked up to the cathedral tower. "It's hard to pretend for so long. To feign grief. I even feel guilty in front of you, someone who genuinely loved and still grieves for her deceased husband."

Heike felt her heart thrumming in triple time. "I may have forced you into rehashing something you'd rather forget, Grace. Don't feel the need to explain."

Grace met her gaze directly. "But I would like to explain, if you'd care to listen. I've kept it in for so long. Now I live with this guilt."

Heike wanted to be there for her friend, but, at the same time, she hesitated. Grace had spoken about tensions with her daughter and son-in-law, concerns for Kathryn. But, in reality, what had she ever told Heike about her marriage? Heike had assumed, like her, Grace suffered deeply as a widow. But she owed it to her friend to stay silent and hear her out. Heike nodded.

Grace looked up. The sun was higher in the sky, and Easter Monday was shaping up to be a beautiful day. The sun shone down on Grace's face and Heike recognized that Grace, so pretty and elegant now, must have been truly stunning in her younger days.

Grace brushed lock of hair from her forehead. "I met Richard when I was a student. Back then, I was quite ambitious. I was studying nineteenth-century English literature. Dreamed of becoming a professor one day." She shook her head. "That seems so long ago. Richard had recently arrived in Durham as an economics professor, and I took his class. I was an unsophisticated girl from outside Durham city, a little mining town in Country Durham. Solidly working class. My father a mechanic, my mother a seamstress. They made sacrifices to send me to school. Were so proud." She trained her gaze on her ceramic cup, fidgeted with the handle. "When Richard trained his attention on me, I was flattered. Of course, it was wrong. But we weren't so hung up on such things at the time. I couldn't believe he would even notice me, let alone invite me over to his flat for dinner."

The waitress came over to clear their cups, and Heike quietly ordered two more.

Grace took a deep breath. "I know how foolish it all sounds, but if you had met the mousey version of me at nineteen, you'd understand. He was fifteen years older. So much more sophisticated. He'd lived in London, travelled the world. I'd never been farther than Newcastle. I couldn't believe he would even learn my name, let alone pay me any special attention." Grace covered her face with one hand. "My naïveté shone through. Such a ridiculous simpleton. Fell into his bed almost right away." She looked up, meeting Heike's eyes, then shook her head. "Pregnant at nineteen. He offered to pay to take care of it." She sighed again. "To take care of my beloved Ellen. It's the one thing I stood up to him about. So by twenty, I was a college dropout and a mother. We married in a small ceremony in town hall. After my father threatened to tear his eyes out." She laughed. "You didn't want to get on the wrong side of my dad."

Their coffees arrived and Grace fell silent for a moment, until the waitress left. "Yes, he married me and ensured our baby was legitimate. Ellen had everything she needed. But he never forgave me. There was never any love in our house."

They both paused to sip from their drinks. Heike found she needed the jolt of caffeine. She'd been around enough to understand you never truly knew what lay beneath the surface once you scratched off the outermost layer. Grace had never alluded to a happy marriage, and yet Heike had assumed it was so. Because hers was. Because Grace was so elegant. And kind. And her new friend. And yet, she'd misread her situation the entire time.

"The last time he tried to seduce me was when I was a nineteen-year-old girl. It was the last time he was kind to me, too. After I gave birth to our daughter, all he did was insult me, tell me how worthless and stupid I was. No better than a whore who fell into his bed to trick him into marriage. Oh, he was clever. He never said it in front of Ellen. She adored him, and he was not indifferent to her worshipful regard. To this day, she still thinks he was a wonderful father and husband." She sipped her coffee. "Credit where credit is due. He was a good father, if not outwardly affectionate. But he was always cruel to me."

Heike shook her head. "I am so sorry, Grace. I truly had no idea."

Grace offered a wry smile. "Why would you? Like most abused women, I was masterful in covering for him. No one knew." She twisted the watch on her wrist. "Oh, he never physically abused me. That wasn't his vice. He was too sophisticated for that, would consider a man who slapped his wife a brute from the lower classes. But he was a master in exerting precise, agonizing mental abuse. Ensuring I felt stupid. And worthless. And not someone who merited his precious attention." She shook her head. "Sometimes, I thought a slap would be more honest." She breathed out slowly, took another sip of her coffee. "I cooked for him. Kept his house. Raised his daughter. Washed and ironed his clothes. I was available for him sexually when he felt the need, but he was clear to me that he had plenty of better opportunities in that department. As the years went by, he took particular pleasure in recounting to me how much younger they were."

Heike watched a tear roll down one cheek, and she handed Grace a tissue. She wanted to reach across the table to enfold her friend in a comforting embrace, but she sensed Grace needed to get through this without interruption, so she sat still and ensured her face showed no judgment.

Grace shook her head. "Do you have any idea what that's like? Being married to an evil man who takes pleasure in rubbing your nose in it? My husband was a well-respected economist, invited all over the world for speeches and conferences. I used to accompany him on some of the earlier conferences. Fewer in the last years, thankfully. But he insisted I pack his bags. And unpack them."

Grace tilted her face up to catch the sun glowing down. She closed her eyes. For a moment, Heike feared she had fallen asleep. Once again, she bit her tongue. A tear slipped out through one closed eye. Heike realized how difficult this revelation was on her friend. She was determined to hear her out. She remained in silence until Grace opened her eyes again.

Grace looked across the table. "I'm sorry," she whispered. "This is so much harder than I thought."

"Do *not* apologize. I'm here for you. I have nowhere else to go. I've got all day if you need it. Take your time, Grace."

Grace offered a tight smile. Slapped her hands gently on her thighs. "Where was I in my recounting of horrors? Ah, yes. The unpacking. Yes, my darling of a husband wanted to rub my nose in it. The clothes that reeked of cheap perfume. The lipstick stains on his collar. The opened box of condoms. Sometimes handcuffs and sex toys." She shook her head. "I had to put them back in their place in his bedside drawers. Then I had to wash the traces of other women off his clothes."

"Oh, Grace ..." Heike's heart ached for her friend. For the cruelty she had endured.

"You'll wonder why I put up with it. What was essentially wrong with me to have allowed him to abuse me day after day. Year after year."

"No, Grace," Heike whispered.

"It's alright." Grace's hands twisted the edge of her sweater as she spoke. "It's no less than what I wondered about myself. Why *did* I put up with it?" She touched her face, stared off across the square. "Only since his death have I truly realized how clever he was. He didn't start all at once. The insults were subtle. He was a groomer, luring me into my own abuse slowly. How much power he must have felt watching me fall into his trap." She wiped the tears gliding down her face with Heike's handkerchief, looked up to the sky and breathed in deeply.

"At first, after some faculty dinners we went to, he'd make comments about my accent, how I was so clearly the least-educated person in the room. He'd pass it off as a compliment, a salt-of-the-earth comment. Even the one topic I loved—literature—he asked me not to discuss with faculty, saying I would embarrass myself. My dreams of becoming a high school English teacher—I'd already given up on my hopes of becoming a college professor—were foolish. Who would want to learn from someone as ignorant as I was? I always sat quietly at those dinners, a little mouse, unless I was helping the hostess or discussing recipes." She laughed. "That was acceptable to him. At first, I would join him at some of his conferences, but I always had to sit through the lectures, join the official meals. Never could I venture out on my own to visit the Louvre or the Prado or enjoy a coffee on those lively squares. Only with him, and only if he had time." She gave a wry laugh. "And he would have had a lot more time if he hadn't started hopping into some young graduate student's bed while I was just down the hallway, locked in like the obedient wife."

"Oh, Grace," Heike whispered, then kicked herself for interrupting.

"I thought about leaving him, but with what money? I was in my twenties and early thirties with a young daughter. Ellen became my excuse for not attending any more conferences. As for our daughter, Richard did love her. In his way. I knew if I tried to leave, he'd fight for custody. Just to spite me. And how would I argue? A college dropout mother with no skills, no work experience, no money if I left my husband. Each year, walking away seemed less possible. I tried to pour everything into my daughter. We always had a fixed teatime each weekend. I took her to parties, swimming classes, art sessions. I was there to fix her tea, help her with homework, to take her out with friends. But she was such a daddy's girl. The less he did for her, the more she adored him."

She shook her head. "I put up with it, thinking at least my daughter would be strong. Have more options than I did. Have more friends, because I never wanted people to get too close and see how gruesome my home life was." She leaned back in her chair. "It didn't do me much good. My daughter found a man not unlike her father. Not as cruel, not abusive to her. But pompous and self-satisfied. Never supportive of Ellen. Quick to jump on to the newest virtue-signaling trend. I ..." she sighed. "I can't help but think this split could be good for Ellen. But I can't explain to her without explaining all the things I hid from her growing up ... trying so hard to pretend we were a normal, happy family."

"Are you sure she suspected nothing?"

"I honestly don't know. She was distraught when Richard died. Heike, this will sound terrible, but all I could feel was elation when they called me from his department to tell me the news. He collapsed. In one of his lectures. The students called an ambulance. Tried to help him. But it was a heart attack. I was silent when the dean called me. He thought I was suffering from shock. Sent his wife over to my house to comfort me." She met Heike's gaze, shook her head. "I *was* in shock. But it wasn't despair. It was elation. I sat in silence as the dean's wife came, made me tea, tried to make me eat as I stared blankly into space. I didn't move, but inside, I felt the old me clawing back. I felt as if God had finally heard my prayers. Do you understand? I was free. Finally free."

Heike felt her heart clench as she observed the pain etched on Grace's face. She reached across the table and placed one hand over Grace's, speaking softly, "I do understand. I can't imagine how you suffered."

"But that's the thing. No one could ever know. Once someone dies, he becomes even more of a saint. I went to his funeral, to services at the college. Listened to his colleagues, his students. I watched all these young women sobbing through his funeral, wondering how many of them had slept with my husband. My daughter was inconsolable. The more she spoke with mourners and his colleagues, the more upset she got. I had to keep acting. Keep pretending to be destroyed by Richard's death. Even if I wanted to, it was too late for the truth to come out. I had no choice but to play along." She looked up, eyes sparkling. "When every day I wake up, thankful he's gone. Thankful he no longer controls my life. No longer fills my soul with despair." She wrung her hands together. "But, in a way, he won. I keep living the same way he trained me to live. This trip to Italy—it was the first time I broke from the role he created for me. The first time I travelled alone. Without my jailer controlling me. And it wasn't even me to make that decision, but my daughter asking me to take her place. But it makes me think I can do other things. It's too late to become a teacher now, but perhaps I can get my certification to become a teacher's aide. Substitute occasionally. I can go see my friend

Nicola in Spain. He would never let me, you see. She never understood why I couldn't visit her, and I was tired of making up excuses. And finally, he'd died and I could do what I wanted. Go to London. On my own. Sleep late and get hotel room service. Visit the museums. Venture outside of hotel rooms."

Heike had been struggling with the internal pain as she listened to Grace's Angst, the horrible secret she'd lived with for so long. How she'd protected that evil man. The shame she must have felt all these years, keeping his secret. But now, watching her friend's face glow with the knowledge she was truly free, Heike felt all that anger for a man cold in his grave seep away. She stood up and wrapped her friend in her arms. "I will be waiting for you in Vienna." She sat back down, holding Grace's hand in her own. "You have been very brave, Grace. For a very long time. You were selfless and did everything to protect your daughter. But now it's time to think about what makes *you* happy." She called the waitress over and whispered in her ear.

The two women waited in silence until the waitress returned with two shot glasses filled with clear liquid. Heike thanked her and placed the two glasses between them. "This deserved more than a third cappuccino. Grappa, this time. That must have taken a lot out of you."

Grace nodded. "It did. But I feel lighter somehow. I'm tired of playing the grieving wife for such an evil man. I won't sully his reputation in town, but I no longer plan to pretend I'm devastated. Not right away, she'll have enough to deal with, but I want to tell Ellen why I shielded her to protect her. I won't tell her the worst of it, but she needs to know that she can't make the same mistakes I did. The irreversible ones you'll regret later." She shook her head. "I don't have any worries for Kathryn. She's a strong girl who will look after herself. Thank God."

"I think you're right there." Heike held up one of the glasses. "But this toast is for you. My new friend. To Grace. For all your strength and goodness and beauty. I'm so fortunate to have met you and to become your friend. And I look forward to your visit to Vienna. And mine to Durham. And a lifetime of new memories." She raised her glass. "Here's to second chances in life."

Grace smiled and raised her glass, her eyes still glossy with unshed tears. "I can toast to that. To second chances in life." She clinked her glass gently against Heike's. "And to new friends."

"Always to new friends." Heike sat back in her seat. The sun was high in the sky now, the square more crowded on this holiday day. She had walked up the hill to town this morning feeling sad and very much alone, but as she sat in the warm glow of this early spring with Grace, she felt an overwhelming sense of love and belonging. And the need for new beginnings. She knew Matthias would be the first to understand.

CHAPTER 33

Chris

CHRIS' NECK AND SHOULDERS WERE TENSE, the total relaxation following his morning massage mere distant memories. "What're you doing? You gave up that shot. You were in the lead! Wanna lose today?" He hollered from the sideline. "Marco, move up on the field. Valerio, you need to stick yourself like glue to that midfielder."

God, these kids were driving him nuts. Practices had run fine, but now every player was out on the pitch playing an individual game. Zero teamwork. They took an early lead and then got lazy, and Orvieto, playing united, clawed their way back. When another team was hungrier than you, it never ended well.

Mark ran over from the opposite sideline. "Lorenzo's limping. We'll need to sub him out."

"Oh, damn. Just what we need. One of our strongest players."

Mark nodded. "True, but Paolo has been getting stronger. I had him warming up, just in case Lorenzo started looking worse. But it's clear now his ankle is worse than he let on. We need to get him out and get some ice on that."

Chris nodded. "Can you speak to the ref for a substitution? He won't understand me. Can we get a short timeout to speak to the team?"

"Good idea. Federico's mom is a nurse. I'll also call her over to look at that ankle."

Mark ran off to alert the ref. The whistle sounded and the universal timeout signal displayed. Lorenzo was staying stubbornly in place, ignoring the whistle.

Chris raced over, slung the gangly boy over his shoulder, and trotted him off the pitch, lowering him to the team bench. He pointed a finger at the boy. "Sports lesson. When you're injured, you tell your coaches so that they can remove you right away. You could have made that worse."

The boy looked at him in confusion. Thinking back, Chris realized he'd never heard him speak English, had always heard Chris' instructions translated. He saw Mark returning with a woman who was kneeling beside Lorenzo, feeling his ankle, murmuring something to the boy in Italian and then reaching into the cooler for the ice.

Chris strode over to the team, Mark at his side.

"What the heck is going on? Where is the team I've seen these past days? This is your chance to win against a bigger team ... on your home field. You're just gonna roll over and let them beat you?"

Marco was rapidly translating Chris' words for his teammates.

"In these past days, I've seen you play as a team. Now I watch you all running around the field as eleven individual players. If you want to win as a team, you need to start doing what Mark and I have been teaching you. Lorenzo is out, but Paolo here," Chris clutched the young boy's shoulder. "He has been working hard, and his footwork is strong. He'll play attack alongside Marco. Then we have Valerio and Kathryn as wings. I want you passing to them. I want you putting into place those drills we've been working on. I want you to make your families and your townspeople proud. Do you hear me?"

Marco finished translating and the team came together in a huddle. "*Sìiiiii!*" they yelled in unison.

"Are you going to get out there and win today?"

"*Sìiiiii!*"

"Are we going to kick some Orvieto butt and show them how it's done?"

"*Sìiiiii!*"

The whistle sounded and the kids ran back on the pitch, bouncing up and down, ready for the remainder of the game. The parents and friends surrounded the field, red and white scarves worn proudly.

And then he spotted it. Chris could see the shift in his teams' behavior. They were standing straighter, their leg muscles flexed, ready to get out there to fight for the win. Play began and Chris was looking at an entirely new team—one hungry for the win. They were aggressive, in possession of the ball and paying attention to where their teammates were on the field to pass effectively.

Mark patted him on the shoulder. "Well done. Your pep talk seems to have done the trick. They're finally playing like they actually want to win. Good news on Lorenzo, too. Roberta says it's a light sprain. Icing and lots of rest. Lorenzo and his mother are headed home so he can elevate it and their doctor uncle can have a look, too. She has the car parked nearby."

Chris nodded. "Good. Can't believe I missed the limping."

"Happens. He was trying to hide it. No way ... Go Kathryn!"

Chris turned to see his English player tearing up the field with amazing speed and impressive dribbling, something they'd been working on all week. But no way was the opposing team going to let a girl score. She was marked by two defensive players.

Chris clasped his hands together. "Pass, Kathryn. Pass," he muttered. He watched her split-second gaze over the field and saw her fake a forward sprint while doubling back and passing to Paolo. Fresh on the field, with a huge grin on his face and a wide opening, Paolo took possession of the ball and charged to the goal with Marco at his side. He sidestepped a robust defender and saw his shot. One leg back, gathering speed, he made perfect contact with the ball. It flew through the air, spinning and arcing gracefully despite its speed. The goalie, a highly talented boy, sailed through the air for it ... as it skimmed a millimeter over his fingers and firmly hit the back net of the goal.

"*Gol*!!" cheered the crowd, waving their red and white scarves in the air. Paolo stood still before the goal, reliving the moment, until Marco threw his arms around him. Paolo looked back at Kathryn and ran over to embrace the wing who'd given him the assist.

Chris and Mark were hopping up and down at the sideline. Chris screamed out, "Two–two! Now take it home! Todi wants a win!"

The tide had turned. You could see it in the Todi teammates' eyes. Finally, they were ready to give it their all to deliver victory to their town. And that would not be done by everyone hogging the ball and playing individually. Chris looked on as the endless drills they'd practiced took beautiful shape on the field. Finally, the kids were being tactical. Aware of where their teammates were on the field. Attuned to when they were too guarded to make a clear shot and which players had a more open field and a better shot of netting the ball. Midfielders and defense were supporting, and tearing back to position themselves to make certain no Orvieto players got any openings on their watch.

Honestly, it was beautiful to see it clicking. To see them coming together as a team, just as Chris knew they could. That hunger in their eyes was what underpinned the whole game. That level of raw desire, combined with skill and well-honed teamwork, was going to make it tough for Orvieto to get ahead. At least, he hoped it would. Chris glanced at his watch. A tie was certainly better than losing, but 2–2 wasn't the victory he craved for this team.

Chris ran along the sideline, following the play. He clapped his hands over his head. "Todi—I wanna see three! Get to work to give me three! Leave everything you've got out on this field!!"

Just then, one of the Orvieto players fumbled the ball, and Alberto, one of their most impressive defensemen, made easy work of stealing it away. That kid had a leg like a catapult, and he shot the ball perfectly across the pitch. Valerio was left wing and he met it, successfully outmaneuvering the closest defender. He was hurtling towards the goal, but a defender and midfielder were ready for him. Chris could see the panic in the boy's face.

"Think, Valerio," Chris whispered. "Think. Marco and Paolo are marked, and Kathryn is over there all by her lonesome."

The cloud washed over Valerio's face, and Chris caught the moment Valerio saw the opening, too. One foot firmly planted on the grass, the other stretching back and unfurling, making perfect contact with the ball. A clean, beautiful shot to Kathryn, who met the pass and ran with it. She was running toward the goal and Valerio was at the same level. Thankfully, pounding into their heads the danger of offsides had yielded some fruits. Chris could feel his heart thundering in his chest as Kathryn neared the goal. The defense was backing up, but they were too slow. It was all on the goalie. The extremely talented goalie. The goalie who would be hellbent to not let a girl score on his goal. Chris clutched his fists at his side, that old, familiar adrenaline raging within.

Kathryn raised her right leg, angling in for the kick. He watched the goalie commit to the white orb that would soar through the air. Chris felt tears spring to his eyes as he realized it was the fake he'd taught the young English girl, who now— only to rub it in—gently tapped the ball into the liberated goal.

Kathryn screamed, jumping up and down. Marco wrapped her in an embrace and, Chris couldn't help notice—wondering if other spectators had as well—also planted a quick peck on her lips. They were immediately swarmed by teammates, all in a huddle yelling "Ca–te–ri–na! Ca–te–ri–na!"

He chuckled. Kathryn had already told him she was becoming used to her Italian name.

Chris clapped his hands together. "C'mon team! Only two minutes left to the game. It ain't over yet! You've got this! Do *not* let them score. Footwork! *Teamwork!*"

The ball went into play, but Chris knew the goal—one scored by a girl, no less, and tapped in like a toddler match— was the final blow to a team that had already initiated its downward spiral of play. He had seen the moment when the energy shifted, and the Todi team finally decided it would claim victory. Whether it was swimming or soccer, watching that mindset-switch-moment was glorious.

Mark came over and patted him on the back. "Hey Coach, congrats!"

Chris smiled and slapped Mark's free hand. "Right back at you, Coach."

"When Giordano comes back from his holidays, he might find he's been supplanted as a coach."

"Ha. If only I could stay."

"And why can't you? You told me you were looking for a new challenge after selling your consultancy. As you see, we could use your talents here in Todi." Mark nodded over to the pitch. "And did you notice my stepson kissed the scorer?"

Chris chuckled. "I did."

"Hey, what kind of discipline are you promoting on this team?" Mark winked.

Chris watched the clock wind down to the final seconds, until the ref blew his whistle and the pitch exploded with red-clad players huddling together and jumping up and down with joy. Around the field, townspeople screamed and waved their red and white scarves in the air, a continuous wave to celebrate the victory over local rivals, who were also clad in red and white, but wearing their white away shirts and slumped at the far corner of the pitch. Rivalries always drove sports, but Chris realized these rivalries were different—had probably existed between competing hilltowns since the Middle Ages. A wide grin spread across his face. "Well, Mark, I am maintaining the kind of discipline that garners us a three-two victory over Orvieto." Dragging Mark by the arm, he said, "Let's go congratulate our hometown heroes."

Chris and Mark edged their way into the celebratory huddle and Chris embraced the youth league victory with the same enthusiasm he'd once dedicated to NCAA championships.

"OH, DAMN. DO YOU COUNTRY MICE know how to party." An exhausted Chris slipped back against the worn leather couch in Mark's office. Mark had built another fire, which may have been overkill. The evening was warm and the window was open.

The victory had been followed by a triumphant march up to the old town, teammates, parents, brothers and sisters, townspeople and neighbors. The mayor's nephew was on the team, so the mayor had diplomatically greeted the other team and invited them up to the Piazza del popolo for postgame festivities. The coach was gracious, but the team was in no mood to prolong its agony. They boarded their bus for home, and the victorious parade wound its way up the steep streets.

Grace had come up to Chris with tears in her eyes and enfolded him in a big hug. He told her to keep encouraging Kathryn once they returned home, that her encounter with aggressive Italian soccer would give her added confidence and skills when she returned home. Grace hurried off to congratulate her granddaughter.

The other unexpected embrace threw him for a loop.

"Congratulations, Coach," she said as she wrapped her arms around him and planted a kiss on his cheek. "Your morning massage and sauna session clearly got you into the right mood for victory."

She pulled back and the late afternoon sun glinted gold in her hair. Without thinking, Chris reached out and stroked one of those locks before quickly retracting his hand and cursing himself for instigating an intimacy he had no right to initiate. But she didn't seem to mind, and it would be written off as a part of the general revelry of the whole-town celebration.

"Thanks, Madison. I didn't know you'd be coming in the end. Did you see the whole game?"

"Okay, so I won't pretend I'm a huge sports fan, but Emma explained to me that you were right—that the whole town would be here and I couldn't miss it."

She reached into her bag and pulled out the now-familiar red and white scarf, wrapping it around her neck, where it looked ridiculously fetching. Chris clamped his hands into tight fists, resolving to not reach out to touch her again.

"I got here a bit late, and it wasn't looking good ... but how exciting to see how you turned it around! And even more exciting to see Kathryn's goal. I was next to Grace and Heike—and I can't tell you the joy on Grace's face."

She extracted her arm from around his waist, and he regretted its absence. Instead, she maneuvered beside him and slipped her arm into his. "I know I can count on you to help me tackle this big, bad slope looming between me and town celebrations way at the top."

He'd laughed and walked with Madison up the steep walk to town, laughing and joking along the way as townspeople came to thank him or slap him on the back. Just a few weeks ago, he'd been devastated to find his wife and best friend betraying him. In his own bed. And here he was, a short time later, on a holiday he had planned with his wife, the temporary town hero, with a beautiful woman on his arm. Was he imagining her interest in him? Was it too soon to jump back in?

Their moments of intimate chatter were short-lived. When they reached the town square, pandemonium reigned. The mayor now wore an official sash with the colors of the Italian flag.

Tables had been set up with local treats baked by the soccer moms. A photographer was placing the team on the stairs of town hall, the medieval buildings forming a picturesque backdrop to their red and white uniforms. "Chris!" the children cried out, and Chris was plucked from the crowd to stand front and center in this tableau, alongside Mark and the mayor, the kids around and above them on the stairs.

He glanced over at Kathryn, who was radiant. Smile wide, cheeks flushed. He could already see the ghost of the beautiful woman she would become, and he hoped she would always look back at this experience and smile. Marco's hand was draped possessively around her shoulders, and this, too, made him smile at the long-ago euphoria of burgeoning first love. He caught Madison's bright blue gaze in the crowd. Could those feelings be rekindled? Even all these years—and heartbreaks—later?

The local newspaper photographer snapped numerous photos, while the team stayed surprisingly still, and the townspeople cheered and sang. Afterward, more tables were ferried to the center of the square and wine and grappa flowed steadily. People were laughing and chatting. The mayor began to speak to Chris, but his English was quite rudimentary, so the mayor quickly dragged Emma over to serve as translator.

"He says the town is thrilled," Emma told a stunned Chris. "Orvieto is the big rival, and they never thought they could win. But the kids made the town proud. The mayor wants to thank you."

"Tell him it was my pleasure," said Chris. "They're a great group of kids, with a lot of potential. It was fun for me."

The mayor continued speaking in rapidfire Italian to Emma, who was patiently listening. When he finished, she turned back to Chris.

"He was told you are a former college athlete. He says you are welcome to stay as coach. Alongside Giordano. Says it looks even more important to have a foreign 'Mister.'" She smiled. "That's the English term they use for soccer coaches here. He also says—and sorry, I'm just the messenger—that their swim team is in pretty dismal shape. He was told you were a competitive swimmer and he wondered if you might consider coaching them to victory." Emma was clearly fighting an attack of giggles.

"Oh, wow. Please tell him I'm flattered. Two job offers in one day. But ... uh ... I do have commitments back home. I'd have to think about it." He placed a hand over his heart. "Even if it is an honor to be asked by this wonderful town."

The mayor reached up to slap his shoulder. "*Bene, bene.* You think about it. We know you be right Mister for Todi," he said in strained English. "I must to go. Reporter want to speak me about it." He shook Chris' hand and hustled off.

Chris shook his head. "That was *not* on my 2019 list of New Years' resolutions."

Emma chuckled. "True. But you must be gracious when you become the man of the hour and hometown hero of a town—and country—that aren't even yours." She turned to Madison, who had materialized at her side, offering her a plastic glass of wine. "Take advantage of speaking to our famed fellow guest, before the adoring crowds hoist him up on their shoulders and parade him around town. If you don't mind, I'm off to check on the twins to ensure their heads haven't swelled too much in all the excitement."

"They deserve a bit of head-swelling, Emma. It doesn't happen too often in one's life," said Chris. "I hope you'll let them bask a bit."

Emma nodded. "I will. See you later!" She disappeared into the crowd.

"So, hero of the day. How does it feel to take Todi by storm?"

Chris smiled. "Honestly? Pretty good. It's certainly never anything I expected. And makes a nice addition to my trip. It's going to be hard leaving here, isn't it?"

Madison smiled up at him, and he tried to pretend her face wasn't as beautiful as it appeared to him in that golden afternoon light. Tried to deny that his heart was beating double time because of her closeness. Tried to keep his desire at bay so he wouldn't pull her into his chest and kiss her so passionately that she'd have to fight to come up for air.

Instead, he held up his plastic cup and silently clinked against hers. "Here's to Todi."

"To Todi," Madison said, stepping in closer. "And you're right. It will be awfully hard. Leaving this place."

The crowds surrounded them as Chris and Madison sipped their wine from their plastic cups, the sun warming their faces as they soaked in its heat and the sound of laughter and joyous cheers of the crowds.

SCOTT HAD ARRIVED IN MARK'S OFFICE, and a new round of whiskey was poured.

"Hey, all over town they're talking about your victory," Scott said, as he sat down beside Chris on the couch and held up his glass. "What the hell? I go away a couple of days, and you get all competitive on me."

Chris shook his head. "I'm no soccer coach. Mark just asked me to step in because the coach was away. But we worked them hard in these days. They're a good team."

"I don't doubt it," said Scott, taking a sip from his glass. "But I'd imagine you're a good coach, too. Not all athletes are, but, when you get that combination, it's impressive. Anyway, the mayor knows I'm a former swimmer, too, and he told me he already approached you hoping you could join me coaching the youth team. Whaddaya say? Wake Forest and UVA teaming up ... years later?" He smiled. "It would make a helluva article for our respective alumni magazines."

Chris chuckled. "That it would. But yeah, I told the mayor I'd think it over to be polite. But even if I'm selling my business, I can't just leave the US to move to Italy and become a youth coach."

Scott leaned forward, his arms on his knees. "Yeah, I get that. I was hoping I could sweeten the pot somewhat."

"What do you mean?"

"Well," Scott looked up at Mark, who was seated behind his desk, going through letters.

"Oh, no," Mark felt the eyes on him and held up both hands. "Don't look at me, Scott. He told me his ideas, Chris, but I said to discuss them with you. I'm only here to use the room." He held up his glass. "And as a pourer of whiskey."

Chris felt confused, but then again, the whole day had been hazy. The relaxation of the massage and the time in the sauna with Madison, looking so hot in that bikini. Then the victory and the adulation of the town. Then the coaching offer and more time getting closer to Madison. And now, being dragged into Mark's studio for something they had apparently discussed, and, as usual, he was the only one in the dark. The last thing his confused brain needed was any more alcohol, but he sipped his whiskey anyway.

"So last time, when we met, I told you I was here opening up a university study-abroad program," said Scott.

"Yeah, Lakeview College. I remember."

"Well, things have been moving along fast, because the donor who left us his villa has deep pockets. Yeah, it has to be retrofitted for students, but believe me when I tell you most of these students won't know what's hit them when they come over for their semester abroad. Am I right, Mark?"

"Ha. Definitely. A whole new level of study-abroad luxury."

"A lot of professors will be coming over to teach, and, of course, we get lots of Italian professors from around here for language and culture courses." He placed down his glass and leaned back in the couch. "But we need a lot of graphics work done. And we'll be doing a school newspaper and other outreach projects. We'd love to have a graphic artist with us, maybe someone to teach a class to students, too. I've spoken to the college after our last conversation, and they agree with me. We think that could be you."

"I'm really flattered," Chris shook his head. "Maybe you don't realize, I'm not a graphic artist. I draw. A bit. But I haven't done anything in the past ten years. I'm not up on all the programs, all the changes. How would I teach college students?"

"Chris, we have a budget for continuing studies. I already floated the idea to our home campus, and they approved it. You can catch up on any training you need, but honestly, it would be great to have you onboard early. And, to be frank, I agreed to coaching the swim team and would love to do that with you. We're new in town, and we want to be good neighbors. Not only professors and students who fly in for a semester and then disappear. This would be a good way to show we're a core part of the community. That and a student paper that spotlights activities at the study-abroad center and in town. Since they'll be in English, we'll make them available to the hotels and the tourist center, free of charge. We already spoke to Mark about distributing them here at The Three Coins, too."

"Look, it's a really interesting offer, Scott. I'm just ... a bit overwhelmed today."

Scott swept his hands in front of him. "I get it. Why don't you stop over tomorrow? See the place? We can talk some more."

"Um ... I already have a trip planned. With the other guests. We're headed to Gubbio."

"Oh, you'll love it." He stood and extracted a card from his wallet. "Here are my contacts. Cell, WhatsApp, email are all there. And the address. If you're free on Wednesday, we can make some time. I can show you around."

Chris looked at the card. "Yeah, sure, Scott. That sounds good." Chris stood and shook his hand. "Seriously, thanks for putting such trust in me. I just need a bit more time to consider it."

"Of course." Scott slapped his thighs. "Mark, thanks for the drinks. And the chat. Chris, looking forward to seeing you soon. *Buona notte!*"

Chris slumped down onto the couch, examining the card before looking up at Mark, who had been observing him. "Wow, quite a day. I'm still in a bit of shock from all the events of today. When he threw out the idea last time, I thought he was joking."

Mark stood and walked around the desk, and held up his glass to clink against Chris'. "To the man of the hour. Whose cup is quite literally running over. Take your time. You need to feel it's right for you. But, speaking from strictly personal experience, I can say moving to Umbria was the smartest decision I ever made."

Chris smiled up at him, but inside, his mind was whirling.

CHAPTER 34

Grace

AS PER HABIT, Grace woke early. Yesterday had been a remarkable day. For years, Grace kept her shame locked inside. Hidden from her family. From her friends. In reality, her shame had ensured she had few real friends. She would chat with the other mothers at the school gate or at party drop-offs, but rarely would she take them up on an offer of tea together or a dinner out. It might mean she would have to return the favor, and she could not risk that.

Only later would she fully understand she was an abused wife. Not physically, the only type of abuse she understood. Mental abuse was more understood today then it was when she was young. Richard had manipulated and abused her. The putdowns. The constant humiliation. He made her feel worthless. Cut her off from friends and acquaintances who might lead her to challenge his control. Even at his conferences, she was largely tucked away in their room, ironing his shirts, typing his notes. The other wives were off shopping and sightseeing together, and he would find an excuse why she could not join them. Why had she not had the courage to embarrass him in front of them? Say, *Why yes, I really would love to join you at the Musée d'Orsay. At what time?* How could he possibly get her out of it then? But she knew he'd find a way to make her pay for her rebellion. And so the cycle of abuse continued, with her serving as her own jailer.

But speaking to Heike had felt like a heavy burden was lifted from her chest and she was finally breathing free once again. What was wrong with her for having kept it bottled up inside for so long, even after his death? For the first time since she was a teenager going off to university in the "big city" filled with a young girl's hopes and dreams, the world once more seemed open and exciting. Potentially filled with adventure. Hers for the taking.

And who illustrated that better, after her therapeutic chat with Heike, than her own granddaughter? Grace had been mesmerized watching Kathryn on the pitch. The only girl in the game. In a language and country that were not hers. How she relished cheering for her fearless granddaughter. No man would ever succeed in making Kathryn feel worthless. How proud she was that her granddaughter was a girl who had more courage in her little pinkie than Grace would ever have.

She'd watched Kathryn step it up when Chris gave them their pep talk. That assist to Paolo. And then her own, glorious goal. Even that was a masterpiece. After faking it, Kathryn could have slammed the ball in, but she chose not to. She exerted control, simply tapping it in. A controlled decision that would exert maximum pain and embarrassment on the team, who had to go back to Orvieto after being bested by a girl. Truly glorious.

After the heady celebrations on the square, they'd returned home and Grace had called her daughter. Kathryn had recounted the excitement of the day, something she knew Ellen needed to hear. Grace needed her daughter to support Kathryn when she returned, to appreciate her talents, not to confuse her and humiliate her, as Grace felt her daughter and Rupert had—perhaps unwittingly– done over the past year.

Although it would be difficult, Grace would also need to speak with Ellen eventually. She should still love and cherish her father, he'd been good to her. But she had to understand why Grace could not honor his memory in the same way, and how dangerous it was to be subservient to a man ... the very same trap she'd watched her own daughter falling into.

Now that she was free, Grace could support her daughter in finishing the doctorate in art history she'd been pursuing when she'd met Rupert and left her studies to support him. It was too late for Grace, but not for Ellen. She didn't want her daughter to look back at her own life with the same regrets Grace harbored within.

She rose from bed and showered before waking Kathryn. "Come on, sleepy football star. Let's have some breakfast in you before we head off to Gubbio."

After ensuring Kathryn had risen from bed and was on her way to the shower, Grace slipped down to the dining room to enjoy her first cappuccino of the day.

THE SKY WAS A BRIGHT, ROBIN'S EGG BLUE and cloudless, a perfect day for exploring. Patrizia was accompanying them around town this morning, but had another job this afternoon, so she would drop them off at lunch and then they would have free time to wander, much more slowly than under Patrizia's tutelage, before Ugo returned to pick them up in the evening and return them home.

The hour-long trip had been a quick one, everyone chatty and in a good mood to explore another beautiful hilltown. Ugo's van was full. Heike, Chris, and Madison joined, as did Kathryn and her new shadow. Although he'd been numerous times, Marco was dressed and ready to depart for Gubbio, insisting he was in the mood to see it again. Emma smiled knowingly and exchanged a wink with Grace. Marco and Kathryn were sitting together in the back, heads close over Marco's phone, reviewing game clips friends had recorded and sent. Grace feared their departure on the twenty-seventh would be a shock for Kathryn. She was already annoyed they couldn't stay an extra day for the friendly match against Perugia, but Sundays were move-in days for the new round of guests. And besides, as Grace pointed out to her granddaughter, the plane tickets were already booked and school began again on Monday.

As they reached the city limits, Patrizia pointed out the sign to town. "Here we are—Gubbio. It says, 'The most beautiful medieval city.' It also indicates which cities it is twinned with. Nothing for Austria, I'm afraid. In the US, it's a town in Pennsylvania—Jessup. And there are two UK towns, Huntingdon and Godmanchester."

"Where are those?" said Kathryn, she was tapping away at her phone. "Oh, two towns side-by-side outside of Cambridge." She looked out the window. "Oh, look! How pretty!"

In the distance, white crenellated towers rose high above other buildings, behind that, a dramatic mountain.

"That's Mount Ingino," said Patrizia. "It's not on our itinerary this morning, but if the weather stays fair, you may want to work off your lunch hiking up. There's a pretty church up there, which is important to the Corsa dei Ceri, a big festival I'll explain to you ... and castle ruins, too. There are also great views over town and the surrounding countryside."

Grace met Heike's gaze, and the look they shared made Grace feel confident she would not be the only one politely declining a post-lunch mountain hike. Leave that adventure to the young and energetic.

"Even if you don't opt for Mount Ingino, which, by the way, is lit up like an enormous Christmas tree each December, I should warn you there are still lots of steps up and down the old town."

Grace and Heike groaned.

Patrizia laughed. "But you're all decked out in good shoes. Even you, Madison, so we should be fine. Now, *papà* will find a place to drop us off, and then we can go explore."

Ugo looped down to the lower part of town, and found a spot where he could stop for a few minutes to unload. They all piled out of the car, and Hugo told them to wait for him in the same spot at seven that evening.

Patrizia led them to a spot at the bottom of a set of stairs. Starting to get a feel for these Umbrian medieval towns, Grace suspected it would be the first set of many staircases they would climb to visit the town. Durham was a great walking city, too, but its hills seemed positively mild compared to what she tackled each day on her Umbrian stay.

"Gubbio has very old roots, tracing back to the Bronze Age," said Patrizia as they all gathered around her. "It was settled by the Umbri people. We'll see the famous bronze Iguvine Tablets in the town museum, one of the largest surviving artifacts with Umbrian text in the world. Like most pre-Roman peoples, the Umbri were conquered when it became part of the Roman Empire in the second century BC. The ruins of the Roman theatre are just on the edge of town. But what I'll be showing you today mostly dates back to the Middle Ages, specifically the twelfth to the fourteenth centuries. That is when Gubbio was at the height of its power." She smiled and looked around the group. "So, are we ready to take Gubbio by storm? Upwards and onwards. We'll meet on the square outside of the Palazzo dei Consoli."

Patrizia turned and took the steps two at a time, Marco and Kathryn running right behind her. Chris and Madison were ascending at a fast clip.

Heike and Grace looked at one another.

"Next time," Heike said. "I think I need to find less athletic travel companions."

"I'm with you one hundred percent," agreed Grace.

The two women began the long slog up, enjoying the medieval buildings, the shops, and the crowds.

"When the Ironman training team goes off to hike the mountain," said Heike, examining the shop windows, "you and I can return and do a little shopping."

"That sounds perfect," said Grace, plucking a water bottle from her bag and taking a long sip. "Before we join the others, I just want to thank you again for our talk yesterday. I didn't want to intrude on your time marking Matthias' birthday, but I guess I needed to get it all out."

"I'm so glad you did, Grace. And you have no idea how happy it makes me if speaking about it has made you feel better. Stronger. You've been bottling a lot inside for far too long. It must have felt cathartic to let it out."

Grace nodded. "It did. It really did. I feel so foolish. Letting him manipulate me like that. For so many years. But he's dead and gone. And I know it makes me sound terrible, but he has no power over me anymore." She sighed. "I have a lot I need to change. I want to work part-time. I want to travel. Heck, first off, I want to take the damn train down to London and explore on my own. I've only been with Richard on his conferences. Only seen what he wanted to see." She stopped on a landing, catching her breath and looking at Heike. "Better late than never."

Heike clasped her hand. "It's not late, Grace. You're finally in charge of your own life. That's the important thing. And go out and do what you want now. You have lots of energy to get started." She chuckled. "Just not all concentrated in those legs."

"Very funny. They're way ahead of us, aren't they?"

"Most definitely," agreed Heike. "But we'll get there. We may miss out on a few millennia of history in Patrizia's detailed explanation, but we're *signore di una certa età* now. Our fashionably late arrival will be expected. And they'll need to wait for us before going on."

Grace slung one arm around Heike's shoulder. "Alright, fellow lady of a certain age. Are we ready to tackle this last flight of steps?"

Heike smiled at her, a glint in her eyes. She raised her arms like a sprinter arising from the starting blocks.

The two new friends continued up the steps, slowly but steadily, to meet what awaited them at the top.

CHAPTER 35

Annarita

"WELL, THIS FEELS LIKE OLD TIMES." Annarita peeled potatoes beside Giuseppe, bumping her hip against his. Sebastiano was back home, already nursed and asleep in his crib, Giulia was being fed and told a bedtime story by *nonna*. Annarita glanced at her watch. "No way does she last more than thirty minutes. Forty minutes, tops."

Giuseppe chuckled. "She has been running on adrenaline since yesterday, hasn't she?" He had his beloved Japanese precision knife out and was making quick work of the carrots, slicing them into fine cubes and throwing them into the metal bowl before him.

With the guests away on a trip to Gubbio and no cooking classes scheduled for this evening, Annarita was assisting Giuseppe in the kitchen to prepare a hearty stew that could be warmed and served when the group returned. Annarita had bounced back quickly after Giulia's birth, but she'd been exhausted following the birth of Sebastiano. Everyone had warned her the jump from one to two children meant adjustment time would take longer. It probably didn't help that Sebastiano nursed around the clock, although he was finally settling into longer sleeping rhythms. And she was starting to think returning longer hours to the kitchen and cooking classes this summer during the busy tourist season might be doable.

Annarita missed regular contact with the guests, the fun of leading those cooking classes. She'd started getting her feet wet this week, but having Heike there, an experienced chef and an English and Italian speaker, had meant that getting her feet wet these past two weeks had, in actuality, only been dipping one toe cautiously into the water.

Annarita chucked. "Adrenaline? Giulia is a full-blown Kathryn Fan Girl. She was crazy at the match. Screaming and cheering, waving her scarf in the air. Good news is ... you know how she never wanted to respond to me in English? Well, now that she knows Kathryn doesn't speak any Italian, she's switched. Says she needs to improve her English with me." Annarita shook her head. "Oh, and she says she also wants to play on the soccer team when she's bigger. I made an executive decision. I said okay, but only after she learns to swim and passes all the levels."

"*Menomale*. We're on the same page. I told her the same." He finished cutting the carrots and went to check on the chicken stock gently boiling on the stove in one of their Chinese army-sized pots.

"It will be nice having you back here with me, but I want you to have as much time as you need with Sebastiano." He turned back to her as he stirred. "We know from experience how quickly that time passes."

"True. You know, I have no idea at all how Concetta does it. Has such a big family." Her sister had called to share the news that they were expecting their seventh, although she had promised—once again—this would be the last. Of course, Concetta had started much younger, and Annarita felt fortunate they had been able to have two. She left the potatoes, laid her knife on the chopping board and came over to Giuseppe's side to plant a kiss on his cheek.

Giuseppe smiled. "What was that for?"

Annarita slipped her arms around his robust waist. "Just to show you how much I love you. How happy I am with our little family life. Our joint professional life."

Giuseppe kissed her on the top of her head. "I'm the lucky one. I didn't think I could find love twice in one lifetime." He stroked her cheek. "I'm happy to have been proved wrong. You, Giulia and Sebastiano have filled my life with joy."

"You know ... it's not that often we have two kids asleep and no guests to serve ..."

"Are you thinking what I'm thinking?"

"Let's hurry up with this soup. The faster we wrap it up, the faster we can hurry home and get to bed."

Giuseppe grinned. "If that's not incentive for a chef, I don't know what is. *Sbrigiamoci ...*"

CHAPTER 36

Madison

THE DAY WAS PERFECT. Following Patrizia's lead, they'd trouped all over Gubbio, admired its picturesque buildings, visited its churches and museums, learned its history. If you squinted your eyes and blocked out the tourists in their brightly colored T-shirts, you really could believe you were back in medieval times.

Patrizia was truly a master at her work. Honestly, Madison's eyes generally glazed over with long, historical explanations, but Patrizia had a way of pulling you in and making you feel a part of it. She'd even managed to make Madison anxious to hear more about the battles and plight of the Guelphs and Ghibellines, let alone to finally understand what those long-ago factions were all about. And now she knew that the Guelphs—and Gubbio—were aligned with the Papacy. She smiled at the thought of slipping that random, newfound knowledge into cocktail-hour chatter back in Columbus.

After cramming a day's worth of sightseeing into a breakneck morning tour, Patrizia had taken her leave after depositing them in an *osteria*, where she had reserved them a table for lunch. Now they all sat, bellies full, the detritus of their lunch around them.

"That was fantastic," said Heike. "And I say this having run a restaurant for years. Every dish was perfect."

"Can't but agree with you, Heike," said Chris, beside her, patting his firm stomach. "No way will I be eating like this back home. You have no idea how much I'm going to miss pasta in wild boar sauce, and wild boar sausages."

They all laughed. The waitress returned to clear up the table and to hear the compliments on the food. As she dictated the dessert menu, shouts went out from all around the table. When the waitress arrived at Madison, she groaned. "No space, but I'll have a *caffè macchiato* while they're enjoying their desserts."

"Are you sure?" asked Chris, before looking at the waitress. "Please bring an extra spoon with mine. I'll try to convince her."

Truth be told—and it isn't something she would have told anyone—Madison had had an uncomfortable relationship with food over the past years. While it was true the camera added pounds and she wanted to stay slim, eating as little as possible had become a badge of honor for her recently. Her diet consisted almost entirely of salads, fruit, and the occasional lean chicken or salmon. Before this holiday, when was the last time she'd consumed pasta? She even recalled vowing not to let any pass her lips during her holiday. Had stuck to that rule at the outset. And yet, once she'd joined the group, started cooking classes, she'd eaten along with the rest of them. And the sky hadn't fallen. True, she'd never walked and hiked up hilltown slopes as much as she had in these days, which probably explained why she wasn't putting on weight. Could this healthier relationship with food accompany her home? There was no way she could prepare elaborate meals daily, but maybe she could replicate some of the recipes on weekends when back.

"So," said Chris. "We still have some time this afternoon before we need to get back and meet Ugo. And the weather's still perfect. Anyone up for climbing up the mountain to Sant'Ubaldo and the castle ruins?"

On the far edge of the table, Kathryn and Marco both nodded enthusiastically. Madison thought it was adorable that, be it the bus, the lunch table, or when they were walking around town, they always found excuses to be together, their hands brushing. During lunch, they'd been holding hands under the table, thinking no one noticed. It wasn't that long ago that Madison had been a pre-teen doing the same thing. Well, honestly, that *had* been a long time ago. But she still remembered it as if it were yesterday.

Back then, she assumed life would be filled with intriguing boys and then men who made her heart thrum in double time. Those stolen touches under the table, eyes that lit up when they gazed on her, a warm hand on hers that convinced her she was the most special girl in the room. Sadly, that had not been the case for many years now, and, as she became increasingly jaded, she wondered if she'd ever feel that way again.

"Hey, Madison."

Chris placed a warm hand on her exposed forearm, and Madison felt a long-dormant spark. Unbidden, her heart beat in double time. *Foolish girl*, she thought. *He just startled you.*

"What do you say to a little hike? The view's supposed to be fabulous."

She paused before responding. His blue eyes were sparkling. His high cheekbones and chiseled face were exactly what she loved in a man. To say nothing about his height and athletic build. More than that, he was kind. Good with kids. And fun. What was wrong with her? It was a simple question, and she stayed silent like a simpleton.

"Yeah, sure," she croaked.

"Makes a difference when you have the right shoes. Right, Madison?" Heike said from the other side of the table. "Grace and I were with her when she finally decided to give a rest to those vertiginous heels and buy something practical."

"True," laughed Madison, looking down at her trusty, smart-casual sneakers. "I have gotten a lot of use out of these shoes in the hilltowns."

"Good, so you're kitted out for our walk," said Chris, before turning to Grace and Heike. "Ladies, care to join us?"

"Heavens, no!" cried Grace. "Heike and I already discussed this. We are feeling our years, and we decided to do some quiet shopping and wander Gubbio's lower levels, while you young people take off on your exhausting adventure."

"I second that. We spotted a charming little bookshop and some clothing shops we'd like to see, so we won't slow you all down on your hike."

"Are you sure?" Chris asked, sounding disappointed.

"Absolutely," said Grace, nodding over at Kathryn and Marco and lowering her voice. "And I suspect our lovebirds will enjoy some time alone. But you will keep an eye on them, won't you Chris?"

He smiled. "Of course I will."

"So it's settled then. As long as everyone is back at our meet-up point a bit before seven."

They paid their bill and exited together, with one group heading up for the trail, while Grace and Heike laughed about how grateful they were to take the easier steps down to the lower town, allowing their leg muscles some blessed time to recuperate.

THE GROUP OF FOUR WALKED UP the well-worn path together, stopping to admire the views over the medieval town. It was obvious Kathryn and Marco wanted to be on their own, so Madison and Chris feigned exhaustion and told them to run on ahead. Honestly, only Chris had to feign exhaustion. For Madison, it was real. Her leg muscles groaned as they ascended the mountaintop. Giving herself the benefit of doubt, the huge meal may not have aided her mountain-scaling abilities.

As they walked up, Chris offered his arm, and she gratefully slipped her arm under his, allowing herself to be gently dragged along, even if her calves and quadriceps were still burning.

"So, Emma mentioned something about job offers flooding in for you," said Madison. "Not just the coaching offer I witnessed firsthand. But university professor, too? Does this always happen to you when you're on vacation?"

Chris chuckled. "Word travels fast. Actually, this is a big coincidence. The coordinator of this study-abroad program was in my sports conference back in my swimming days. So he kind of knows me."

"That is a coincidence. And he's in Todi, too?"

"Yeah. It's a new study-abroad program. Lakeview University. The first semester abroad students will arrive in the late summer, so they want someone on board for setup. And eventually teaching graphic design."

"How do you feel about that?"

"Hard to say." Chris sighed. "Obviously, it was so unexpected. I used to love graphic design, but it's been a whole decade since I've done it. I'd need to catch up on all I've missed. Don't know if you can teach an old dog new tricks."

"You're hardly old."

"Depends on the day." Chris smiled. "Anyway, Mark says I'll be blown away by the place. The alum donated an amazing villa. And all the money needed for it to be adapted to a university structure, plus operating fees. Mark says I should at least go there to see what I think."

"Hmmm. And is there a part of you that can picture yourself staying in Italy?"

Chris looked at her, and those blue eyes had that same tempting sparkle.

"It's a good question. I mean, how can I really judge? I've been here a week and a half." He tugged her arm closer. "An amazing week and a half, but how can one judge from a holiday if you really see yourself staying long-term? But, on the other hand, I did want a change. I'm selling my consultancy, and that's moving forward. Maybe a break—starting something new— would be good for me. Even if I don't like it, I stay for a year, maybe two. Shake up my resumé, and then return home. Plus I have all this great food and wine. Learn Italian. Travel. It's honestly tempting."

"Hell yeah, it's tempting. Where do I sign up? Do they need journalism instructors, too?"

Chris broke out in a wide grin. "As it turns out, they do. Part of what I'd be doing on the graphics—and why I need to brush up on InDesign—is helping organize a student-run school newspaper. It would actually be broader. They want to give back to the community. Cover events at the school, but also Todi and surroundings. Have them at the visitor's center and local hotels. The Three Coins Inn, too. So, you see. I could use a colleague who actually knows journalism to get those articles between the spectacular design I'll set up."

She laughed. She looked up and caught his gaze. Instead of the joking exterior she'd expected, he was studying her carefully. But he must be joking. She cracked a smile. "Yeah, well, if salary negotiations don't go the way I want, I might just take you up on that."

They kept walking up the path. Madison hadn't heard a peep out of Rita since that ill-fated call. True, she'd finally started having a good time here. Meeting her fellow guests. Enjoying being beside such a handsome man like Chris. A little harmless flirtation could help dust off the old, battered ego. But *should* she be worried at the radio silence? She was headed home on Saturday, and still no news about what she would be expected to find there.

"Here we are," said Chris.

To her surprise, she saw they had reached the top. Marco and Kathryn had climbed the ruin of the castle tower and were waving down. It didn't look incredibly stable, but if there were guardrails and steps, it must be meant for visitors to climb. Chris was already on his way up, dragging out his cellphone. At the top, he said. "Okay, photo of my two favorite soccer stars, with all of Gubbio beneath them." He clicked away. Marco and Kathryn needed no excuse to squeeze together.

Madison reached the top and Chris smiled. "Okay, group photo. Young and old together." He winked at Madison.

They all squeezed together for the selfie clicks.

"Now we have proof for your mom and grandma that we did actually make it up here to the castle." He looked around him. "Although, honestly, it's not much of a castle. I know I'm spoiled after all the amazing things we've seen, but I think the San Ubaldo church we left for the way back is going to be more exciting than this ... even if the view from up here is impressive."

"Yeah, Chris. We were talking. I don't think we're up for another church," said Marco.

"But don't you want to see the Saint's statue they run up from town to Saint Ubaldo each year on Saint Ubaldo Day? It's supposed to be over 600 pounds. That would make a pretty cool soccer training workout." Chris winked at them.

"Funny," said Marco. "But no. We had all our history this morning with Patrizia. From up here," he pointed in the distance, "we saw a soccer pitch and kids playing on it. We want to head down there."

Chris made a face. "But will you get back to the van on time? Do you know where the pickup place is? Kathryn, I promised your grandma I'd keep an eye on you."

Marco made a face that foreshadowed the teenage years just around the bend. "You're forgetting I speak Italian a lot better than all of you. I'll have no problem finding our way back, or asking directions, if needed. And Gubbio's not exactly a big, dangerous city. We can handle it, Chris."

Madison stifled a giggle as Chris tried to hide his shock.

"Thanks, Chris," said Kathryn, touching his arm. "We'll be fine, and we'll stick together. Sorry—we just agreed we can't handle another church." She smiled. "Plus, it's a chance for you two to enjoy some time together."

"Yeah, sure," said Chris. "But take care. Be careful."

"We will!" said Marco and Kathryn, in unison, as they scrambled down the steps and ran away before any adult could change his or her mind.

Madison waited until they were safely out of earshot and then she broke out in the laughter she'd been holding in. "Oh ... my ... God!" She sucked in breath after each word. "They couldn't get away fast enough."

"I know! It's the first time I feel sorry for the elderly aunts and uncles I was always trying to escape from when I was a kid." He looked out over the panorama. "I dunno. I'm a bit scared now. If I suggest visiting Sant'Ubaldo, are you going to take off running away from me, too?"

"Ha. You may have better luck with me—since you'll be able to outrun me in no time."

THE BASILICA WAS SURPISINGLY large. They entered though the grand courtyard and walked into the darker interior. The glass sarcophagus of Sant'Ubaldo, the twelfth-century bishop who served as Gubbio's patron saint, took pride of place. They looked at the heavy statue that was heaved through the streets of Gubbio and run up by a team of costumed men decked out in golden-colored, medieval finery to this very basilica.

"Each May fifteenth, it says. Sant'Ubaldo Day," said Chris, reading the placard. "If I'm still here, I'll have to come see it."

"Rubbing it in, I see."

"Well, I can't really miss a sporting event. One with medieval roots. You see, it's a competition between three medieval guilds. Those racing with the Ubaldo statue are the masons, dressed in gold. The merchants wear blue and carry Saint George. And the peasants wear black and carry Saint Anthony. The statues are called *ceri*. That's why it's called the *Corsa dei Ceri*."

"It really does sound amazing. And I only missed it by a few weeks."

"Unless you come back and teach journalism in Todi." Chris winked.

Madison shook her head. "Hmm. Today I have ticked all the boxes on learning about the history and culture of Gubbio. I've eaten a huge lunch of local specialties. And I even got hiking in ... and believe me, my legs are feeling it." She rubbed her sore quadriceps. "I saw a café over on the edge of the basilica, with views over town. What do you say to a nice stop-off there ... and maybe an *aperitivo* .... before we start the hike down?"

Chris placed one hand on her shoulder. "That's a brilliant idea. Wish I'd thought of that myself."

They exited the church and crossed the courtyard on their way to the café. From the terrace they had clear views over the town. When the waitress arrived, they both ordered Aperol spritzes like experts.

When the drinks arrived at the table, they picked them up to clink them gently.

"*Salute*," they both said in unison.

Madison laughed. "Listen to us, sounding like a pair of locals."

"True, but a solid week and a half of nonstop eating and drinking will do that to one."

"*Touché.*"

"Life's weird sometimes." Chris said, looking out on the landscape unfurled beneath them. "This holiday. All we've seen and learned. The recipes I now know how to cook, which has just upped my repertoire by about a thousandfold." He grinned.

"You and me both," said Madison, before taking a sip of her drink.

"And this fabulous rapport that's developed between all of us, the Three Coins guests. I wasn't expecting that."

"It's a nice group, isn't it?" Madison agreed. "It probably helped that you ingratiated yourself to both management and fellow guests by coaching their kids and grandkids to never-before-seen heights of soccer victory. Thereby practically making you a local hero worthy of the keys to the city."

Chris laughed. "You exaggerate slightly." He sipped his drink. "That said, it was fun. The kids are great." He tilted his head. "Except, you know, for being unceremoniously dumped by my two star players back there." He nodded in the general direction of the peak they had left.

"Yeah, well. First love can do that to kids." She swept a hand through her hair. "Even those far beyond childhood years. Those who should know better."

"Speaking of that." Chris leaned in. "Earlier, you broke my train of thought. As I was reflecting on all the unexpected surprises of this past week and a half, I also wanted to mention meeting and getting to know you."

Madison was ready to respond with a quip, but as she sipped her drink and caught his gaze, she sensed Chris was serious.

"I hope I'm not speaking out of turn," he continued. "But I've really enjoyed getting to know you, Madison. I wasn't expecting it, but I feel there's a spark. I hope I'm not imagining it." He paused.

Madison could feel the blood coursing through her body. Her heart, already racing from the earlier exercise, was sprinting along at double pace now.

Chris sighed. "As I'm met with silence, I realize the feeling might not be mutual. Or the sentiments welcomed." He shook his head and swept one hand over the view below. "I can only blame my outburst on this ridiculously romantic backdrop." He raised his glass. "And these jewel-like drinks that light up under the sun and set the scene. I'm sorry, Madison. I didn't mean to make you uneasy."

She placed her hand on his wrist, where his rolled-up shirt had fallen away. His skin felt warm to her touch. Set off a spark that reached her heart. "You didn't make me uneasy, Chris. It came as a surprise, yes. But that doesn't mean I haven't been developing feelings for you."

He looked down at her hand, then up into her eyes, before slipping one large hand over hers. "Wow. Now I'm glad those two little brats took off and deserted us."

She laughed.

He held up his glass. "Shall I impress you and order us two more with my spectacular Italian?"

"*Per favore*. But don't go getting a big head about it, now that you're considering becoming a local."

"Hardly." He called the waitress over and gave his order. She cleared their glasses away. He reached in his back pocket. "Oh, shit!"

Madison saw the panic in his face. He stood, patting down his pockets.

"What's wrong?" she asked.

"Damn. It's my wallet." He slumped back into his seat, closing his eyes and rubbing his temples. "The last place I had it was the restaurant. I took it out to pay. And I seriously *left it there*? How could I be such an idiot?"

"Don't be so hard on yourself. It was chaotic and we were all debating what to do next."

He grabbed her hand. "Madison, don't be angry, but I need to run down there to see if they have it. I am so screwed if they don't. My driver's license, credit cards, ATM are all inside. Do you mind? I'll sprint down and back, and be back in a jiffy. Ideally with my wallet. Are you okay?"

"Yeah, sure. Go ahead, Chris. I'll keep guard over our drinks when they arrive."

He smiled and leaned over the table, planting a warm kiss on her cheek. To her shame, she felt a blush blossoming on the spot.

"Hurry now. Or I may just drink them both. Or invite some handsome Italian over to help me."

He squeezed her shoulder. "Please do not do that. I'll be fast. Promise."

No sooner had he left than their drinks arrived. *Because of course they did*, thought Madison. She smiled at the waitress as she placed them down. Sitting back in her seat, she felt the afternoon sun caressing her face and breathed in deeply. Wow, Chris. If she were honest, she had felt something in the past days. How could a girl not? He was gorgeous. And funny. And someone who could, without even trying, turn himself into a hero. But the last days into a two-week holiday? Did she need this complication? She should wait for his return, but her sparkling drink beckoned. She took a sip and felt her nerves calm. A bit of romance—even of the star-crossed variety— never did a girl any harm. And he still had to decide if he'd truly stay in Italy. Maybe he'd hate the place when he went. And who knew, she may get hired in a small Virginia market. It would certainly be better than Ohio. She sighed and looked over the countryside, bathed in an otherworldly golden light, because this was Italy, and beauty and romance went hand in hand.

An unfamiliar ringtone exploded in her ear. She looked down and saw the cellphone on the table, vibrating. Damn, Chris must have left the phone here as he was running off. She took another sip of her drink. "Kaitlyn," the screen display announced. She watched it vibrate with each ring, until it stopped.

She looked around the terrace, at all the families and couples sitting and enjoying their drinks. Like her, enjoying a day out in Gubbio in this glorious spring weather. She looked down at her watch. Still a little over an hour before Ugo would be back to pick them up for the drive back, a light supper, and maybe some time to chat privately with Chris over the crackling fire?

Her train of thought was interrupted by the annoying ringtone once more. She startled, then noticed disgruntled customers at the tables around her, clearly wondering why she didn't answer it. Or at least lower the thunderously loud ringtone. And honestly, it was grating.

On the screen, "Kaitlyn" was once more displayed. Why did she call twice in such close succession? What if it were an emergency? A sister, a colleague, desperately trying to get through to Chris. After another man at a nearby table shot silent daggers with his stare, she plucked up the phone and responded, quietly.

"Hello. Chris' phone."

There was silence on the other end, then an angry voice. "Who the hell are you?"

Madison turned away from the nearby tables, looking out in the distance. "I'm a friend of Chris. He isn't here, but I'll have him call you back. Kaitlyn, is it?"

"This is un-freaking-believable. Do you even know who I am?"

The silence stretched on.

"This is Kaitlyn. As in, Kaitlyn His Wife. Bet he forgot to mention that to you. Or maybe he did and you're the type who doesn't care."

Madison's free hand was shaking. She placed it on her lap and tried to remember how to breathe. In-out-in-out.

"Are you there?"

Madison rubbed her hand over her face. This couldn't be happening. Not a second time. He was *married*? Of course he was. They always were. It didn't matter how nice they appeared to be. And now his wife was on the line, trying to make her feel like a slut. Again.

"I said, are you still there? What's your name? I'm guessing you're young and blond. That's how Chris likes them. But don't forget, I'll still be here when his little Italian fun is over. Is it nice to be the local slut?"

No. She wasn't starting with this again. Without another word she ended the call, gazing around wildly. She waved the waitress over. "I'd like to pay. I need to go." The waitress took her euro bills. "I'm sorry, but my friend will be returning here. Could you please hang on to the phone until he returns? Tall guy. Broad shoulders. Blond hair."

"*Certamente*," said the waitress, placing the cellphone in her apron pocket.

Madison looked around, confused. She couldn't risk taking the same path down, bumping into him. She was too upset. She turned back to the waitress. "Will this path to the right get me back down to the lower town, too?"

The waitress nodded. "*Sì*. Is longer. It take more time to go down long steps, but it get you to low town."

"*Grazie*," said Madison, rushing away. She pressed another large bill into the young woman's hand and raced away from the terrace.

Her chest burned with anger and humiliation, but she refused to cry. No man would put her through that again. Least of all, yet another married player, intent on having his fun at her expense. Let Kaitlyn suffer with him. She was done.

CHAPTER 37

Heike

"THANK YOU FOR COMING WITH ME," said Heike. "But I feel terrible taking you away from your granddaughter with only a few days left."

Grace shook her head and took a sip of her cappuccino. "Are you kidding? Kathryn is off playing football this morning, then going to the birthday party of a new friend on the team, a classmate of Marco and Valerio's. Laser tag or some such nonsense. She'll be having the time of her life, and the last thing she'll want is her grandmum tagging along." She placed down her cup. "And this was too perfect to pass up."

"It means a lot to me to have you here. Matthias and I always wanted to come here together. This is what we planned when we decided on this Umbria trip. Assisi and the San Francesco basilica. Giotto's frescoes. With all the other trips, this was the only day Ugo could manage. I would have come alone, but I'm so pleased you agreed to join me."

"I have to admit back-to-back trips wear me out a bit, but I wouldn't miss seeing Assisi. And it's nice to spend some time alone together. What with Kathryn having other plans, and Chris off to see this university program that offered him a job. And then ..." Grace took another sip of her cappuccino. "I imagine I'm not the only one who noticed the tension between Madison and Chris yesterday. They sat on opposite ends of the bus. Barely spoke to one another. Then Madison skipped out on dinner and I saw her on the way to the spa today. Said she had the whole day booked. I didn't see that coming. Did you?"

"Not one bit. All morning in Gubbio and at lunch, I thought they were lovebirds. I had no idea they wouldn't be talking by day's end."

"Kathryn doesn't get it either. She said they all went up to the castle together. Here." Grace flipped through her phone and found the photo Chris had sent her and Kathryn. All four of them on a tower, Gubbio and the countryside behind them, far below. "Do they look like they hate one another there?"

Heike shook her head. "Not at all. But who understands young people today? My grandchildren seem to break up with their respective boyfriends and girlfriends all the time. I don't bother learning names anymore unless I've met them at least three times." She chuckled. "It almost never comes to that."

Heike called the waitress over and ordered another cappuccino. "I'm sorry," she said to Grace. "I slept poorly. Would you like anything else?"

"Go on, twist my arm. I'll join you in cappuccino gluttony. Won't have that chance much longer."

"*Due cappuccini, per piacere*," Heike said.

"Why did you sleep poorly?"

"I had a late-night chat with my daughter."

"Oh."

"Yes, it wasn't so pleasant. It was a second attempt. She asked for more money. For the restaurant. I said I already gave her too much. And it's been lost. She said she would have to take some of the money out of the college accounts for my grandson and granddaughter. It's true they'll most likely study in Vienna and won't have to worry about expenses. But Matthias and I scrimped and saved to put that money away for them so they could study abroad, or have a whole year in the US, a gap year, if they wanted."

"Oh, I can understand that must be upsetting."

Their cappuccini arrived and they waited while the waitress set them down.

"The worst was, I had to explain to Anneliese that her husband would simply lose their children's money, too. That their idea for a restaurant would never work. They have chased away all our regular clients and gained very few new ones." Heike shook her head. "I reminded her they took over the management of the restaurant, but that I was still the owner. I gave her two options. Either we sell it outright, and I'll give them a small portion of the sale. Or we go back to the original formula—maybe with a modern twist."

Grace sipped from her cappuccino. "What kind of modern twist?"

"Well, I was so upset when they got rid of all the Alpine furniture. You see, my father-in-law was a *Schreiner* ... I mean, a carpenter. My brother-in-law, too." Heike plucked the sleeve of her jacket. "It was probably too close to the funeral, and it hit me the wrong way. But maybe it was a bit dated. We could have more modern furniture in an Alpine theme. My nephews in Tirol are also carpenters. We could give them business and also get a discount. I suggested we can offer the classics on the menu, but also specials. I know my son-in-law likes Asian cuisine. When he's not insisting on fusion, he's actually quite good at it. I suggested we could have Asian special plates on the weekend. Maybe even some of the Italian dishes we've been learning here."

"Oh, that's wonderful!" said Grace. "So that means when I come to visit you in Vienna I can enjoy Schnitzl and Apfelstrudel and pasta in wild boar sauce?"

"We call in *Wildschwein*, but yes, you can. Plus, Giuseppe gave me another great idea. He says they have a lot of well-traveled Italian and European tourists. He said he'd be happy to mention my restaurant for those going to Vienna. Maybe have some of my flyers on hand. And he suggested to me dedicating one evening a week to cooking classes. Bilingual, in German and English. He said they could promote our Viennese cooking, and we would do the same for those thinking of a holiday in Umbria."

Grace clapped her hands together. "That's an amazing idea!"

"Of course, it might take time to build up tourists stopping through, but Anneliese and Hans know a lot of younger people who don't cook anymore. We would also advertise through the local parish. The traditional recipes weren't handed down in some families, so they'll happily come to learn from us. Anneliese said it could be a fun night out for young people wanting to make acquaintaces. Cooking, eating and drinking together." Heike felt her cheeks grown pink. "And Giuseppe says I have a natural talent for cooking classes. I don't know how he can tell when I was only translating for him ..."

"Heike, you are being far too modest. You were wonderful with all of us. So patient and excited to see our progress. I agree, that can't be taught. You do have a natural talent."

Heike shook her head. "Anyway, Anneliese said it didn't sound like a horrible idea. That she would speak to her husband and we could discuss it together when I return."

Grace smiled. "And how do you feel about going back to work?"

Heike sighed. "I feel good. Matthias and I dreamed about working less. Retiring. But losing him, and then having everything that was familiar taken away at the same time. It was all too much. I spent too much time alone. Lost track of friends and neighbors. Then Anneliese and Hans were struggling. It hasn't been an easy time for any of us. But I think this will work."

"I'm so pleased for you."

"That doesn't mean I won't ever travel. Once we get things back on track, my daughter and son-in-law will be able to take over for me, and I for them, for holidays and breaks. I want to come to Durham. And I hope you'll come to see me in Vienna. And I've already told Emma and Mark I want to return to Todi."

"Oh, let's plan that return together!"

"I'd love that, Grace." She lifted her ceramic cup and clinked it against that of her new friend. "Now, let's finish these drinks. Giotto is awaiting us."

CHAPTER 38

Chris

"I DON'T KNOW WHAT TO SAY. This would be my suite?"

"Yup," said Scott. "Pretty sweet, isn't it? The student dorm rooms are simpler—but still a whole other level from what they're used to back on campus, but the professors have mini-suites, including those who are based here full time. That would be you, me, some admin staff—they have these somewhat larger suites with kitchenettes. Of course, there will be dinner service here, so you could also eat here when classes are in session. Oh, and by the way, any interest from the fellow guest you mentioned? The journalist? I'm sure I could make the case for someone to run the paper and comms classes here. We don't have the capacity on campus to send someone over right away."

"Ah, yeah. No, not looking that way. She needs to get back to her job."

"A shame, that. Will keep looking."

Chris stepped out onto the balcony, directly above the backyard pool that would be in use in a few weeks. This was a large property, already kitted out with tennis courts, a soccer field, and trails through the countryside for jogging. Beyond, up on the hill, was Todi, displaying its medieval splendor. It was a different angle from the now familiar views at The Three Coins Inn, but equally spectacular.

Living and working in the same place could become a bit claustrophobic, but it would cut back on expenses and be a great way to set aside money. Plus, weekends and more generous academic holiday schedules were all his to travel or spend time as he wanted. And he could join Scott in coaching the local swim team, even help Mark out with soccer occasionally. Scott made it clear they wanted faculty to spend time with community activities, needed to show they were an important part of the community fabric. Scott even competed with a Masters swim team—he'd helped add points to Todi's roster. He said if Chris joined, too, the team would be thrilled. They travelled around Italy on weekends, competing in meets. It was a great way to meet people locally, too. To learn Italian.

Standing here in this beautiful building, Chris couldn't help picturing himself constructing a new life for himself. What better way to break away from his old life than starting fresh in a new country across the ocean? Returning home, he'd need to see through the divorce, the sales of the house and the business, and then send out resumés or begin the long slog of opening a new company. Yet, he had no desire to jump back into consulting right away. A new challenge at the university would give him the chance to separate himself from his old life, while also requiring him to tackle a new learning curve, make new friends, learn a new language.

The more he thought about it, the more convinced he became.

"Look," said Scott, stepping out on the balcony. "I know it's a lot to take in, and I've ambushed you in your last days in

Italy. I have a proposal. Why don't you extend your holiday by a week, maybe two? Check out on Saturday, as you planned, and come test-run this room." Scott looked back at the suite. "I can introduce you to some of the skeleton staff here and we can videoconference with some of the administration back on the main campus, so you know them better. We can also talk about the graphic design training you might need to be prepared. We'll find out how to get that to you between now and end of August, when the semester begins. I can also introduce you to some of our Italian collaborators here in the area and, if you want, you can come up to one of my swim practices to meet the Masters team." He grinned. "Big, generous move on my side because right now they think I'm amazing. If you've still got it, you might cast some shadow my way, so I hope you appreciate what a generous offer I'm making." He laughed.

"Wow, that would be great. It's hard to make a decision on such short notice, but a week or two here would give me a little more time to concentrate on the work and if we'd be a good fit." He frowned. "What if I decide it's not the right fit?"

"No hard feelings. I promise. Listen, my grandparents are Italian and I've always wanted to come live here. They were from Perugia—so not far away. But I get it's not for everyone. What do you say. Shake on it?"

Chris offered his hand, still shocked at how quickly things were moving. But he knew he'd regret not giving it a chance and keeping an open mind. He grinned as he shook Scott's hand.

An extra two weeks in Todi.

"HEY, LOOK AT YOU TWO hanging out at the fountain, not a care in the world."

Emma laughed. "Sadly, we have a few too many cares, which is why we're here having a coffee, pretending they don't exist. A plumber was just here to fix a leaky pipe. And Mark just adjusted the chicken coop—again—after some loose boards from the last adjustment collapsed and our chickens escaped." She sipped her espresso. "Needed this more than ever. Care to join us?"

"Sure. Thanks," said Chris, pulling out a chair and sinking into it. The fountain gurgled before him. He remembered this being his first glimpse of the inn a little over a week ago. How time had flown.

"So how was your time at the new university? As luxurious inside as I saw from the original plans?" asked Mark.

Chris whistled. "You weren't kidding. They've pulled out all the stops there."

"Bankrolled rather generously by a benefactor with deep pockets," said Mark. "But it's a nice addition to town. Todi's happy to have them. It'll add a lot to the economy. A lot of students who'll spend many nights in town, with parents and relatives who'll visit them and fill up hotels. And town coffers. And they'll offer some seminars, Model UN and the like for local high school students. Seems like a win-win all around." Mark drained his cup and fixed Chris with a sharp gaze. "Will you be a part of it?"

Chris laughed. "Right to the point, I see. I might be. Scott suggested I stay on a week or two in Todi. On Saturday, I'll move over there, probably for two weeks, and give it a try. Seems a good solution because it's all happening a bit suddenly, and I'd like to have a better idea before I make a decision."

"That makes a lot of sense," said Emma. "We'd love having you as a neighbor, but I'm pleased you can give it a test run first."

"Great news, Chris." Mark gathered up the cups. "Sorry to run, but the electrician is stopping by for another needed fix. The fun never ends for an innkeeper. Let's talk later."

Mark left and Emma and Chris sat in silence, listening to the gurgling water rushing over marble.

Emma sighed. "I have a million things to do, but sometimes I need to recharge here."

"Yeah, I get it. We're a lot of work." He smiled.

"But pleasurable work. Chris, I hope you won't think me overstepping, but I had a chat with Madison today."

Chris' head snapped up. He tried to keep anger from clouding his face.

"She was ... well, rather upset upon learning you had a wife."

"Soon-to-be ex-wife," interjected Chris, a bit more stridently than he'd intended.

"True," said Emma. "But she obviously didn't know that. She felt you'd lied to her. Or deliberately kept pertinent information from her."

Chris began to tap his foot angrily. "I may not have been completely open with her. But Madison seems to have a lot of information she doesn't share either. A simple Google search revealed she's not hiding out for a better contract with a higher salary, as she's been claiming. She's hiding out after sleeping with her married producer. And escaping the on-air meltdown of his wife taking it up with his mistress. I'd say she wasn't sharing pertinent information with me, either."

"It's not my place to intrude," said Emma gently, "but you may both be jumping to hasty conclusions, with only partial information. I told her that myself today. I hope you won't be angry with me, but I told her you discovered your wife cheating and were in the middle of a divorce. I made her swear not to tell anyone else. But I also think it's only fair I told you that Madison thought her producer was single. He asked her out and never made any mention of his family. She learned that little nugget while being made a fool of live on air, and, well, you know the rest. I might add that the cheating husband seems to be emerging from the scandal much better than the single reporter who had no clue." She slapped her legs and stood up.

"Again, I would ask you not to share that information more widely. Of course, it's none of my business. But I hate to have two guests thinking poorly of one another, especially when they are basing that judgment on false assumptions." She sighed. "And especially when they seemed to be getting along so well."

Chris looked up and caught her eye.

"I'm not generally meddlesome, Chris. Let's just say, I speak from experience. Well now, this break has been lovely, but I need to get back to work." She began walking and turned her head back for a moment. "Oh, I forgot. Apropos of absolutely nothing, Madison did mention to me that she was going up to town to climb the San Fortunato belltower." Emma looked at her watch. "I believe it reopens at three p.m. Also apropos of nothing, were a fit, young man to hightail it up to town, he would probably find her sitting on the stairs of San Fortunato, waiting for the opening. *Ciao*, Chris." She winked at him and walked back to the inn.

Chris shook his head as he watched the water course over the nymphs' heads as it rushed into the basin. The birds tweeted from the branches above. Chris closed his eyes and took a deep breath.

CHRIS PRIDED HIMSELF ON STAYING IN SHAPE, but even he was proud of the speed with which he ran up the steep hills leading up to town. This time in Umbria had toughened him up, certainly when it came to hills.

He wound through the twisting streets of Todi, waving to now familiar faces—kids on his team and their parents. But he motioned to them he was in a hurry. Now wasn't the time to stop and talk when he had an end goal in mind. He continued briskly to his destination, scanned the multidirectional stairs leading up to San Fortunato. There were people sitting there— chatting or drinking from their water bottles. One harried mother tried to keep her three charges still with snacks, as she attempted to type out a text message. But Madison was clearly not among those waiting on the steps.

Looking up to the fifteenth-century church's unfinished façade, Chris noted with disappointment that the doors were open. He glanced down at his watch. Damn, he wasted time sitting before that fountain at the inn contemplating what he wanted to do for too long, rather than going out and being decisive. The church had opened and Madison must have gone immediately to the belltower. He looked up at that iconic tower that had been their view all this time down at the inn. Its pointed roof sported a cross. Three arched windows graced each side of the tower—he knew the views out from them over the town and the surrounding countryside would be spectacular. Something he had wanted to see with Madison, after apologizing to her as she waited on these churchfront steps.

His frustration mounted. He took the steps three at a time in a race to the top. He located the booth to purchase tickets to the tower, and whipped out his wallet.

"*Buongiorno,*" he said to the young woman at the counter. "*Campanile.* Up. One ticket." Okay, so if he did stay, learning Italian would become priority. "Did you see a beautiful blond woman go up?"

She looked at him quizzically. "French? German?"

Oh, damn. He was wasting time. "No problem, no problem. One ticket, *per favore.*" He handed her the euro and took his ticket, praying that there was only one staircase up and down, and that she was even here.

He began his upward slog, and it soon opened onto a staircase that hugged the tower walls, making it apparent there was only one staircase. It was tiring, especially after the sprint up the hill to Todi, but he raced up steadily. Regardless, the stairway was narrow for two-way traffic and a scouting group was making its way down, forcing Chris to press himself against the wall as they passed. The rough stone dug into his back as he inwardly cursed their slowness. They were eight-year-olds, for Christ's sake, they should have been eating these stairs up on their way down. Instead, they were lingering, chatting, joking with one another on their snails' pace descent. All the while, his blood boiled and he clutched angry fingers across those rough-hewn medieval tower walls.

Hurry it up, he urged them mentally, but to no avail. The troop leaders were no faster than their charges, and they smiled politely and greeted him as they went down and his blood pressure rose. Finally, the last straggler in a group of slowpokes made his way down and Chris continued his sprint up, almost shouting for joy when he saw the last set of metal stairs and the door opening to the belltower landing.

He opened it with such force that a loud bang sounded through the air and set a pair of cooing pigeons in flight. On the other side of the belltower, the sole visitor startled and turned back.

As she did, the sunlight glowed on her hair, setting it ablaze. Her bright blue eyes shifted from shock to recognition as she dropped the hand she had instinctively raised to her chest. "Oh. It's you," she said.

Chris noted the relief in the recognition, despite detecting no underlying sense of tenderness. He firmly closed the door, as the sign instructed in several European languages. His heart was still pounding wildly, though not from the hundreds of stairs he'd run up.

He crossed the distance between them. "Madison, it's great seeing you here."

She hesitated. "Yeah, weird coincidence we both chose the same time to climb up." She indicated the breathtaking view before her.

The town laid out beneath them. Tiled rooftops, belltowers, the Piazza del popolo and the façade of the cathedral directly in front of them. And beyond, undulating waves of green and gold of the Umbrian landscape surrounding the town. It was perfect. One of the most beautiful views he'd ever seen. And yet, he cared not one whit for any of it, only the lovely face right before him, the one studying that view.

"I don't know. I actually didn't come up here for the view."

Madison turned, her brow furrowed. "What do you mean you didn't come for the view? Why else would you climb all those steps?" She swiveled back, indicating the center of the tower with her thumb. "Unless your Fanboy the mayor asked you to become the official town bellringer."

Chris turned to his right. He hadn't even noticed the giant bells there when he had emerged onto the landing. Four giant black bells, slightly green with moss or age. He cracked a smile. "No, I haven't been given that honor, I'm afraid. But based on how fast I ran up, an offer could be in my future." He made a face. "Well, if it weren't for that scouting group slowing my upward progress."

Madison smiled. "Yeah, they were up here when I first got here. Complete chaos. I was enjoying the solitude once they left me alone to head back down."

"And I destroyed that solitude," said Chris.

She looked up at him. "Yes. Yes, you did. And now you tell me you didn't even come for the view. So why exactly are you here?"

Chris took a deep breath. "For you."

Madison shook her head. "Why, Chris?" She turned away from him, looking out once more over the town.

He watched her profile, that angry furrow in her brow. She looked so beautiful. And so very angry at him.

Madison took a deep breath. "Chris, I just don't need any of this now. I admit I was starting to feel something for you." She raised her hands, stroking her hair away from her face.

Chris watched it falling back in waves across her shoulders, wanting desperately to touch it, but knowing he had no right.

"It was humiliating on that terrace in Gubbio. The caller hung up, and called again immediately. I only picked it up because I thought it might be an emergency. Silly me." She laughed a bitter laugh. "You failed to mention to me you have a wife."

Chris touched her shoulders, turned her gently around to face him. "*Had* a wife, Madison. We're getting a divorce. But yes, you're right. I should have told you." Chris took a deep breath. "I was ashamed. I had organized this trip as a surprise. A holiday together. I didn't expect to catch her in bed with my best friend and business partner. That's why I wanted to sell the business so quickly." He saw compassion in her face, not judgment.

"I truly am sorry. That's just awful. If it makes you feel better, she hardly ingratiated herself to me over the phone."

Chris stifled a grin. "I needed that. Thanks. She obviously had no right to speak that way to you. But I admit I was wrong not to tell you. I would have when I told you my feelings for you. If that little wallet snafu hadn't happened." He looked out fleetingly to the view over the town that had become so meaningful to him in such a short period of time. "You know. It was so hard. So humiliating and unexpected. It took a lot to come here alone after hitting rock bottom." He looked into her eyes. "I thought it would be hard, but I wound up having a great time. New friends, new places." He cracked a smile. "New cooking skills. I didn't want to put a damper on it with my problems. It felt better to pretend I wasn't married and to push it to the back of my mind. But I did talk with Mark. And learned that both he and Emma had survived divorces with cheating spouses. And that pain brought them together. It gave me hope ..."

Madison nodded. "Yes, Emma told me. But I also confided in her my problems. Why I'm especially sensitive about married men lying to me."

He placed his hands back on her shoulders. "I know. I Googled you."

"You what?" She looked furious.

"Only after Gubbio. Don't worry, Emma just set me straight on that, too. I'm sorry."

Madison shook her head. "I guess neither of us was fully honest with one another."

Chris placed one hand on her cheek. "Madison, it's early days. We're only getting to know one another. And we were both escaping from recent hurts, probably embarrassed. We could take it from here and promise complete honesty from now on. What do you think?" He tilted his head.

"I'd like that," Madison whispered.

"Good, because as soon as Emma told me I was wrong, I ran like a maniac up that endless hill and then up this belltower to see you. You're lucky I didn't have a heart attack."

Madison smiled and placed one hand against his chest. "Yeah, it does seem to be galloping along at a pretty fast pace."

Chris placed his hand over hers, holding it in place. He shook his head. "I can't blame that on the hill up to Todi or the belltower steps. Not even on those annoying scouts hampering my efforts by moving like human sloths." He looked down into her beautiful face tilted up at his. "My heart racing is all the fault of my feelings for you." He placed one arm around her, and brushed away a lock of hair with his other. "And my hopes you might feel the same."

She held his gaze and smiled. "I could be persuaded by enjoying this spectacular view with the town's favorite son. You have a way of making a good impression on people."

He tilted his forehead down to rest against hers. "That's great to know, but, honestly, right now I'm only interested in making a good impression on one special person."

She cocked one eyebrow. "You may be pleasantly surprised," she whispered.

Chris crushed her into his chest and brushed his lips against hers, gently at first, with increasing urgency. She wrapped her arms around him and he felt a passion he hadn't felt for some time, even long before that horrible night, if he were honest. He threaded his fingers through that long hair, barely coming up for breath. Pressed against her chest, her heartbeats matched his own racing chest.

"Dong, dong."

The belltower reverberated and, startled, they broke apart. They turned towards the source of the noise.

Chris laughed. "The bells, chiming the hour."

Madison smiled. "Taking your town bellringing duties as trainee bellringer a bit too seriously, I see." She looked up and smiled. "They don't bother me, if they don't bother you. Anyway, we were in the middle of something."

She leaned in to press her lips against Chris' and they began where they had left off. The bells clanged noisily around them, the wonders of Todi's views sprawled out before them, but Chris and Madison noticed none of it.

CHAPTER 39

Grace

"FANCY SEEING YOU HERE!" exclaimed Grace. "Squeezing in that last day of pampering, too?"

Heike sat up in the sauna and smiled. "Absolutely. I won't have this back home. Angela gave me a neck and shoulder massage. I'm feeling fabulous."

"Great minds think alike. I just did the same. Set for my flight tomorrow. I've also packed up, even if Kathryn was pestering me the whole time to see if we couldn't stay an additional week." She chuckled and took a place on the wooden benches, leaning back against the warm wall. "Although, if I'm being honest, I wouldn't mind it either. But real life awaits, right?"

"True," said Heike. "But I'm excited, too. Anneliese and I will speak on Sunday. She's coming over for lunch, without Hans for our first talk. I think she realizes she lost a bit of control with her husband, and that his business plan wasn't as well-thought-out as he'd insisted."

"That's really good news, Heike. I know you can turn this around."

Heike sighed. "I hope so, because I forked over too much of the retirement money Matthias and I saved to my son-in-law's unrealistic plans. We need to earn that back. But I honestly think we can. And I think Giuseppe's ideas for cooking classes can help."

"And I can't wait to take them."

"I know you need to see to the situation back home, but, once you do, I hope you'll book that flight to Vienna. I have plenty of space to host you at my place. Summer in Vienna is lovely."

"Absolutely, I'm so excited to finally see it." Grace made a face. "And so happy the city isn't ruined for me by having been locked into some Viennese hotel to carry out servant duties for my husband on some long-ago Austrian conference."

"I'm glad you can laugh about it now. But it may take time. Call me if you ever need to vent."

Grace nodded. "I will."

"And how is our favorite lovestruck preteen handling imminent separation?"

"Ha. About as well as one could expect. But they're spending every moment together until the inevitable parting. With you taking the train and Chris staying here, Marco has even wiggled his way into the departure van to Rome to 'help Madison and Grace with their bags,' since he claims Ugo can't do it all on his own."

"Clever boy," chuckled Heike. "So it will be an airport farewell."

"Yes. I also gave a little warning to Kathryn that all was not well at home. Originally, I promised not to interfere, but it seemed unfair to hit her when she'd be down and missing Marco."

"How did it go?"

"She was upset, but not as upset as I'd thought. She realized home life was tense. I think my daughter will be more involved now that Rupert isn't influencing her. She's already told Kathryn she wants to start attending more of her matches, which really made Kathryn happy. And I'll be there, too. This trip has been good for Kathryn and me. We've already scheduled a weekly Italian dinner at my place, just for the two of us. We'll continue our recipes and it will also give Ellen a free evening. We'll speak more when I'm home, but she said she'd check out requirements to finish her doctoral degree in art history."

"Oh, that's wonderful, Grace. For your daughter. And Kathryn. I'm looking forward to some more time with my grandchildren, too. I've missed that in these past months. We have an Italian dinner scheduled, too, for next week."

"That's fantastic. I hope I can meet them on my visit. Oh, and I'll start training to be a teacher's aide. Not full time, but a substitute. I like the idea of meeting my old dream of being a teacher halfway. And I'll join a book club at the local library. Richard always looked down upon that, since it wasn't intellectual enough for his lofty standards. But he's not here to boss me around anymore. I don't know why it's taken me so long."

"Don't be hard on yourself. Old habits die hard." Heike broke out in a grin. "And speaking about second acts for the younger set. Did you see Madison today? She was here earlier when I was in the Jacuzzi."

Grace shook her head. "I don't think I've seen her since she was so miffed on our trip back from Gubbio."

"Oh, my. You've missed a lot. She was angry because she discovered Chris is married."

She gasped. "Chris is married?" Grace was genuinely surprised.

"In the middle of a divorce. The wife slept with his best friend. Chris discovered them *in flagrante*."

"Oh, poor Chris," said Grace, clutching her chest. "What a terrible, despicable woman to do that to such a wonderful man."

"I fully agree. It seems Madison has problems with her job because she got involved with a co-worker, and he lied about not being married. All hell broke loose when the wife found out. Live, on air. She's on leave from her job."

"Oh, goodness. All this drama around us. And we were none the wiser."

"Well, maybe it all turned out for the best. It led Chris and Madison to one another."

"You're kidding me!" Grace clapped her hands. "What a wonderful couple they would make."

"That remains to be seen, of course. Madison had that telltale glow of new love. But, as you know, Chris may be staying on here in Todi. And it seems they also need a journalism teacher, one who can run the student newspaper. So there's a spot for Madison if she decides to return to Todi."

Grace found herself inexplicably tearing up. How could one vacation lead to all these wonderful connections, and even blossoming love? "What an eventful holiday this has been, hasn't it? Now, I've reached my sauna limit. How about some time in the relaxation room and a nice cup of tea?" Grace shook her head as they left the sauna together. Truly, this had been an extraordinary holiday.

CHAPTER 40

Emma

DEPARTURE SATURDAYS WERE ALWAYS trying, but this one even more so than usual. Emma helped out with the breakfast service, while trying to deal with Marco's mercurial mood. She hadn't insisted that he not go with the van to the Rome airport, knowing he'd only mope were he not allowed to see his first girlfriend off at the airport. How things would end, she had no idea. But first loves were first loves, and she did not want to be seen as coming in the way of their goodbye.

In a rush, all the guests were checking out and Ugo had his van out front. She had ordered another taxi service to bring Chris and his luggage to the nearby villa, then to continue on to Perugia, where he would drop Heike off at the train station for the trip back to Vienna. She even made him promise to help her organize her many ceramic purchases in her cabin.

Now that everyone stood together chatting out front, she realized what a remarkable seasonal opening the first two weeks had been. She plucked up her cellphone and marched out to see them.

"Everyone," she called. "I have one last request." She placed a coin in each of their hands and herded them together in front of the fountain. "I met my two closest friends while viewing the film that is the namesake for this inn. And I've been thrilled to see all these new friendship groups forming these past two weeks. Maybe even new love." She smiled. "It's not the Trevi Fountain, but we do what we can in Umbria. I want a photo of all of you tossing those coins into the fountain and making a wish."

They all laughed and placed bags and purses to the side, following Emma's directions to stand towards the camera and to throw coins over their shoulder. While not a guest, Marco asked for a coin to stand beside Kathryn for the tossing ceremony, and who was Emma to refuse?

"*Uno—due—tre!*" she called, snapping photos as they tossed their coins and made wishes.

"I'll send you the photos. Now, our airport passengers and train passengers need to get started." Ugo and the other taxi driver initiated packing suitcases in the cars and everyone began giving hugs and kisses and wishing one another pleasant journeys and promises to stay in touch. From the corner of her eye, she noticed Madison and Chris and their tender kisses. Emma smiled.

She hugged each guest, wishing them a pleasant journey, and ensuring they made their way to their transportation. Ugo's van and the car both departed at the same time, enthusiastic hands waving from open windows. She watched until they were specks on the horizon.

Annarita emerged from the inn with two coffee cups. "Departure days always mean a ton of work. The cleaning crew will be here in a half hour. Let's take a needed break." She held up a mug. "Look what Mark had made."

Emma examined the mug, smiling at Chris' new logo on it. She traced it with her finger.

Both women sat beside the fountain, delighting in the morning light and the gentle gurgling of the water.

"How's Marco handling separation?" asked Annarita.

"Well, obviously not that well since he's in the van. I'll have to hope he won't make a break for the airplane. I admit to having hidden his passport, just in case."

Annarita chuckled. "And Giuseppe tells me we may have another Three Coins Inn couple."

Emma smiled. "I hope so. Chris and Madison."

"There's a couple that would make heads turn in a crowded room. But isn't he staying here?"

"He'll be at the Lakeview College villa for two weeks. A kind of a test run. He promises to come back during his stay and let us know what he decides. It would be nice to have him in Todi. Madison is going back, but she says she's thinking it over. Things aren't great with her job, and she likes the idea of a change, so we'll see what happens there."

"And I hear from Giuseppe our chef extraordinaire these weeks, Heike, also made a new friend."

"Ah, yes. Heike and Grace are thick as thieves now. Grace says she'll be going to Vienna this summer, and Heike will visit Durham in the autumn. And they both say they'll book to come back here next year. I don't know the full story, but I understand from something Grace told me that Grace's marriage was not a happy one, and that she suffered under a manipulative husband. I think both Grace and Heike found one another in the right moment." Emma reached out and clasped Annarita's hand. "And we both know firsthand how life-changing that can be."

"We certainly do," said Annarita, holding up her mug. "To The Three Coins Inn."

Emma smiled back and clinked her mug against Annarita's. "To The Three Coins Inn. And to new friendships and new starts."

Both women drank their coffee, allowing the sun to warm their faces as they listened to the peaceful sound of water cascading over the fountain, enveloping the shiny, new coins now at home in its basin.

They knew they had a long day ahead of them to prep for the next set of guests, and this brief break would fuel them for the tasks they faced. Plus, both women knew how important it was to honor new friendships that could change lives. After all, it had happened to them, too.

Acknowledgements

This novel is my first attempt at a series. *Three Coins* was my first-ever novel, and since I published it over three years ago, I've gone on to other projects, publishing novels and short stories while my début sat quietly on the bookshelf. But Emma, Tiffany and Annarita have remained stubbornly in the back of my mind, and I've often found myself wondering what happens to them. (And yes, if you haven't realized this yet, we writers are a decidedly odd lot, and the characters we make up truly do live on in our minds.)

So, even if it wasn't my original intention to create a series, I felt Emma and Annarita's decampment to The Three Coins Inn offered me the perfect opening. After all, if those three very different women could forge a deep friendship that could change their lives forever, why couldn't the same happen to the guests at their hotel?

And what a wonderful opportunity for a committed travel addict like me – the chance to base stories centered around a hotel in beautiful Umbria. After all, I'm a firm believer that travel is the cure to all of life's trials and that a plane ticket to a new destination clutched in one hand and a passport in the other is pretty much the equivalent of a winning lottery ticket. There's just something about being in a new environment, with new cities and towns to explore, a new language caressing your ears, new foods and new people that excites all the senses and allows you to forget those nagging concerns of daily life. I had fun with my first batch of Three Coins guests, and I'm already at work on the next set. I'm hoping you'll enjoy these excursions to The Three Coins Inn as much as I enjoy dreaming them up.

As a writer, I am grateful for the wonderful support of fellow writers, readers, collaborators and friends that get me past the finish line for all my projects.

As always, the wonderful Women's Fiction Writers Association is a valuable support for all my work. WFWA critique partners Patty Warren and Jarmila Sawicka helped improve opening chapters. And WFWA's classes, sessions and affinity groups keep me among such talented and fun likeminded authors who inspire me to create my stories.

I am deeply grateful to The History Quill/ Niche Readers beta readers, who are avid readers of women's fiction and returned with thoughtful suggestions that allowed me to improve my manuscript. While all reader feedback is valuable, I was especially moved by reader C.C., who told me reading this book at a difficult time in her own life was cathartic. "It truly felt meant to be for me to find myself part of the beta team for this book, as it resonates so much with me, and was honestly very healing and inspiring for me to read. This was a timely read for me given what's going on in my own life. I would immediately recommend it to anyone going through something similar. I found it to be healing, inspiring, and hopeful." Both as a reader who has stumbled upon the "right" book to accompany my emotions at the moment, and as a writer whose heart soars to read these words, I'm so thrilled when my stories resonate with readers. *Grazie*, C.C., your words meant the world to me!

It is always a pleasure to work with my editor, Valerie Valentine, who consistently offers a fresh set of eyes, an appreciation for Italy, and concrete suggestions to improve my work. Thanks, also, to Roxana Coumans for her excellent proofreading assistance.

Gratitude always to my favorite designers, Joanne Morgante and Roberto Magini of Maxtudio, for partnering with me to create my beautiful cover art. I love reaching the point when we can start chatting covers – and being consistently stunned by your beautiful creations. *Grazie*!

Special thanks to my mother and my husband and sons, Francesco, Alessandro and Nicolò, for their constant support that allows me to moonlight as an author.

And lastly, as expressed in my dedication, I am fully aware that it is my treasured readers who allow me to write my stories. It is you who allow me to continue creating my tales. Thank you for your greatly valued support. If you enjoyed this novel, please consider leaving a review at Goodreads, Amazon, Kobo and other sales sites. Reader reviews – even if only a sentence or two – are the best way to ensure that new readers discover my work. As an indie author, I'm especially grateful for this precious word-of-mouth publicity.

If you want to keep up with my work, new releases, travel stories, and short book reviews for novels I've enjoyed, please sign up for my newsletter at my author website: www.kimberlysullivanauthor.com

Thank you for reading!

About the author

KIMBERLY SULLIVAN grew up in the suburbs of Boston and in Saratoga Springs, New York, although she now calls the Harlem neighborhood of New York City home when she's back in the US. She studied political science and history at Cornell University and earned her MBA, with a concentration in strategy and marketing, from Bocconi University in Milan.

Afflicted with a severe case of Wanderlust, she worked in journalism and government in the US, Czech Republic and Austria, before settling down in Rome, where she works in international development, and writes fiction any chance she gets.

She is a member of the Women's Fiction Writers Association and The Historical Novel Society. She has published five novels: *Three Coins, Dark Blue Waves, In The Shadows of The Apennines, Rome's Last Noble Palace* and *Easter at The Three Coins Inn,* and one short story collection, *Drink Wine and Be Beautiful.* She also coedited the historical fiction anthology *Feisty Deeds: Historical Fictions of Daring Women.*

After years spent living in Italy with her Italian husband and sons, she's fluent in speaking with her hands, and she loves setting her stories in her beautiful, adoptive country.

kimberlysullivanauthor.com
Instagram: kimberlyinrome
Twitter: @kimberlyinrome
BookBub: kimberly-sullivan

www.ingramcontent.com/pod-product-compliance
Lightning Source LLC
Chambersburg PA
CBHW071349300726
48976CB00006B/1824